# DEXTER'S
# FINAL CUT

## ALSO BY JEFF LINDSAY

Darkly Dreaming Dexter

Dearly Devoted Dexter

Dexter in the Dark

Dexter by Design

Dexter Is Delicious

Double Dexter

# JEFF LINDSAY
# DEXTER'S FINAL CUT

First published in Great Britain in 2013 by Orion Books,
an imprint of The Orion Publishing Group Ltd
Orion House, 5 Upper Saint Martin's Lane
London WC2H 9EA

An Hachette UK Company

1 3 5 7 9 10 8 6 4 2

A CIP catalogue record for this book is
available from the British Library.

ISBN (Hardback) 978 1 4091 4490 8
ISBN (Export Trade Paperback) 978 1 4091 4491 5
ISBN (Ebook) 978 1 4091 4492 2

Printed in Great Britain by Clays Ltd, St Ives plc

The Orion Publishing Group's policy is to use papers that are natural,
renewable and recyclable products and made from wood grown in sustainable
forests. The logging and manufacturing processes are expected to
conform to the environmental regulations of the country of origin.

www.orionbooks.co.uk

For Hilary, who gives meaning and structure to life,
as well as to stories.

# ACKNOWLEDGMENTS

I am deeply indebted to my research assistants—Bear, Pookie, and Tink—who helped me so very much in coming to understand pre-adolescent behavior. Thanks are also due to Dunny O'Toole and Julio S. for their invaluable assistance on security, technical background, and in-depth knowledge of *pastelitas.* Many thanks, too, to my many friends in The Biz for their years of moral support, friendship, and acting tips.

Thanks to my editor, Jason Kaufman, for his belief and support.

And finally, *Dexter* would never have happened without my agent and friend, Nick Ellison. Thank you, St. Nick. What a ride . . .

# DEXTER'S
# FINAL CUT

# INTRODUCTION

I t's not that bad being dead. Surprising, really, when you think about it. I mean, everyone always seems so very terrified of the whole thing, weeping and moaning and spending years of anguish brooding about the possibility of an afterlife. And yet, here I lay in peaceful repose, quiet, pain-free, without a care in the world, doing nothing more metaphysically complicated than remembering my Last Meal—an excellent pastrami sandwich. It was brought to me, still warm, only forty minutes ago as I sat in a comfy folding chair, and I remember wondering, Where did they find such succulent pastrami in Miami nowadays? The pickle was quite tasty, too. And just to be ethnically authentic, I'd had a cream soda with it, something I hadn't tried in a very long time; delicious. Altogether, a culinary experience that made being dead seem like a very minor inconvenience.

—although to be truthful, which is sometimes unavoidable, lying here unmoving on the pavement was starting to get just the tiniest bit tedious. I really hoped I would be discovered soon; death was not really enough to keep the mind occupied, and it seemed like I had been here quite a while. I know it might not seem like the first thing you would object to about being dead—long hours and no real challenge to the work—but there it was. I was bored. And the pavement underneath me was hot and beginning to feel very hard. On top of that, there was a puddle of sticky red nastiness spreading out around me that made me feel quite uncomfortable—of course, I mean it would have made me uncomfortable, if I had actually been alive. But if nothing else, it was certainly unsightly; I must look terribly unattractive.

Another odd concern for the newly dead, perhaps, but true. I was bound to be an uninviting sight. It was unavoidable; there's very little charm to a corpse killed by gunshot wounds, and no dignity at all to lying in the street in the Miami sunlight and waiting in a pool of sticky red mess for someone to find your body. And when my poor, bullet-riddled corpse was discovered at last, there would not even be a genuine flood of sentiment, no heartfelt outpouring of anguish and regret. Not that I ever found real emotion terribly moving, but still, one would like to be really mourned, wouldn't one?

But not today, not for poor Dead Dexter. After all, who could mourn a monster like me? No, it would be purely pro forma, even less convincing than usual, and I, of all people, could not really complain. I had spent my entire professional life—and a great deal of very rewarding hobby time— around dead bodies. I knew very well that the most natural reaction to finding a gore-soaked corpse was something like, "Ooh, gross," as your Finder guzzles an energy drink and turns up the volume on the iPod. Even that was more honest than the overblown and empty teeth-gnashing I knew I would get when my pitiful corpse was discovered. I could not even hope for a classy statement of grief and loss like, "Alas, poor Dexter!" Nobody says "alas" anymore; for that matter, I doubt anyone really feels it nowadays, either.

No, there would be little real grief for Dear Departed Dexter; no one can express it for the simple reason that no one is capable of feeling it. I may be the only one honest enough to admit that I don't, but I have never seen any compelling evidence that anyone else does, either. People are far too callous and fickle, and even in the best of times—which this was not—I could hope for no more than a moment of revulsion at the compost heap that was my human (more or less) body, and a twinge of irritation at having one more mess to deal with. And then no doubt the conversation would turn to football, or plans for the weekend, and the memory of my pastrami sandwich would last far longer than anyone's sense of loss at my untimely demise.

But after all, there was no alternative. I just had to make the best of it, and lie here like a lox until I was discovered—which seemed to me to be a long-overdue event. I had been sprawled here in direct sunlight for at least half an hour: Can a corpse get a sunburn? I was certain dead people avoided *tanning booths—even in zombie movies—but here in the midday sun, was it possible for dead skin to tan? It didn't seem right; we all like to think of cadavers as pale and ghostly, and a healthy sun-kissed epidermis would certainly spoil the effect.*

*But now I hear a rising chorus of fuss and bother nearby: A metallic door thumps shut, hushed voices murmur urgently, and finally I hear the sound for which I have been yearning: the hurried clatter of approaching footsteps. They stutter to a stop beside me and a woman gasps and cries out, "Nooo!" At last: some real concern for my tragic condition. A trifle melodramatic, perhaps, but it's touching, and would even be heartwarming, if only Dexter had a heart to warm.*

*The woman bends over me, and in the bright halo of sunlight surrounding her head, I can't make out her features. But there is no mistaking the shape of the gun that appears in her right hand. A woman with a gun—could this be Dexter's dear sister, Sergeant Deborah Morgan, stumbling across her beloved brother's tragically murdered self? Who else could possibly put on such a rare display of well-armed grief for me? And there is real tenderness in her left hand as it drops to my neck to feel for a pulse: in vain, alas, or whatever it is we say instead of "vain" nowadays. Her left hand drops away from my neck and she raises her head to the heavens and says through a tightly clenched jaw, "I'll get the bastards who did this. I swear it. . . ."*

*It is a sentiment I approve completely—and actually, it does sound a little bit like Deborah, but not quite enough. There is a hesitant, musical fluctuation in the voice that my sister would never permit.*

*No, this is not Deborah, but some histrionically tender imitation. And it sounds even less like my ferocious and foulmouthed sister when she adds, in a slightly nasal and very cranky tone, "Goddamn it, Victor, there's a shadow right across my face the whole goddamn time!"*

*A man who sounds like he has just lived through an endless stretch of fatigue that has taken him far beyond the point of mere human exasperation calls out, "Cut. Where's the fucking key grip?"*

*Victor?*

*Key grip?*

*What can this be? What, indeed, is happening? How can there be such a bizarre reaction to the tragic passing of one so young, so talented, and so deeply admired—at least by me? Is this some cosmic hiccup, a loony hallu-*

cination caused by passing through the Veil and into the Beyond? Perhaps some confused moment of transition into Oneness with All Things, as Dexter shuffles off the mortal coil and heads for the Last Roundup?

And now it gets even stranger, as a surreal scene of swarming activity begins to swirl around my body. Dozens of people, silent and hidden until now, leap out onto the sidewalk and explode into furious and focused frenzy, as if it was the most natural thing in the world to amble past a gore-soaked Dexter and whirl into antlike action. Two men and a woman step right over my tragic cadaver and begin to wrestle with large tripod-mounted lights, reflectors, and bundles of electric cable, and one really has to wonder: Is this how it all ends, for all of us? Not with a Bang but a lighting change?

Unfortunately for metaphysical discovery, we must wait a little longer to answer all these very good questions. Because today is not, in fact, that long-dreaded day of infamy when Dexter Dies. It is, instead, a very small and harmless fraud: Dexter's Deception. For today, Dexter has entered the swinging swirling world of big-time professional show business. We have been granted the great and humbling boon of a real Acting Job, and today we are performing, playing a role for which we have done a lifetime of research. We have been cast as an extra, a playtime corpse, a small and motionless pawn on the great chessboard that is Hollywood.

And now, the woman who is not Deborah pats my face and stalks away to her trailer, muttering homicidal comments about those who would allow shadows on her near-perfect visage. The crew have all busied themselves with their obscure and energetic tasks, and above it all the more-than-tired voice of Victor chants a series of weary orders, and then adds, "And you need to get to wardrobe, and get cleaned up for another take, okay, Derrick?"

"It's Dexter," I say, rising up from the dead and into a sitting position. "With an 'X.'"

Victor shows no sign that he has heard me, or even that I exist at all. "We are already three days behind schedule, people," he moans. "Can we all move a little faster?"

I do not notice that anyone actually does move any faster, which seems perfectly fair to me. After all, if Victor chooses to ignore me, he can't really object if others ignore him, can he?

An elegant young man has appeared at my side, and he squats down beside me, bringing with him the distinct aroma of some floral cologne. "Really nice," he tells me, patting my arm. "You soooo looked really dead?"

*"Thank you," I tell him.*

*He lays his soft hand on my arm. "Let's get you cleaned up?" he says. Almost everything out of his mouth so far has been a question, even simple statements like, "Hello, my name is Fred?" I do not hold it against him— although I am beginning to suspect that Fred would very much like me to hold something against him. But even if I were so inclined, and available, which I am not, it could never work out. He is a mere wardrobe assistant, and Dexter is Talent—it says so on the contract I signed!—and so I stand up with great dignity and follow along to the large trailer occupied by Fred and his associates. And as I walk, I ponder, and perhaps the very question is a cliché, an absurd echo of the human obsession with finding meaning where there is absolutely none. But as I look around me at all the absurdly expensive fuss and clutter, I ask it anyway.*

*How did I get here?*

# ONE

**I**T ALL STARTED SO PEACEFULLY, JUST A FEW SHORT WEEKS AGO, on a lovely day in early autumn.

I had driven in to work as I always did, through the happy carnage that is rush hour in Miami. It had been a bright and pleasant day: sun shining, temperature in the seventies, the other drivers cheerfully honking their horns and screaming death threats, and I'd steered through it with a blissful feeling of belonging.

I had pulled into a spot in the parking lot at police HQ, still completely unaware of the lurking terror that awaited me, and carefully carried a large box of doughnuts into the building and up to the second floor. I'd arrived at my desk punctually, at my usual time. And I made it all the way into a seated position in my chair, a cup of vile coffee in one hand and a jelly doughnut in the other, before I ever for a moment suspected that today would be anything other than one more day of peaceful routine among the newly dead of Our Fair City.

And then the phone on my desk began to buzz, and because I was stupid enough to answer it, everything changed forever.

"Morgan," I said into the receiver. And if I'd known what was coming I would not have said it so cheerfully.

Someone on the other end made a throat-clearing noise, and with a jolt of surprise I recognized it. It was the sound Captain Matthews made when he wanted to call attention to the fact that he was about to make an important pronouncement. But what momentous declaration could he possibly have now, for me, before I even finished one doughnut, and why would he speak it on the phone to a mere forensics wonk?

"Ahem, uh, Morgan," the captain said. And then there was silence.

"This is Morgan," I said helpfully.

"There's a, um," he said, and cleared his throat again. "I have a special assignment. For you. Can you come up to my office? Right now," he said. There was another slight pause, and then, most baffling of all, he added, "Uh. Please." And then he hung up.

I stared at the phone for a long moment before I replaced it in its cradle. I was not sure what had just happened, or what it meant: "Come up to my office right now"? Captains do not hand out special assignments to blood-spatter analysts, and we do not visit captains' offices socially, either. So what was this about?

My conscience was clean—most mythical objects are—but I felt a small twinge of unease anyway. Could this be trouble—perhaps a confrontation over some emerging evidence of my Wicked Ways? I always cleaned up thoroughly—No Body Part Left Behind!—and in any case, it had been quite a while since I had done anything at all worth not talking about. In fact, it had just recently started to seem like much *too* long, and the past few evenings I had been fondling my little candidates list and thinking about a new Playdate. My last Enchanting Encounter had been several months ago, and I certainly deserved another soon—unless I had somehow been discovered. But as I thought back on that wonderful evening, I could remember no slipup, no lazy shortcut, nothing but painstaking perfection. Had Somebody Somehow found Something anyway?

But no: It wasn't possible. I had been meticulously neat, as always. Besides, if my handiwork had been detected, I would not have received a polite invitation to come chat with the captain—with an actual "please" tacked onto it! I would instead be looking up at the Special Response Team clustered around my desk, peering at me through their laser-guided telescopic sights and begging me to try something.

There was clearly some other, simpler explanation for why Captain Matthews would summon me to Olympus, but no matter how diligently I pushed my mighty brain through its paces, it came up with nothing more than an urgent suggestion that I eat the doughnut before I entered the captain's august presence. It was not actually an answer, but it was a good and practical thought, and it was followed by another: It didn't really matter what he wanted. He was the captain; I was a lowly blood-spatter analyst. He gave commands and I obeyed them. That is all you know in this world, and all you need to know. And so with a rising chorus of "Duty Calls" skirling on my mental bagpipes, I got out of my chair and headed out the door, finishing my doughnut as I went.

Because he was a real captain, and very important in the general scheme of things, Matthews had a secretary, although she liked to be called an executive assistant. Her name was Gwen, and she had three virtues far above anyone else I had ever known: She was astonishingly efficient, unbearably serious, and uncompromisingly plain. It was a delightful combination and I always found it irresistible. So as I hurried up to her desk, wiping the residue of the doughnut off my hands and onto my pants where it belonged, I could not help attempting a very small bon mot.

"Fair Gwendolyn," I said. "The face that launched a thousand patrol vehicles!"

She stared at me with a slight frown. "He's waiting for you," she said. "In the conference room. Go right in."

It was not much of a zinger, but Gwen had never been known for her sparkling sense of humor, so I gave her my best fake smile anyway and said, "Wit and beauty! A devastating combination!"

"Go right in," she repeated, with a face that might have been carved from stone, or at least very hard pudding. I breezed past her and went through the door and into the conference room.

Captain Matthews sat at the head of the table, looking earnest, manly, and at least semi-noble, as he almost always did. Sitting to one side of him was my sister, Sergeant Deborah Morgan, and she did not look happy. Of course, she very seldom did; between her carefully cultivated Cop Scowl and her general outlook of surly watchfulness, the most cheerful expression she had ever managed in my presence was a look of grudging acquiescence. Still, this morning she looked very much displeased, even for her. I turned my gaze to the other three people sitting around the table, hoping for some clue to my sister's malaise.

Sitting closest to the captain was a man who was clearly Alpha Dog of the group. He was about thirty-five and wore what looked like a very expensive suit, and Matthews had inclined his head toward the man in a way that went beyond deferential and nearly approached reverence. The man looked up at me as I entered, scanned me as if he was memorizing a row of numbers, and then turned impatiently back to Matthews.

Sitting next to this charming individual was a woman so startlingly beautiful that for a half moment I forgot I was walking, and I paused in midstep, my right foot dangling in the air, as I gaped at her like a twelve-year-old boy. I simply stared, and I could not have said why. The woman's hair was the color of old gold, and her features were pleasant and regular, true enough. And her eyes were a startling violet, a color so unlikely and yet so compelling that I felt an urgent need to move near and study her eyes at close range. But there was something beyond the mere arrangement of her features, something unseen and only *felt*, that made her seem far more attractive than she actually was—a Bright Passenger? Whatever it was, it grabbed my attention and held me helpless. The woman watched me goggle at her with distant amusement, raising an eyebrow and giving me a small smile that said, *Of course, but so what?* And then she turned back to face the captain, leaving me free to finish my interrupted step and stumble toward the table once more.

In a morning of surprises, my reaction to mere Female Pulchritude was a rather large one. I could not remember ever behaving in such an absurdly human way: Dexter does not Drool, not at mere womanly beauty. My tastes are somewhat more refined, generally involving a carefully chosen playmate and a roll of duct tape. But something about this woman had absolutely frozen me, and I could not stop myself from continuing to stare as I lurched into a chair next to my sister. Debs greeted me with a sharp elbow to the ribs and a whisper: "You're drooling," she hissed.

I wasn't, of course, but I straightened myself anyway and summoned the shards of my shattered dignity, looking around me with an attempt at regaining my usual composure.

There was one last person at the table whom I had not registered yet. He had put a vacant seat between himself and the Irresistible Siren, and he leaned away from her as if afraid he might catch something from her, his head propped up on one elbow, which was planted casually on the table. He wore aviator sunglasses, which did not disguise the fact that he was a ruggedly handsome man of about forty-five, with a perfectly trimmed mustache and a spectacular haircut. It wasn't possible to be sure with the sunglasses clamped to his face, but it certainly seemed like he hadn't even glanced at me as I'd come clown-footing into the room and into my chair. Somehow I managed to conceal my crushing disappointment at his negligence, and I turned my steely gaze to the head of the table, where Captain Matthews was once again clearing his throat.

"Ahem," he said carefully. "Since we're all here, um. So anyway." He nodded at Deborah. "Morgan," he said, and he looked at me. "And, uh—Morgan." He frowned, as if I had insulted him by choosing a name for myself that he'd already said, and the beautiful woman snickered in the silence. Captain Matthews actually blushed, which was almost certainly something he hadn't done since high school, and he cleared his throat one more time. "All right," he said, with massive authority and a sidelong glance at the woman. He nodded at the man in the impressive suit. "Mr., ah, Eissen here represents, um, BTN. Big Ticket Network." The man nodded back at Matthews with a very deliberate display of patient contempt. "And, um. They're here, in town. In Miami," he added, in case we'd forgotten what town we lived in. "They want to shoot a movie. A, um, TV show, you know."

The man in the sunglasses spoke up for the first time. "A pilot," he said, without moving his face, parting his lips only enough to reveal a blinding set of perfect teeth. "It's called a pilot."

The beautiful woman rolled her eyes and looked at me, shaking her head, and I found myself smiling eagerly back at her, without any conscious decision to do so.

"Right," said Matthews. "A pilot. Okay. So here's the thing." He slapped the table softly with both hands and looked back at Deborah. "Mr. Eissen has asked us for our cooperation. Which we are very happy to give them. Very happy," he said, nodding at Eissen. "Good for the department. Positive image, and, uh, ahem." He frowned again, drummed his fingers on the table, and stared at Deborah. "So that's what you do, Morgan." He frowned again and shook his head. "And, uh, Morgan. Both of you."

Perhaps it was merely because I hadn't finished my cup of awful coffee, but I had no idea what Matthews was talking about. And so, since Dexter has always been a quick study, I cleared my throat, too. It worked; Matthews looked at me with an expression of surprise. "I'm sorry, Captain," I said. "But exactly *what* am I supposed to do?"

Matthews blinked at me. "Whatever it takes," he said. "Whatever they ask you to do."

Mr. Mustache spoke up, again without moving any facial muscles. "I neeeed," he said, drawing out the word pointlessly, "to learn Who. You. Are."

That made even less sense than what Matthews had said, and I could think of no reply more penetrating than, "Oh, uh-huh . . ." It must have sounded just as feeble to him as it did to me, because he moved at last, turning his entire head in my direction and flipping up the sunglasses with one manicured finger.

"I need to watch you, learn to do what you do, figure out how to *be* you," he said. And he flashed his perfect white teeth at me. "Shouldn't take more than a few days."

The beautiful woman next to him snorted and murmured something that sounded like, "Asshole . . ." The man's face gave a very slight twitch of irritation, but otherwise he ignored her.

"But why?" I said. And because I like to give as good as I get, I added, "Don't you like who you are?"

The Goddess snickered; the man merely frowned. "It's for the part," he said, sounding slightly taken aback. "I need to research my character."

I think I still looked a bit confused, because the beautiful woman gave me a dazzling smile that curled up my toes and made me happy to be alive. "I don't think he knows who you are, Bob," she said.

"Robert," he grumbled. "Not Bob."

"Some people actually haven't heard of you, you know," she said, a little too sweetly.

"He probably doesn't know who you are, either," Robert snarled back at her. "Unless he reads the tabloids."

Mr. Eissen, the man in the wonderful suit, tapped one fingertip on the table. He did it very quietly, but everyone got silent and sat up a little straighter. Eissen gave me a microscopic smile. "Robert," he said, emphasizing the name slightly, and then adding, "Robert Chase." He gave a slight, dismissive shake of his head. "Robert is a well-known actor, Mr. Morgan."

"Oh, right," I said, giving Robert a friendly nod of the head. He flipped his sunglasses back down.

"Most actors like to get a sense of the . . . *reality* . . . behind the part they're going to play," Eissen said, and somehow he made it sound like he was talking about small children going through an unpleasant phase, and he gave me another condescending smile to go with it. "Jacqueline Forrest," he went on, with a little flourish of his hand to indicate the beautiful woman. "Jackie is playing a hard-as-nails woman detective. Like your Sergeant Morgan." He smiled at Deborah, but she didn't smile back. "And Robert is playing the part of a forensics whiz. Which we hear is what you are. So Robert would like to follow you around at your job for a few days and see what you do, and how you do it."

I have always heard it said that imitation is the sincerest form of flattery, but I did not recall anyone ever adding that flattery was actually a good thing, and I admit that I was not terribly pleased. It's not that I have anything to hide—I've already hidden all of it—but I do like my privacy, and the idea of having somebody following me around and taking notes on my behavior was a bit unsettling.

"Um," I said, and it was good to hear that my customary eloquence had leaped to the fore, "that's going to be, um, kind of difficult—"

"Doesn't matter," Captain Matthews said.

"I can handle it," Robert said.

"I can't," Deborah said, and everyone looked at her. She looked even more surly than she had when I came in, which was quite an achievement.

"What's the problem?" Eissen said.

Debs shook her head. "I'm a cop, not a fucking nanny," she said through clenched teeth.

"Morgan," Captain Matthews said, and he cleared his throat and looked around to see if anyone had noticed the bad word.

"I don't have time for this shit," Debs went on, using yet another bad word. "Brand-new this morning I got a drive-by shooting in Liberty City, an overdose at the U, and a beheading in the Grove."

"Wow," said Jackie, with breathy wonder.

Matthews waved a hand dismissively. "Not important," he said.

"The hell it isn't," my sister said.

Matthews shook his head at her. "Pass it off to Anderson or somebody. This," he said, rapping a knuckle on the table, "has priority." And he gave Jackie his most dazzling thoughtful-but-macho smile. She smiled back, apparently paralyzing Matthews for several seconds, until once more Deborah broke the spell.

"It's not my job," she insisted. "My job is taking down perps—not babysitting a model."

I looked at Jackie to see how she would take that; she just looked at Debs with awe and shook her head slowly. "Perfect," she said softly.

"Your job," Matthews said sternly, "is to follow orders. My orders," he added, glancing again at Jackie to see if she was impressed. But Jackie hadn't taken her eyes off Deborah.

"Goddamn it, Captain," Debs said, but Matthews held up a hand and cut her off.

"That's enough," he snapped. "I am assigning you to be technical adviser to these people. Period. Until further notice." Debs opened her mouth to say something, but Matthews plowed right over her. "You'll do it and do it right, and that's it, all of it, end of discussion." He leaned toward my sister slightly. "And, Morgan—watch your language, all right?" He stared at her, and she stared back, and for a moment that was all that happened, until Eissen finally broke the spell.

"Good, that's settled," he said, and he put on a fake smile to indicate that everyone was happy now. "Thank you for your cooperation, Captain. The network is very grateful."

Matthews nodded. "Well, that's, ahem. And I'm sure this is a good thing." He looked at me and then at Deborah. "For all of us," he said, glaring at my sister.

"I'm sure you're right," Eissen said.

"This is going to be *awesome*," Jackie gurgled.

Deborah did not appear to agree.

# T W O

"ISTEN," ROBERT CHASE SAID TO ME AS WE WALKED DOWN THE hall together toward my lab. "We need to get a few ground rules straight, all right?"

I looked at him, seeing only his profile, since he was staring straight ahead through his sunglasses. "Rules?" I said. "What do you mean?"

He stopped walking and turned to face me. "It's Derrick, right?" he said, holding out a hand.

"Dexter," I said. "Dexter Morgan." I shook his hand. It was soft, but his grip was firm.

"Right. Dexter," he said. "And I'm Robert. Okay? Just Robert." He held up a warning finger. "Not Bob," he said.

"Of course not," I said. He nodded as if I had said something thoughtful and continued walking down the hall. "Okay," he said, holding up the palm of his hand and waving it. "I'm just a regular guy. I like the same things you like."

That didn't seem possible, considering what I actually like, but I decided not to challenge him. "Okay," I said.

"I don't ride around in a Ferrari, or snort coke off a hooker's tits, all right?"

"Oh," I said. "Well, good."

"I mean, don't get me wrong," he said, with a thoughtful and manly smile. "I like the ladies. Absolutely love 'em." He glanced at me to make sure I believed him, and then went on. "But I don't do the whole . . . *celebrity* thing. Okay? I'm a working *actor*, not a star. I do a job, just like you do, and when I'm done for the day I like to relax, have a few beers, watch a ball game. Perfectly normal stuff. You know? Not clubbing and groupies and party all night. That's . . ." He shook his head. "That's bullshit."

It was all very interesting, but I have found that most of the time, when someone underlines something that much, they are either trying to convince themselves—or trying to disguise something very different. Maybe he really did snort cocaine from hookers' tits, and just didn't want to share. But of course, my experience with Hollywood Leading Men had been limited to watching them on TV with less than half of my attention, so it was also possible that Robert Chase was making a real point with a monologue from some past role. In any case, he did seem to be going on a bit about having "normal" tastes in women and sports, and I really had to wonder whether it was actually leading to some kind of point. "All right," I said. "So what's the rule?"

He twisted his head slightly, as if he hadn't heard me. "What do you mean?" he said.

"Ground rules," I said. "You said we were going to get the ground rules straight."

He stopped walking and turned to look at me with no real expression on his face. I looked back. Finally, he smiled, and then patted me on the shoulder. "All right," he said. "I guess I got a little . . . what. Pompous."

"Not at all," I said, lying politely.

"The point is," he said, "I don't want any kind of, you know. Special treatment, or whatever. Just do what you normally do, and act like I'm not even there. Do what you always do, okay?"

I had to believe he meant what he said, but even one brief moment of actual thought should have shown him how impossible his First Rule really was. In the first place, he was already getting special treatment, because I had been ordered to give it to him. And in the sec-

ond, if I truly did what I always did, he would almost certainly run
screaming from the room. Still, life teaches us that human thought
almost never walks hand in hand with Logic, and it is usually coun-
terproductive to raise the point. So I simply nodded as agreeably as
possible, as if he was really making sense. "Sure," I said. "Anything
else?"

He glanced around him in the hallway—a little furtively, I
thought. "I don't like . . . blood," he said. He swallowed. "I'd kind of
like to, um. Not have to see it too much."

So far, Chase had struck me as somewhat humorless, but this
statement was so wildly unlikely that I stared at him to see if he was
kidding. He didn't seem to be; he glanced at me, looked around again,
and then down at his shoes. They were worth looking at. They probably cost more than my car.

"Um," I said at last. "You did know that I do *blood* spatter, right?"

Chase flinched. "Yeah, I know, but . . ." He twisted his head like
he had a knot in his neck, flexed his hands, and then gave a sort of
half chuckle that was not nearly as convincing as it should have been,
coming from a Working Actor. "I just, uh," he said. "I don't like it.
It, uh . . . it makes me kind of . . . queasy. Just even thinking about
it running around inside you, or even looking at where it's been, I
can't—and to see it right *there*, like, on the floor, *splattered* . . ." He shiv-
ered and then jerked his head around to look at me, and for the first
time he seemed like a real, live, less-than-perfect human being. "I just
don't like it," he said, in a voice that was close to pleading.

"All right," I said, since there wasn't much else to say. "But I don't
know if I can show you how blood spatter works without showing
you blood."

He looked at his feet again and sighed. "I know," he said.

"Oh. My. *God!*" said an awestruck voice behind me, and I turned
to look. Vince Masuoka was standing there, both hands on his face
and his mouth wide-open, looking for all the world like a twelve-
year-old girl who had just run into the entire cast of *Glee*.

"Vince. It's me," I said. But apparently it wasn't; Vince ignored me
and pointed one trembling hand at Chase.

"Robert *Chase*, oh my God oh my *God!*" he said, and he bounced
up and down as if he had to go to the bathroom badly. "It's you; it's

really you!" he added, and even though I couldn't tell whether he was trying to convince himself or Chase, I found his performance profoundly irritating. But it seemed to be exactly what Chase needed; he straightened up, instantly looking serene, in command, and more perfect than a mere human being should ever be.

"How are you?" he said to Vince, although it must have been obvious that the answer was, "Completely insane."

"Oh my God," Vince said again, and I wondered if I could get him to stop saying it if I slapped him a few times. But such logical and rewarding actions are discouraged in the workplace, even when they make perfect sense, so I reached deep inside and found enough iron control to stifle my wholly natural urge.

"I see you know Robert," I said to Vince. "And, Robert, this is Vince Masuoka. He used to do forensics before he lost his mind."

"Hey, Vince," Robert said. He stepped forward with his hand out and a manly smile on his face. "Pleased to meet you."

Vince stared at the outstretched hand like he'd never seen one before. "Oh. Oh. Oh. Ohmygod," Vince said. "Ohmygod. I mean . . ." He grabbed onto Chase's hand as if he was drowning and it was a life jacket, and clutched it between both his hands while he stared at Chase and burbled madly on. "This is just unbelievable—I am soooo . . . I mean, *forever*— Oh, God, I can't believe it—" And even odder, as he stood there clinging to Chase's hand, his face began to flush, and he lowered his voice to a weird, husky whisper. "I absolutely *loved* you in *Hard and Fast!*" he said.

"Yeah, well—thanks," Chase said, somehow prying his hand from the moist trap of Vince's grip, and adding modestly, "That was a while ago."

"I have the DVD," Vince gushed. "I've watched it, like, a million times!"

"Hey, great," Chase said. "Glad you like it."

"I can't believe this," Vince said, and he hopped up and down again. "Oh my God!"

Chase just smiled. He had apparently seen this kind of behavior before, but even so, Vince's seizure had to be getting a little bit uncomfortable. Still, he took it manfully in stride, and patted Vince on the shoulder. "Hey, well," he said. "Derrick and me have to get going." And he turned toward me, nudged me, and said, "But I am really looking forward to working with you. See you around!"

Chase clamped one hand on my elbow and urged me along the hall. I needed very little urging, since Vince had lapsed back into moaning "Ohmygod, ohmygod, ohmygod," and it is never pleasant to linger in the presence of someone who has once been a friend and is now a poster boy for the tragedy of mental illness. So we left Vince in the hall and dodged into the shelter of my little office, where Chase leaned one haunch on the edge of my desk, crossed his arms, and shook his head.

"Well," he said. "Wasn't expecting that here. I mean, I thought cops were a little more, I dunno." He shrugged. "Um, tougher? More macho? You know."

"Vince isn't actually a cop," I said.

"Yeah, but still," he said. "Is he gay? I mean, that's fine and all; I was just wondering."

I looked at Chase, startled, and to be truthful, a large part of my surprise was at myself. I had worked with Vince for years, and I had never actually asked myself that question. Of course, it was completely irrelevant, and none of my business. After all, I wouldn't want him prying into *my* private life. "I don't know," I said. "But last year for Halloween he was Carmen Miranda. Again."

Chase nodded. "One of the warning signs," he said. "Well, shit, I don't care. I mean, there's, uh, fags everywhere these days."

I wondered at his use of that word, "fags." It seemed to me to be a word that was not actually au courant in more liberal circles, as I had thought the Hollywood community to be. But it may be that Robert just wanted to fit in, and he had assumed that I routinely said things that were not Politically Correct because I was a rough and macho member of the Miami Law Enforcement Community, and everyone knows we all talk that way.

In any case, I was more interested in his reaction to Vince's attack of Teen Girl Syndrome. "Does that kind of thing happen to you a lot?" I asked Chase.

"What, the whole freaking-out-and-hopping-on-one-foot thing?" he said matter-of-factly. "Yeah," he said. "Everywhere I go." He poked at a file folder on my desk and flipped it open.

"That must make grocery shopping a little difficult," I said.

He didn't look up. "Uh-huh," he said. "Somebody does that for me. Anyway"—he shrugged—"it's different in L.A. Out there, everybody thinks they're in the business with you, and nobody wants to look like a geek." He began to flip through the pages of the report, which I found a little irritating.

"I have some lab work to do," I said, and he looked up anxiously, which made me feel a little better.

"Is it, I mean," he said, "um, a murder? Blood work?"

"I'm afraid so," I said. "I need to work with some samples from a crime scene." And because Dexter is actually not very nice sometimes, I added, "The killer slashed through the femoral artery, so there was blood everywhere."

Chase took a long breath in through his teeth. He let the air back out again, took off his sunglasses and looked at them, then put them back on. I watched him for a moment, and it may not say good things about me, but I was enjoying the way he had gone slightly pale under his tan. Finally he swallowed and took in another long breath. "Well," he said. "I guess I'd better tag along and watch."

"I guess so," I said.

Chase swallowed, took another breath, and stood up, trying very hard to look resolute.

"Okay," he said. "I, uh. I'll just look over your shoulder . . . ?"

"All right," I said. "I'll try not to splatter too much."

He closed his eyes, but he followed.

It was a small triumph, but it was just about the only one I got for the rest of the week. As I trudged through my daily routine, Robert trudged along with me. He did not really get directly in my way too often, but every time I turned around he was there, a frown of concentration on his face, and usually some kind of inane question: Why did I do that? Why was it important to do that? Did I do that often? How many killers had I caught by doing that? Were they serial killers? Were there a lot of serial killers in Miami? A lot of the time the questions were completely unrelated to whatever I was doing, which made the whole thing seem even more pointlessly annoying. I could understand that it was a little hard for someone like him to frame intelligent questions about gas chromatography, but then, why watch me do it in the first place? Why couldn't he just go sit in a sports bar and text me his questions while he sipped a beer and watched a ball game?

The stupid questions were bad enough. But Wednesday, he took things to a new level of persecution.

We were in the lab once more, and I was looking into the microscope, where I had just found some very interesting similarities between tissue samples from two different crime scenes. I straightened up, turned around, and there was Chase, frowning thoughtfully, with one hand massaging the top of his head and the other covering his mouth. And before I could ask him why on earth he was making such a ridiculous gesture, I realized that I was doing exactly the same thing.

I dropped my hands. "Why are you doing that?" I said, keeping most of the irritation out of my voice.

Chase dropped his hands, too, and smiled, a cocky little smile of triumph. "That's what you do," he said. "When you find something significant. You do that with your hands." He did it again briefly, one hand on his head and the other over his mouth. "You do that," he said, letting his hands fall away, "and then you stand there and look really thoughtful." And he made a half-frowning face that said quite clearly, *I am being really thoughtful.* "Like that," he said.

I suppose I might well have been doing that and many other things my entire professional life without knowing it. There are very few mirrors in a forensics lab to show me what I looked like as I worked, and frankly I preferred it that way. We all have unconscious patterns of behavior, and I have always thought mine were just a little bit more restrained and logical than those exhibited by the mere mortals surrounding me.

But here was Chase, showing me quite clearly that my mannerisms were just as ridiculous as anyone else's. It was unbelievably infuriating to have him copy me right back at me, and it still didn't explain the most important part of the question. "Why do *you* have to do it, too?" I said.

He shook his head, one quick jerk to the side, as if I was the one asking stupid questions. "I'm *learning* you," he said. "For my character."

"Couldn't you learn Vince instead?" I said, and even to me I sounded peevish.

Chase shook his head. "My character isn't gay," he said quite seriously.

By the end of work on Thursday, I was very willing to become gay myself if it meant that Chase would stop copying me. I watched him as he aped everything I did, each small unconscious tic, and I learned that I slurped my coffee, washed my hands too long, and stared at the ceiling pursing my lips when I was talking on the phone. I have never had any problems with my self-esteem; I like Dexter very much, just the way he is. But as Chase's performing-monkey act went on and on, I discovered that even the healthiest self-image can erode under a barrage of constant, solemn mockery.

I did my best to soldier on. I told myself that I was following orders, and this was all part of the job and I really had no choice in the matter, but it didn't help. Every time I turned around, there was a mirror image of whatever I was doing, but with a neat mustache and a perfect haircut. Worse than that, every now and then I would turn and see him simply staring at me, with an otherworldly expression of abstract longing on his face that I could not decipher.

The days wore on and his presence became more and more exasperating. It was bad enough to have him following, watching, copying me—but even setting all that aside, I found it impossible to like Robert Chase. I admit that I rarely manage to achieve the kind of warm personal bond that humans routinely forge, mostly because I do not actually have human feelings. Even so, I fake it very well; I have survived among people my whole life and I know all of the rituals and tricks of social bonding. None of them worked with Chase, and for some reason I found myself reluctant to keep trying. Something about him was wrong, slightly off, unattractive, and although I could not have said why, I just didn't like him.

But I had been commanded to tow him through the stormy waters of my life in forensics, and so tow I must. And I have to admit that at least Chase was diligent. He showed up every morning, almost exactly at the same time I did. Friday morning he even brought in a box of doughnuts. I must have looked surprised, because he smiled at me and said, "That's what you do, right?"

"Sometimes I do," I admitted.

He nodded. "I asked around about you," he said. "They all told me, 'Dexter does doughnuts.'" And he grinned at me as if alliteration was some kind of wonderfully clever form of wit.

If I had been irritated by him before, now I was positively seething. He had gone beyond mere mockery; now he was "asking around" about me, prying into my character, encouraging everyone around me to unload about all of Dexter's quirks and peccadilloes. It made me so angry that I could calm myself only by picturing Robert duct-taped to a table, with me standing happily above him clutching a fillet knife. Still, I ate his doughnuts.

That afternoon provided the only relief I'd had all week. And it seemed only fitting that it came in the form of a homicide.

Robert and I had just returned from lunch. I had allowed him to persuade me to take him for some Real Cuban Food, and so we'd gone to my favorite place, Café Relampago. The Morgans had been going there for two generations—three now, if you counted the fact that I had taken my baby, Lily Anne. She loved the *maduros*.

In any case, Robert and I had dined lavishly on *ropa vieja, yuca, maduros*, and, of course, *arroz con frijoles negros*. We had washed it all down with Ironbeer, the Cuban version of Coke, and finished with flan and a barrage of *cafecitas*. Robert had insisted on paying, perhaps trying to buy his way into my affections, so I was in a slightly mellower mood when we returned to our job. But we didn't get a chance to settle into our chairs to reflect and digest, because as we strolled in, Vince came rushing out clutching the canvas bag that held his kit.

"Get your stuff," he said, hurrying past. "We got a wild one."

Robert turned to watch him go, and his air of relaxed confidence seemed to drain out and puddle at his feet. "Is that . . . Does he mean, um—"

"It's probably nothing," I said. "Just a routine machete beheading or something."

Chase goggled at me for a moment. Then he turned pale, gulped, and finally nodded. "Okay," he said.

I went to fetch my gear, feeling a warm glow of satisfaction at Chase's obvious distress. As I said, sometimes I am not a very nice person.

# THREE

THE BODY WAS IN A DUMPSTER IN AN ALLEY ON THE EDGE OF the downtown campus of Miami-Dade Community College. The alley was dark, even in the midday sun, shaded by the surrounding buildings, and it had probably been even darker at night, when some wicked Someone had chosen the spot for his fun and games, most likely for that very reason. Judging by the condition of the body, that had been a very good idea. The things that had been done to what had once been an attractive young woman were best left unseen.

The Dumpster was at an angle in the back corner of the alley. One side of the lid was propped open, and even from ten feet away you could hear the buzz of the nine billion flies whirling around it in a huge dark cloud. Angel Batista-No-Relation was dusting the outside of the Dumpster for prints. He worked carefully along the top edge, dusting with one hand and waving flies away with the other.

Vince was on one knee on the near side, beside the Dumpster, where some of the sloppier garbage had spilled over onto the pavement. He was gingerly sifting through the filthy glop with his rubber-gloved fingers. He didn't look happy. "Jesus," he said to me without looking up. "I can't breathe."

"Breathing is overrated," I told him. "Find anything?"

"Yes," he said, and he was almost snarling. "I found some garbage." He gritted his teeth and brushed at something that clung to his gloves. "If we get another one like this, I'm transferring to Code Enforcement."

I felt a small dark tickle of interest from the Passenger. "Another?" I asked. "Are we likely to get another one?"

Vince cleared his throat and spit to one side. "Doesn't look like a casual kill," he said. "Definitely not a fight with the boyfriend. Jesus, I hate garbage."

"What does that mean, another?" Chase asked from his position at my elbow. "Do you mean it could be, like, a serial killer?"

For a moment, Vince forgot that he was on his knees in garbage, and he beamed up at Chase with sheer adoration. "Hi, Robert," he said. After a full week of seeing Chase every day, Vince still came close to swooning in his presence. But at least he wasn't moaning "ohmygod" anymore.

"So why do you think that?" Chase said. "That, you know, it's not casual?"

"Oh," Vince said. "It's just, you know. A little bit . . . baroque?" He waved one hand merrily, sending a small glob of garbage flying through the air and onto my shoe. "Oops," he said.

"Baroque," Chase said thoughtfully. "Like what. You mean, um . . . what?"

Vince kept smiling. Nothing Chase said, no matter how stupid, could put a dent in his bright and shiny armor. "Complicated," Vince said. "Like, you know. He didn't just want to kill her. He had to *do* stuff to her."

Chase nodded, and even in the shadows of the alley, I thought he turned a few shades paler. "What, um," he said, and he swallowed. "What kind of stuff?"

"Take a look," Vince said. "It's kind of hard to describe."

Chase shifted his weight from one foot to the other, clearly wishing he was almost anywhere else. But for my part, I could wait no longer. I would like to say that I felt an urgent sense of duty to the city of Miami, which paid me to investigate these things. But in truth, the weight of my professional obligations was nothing compared to the rising tide of eager whispers from the deepest basement of Dexter's Dark Keep, urging me to peek into the Dumpster and delight in what we might find. So I stepped around Vince to where Angel No-Relation was meticulously photographing the dozens of smudged fingerprints he had found.

"Angel," I said. "What have we got?"

He didn't look up; he just made a face of terrible disgust and nodded at the Dumpster. *"Mira,"* he said.

I looked inside. The Dumpster was two-thirds filled with a delightful medley of paper, plastic, and rotting food scraps. Sprawled across the top of the fragrant mess was the nude and mutilated body of a young woman. I stepped forward for a closer look, and even before any of the details registered with me consciously, the picture clicked into focus in a dim dry place inside and I felt the Dark Passenger slither up out of its slumber with a stirring of leather wings and a rising sibilance of not-quite-words, whispering its way up the shadowed staircase from the deepest basement of Castle Dexter and onto the ramparts for a ringside view and softly saying, *Yes, Oh, yes, yes, Indeed*, and with a new sense of respect, I looked very carefully to see what had awakened the Passenger from its dark dreams.

She was turned half away from me, slipping partway down the slope of the heaped-up garbage, but from what I could see in profile, her death had not been an easy one. A large handful of golden hair on the side of her head had been ripped out by the roots, revealing a partially chewed-off ear.

The visible part of her face was so savagely damaged that her own mother would never recognize what was left. Her lips had been hacked off clumsily, leaving only a jagged red ruin. Her nose was mashed into a flat red pulp, and the visible eye socket was empty.

The rest of her seemed to be just as thoroughly ravaged; her nipple was missing, apparently chewed away like the ear, and her stomach had been slit open right below the navel. I could see at least three wounds that might have killed her, and a dozen more that would have been horrible enough to make death seem like a good idea.

But before I could take more than one quick glance, I heard a dreadful sound behind me, as if someone was strangling a large animal, and I turned to see Chase backing rapidly away with both hands clamped over his mouth, his face turning pale green almost as fast as he retreated. With a feeling of real pleasure, I watched him sprint for the perimeter. It was a common reaction to seeing messy death for the first time, but in this case it was very satisfying. It also left me in peace to take a longer look at a more leisurely pace, and I did.

I scanned the body head to toe, marveling at the thoroughness of the devastation, and the Passenger murmured its appreciation. Someone had spent a great deal of time and effort doing this, and although the results were certainly not up to my high artistic standards, they still showed a certain primitive vigor and abandon that were admirable, even infectious. The technique was clumsy, inefficient, even brutal, but it spoke of a wild experimental joy in the work that was a pleasure to see. After all, so very few of us seem to enjoy our jobs nowadays. Whoever did this clearly did enjoy it. Just as clearly—at least to me—the killer was exploring, seeking something he had not quite found, in spite of a very thorough search.

I took one more long, studious look at the whittled-away remains of the young woman, and I did not need the Passenger's whispered endorsement to agree with Vince. This might be the very first time Our Perp had done this, but it would not be the last. Things being what they were, it would be a very good thing to catch him before he turned too many more young women into fish bait, and that meant it was time for Dexter to push his mighty brain online and get busy. There was real and compelling work to do, and with Chase in exile at the perimeter tape, I was at last free to do it.

But I had done no more than find a relatively clean place to set down my bag when I heard what sounded like a spatter of applause coming from the perimeter. I have been at the scene of hundreds of homicides, both professionally and in pursuit of my hobby, and I have seen and heard many surprising things. I can truthfully say, however, that I had never before heard a mutilated body receive a standing ovation. I turned to look with more than a little curiosity.

Deborah was just ducking under the yellow tape, and for half a second I wondered whether she was somehow finally getting the public appreciation she so richly deserved for her years of hard toil in the service of Justice. But no—a few steps behind my sister, a perfectly tousled golden head bobbed into view, and I realized that the eager spatter of approval was actually directed at Deborah's shadow, Jackie Forrest. She paused at the tape to give the crowd a wave of the hand and a dazzling smile, and the people around her pushed forward—not as if they meant to grab her or touch her, but more like they couldn't help themselves, that there was just something about her that made them move closer.

I watched as Jackie traded words with a few of the eagerly, mindlessly smiling people, and I found it strangely fascinating. What was it about her that acted like catnip on these people? She was famous, yes, but so was Robert, and the crowd's reaction hadn't been anything like this. And she was pretty—but I could see at least three women in the crowd around her who were, quite frankly, better-looking. And yet they all surged forward toward Jackie, apparently without knowing why.

I watched as Jackie gave the crowd a few final words, a last smile, and then ducked under the tape and moved toward the Dumpster. They watched her go, unable to take their eyes off her, and I realized that I was no better. Now that I had seen a brainless and drooling crowd staring at a TV actor, I felt compelled to watch her, too. I told myself that I was just trying to understand why the unwashed mob found her so mesmerizing, but myself didn't seem to believe it.

I finally peeled my eyes away and went to join my sister. Debs was already peering into the Dumpster with a very hard look on her face. "Jesus Christ," she said. "Jesus Fucking Christ." She shook her head. "You got anything yet?"

"I just got here," I said.

"Who's got the lead?" she said, her eyes flicking over the body.

"Anderson," I told her,

"Shit," she said. "He couldn't find his ass with both hands."

"What is it?" said a husky voice, and Jackie Forrest joined us.

"You might not want to look," I said, but she had already pushed past me to stare into the Dumpster. Remembering Chase's reaction, I braced myself for the inevitable explosion of horror, dismay, and vomit, but Jackie just stared.

"Wow," she said. "Oh, my *God*." She glanced at Debs. "Who could do that?"

"A lot of people," Deborah snarled. "More every day."

"Wow," Jackie said again, still looking at the dead girl, and then she frowned. "So what do you do now?"

"Nothing," Debs said through her teeth. "It's not my case."

"Okay, right," Jackie said with an impatient wave of her hand. "But if it *was* your case, what would you do?"

Deborah turned away from the body and stared at Jackie. After a very long moment, Jackie ripped her gaze away from the thing in the Dumpster and faced my sister. "What?" she said.

"That doesn't bother you?" Debs said, nodding at the corpse.

Jackie made a face. "Of course it bothers me," she said, her voice rich with irritation. "But I'm just trying to be, you know. Professional. I mean, doesn't it bother *you*?"

"It's my job," Deborah said.

Jackie nodded. "Exactly," she said. "And right now it's *my* job, too. I need to learn about this. I mean, what. You want me to go all girly-girl, and squeal and pass out?"

Deborah studied her for another long moment. Jackie studied her right back. "No," Debs said at last. "I guess not."

Jackie nodded. "All right then," she said. "So if it's your case, what do you do now?"

Deborah looked at her. Then she nodded. She jerked her head toward me. "Usually, I talk to him," she said, and Jackie turned her violet eyes on me. I will not say that my knees went weak and wobbly, but I definitely felt like I should bow, straighten my tuxedo, and hand her an orchid.

"Why him?" she said.

"Dexter is forensics," Deborah said, "and sometimes he gets lucky, finds something that can help me. Also"—she shrugged—"he's my brother."

"Your *brother*!" she exclaimed with what looked like real delight. "That's perfect! So *you're* the tough cop and *he's* the nerd! Just like the show!"

"The preferred term is *geek*," I said. "Although *wonk* will do in a pinch. But never *nerd*."

"Oh, I'm sorry," she said, and she put a hand on my shoulder. I could feel the warmth of it right through my shirt. "I didn't mean to insult you. I'm sorry."

"Um," I said, horribly aware of her warm hand on my shoulder. "Perfectly all right."

She smiled and took her hand away. "Good," she said. "So, um, have you found anything that's, you know. Something that might help?"

In fact, the only thing I had found was a fondness for having her hand on my shoulder, and for some reason that was tremendously irritating. After all, I had gone my entire life without feeling even a small zephyr from the hurricane winds of human lust—why should I start now, with an unobtainable golden-haired goddess? And seriously, I had much more important things to do, many of them involving duct tape and fillet knives. But I fought down my rising crankiness and, in the spirit of cooperation mandated by Captain Matthews, I gave her an answer.

"In the first place," I said, "you're supposed to say, 'What have you got?' Not, 'Um, have you found anything?'"

Jackie smiled again. "Okay," she said, and added, "what have you got?"

"Don't look so happy," I said. "It's kind of a casual, short-tempered snarl. Like this." I set my face in my very best imitation of Deborah's Cop Face and said, "What have you got."

Jackie laughed. It was such an infectiously cheerful sound that for a moment I forgot we were standing by a mutilated corpse dumped on a heap of garbage. "Okay," she said. "So you're not just a forensics geek; you're an acting coach, too, huh? All right. How's this?" And she twisted her face into a cranky-fish mask that actually looked a lot like Deborah's expression. "What have you got," she deadpanned. Then she chuckled again, and I felt an answering smile creeping onto my face.

Deborah, however, did not seem to share our good spirits. She scowled even more, and said, "If you two Twinkies are done clowning around, we still got a chopped-up body here."

"Oh," Jackie said, immediately looking serious again. "I'm sorry, Sergeant. Of course you're right."

Although I couldn't help thinking that Debs was a little bit of a buzz-kill, I also knew she was right. And in any case, I didn't like the bizarre human feelings that Jackie was causing in me. So I gave them both a short, very professional nod, and went back to work.

I had only been working at it for a very short time when I heard someone gag and say, "Oh, Jesus. Oh, my God," and since I was fairly certain Robert had not come back for another peek at the party, I turned to look at Vince to see what had caused that kind of reaction in someone who was usually so unflappable, even in the face of the most extreme carnage.

Vince had dragged a box over to the Dumpster. He was standing on it and very carefully examining the body, but something had frozen him in place, absolutely motionless, half bent into the Dumpster, and I felt a new hiss of interest from the Passenger.

"What is it," I asked him, fighting to keep the eagerness out of my voice.

"Oh, holy fuck," he said. "I can't believe this."

"Believe what?" I said, more than a little irritated at the way he had to emote his way through a long dramatic buildup instead of simply answering my question.

"Semen," he said, shaking his head and turning to face me with a look of complete disgust. "There's semen in the eye socket."

I blinked; I have to admit that seemed extreme, even to me. "The eye socket? Are you sure?" I said, and it is an indication of how shocked I was that I said something that stupid.

"I'm sure," he said, turning back to look at the body once more. "It's actually *in* the fucking eye socket, which means— Oh, Jesus Fucking Christ."

I stepped over beside him and looked again at the shattered remains of the young woman. She was still dead. Vince had turned her head slightly so the far side of her face was now visible, and although it was just as damaged, her other eye had not been torn out. It was wide-open, staring straight ahead at the improbable death that had come for her. I wondered what she had done to bring this kind of monstrous end to her life. Not that I am parroting the Homicidal Rapist Party Line of, *She deserved it; she had it coming for dressing like that*, and so on. I was quite sure that whoever this young woman had been, she had done nothing to deliberately provoke anything like this.

But there is always something the victim does unconsciously, some special trigger that brings a Passenger up out of the shadows and into the driver's seat. Every Monster has his own specific flash point that ignites the Need, and it is almost always different.

And every Monster reacts in his own distinctive way, following a program that provides unique satisfaction, a series of rituals that makes sense only to him and ends in the way it absolutely *must*, no matter how bewildering it may seem to the casual human witness. And when the press and an outraged public recoil in horror and demand a reason, and wail their baffled chorus of, "Why would someone do *that*?" those of us in the know can only smile and say, *Because*. It will never make sense to you, or to anyone else, and it doesn't need to. It only has to satisfy *Me*, fulfill *My* special fantasy. It is an E ticket to a ride with only one seat, *Mine*, and no one else will ever get to feel this *Me-Only* roller-coaster thrill, the one thing that provides just *Me* with the ultimate in satisfaction, and whether it is slowly and joyously slicing up a carefully selected playmate, or butchering a young woman and filling her empty eye socket with semen, it is always the same solo act with the same conclusion of release, satisfaction, fulfillment.

But this—

I know very well that we all feel sexual urges, to one degree or another, even those of us in the Dark Brotherhood. It may be the most basic and pervasive piece of the human clock; we all tick toward sex. But the hands move at different speeds for all of us, and the thing that sets off the chimes is almost always unique. Even so, this was well outside the range even of my understanding. I could not remember seeing something quite this uniquely lustful.

Semen in the eye socket: a release that was actual as well as metaphorical. What did that mean? Because it always means something. It is always a fundamental symbol in a world of personal meaning, a basic key to understanding who had done this. Semen left on dead bodies is actually very common, and the specific place where it is found is always important. It indicates a desire to control, degrade, conquer that particular spot. So it was quite possible that the killer had some very special issues with vision, or watching—or it could just as easily be a problem with blue eyes, or contact lenses, or someone winking.

Still, it was a starting point for someone with my special skills—the professional ones—and I pondered it as I worked. It was, after all, an area of real personal interest to me. And additionally, if this had been Deborah's case, she would almost certainly have demanded some kind of special insight from Sick and Twisted Me. So I thought about it, and although I came up with nothing helpful, at least it passed the time.

Because we had arrived at the Dumpster so late in the day, after lunch, it was well past quitting time when we finally wrapped it up at the scene. I packed up my samples, grabbed my bag, and turned to go. Chase was standing at the yellow perimeter tape, chatting with a couple of uniformed officers. He was apparently no longer fighting to hold down his lunch; in fact, he seemed to be in the middle of some spellbinding narration, and the officers were following his every word with awestruck interest. Not really wanting to interrupt such a chummy little scene, I gave them a wide berth.

But Chase appeared at my elbow the moment I was under the tape. "What did you find?" he asked me. "Is it a serial killer?"

To be honest, I was getting a little bit annoyed at his obsession with serial killers. Why does everyone assume that Miami is overrun with serial killers? Besides, Robert made them sound like oddities, freaks, some kind of savage, ravening, subhuman beast, and as I could have told him, they really aren't. They're perfectly normal. I mean, most of the time.

But honesty is not always the best policy, no matter what the Boy Scouts may tell you. So I just shook my head at his inane question. "Too soon to tell," I said.

He stayed with me all the way back to headquarters, asking questions that could easily have been answered directly if only he had watched me work: what had I done at the scene, what had I found, what kind of samples did I take, why did I want that, what would I do with it, what happened next. It was all extremely annoying and I couldn't help thinking that Jackie Forrest would almost certainly have asked more intelligent questions—and looked a great deal better asking them, too.

Chase stayed with me all the way up to the lab, and watched as I hurried through the routine of logging in the samples I had brought from the crime scene. I was hungry, and his questions made things take longer than they should have, since I had to explain every single step of the process. At least he had heard of chain of evidence, which saved a few minutes. But when I finally finished and was ready to hustle down to my car and away into the weekend, he stopped me one last time.

"So that's it, right?" he said. "I mean, Friday night. The weekend. So, um, nothing happens with all this until Monday morning?"

"That's right," I said, maintaining a wonderful balance between answering politely and edging for the door.

"So, okay," he said. "So then, what. You, uh—you just, um . . ." He looked away, and then whipped his head back to me abruptly enough to startle me. "What do you do with your weekends?"

I really wanted to say that I looked for people like him and made them go away into neat bundles, carefully packed into heavy-duty garbage bags. But I realized that it was probably not the most politically correct answer. "I'm married," I said. "I spend time with my wife and kids."

"Married," he said, as if I had told him I was an astronaut. "So, what, you take the kids to the park? Playdates with other children, that kind of thing? How old are your kids?"

Deep inside, very deep, in the snuggest, darkest corner of Fort Dexter, I heard a very small and leathery sound, a mere throat clearing, not even a rustle of wings—but definitely a sign that the Passenger had perked up ever so slightly for some reason, not as if there was any danger to me, not at all, but instead . . . what? Something.

I looked at Chase, hoping for some kind of clue about what might have tripped the Passenger's almost-alarm. But he just stared back, and I felt no menace of any kind from him, even though he was looking at me just as intensely as he had when asking about forensic procedure. "Is this about your character?" I asked him.

He licked his lips and looked away. "No, I— Sorry. I didn't mean to pry. I just, you know." He shrugged and put his hands in his pockets. "I, um. I never got married. Came close once, but . . ." He took his hands out again and made a helpless gesture. "I don't know. I never had kids, and I always wondered, you know. If I could have done it, been a father." He looked up at me and quickly added, "I mean, not the physical—the biological part, because you know. Never any problem there." He flashed me a quick, odd smile, then looked away and took a deep breath. "Just, the other stuff. Everyday things, like teaching her to ride a bicycle, and putting a Band-Aid on her knee, and, you know. The stuff you do all the time." And he looked at me with that expression again, the one that said he wanted something but had no idea how to get it.

And once again I felt a small and hesitant murmur from the Basement, and once again I had no clue why. Chase was certainly not threatening me in any way—and the murmur from the Passenger had not indicated an immediate threat, just some kind of vague discomfort. But why?

So I looked at Robert and thought about what he had said. It was not dark and threatening, but it was slightly off in some way I could not pin down. If he truly liked kids, why not have a few? And if he was unsure, he could afford to rent half a dozen to try it out.

But I had no answer, and I got none from Chase, who had turned away and looked like he'd forgotten there was anybody else in the room with him. He was staring into the distance, slumped into his own thoughts and cocking his head as if he heard some faint music playing somewhere. He took a long ragged breath, and then abruptly jerked upright again and looked back to me, startled. He shook himself. "Anyway," he said brightly. "You have a great weekend. With your wife . . . and kids." He slapped me on the shoulder, squeezing just for a second, and then he strode away, out the door and downstairs into the lonely Miami night.

I thought about Chase and his odd performance all the way down to my car. There was clearly a little bit more to the man than I had suspected, a depth of feeling that he kept well hidden behind his everyday mask of self-involved inanity. Or his several masks, since he certainly hid all kinds of things about himself, like why he disliked Jackie so much. Probably all part of being a Leading Man. He would have to hide everything that didn't fit perfectly with his macho-but-sensitive public image. So he couldn't let anyone know it if he liked fluffy little white dogs, or liked to read romance novels. If the public learned about it, that sort of thing could cost him his career. They might think he was a sissy, or worse—even a Liberal! It wouldn't do.

But in all truth, it didn't matter, not even a little bit. It was just one more of the dozens of dopey contradictions making up the many-sided mess that was humanity, and all things considered, it was much less interesting than thinking about what Rita might have cooked for dinner.

I started my car and put Chase out of my mind as I nosed out into the merry brutality of Friday-night traffic in Miami.

# FOUR

BECAUSE I HAD STAYED SO LATE AT THE CRIME SCENE, DIN-nertime had come and gone when I finally got home. The foyer inside the front door was crowded with three tall stacks of card-board boxes that hadn't been there that morning, and I had to hunch in beside them to close the door. Rita and I had recently taken advan-tage of the collapsed real estate market and bought a foreclosed house, larger than our current one, and equipped with a swimming pool. We had all worked ourselves up into an absolute lather at the thought of our palatial new house, with more room for all, and our very own pool, and even a brick barbecue in the back. And then—we waited.

The local office of the bank gave us a number to call. We called the number, and our calls were shunted away to an office in Iowa, where we were offered a complicated recorded menu, put on hold, and then disconnected. We called back, trying all the selections on the menu, one after another, until we finally reached a nonrecorded human voice, which told us they couldn't help, we had to go through the local office, and hung up.

We went back to the local office, who explained that their bank had just been bought out by a larger bank, and now that the merger was complete everything would be quick and simple.

We called the home office of the new bank, where we were offered a complicated recorded menu, put on hold, and then disconnected.

Those who know me best will tell you I am a mild and patient man, but there were more than a few moments in our epic struggle with our nation's great financial system when I was sorely tempted to pack a few rolls of duct tape and a fillet knife into a small bag and solve our communication problem in a more direct way. But happily for all, after eighteen encounters with different Assistant Vice Presidents for Repeating Annoying Redundancy, Rita stepped in and took over. She had spent her career in the world of big-dollar bureaucracy, and she knew how Things worked. She finally found the right person, called the right number, filed the correct form, got it to the correct office, and the paperwork entered the system at last.

And then we waited.

Several more months went by while the bank busily lost the papers and forgot to file forms, and then sent us threatening letters demanding outrageous fees for all kinds of things we had never done and never even heard of. But miraculously enough, Rita was persistent and firm and the bank finally ran through its entire arsenal of reptilian bureaucratic blunders, and reluctantly allowed us to close on our new house.

Moving day was now approaching rapidly, only two weeks away, and with her customary savage efficiency Rita had been spending every free moment stuffing things into cardboard boxes, taping them shut, labeling them with Magic Markers—a different color for each room in our new house—and stacking them in well-ordered piles.

But as I squirmed past the boxes and into the living room, where Lily Anne was sound asleep in her playpen, I discovered that tonight Rita had done a great deal more than simply fill boxes; one quick sniff was enough to fill my nostrils with the lingering aroma of roast pork, one of Rita's signature dishes. There would almost certainly be a plate of leftovers waiting for me, and at the thought of it my mouth began to water. So I hurried through the living room and into the kitchen.

Rita stood at the sink, pale blue rubber gloves pulled up onto both hands as she scrubbed the roasting pan. Astor slumped beside her, drying dinner plates with a sulky expression on her face. Rita looked up and frowned. "Oh, Dexter," she said. "You're finally home?"

"I think so," I said. "My car is out front."

"You didn't call," she said. "I didn't know if— Astor, for God's sake, can't you go a little faster? And so I didn't know when you'd be home," she finished, looking at me accusingly.

It was true. I hadn't called, mostly because I forgot. I had been so distracted by Chase, and Jackie, and thinking about the dreadful, fascinating mess in the Dumpster, that it just slipped my mind. I suppose I took it for granted that Rita would know I was coming and save me some dinner.

But from the way she was looking at me now, I began to think that perhaps that had been a mistake. Human relationships, especially the whole Being Married Thing, were foreign territory for me. It was clear I should have called to say I would be late—but could the consequences really be this calamitous? Was it really possible that there was no plate with Dexter's name on it, filled with succulent roast pork and who knows what other wonderful things? A fate far worse than death—at least, worse than someone else's death.

"We had a really bad one today," I said. "We got the call late in the day, after lunch."

"Well," Rita said, "I do need to know when you're coming home. That's enough, Astor. Tell Cody to take his bath."

"I want a bath, too," Astor snarled.

"You take forever," Rita said. "Cody will be in and out in ten minutes and then you can take all the time you want."

"With his gross germs all over the tub!" Astor said.

Rita raised an arm and pointed. "Go," she said sternly.

"I'm sorry," I told Rita, as Astor stalked past me, looking like Miss Preteen Rage of 2013. "Um, we just got really, uh, tied up, and— So, is there any roast pork left?"

"It's practically bedtime," Rita said, slapping the roasting pan into the dish drainer. "And we were supposed to watch that new penguin movie tonight, remember?"

As she mentioned it, I did, in fact, remember that we had talked about having some quality family time, watching a DVD together. Normally, I would have accepted it as one of those annoying tasks that I simply have to perform in order to maintain the polite fiction of my disguise: Daddy Dexter, Pillar of Family Life. But under the circumstance, it seemed to me that Rita was avoiding the only subject of any real interest—was there, in fact, some roast pork left?

"I am sorry," I said. "If it's too late, maybe we could, um . . . Is there? Some pork left for me?"

"Pork?" Rita said. "That isn't— Oh, of course there's some pork. I wouldn't let— It's in the fridge. But, Dexter, really, you have to be a little more . . ." She fluttered one hand, and then began to pull off the rubber gloves. "I'll heat it up for you. But Cody has been wanting to— I suppose we can see the movie tomorrow night, but still . . ."

She hustled over to the refrigerator and started taking out the leftovers, and a great sense of relief washed over me. In fact, as the microwave began to heat my dinner and reignite the wonderful aroma, I actually felt smug. After all, I was getting an excellent dinner without having to watch another animated movie about penguins. Life was good.

It was even better when I finally sat at the kitchen table with my plate and began to ply my fork. There were fried *plátanos* as well as roast pork, and tortellini in a garlic sauce, instead of the more traditional rice and beans. But I lost no time bemoaning the fall of an institution. I set to with a will, and in only a few happy minutes I was sated, and already sliding into the dopey half-asleep state that follows when you add a good meal to a clean conscience. Somehow, I managed to make it onto my feet and stagger to the couch, where I sloshed onto the cushions and began to digest my meal and think profound Friday-night thoughts.

Because I was in such a deep state of contentment, I pushed away all the nagging disagreeable trivia of the week and concentrated on more pleasant things. I thought about the body in the Dumpster, and it occurred to me that a Dumpster was an odd place to dump a body that had been so thoroughly and distinctively whittled away— especially a Dumpster right there on the edge of the campus, a few blocks from the busiest part of downtown Miami. As I know very well, it is incredibly easy to put a body where it will never be found— especially here in the tropical splendor that I call home. Practically right outside my front door was a delightful aquatic graveyard that was nearly bottomless. And then there was the Everglades, with its lovely gator holes, and the scrublands so full of sinkholes—South Florida was truly a corpse disposer's Paradise.

There were so many wonderful options for dumping bodies, even for someone with the most limited imagination. And so, in my experience, when the leftovers are placed where they must be discovered, it is usually because discovery is an important part of the entire artistic statement. *Look what I did; can't you see why I had to do it?*

I did not see, not yet—but just the thought of that word, "see," reminded me of the most disturbing detail: the semen in the eye socket. There was no mystery about how it got there, but the *why* of it was clearly the most important piece of the puzzle. It was the consummation, the literal climax to the whole event, and understanding what made it necessary was the key to knowing who had done it.

And as I pondered this in my pork-induced demi-doze, a soft and sibilant voice that had not been fed and so was not at all sleepy whispered one sly question in my inner ear: *Was she still alive when he did it?*

The shock of that thought brought me upright. Had she been alive at the end, when he ripped out one eye? Had she been watching with the other eye as he began his ultimate violation? I tried to picture it from her point of view: the unbearable pain, the shattering knowledge that Things had been done that could never be repaired, the slow and brutal approach of that final ocular indignity—

Deep in the shadows of Castle Dexter I felt the Passenger jerk upright and hiss an uncomfortable objection. What, after all, was I doing? There was absolutely no point to such a meaningless act of imagination, and I was in very grave danger of trying to feel empathy, a completely human flaw of which I had only academic knowledge. And I knew nothing about being a mutilated, helpless victim, either. On the whole, I had to believe that was a good thing.

No: It was the predator's perspective that was important for understanding this—an angle that was far more natural for me. I sent a silent apology to the Passenger, and changed my mental point of view.

All right: The basics of stalking, capture, bondage, all the other bits of foreplay were standard, uninteresting. Then the real work begins, and I leaned back on the couch and tried to see how it had happened. Around me in our little house I could hear the clamor of bath, brushing, bedtime, and I closed my eyes and tried to shut it out while I concentrated.

Breathe in, out, focus; I picture the damage to the body, see how it must have happened, each wild bite and slash. The girl thrashes, terrified, eyes bulging, not knowing what will happen next but knowing it will be beyond horror, and in my imagination I raise up the knife—and I realize there is something atypical here, a first significant variation. Because it was My Imagination, I had pictured a knife going up—it is, after all, how I do it. It is a wonderful moment: to see the eyes widen, the muscles knot against the duct tape, the breath hiss laboriously in for a scream that will never get past the gag. I always use knives and other hardware, with never an exception. It is not merely an aesthetic choice, a pride in making neat and clean cuts; the thought of getting any vile body fluids on my hands is repulsive, unspeakable, a dreadful corruption.

From my professional experience, though, I knew very well that many fellow hobbyists prefer the hands-on approach, even require it for fulfillment. Picturing direct contact with pulsing wet leaking flesh gave me a feeling of creeping disgust, but I could at least understand it, and even accept it. After all, we must all try to be tolerant of others. Some of us want to get our hands, feet, and teeth into the work; some of us prefer the more civilized approach of working at a distance with cold steel. There is room for all; different strokes for different folks.

But this time it was something else. This time the killer had used a combination of techniques. The victim had been slashed and stabbed with some kind of blade, but the more meaningful damage, the real signature work, had been done with teeth, fists, fingernails, and other, more intimate body parts. It was an unusual approach, and it almost certainly meant something very important.

But what? I knew very well what knife work was about; it was the perfect way to take control, to cause neat and permanent damage. And then the biting—a desire for contact, for the most intimate possible interface with agony? Except that what had been done to the eye socket was far more than a twisted cuddle. It was a declaration of total power, a statement that *I* own *you and I can do anything I want to you.* And it was a commanding bellow of, *Look at me!* More: it was a punishment, a way to say that *Your eyes did me wrong; you should have paid attention and* seen *me but you did not and now I will teach you and I will do* this.

Down the hall the bathroom door slammed with cataclysmic force and my eyes jerked open. I listened for a few moments as Astor's voice rose from whining to threatening and all the way up into shrill fury above Rita's calm and commanding words, finally subsiding into a muted grumble of general discontent. The door slammed again; Lily Anne began to cry, and Rita's voice turned soothing, and a minute later peace was restored, and I returned to my happy pastime of imagining intimate carnage.

The killer wanted to be noticed—by all of us, of course, which was why the body had been displayed so publicly. But far more important, he had wanted the victim to pay attention to him, truly and completely *see* him, appreciate his significance. I thought about that for a minute, and it felt right. *You should have noticed me, but you didn't. You ignored me and now your eye will pay for what your eyes failed to do.*

I closed my eyes again and tried once more to *see* it, picture the way it would be: to make her feel Me and understand how stupid she was not to know that I was there and seeing her and needing her to see Me and she does not and so I take her and I teach her and I work her through the terror, the pain, the passion of carnage, and I feel the slow approach to fulfillment until at last she understands and she is ready and so am I and I see that beautiful battered head with its golden hair and my arousal grows and I am ready for the finale—

It must have been the roast pork. Combined with the extra-long workday, and the added stress of having Robert follow me around all week, the roast pork had simply worn me out. In any case, I fell asleep. But I did not fall into the timeless, dreamless darkness that usually rewards me when I close my eyes at night. Instead, the visions continued: *I stand there above the still-living body and look down at what I have done, and I feel such a sweet rising pitch of bliss and fulfillment and I kneel beside the body and grab a fistful of beautiful golden hair and yank the head around so it must look at me. And the face turns slowly to me and I hold my breath as the features become clear and it is a perfect face, unmarked and filled with longing for me, for what I am going to do, and as I look down into*

*the bottomless violet eyes I realize that this is Jackie Forrest, and what I am
going to do suddenly begins to change.*

*And I put down my knife and look at her, look at the perfect curve of her
lips and the spray of freckles across her nose and those deep improbable eyes
and somehow her clothes are gone and I lean closer to her face and it leans
up toward me and there is an endless moment of almost touching, almost
completing something that is just barely out of reach—*

I opened my eyes. I was still on the couch, and the house had
grown dark and quiet around me, but the image of Jackie Forrest's
face was still with me.

Why had I thought of her? I'd been having a very nice daydream
about perfectly normal vivisection, and she had shouldered her way
in and ruined it with her demands that I put down the knife and try
something more human. I didn't want to have her kind of fantasy;
this was not me, not Dexter the Destroyer. She was forcing me to
become some new and freakish being, a creature that rushed into
passionate seduction and reveled in actual human feelings and a
longing for something that was as far beyond the reach of the real me
as if it was on Mars.

I know it was totally illogical, but I found myself vastly annoyed
with Jackie, as if she had butted in on purpose. But to my much
greater surprise, I found that I was still aroused in reality, and not
just in my imagination. Was it from thinking of the victim—or from
thinking about Jackie Forrest? I didn't know, and that was even more
annoying.

There was just something about her that I found intriguing, even
compelling. It was not that she was a famous actress—I'd had no idea
who she was, had to be told that she was, in fact, a star. Celebrity had
never interested me before, and I was quite sure it didn't now. And
I was certainly far too set in my wicked ways to be interested in any
kind of dalliance that was merely sexual. When Dexter has a fling,
his partner's afterglow lasts forever.

And yet there was Jackie, crowding the screen in my private inter-
nal television, tossing her mane of perfect hair and smiling just for
*me* with a gleam of intelligent amusement in her eyes, and for some
maddening reason I liked it and I wanted to—

Wanted to what? Touch her, kiss her, whisper sweet nothings in her perfect shell-like ear? It was absurd, a cartoon picture, Dexter in Lust. Such things did not happen to our Dreadful Dark Scout. I was beyond the reach of mere mortal desire. I did not feel it, *couldn't* feel it; I never had, didn't want to—and whatever the thought of Jackie Forrest might be doing to me, I never would. This was no more than a Method-actor moment, a fleeting identification with the killer, a confusion of roles, almost certainly brought on because the process of digesting pork had taken all the blood away from my brain.

Whatever it really was, it didn't matter. I was tired, and my poor undernourished brain was running away from me, down a path I didn't like and could never walk. I could sit here grinding my teeth and worrying about it, or I could go to bed and hope that a good night's sleep would send these disturbing, absurd thoughts back into the dark jungle where they belonged. Tomorrow was another day, and it was Saturday, a day for doing nothing, which was known to be a sovereign cure for what ails you.

I stood up and went to bed.

# FIVE

I WOKE THE NEXT MORNING TO THE CLATTER OF PANS, AND THE smell of coffee and bacon floating down the hall from the kitchen. I started to lurch up out of bed, and then I remembered that it was Saturday, so I took a few extra lazy moments to loll in bed and enjoy the thought that I had nowhere to go and nothing to do and Rita was making me a wonderful breakfast anyway. I could just lie here snug and smug, secure in the knowledge that all was right with the world and this morning there were no dragons to slay. I had an entire day to devote to doing nothing—and even better, doing it without anyone following me around and taking notes on how I did it.

I lay in a partial doze, drifting on the pleasant stream of breakfast aromas and letting my mind wander willy-nilly, which was fine until it wandered back to the brief dream I'd had last night on the couch, and as the memory of Jackie Forrest's face barged in again I jerked upright in bed, irritated. Why couldn't she leave me alone?

All peace was gone; I got up, trudged into the bathroom, showered, dressed, and went to the kitchen table, hoping that breakfast would set me right again. Lily Anne was in her high chair, attacking some applesauce, and as I came in she kicked her feet and yelled out, "Dadoo!" which was her new name for me.

I stood beside her chair and tickled under her chin. "Lily-Willy," I said, and she gurgled. I wiped the applesauce from my finger and sat at the table.

Rita turned around at the stove and smiled. "Dexter," she said. "There's coffee. Would you like some breakfast?"

"More than life itself," I said, and seconds later I was staring down at a steaming mug of coffee and a stack of Rita's French toast. I don't know what she puts into it, but it tastes better than any other I've ever had, and after four pieces of the French toast, a slice of perfect, ripe cantaloupe, and three crisp strips of bacon, I pushed back from the table and poured a second cup of coffee, feeling like there might be some point to this short and painful existence after all.

I was halfway through my third cup before Cody and Astor made their appearance. They came in together, both of them grumpy and tousled from sleep. Cody wore Transformers pajamas, and Astor had on an overlarge T-shirt bearing a picture of what appeared to be a platypus, and they collapsed onto their chairs as if somebody had stolen all their bones. Cody tore into the French toast without a word, apparently still half asleep, but Astor stared at her plate as if it was loaded with grub worms.

"I'll get fat if I eat this stuff," she said.

"Then don't eat it," Rita said cheerfully.

"But I'm *hungry*," Astor whined.

"Would you like a yogurt instead?" Rita said.

Astor hissed. "I *hate* yogurt."

"Then eat your French toast," Rita told her. "Or go hungry. Whatever you want. But stop whining, all right?"

"I'm not whining," Astor whined, but Rita ignored her and turned back to the stove. Astor stared at her back with a look of venomous contempt. "This family is so lame," she muttered, but she began to pick at her food, and as I sipped the last of my coffee she somehow forced herself to eat all of it and take seconds.

I had almost slid back into a more alert version of the contented state I'd been in when I woke up, when Rita jolted me out of my reverie. "Finish up, everybody," she said happily. "We have an awful lot to do today."

It seemed like an ominous pronouncement. A lot to do? Like

what? I tried to recall whether I had seen a lengthy list of tasks to perform—tasks so urgent that they could invade and conquer a Saturday I had hoped to dedicate to loafing. Nothing came to mind, and no list appeared. Rita was clearly so focused on whatever the jobs might be that she assumed we could all get our instructions from her telepathically. Perhaps my psychic antenna had blown down, but I had no idea at all what I was supposed to prepare for, and it seemed a little bit churlish to ask.

Luckily, Astor was not quite so shy. "I wanna go to the mall," she said. "Why do I have to do stupid chores with *you* guys?"

"You're too young to go to the mall," Rita said. "And anyway—"

"I'm almost *twelve*," Astor interrupted with a hiss, making "twelve" sound like an age so advanced that it required regular geriatric care.

"Well, that may seem old enough to you," Rita said. "But the first sign of maturity is— Cody, stop drumming on the table. Go get dressed—and wear old clothes."

"I only *have* old clothes," Cody said in his too-quiet voice.

"Why can't I ever just do what *I* want to do?!" Astor demanded, and Lily Anne began to shout, "Wanna wanna wanna," pounding her tray rhythmically with her spoon.

"Because you are part of this family, and we all have to— Dexter, can you make the baby stop that?"

"I don't want to be part of a family," Astor said.

"Well," Rita told her, pushing back from the table and grabbing at the dirty dishes, "if you can think of a better way to get your Own Room in a New House— Dexter, *please*, Lily Anne's noise is giving me a headache."

"It's not a *new* house," Astor grumbled, but she was clearly winding down at the thought of her Own Room. The only real enthusiasm I had seen from her recently had been when she was thinking about moving to the new house, where she would have private and personal space for the first time—but, of course, she couldn't just cave in and admit that she was excited.

"It's new to us," Rita said, "and it will seem even newer when we paint it and— Dexter, for God's sake, *please* take the baby and get her dressed?"

I stood up and went to the high chair, where Lily Anne had moved into march time with her spoon-pounding. But as I approached, she raised both arms in the air and shouted, "Dadoo! Uppy uppy!" I unsnapped the chair's metal tray and lifted her up, and with the pure and heartfelt gratitude that only the very young can display, she smacked me on the nose with her spoon. "Dadoo!" she said happily, and as I stood holding her, with tears in my eyes and applesauce on my nose, I could think of nothing else to say but, "Ouch."

Astor had dropped her complaints into a kind of background rumble as I carried Lily Anne away to the changing table. I was pleased that I had discovered what important tasks awaited me: "old clothes" for Cody and "paint it" to Astor. With my legendary powers of deduction it was the work of a mere moment to conclude that we were going to be working on the new house, most likely with rollers and brushes and buckets of pastel paint. It wasn't the idle day of couch-warming I'd had in mind, but there are far worse fates than spending a day painting your very own new house.

I got Lily Anne cleaned and changed, and put her in the playpen. I washed the applesauce and related goo off myself, and re-dressed in some appropriately grubby clothes, and then loaded all the paint, brushes, and drop cloths stacked in the carport into the car.

Then I went back into the house and sat for half an hour, marveling at the chaotic din that ebbed and flowed through the house as the rest of my little family got ready. It was really remarkable how complicated they could make the simplest tasks: Astor couldn't find old socks that matched and flew into a towering miff when I suggested it didn't matter whether they matched, since she was just going to get paint on them. Then Cody appeared in a T-shirt with a picture of SpongeBob on it and Astor began to scream that it was *hers* and he better take it off right now, and they fought about whose shirt it was until Rita hurried in and solved it by taking SpongeBob and giving Cody an *Avatar* shirt, which he wouldn't put on because he still liked *Avatar* and didn't want to get paint on it. Then Astor appeared in a pair of shorts so small they might have been denim underwear and fought Rita for the right to wear what she wanted to wear for another ten minutes.

Cody finally came out and sat next to me, and the two of us waited in silent camaraderie and watched as Rita and Astor changed shoes, shirts, shorts, hair scrunchies, and hats, fighting every step of the way. By the time they were finally ready, I was so exhausted just from watching them that I wasn't sure I could lift a paintbrush. But somehow, we all got into the car, and I drove us over to the new house.

It was a surprisingly peaceful day. Cody and Astor stayed in their separate rooms, slopping paint over almost everything, every now and then even getting some on the walls, where it was supposed to go. Rita painted the kitchen and then the dining room, running back and forth between roller strokes to supervise Cody and Astor, and Lily Anne stayed in her playpen in what would someday be our family room, yelling instructions.

I worked around the outside of the house, pulling weeds, painting trim, and discovering two fire ant nests the hard way, by stepping on them. I found a few other things even less pleasant—apparently there was a very big dog living in our new neighborhood. Luckily, there was a hose still hooked up to the side yard's faucet.

At noon I drove out to Dixie Highway and picked up two large pizzas, one with just cheese and the other with double pepperoni, and we all sat in the screened enclosure by what would someday be our swimming pool, if we could figure out how to get all the green floating crud out of the water. Large chunks of the screen hung from the pool cage's frame like Spanish moss, and several of the metal ribs were bent or missing, but it was all ours.

"Oh, my God," Rita said, clutching a slice of cheese pizza and staring around her at her new kingdom. "This is going to be so . . ." She waved the pizza in a way that was intended to convey unlimited magnificence. "I mean, to have our own— Oh, Dexter, Carlene says her nephew has a pool service?"

"Carlene's nephew is a lawyer," I said. I remembered quite clearly meeting him at Rita's office Christmas party, and coming home with three of his business cards.

"What?" Rita said. "Don't be silly; why would a lawyer have a pool— Oh, you mean *Danny*." She shook her head and took a bite of pizza. "Mmp. This is Mark. Danny's younger brother." She said it through a mouthful of pizza and still made it sound as if she was explaining shoelaces to someone with brain damage. "Anyway, he can get all the gunk out of the pool and make it totally— But we could save a lot of money if . . ." She took another bite of pizza, chewed, and swallowed. "I mean, it can't be that hard. And we still have to get a new pool cage, which costs— But we can buy the chemicals at the pool store? If you don't mind doing— Cody, you've got tomato all over your— Here, let me get that." She leaned over to Cody and scrubbed at his face with a paper towel, while he scrunched up his eyes and looked annoyed.

"Anyway," Rita said, leaning back away from Cody. "It would save some money. Which we will need for the new pool cage, because they are very pricey."

"All right," I said, not completely sure what I was agreeing to do.

Rita sighed and smiled happily. "Anyway," she said again, and I had to agree.

It was five thirty when we decided we'd had enough. We cleaned our paintbrushes, and ourselves, as much as possible, and climbed into the car. I turned the air-conditioning to high for the drive home; we'd all been without for the whole day, since the power was not on yet in the new house, and even though it was a pleasant fall day, we were all sweaty.

The next day was a repeat of Saturday, except that we started an hour later, since it was, after all, Sunday. The only difference was that I got our lunch from a nearby Burger King. I found that I didn't really mind the work. In fact, I slipped into a kind of Zen state of not-painting, letting the paint apply itself without any conscious effort on my part, and it was a great shock to me to see how much I'd done when we all knocked off for the day. I stood and looked at the vast expanse of newly painted house, and for the first time I began to feel a real sense of ownership. I walked around the whole house one time, letting it sink in that soon I would be living here. It was not at all a bad feeling.

And so Monday morning I arrived at work slightly stiff from all the physical labor, but remarkably cheerful in spite of it. I had gotten almost all of the paint out of my hair, off my hands, and out from under my fingernails, and I still had a sense of smug satisfaction with things that lasted all the way up to my desk, where I found Robert Chase sitting in my chair and eating a guava *pastelito* and slurping coffee from my personal mug. A large white pastry box sat on the desk in front of him. There were two big Styrofoam cups with lids beside the box, which made me realize with a bright flash of irritation that he'd used my mug merely because it was *mine* and he was starting out the new week by being Me.

"Hey, Dexter," he said with a jolly smirk. "How was the weekend?"

"Very nice," I said, sliding into the ratty folding chair I keep for visitors.

"Great, super," he said. "Hung out with the kids? Playground and so on? Push 'em on the swings . . . ?"

I looked at him sitting there at my desk, in my chair, drinking from my mug, and I discovered that I did not want to have a pleasant chat with someone who was working so hard to become me. But what I really wanted to do with him required a little more privacy than we had here in the heart of police headquarters, as well as a long stretch of uninterrupted time and a few rolls of duct tape. But of course, someone at the network might miss Robert sooner or later, and so the realities of civilized discourse left me no choice except to play the game properly. So I reached across the desk—*my* desk—and grabbed a *pastelito* from the box.

"All work and no play," I said, taking a bite of the pastry. "I'm afraid it was very dull."

"No, no, not at all," Robert said. "I mean, spending time with your kids, that's . . . You know. It's important."

"I guess it is," I said, and I took another bite. It was pretty good. "And you?" I said, out of mere politeness. "How was your weekend?"

"Oh," he said, and shrugged. "I flew down to Mexico."

"Really," I said. "And you lived?"

He sipped coffee—from my mug!—and looked away. "It's, uh," he said. "I go there all the time. There's a place where, you know." He sipped again. "It's a, um. Kind of a private resort. They know me there, and I can just, um. Relax. No biggie. So," he said, slapping the desk and turning back to me with a bright smile. "What'd you do with your kids? You said there's three of 'em?"

I looked at him sitting there at my desk, and clearly trying very hard to pretend he was interested in my little life—at the same time underplaying the whole idea that he was the kind of guy who flew to Mexico for the weekend and it was no biggie. And because I really was starting to dislike him a lot, I decided not to let him.

"Wow," I said. "That must be expensive. Airline tickets on a whim—and *you* would have to fly first-class, wouldn't you? I mean, just so nobody would bother you. So that's probably, what. A couple of thousand dollars? And then a *private* resort? I've never even heard of such a thing. That can't be cheap, either."

He looked away again, and to my great delight he began to blush under his perfect tan. He cleared his throat and looked very uncomfortable. "That's . . . that's . . . you know," he said. "The, uh, frequent-flier miles . . ." He waved his hand in a kind of spastic dismissal, unfortunately forgetting that he was still holding my coffee mug. A glob of coffee spattered onto my desk, and he gaped at it with his mouth hanging open a half inch or so. "Oh, shit," he said. "I'm sorry." He lurched up out of the chair and plunged past me through the door. "I'll get some paper towels," he said over his shoulder.

I watched him go for a second, marveling that such a truly awkward performance came so easily to such an apparently perfect man. It was so odd that for a moment I thought it had to be deliberate— perhaps a way to change the subject? Could he really be that uncomfortable talking about his affluent ways? Or was he hiding something even more nefarious than wealth?

But of course that was absurd. I was just being my normal, nasty, and suspicious self, seeing wickedness lurking in every shadow— even when there wasn't actually a shadow. I pushed the thought away and stepped over to my desk to see whether any real damage had been done. The coffee had spilled right in the center of the blotter, which was lucky. One small tendril had splatted onto a file folder on the right-hand side, but only enough to leave a small stain on the outside, and not enough to soak through to the papers inside.

Robert hustled back clutching a fistful of paper towels, and I stepped away to let him blot up his mess, which he did with a jerky frenzy, the whole time muttering, "Sorry. Damn. I'm sorry." It was a pathetic performance, almost enough to make me feel sorry for him. But of course, feeling sorry is not something I can actually do, and even if I could, I wouldn't waste it on Robert. So I just stood and watched him, and for the most part I managed not to smirk.

Robert had most of the spill wiped up when the phone on my desk rang. I reached past him and picked up the receiver. "Morgan," I said.

"I need you in my office," said a familiar voice that was grumpy but authoritative. "Bring the case file."

"What case file?" I said.

"The girl in the *Dumpster*," Deborah hissed at me. "Jesus, Dexter." She hung up, and I stared at the phone for a moment, wondering what my sister was up to. This was not her case—Anderson had the lead, and Deborah was theoretically not involved in it at all, except as an observer, a guide assigned to take Jackie Forrest through the maze of her first real homicide case. Perhaps she was going to show Jackie what the forensic file looked like. That probably meant that Jackie was there with her now, and at that thought a small sparkle of anticipation lurched up inside me, until I remembered I was angry with her for making me think of her so often and so pleasantly. But I couldn't ignore Deborah's summons without risking one of her blistering arm punches, so I would just have to take the chance of being assailed by more of the dreadful human feelings of delight caused by exposure to Jackie.

I hung up the phone. Robert had finished his cleanup and stood behind the desk with the wad of coffee-soaked paper towels in his hand. "What's up?" he said.

I pulled the coffee-stained blotter off my desk and dumped it into the trash can. "We have been summoned," I said. "Bring the pastries."

# SIX

EBORAH'S DESK WAS IN AN AREA OF THE SECOND FLOOR where the homicide cops clustered. Like me, she kept a folding chair for her visitors, and as I led Robert in, that chair was occupied by Jackie Forrest. Her hair was pulled back into a tight ponytail that did nothing to hide the glow that seemed to come out of each individual strand of it. If she was wearing makeup I couldn't see it, but her face was smooth and flawless, her eyes sparkled with intelligence and wit, and she looked so perfect she might have been some kind of idealized picture of what DNA could do if it was really trying. She looked up as we came in and gave me a bright smile, and then turned away with a frown when she saw Robert trailing in behind me.

"What took you so long?" Deborah said, and I was touched by the warmth of her greeting.

"Traffic was a bitch," I said. "And how was *your* weekend?"

She snatched the case file from my hand and flung it on her desk. "This fucking case," she said.

I had known that Deborah would be bothered by the unusual brutality of this murder, enough to want to do something about it—

but technically speaking, she couldn't. "I thought this was Anderson's case," I said.

"Anderson couldn't find an ocean of shit if he was swimming in it," she said.

"Detective Anderson?" Robert said. "He seems like a good guy."

Deborah flicked a quick glance at Robert; Jackie rolled her eyes. I took the high road and simply ignored him.

"Well," I said, "even Anderson has to get lucky sometime. And it's his case."

Debs gave her head an irritated shake. "He's got the whole weekend and he can't even get an ID," she said, and I blinked in surprise. Finding the victim's name was the most basic first step, and for forty-eight hours to go by without learning who this was seemed to take the Art of Clueless to an epic level.

"That's pretty spectacular," I said, and because I knew my sister very well, I added, "So what are you going to do about it, against all orders and contrary to department regulations?"

Deborah looked at the folder on her desk, and then at Jackie. The two of them shared a moment I couldn't quite read. "I would never go against orders or department regulations," she said, which did not really agree with history as I had lived it. But Debs said it with a straight face. Then she looked up at me and, wonder of wonders, she smiled. It was so unlike her that for a moment I thought she must have been possessed by demons, and I almost took a step backward to protect myself. But she didn't unleash any gouts of fire, or even speak in tongues. She just kept smiling and tilted her head at Jackie.

"Jackie thought of it," she said, and she turned to face the actress again. This time the smirks they traded were clearly looks of great mutual satisfaction. "We are going to run a mock investigation to teach Jackie how it is done," Deborah said, and then her words took on an odd lilt, as if she was reading from an official report. "In this way, we will parallel the department's actual investigation, without interfering in the official process or compromising the investigating officer's mandate, while at the same time constructing a valid simulation and comparing our results to those achieved by Detective Anderson, which will allow our subject, Ms. Forrest, to understand the subtleties of a homicide investigation and all its procedural complexity as such things are conducted in real time by the Miami-Dade Police Department." She looked back at me again, still smiling. "Pretty cute, huh? I get to slip around Detective Dumbfuck and track this asshole down, and Matthews can't say anything, because I am doing exactly what he ordered."

"Plus," Jackie said. "If we actually come up with something—"

"When we come up with something," Deborah said.

"Then it's spectacular publicity. For the show and the department."

I looked at Jackie with new respect. "Ingenious," I said, and she gave me a smile that made me want to sing.

"So," Deborah said, jerking me back to reality, "I wanted to go over the whole thing with you, and see what we got." She tapped the folder with her finger. "Starting with the forensic stuff." She gave Jackie another smirk. "You know. So Jackie can see how it's done."

"In theory," Jackie said, smirking back.

"Right," Deborah said.

I was very pleased that my sister had found a new Best Friend for Life, but their Ain't We Cute act was getting a little annoying. Happily for me, Robert felt the same way, and he was not nearly as bashful about saying so.

"Well, hey," he said. "I need to be in on this, too." Deborah gave him a blank look, and Jackie got very interested in her fingernails. "I mean," he said, "this is like a perfect way for *me* to learn stuff, too, right?"

Deborah flicked her eyes at me, then back to Robert. "Sure," she said flatly.

"Great," Robert said. He leaned back against the windowsill and folded his arms across his chest, clearly a man taking command of things. "So what would my character do first?"

"Whatever I tell him to do," Jackie said, and he glared at her. She shrugged. "I'm the detective. My character is. So it's my case. You are only here to feed me clues."

Robert looked very unhappy. He unfolded his arms and put his hands in his pockets. "All right, sure," he said. "But that's . . . I mean, I've got to have some kind of . . . I mean, my *character* has to have, you know. Respect."

Jackie's face got hard. She slapped the desk. "Respect is *earned*," she said. "Now what have you got for me?"

Robert's mouth flapped open, then closed. He looked like a man who had just been thoroughly scolded. I, on the other hand, realized what Jackie was doing. It was a near-perfect imitation of Deborah, and I was very impressed.

"Wow," I said. "That's good. Just like her."

Jackie gave a low gurgling laugh that made my toes curl and beamed at me. "Thanks," she said. "Sergeant Morgan—your sister—we worked on it this weekend. At Bennie's." Bennie's was a cop bar, a place where off-duty police officers hung out—and sometimes stopped in for a quick snort while on duty. The clientele was not known to be friendly to non-cops who wandered in. If Deborah had taken Jackie to Bennie's, they had clearly bonded even more than I'd realized. "It's a really good place for background," Jackie said. "I have to send the writers there to see it." She winked at Deborah. "We did tequila shots. She's not so tough with a couple of drinks under her belt." Debs snorted, but didn't say anything.

"Sounds like quite a party," I said, and oddly, I almost wished I'd been invited. "So now that you're actually my sister, what would you like me to do?"

For a moment it looked like Jackie was going to say something, but then she bit her lip and picked up the file. "Let's go over the labs," she said, and then she glanced at Deborah. "Is that right?"

"No," Debs said. "The lab work is just background bullshit."

"Thank you very much," I said.

"Is anything in there important?" Deborah said.

"Rope burns on the wrists," I said. "Nylon fibers probably mean clothesline."

"Which could have come from any grocery store in the world," she said.

"She was gagged with her own panties," I said. "They found 'em in the Dumpster."

"I said important," Debs said. "That's all standard crap."

"Well," I said, "there's nothing on her, nothing in the Dumpster or the immediate vicinity to give any clue about who she was."

"And that's what we need the most," Deborah said. "To get an ID on the victim."

"Why is that so important?" Robert asked, and the two women swiveled their heads and gave him matching expressions of disdain. Robert looked very uncomfortable. "I mean," he said, "the forensic evidence is, you know. There's a lot of stuff there." He nodded at the folder. "We might get like, you know. A fingerprint."

"We did," Deborah said. "In fact, we got about three dozen finger-prints. We always get lots of fingerprints. You know how many times we caught somebody from a fingerprint?"

"No," Robert said. "How many?"

"In round numbers? Zero," Debs said. "Even when it's a match with the perp, a decent lawyer will get it thrown out. Fingerprints are for Sherlock Holmes."

"I'm not sure he actually used them," I said helpfully.

"Oh, he did," Jackie said. "There was one story—I forget the name? But he caught the guy from his fingerprint."

"To catch a killer in real life," Deborah went on patiently, "you need to backtrack from the victim. Because ninety-nine percent of the time they knew each other; they were seen together; they got some connection. So first we need to know who the victim is."

"Oh, okay," Robert said. "Well, so how do we find that out? I mean, if we can't use fingerprints, and the lab work is bullshit—what do we do?"

"Yeah," Debs said. "Good question." And even before she turned to look at me, I knew what was coming, because although she would never admit it, whenever my sister was stuck, it somehow became *my* problem. I sometimes thought she must have a secret tattoo some-where on her body: "WWDD?" What Would Dexter Do? And sure enough, as Robert's question was still echoing in the air, her head swiveled my way.

"Dex?" she said expectantly.

Oddly enough, it was Robert who managed to say what I was thinking. "Why Dexter?" he said, and I felt like applauding. "I mean, he does the lab stuff, and you said it was useless, so—you know," he said, looking at me. "Not that I think you're useless, or anything, buddy. But what is he supposed to do?"

Deborah stared at Robert, just long enough to make him uncomfortable, before she answered. "Sometimes Dexter gets these . . . insights," she said. "About the killer."

It is a scientific fact that most situations in life go from bad to worse—I believe it's called entropy. Any scientists who happened to be observing us at this moment would have been quietly satisfied to see that this natural law held true. As Deborah had said, I really did get insights into the sick and twisted creatures of the night. But that was because I was one of them. Deborah was the only living person I had ever talked to on the subject. After all, I didn't want people walking around and saying things like, "Gee, Dexter thinks just like a killer. Wonder why?" Additionally, since these thoughts came from a private place, deep inside Dexter's Dungeon, discussing it always made me feel slightly naked. I thought my sister understood that, but every now and then, like now, she dragged me stripped and flinching into the spotlight.

Robert and Jackie both looked at me, and I began to feel even more uncomfortable. "What," Robert said. "Like he, uh, *profiles*?" I'd never heard it used as a verb before. It didn't make me feel any more at ease.

"Kind of," Deborah said.

"Wow," Jackie said, and she looked at me with new respect. "How did you learn to do that?"

Of course, that was exactly the question I did not want to answer. The only honest reply was not something I felt I could profitably discuss with Jackie. So I did my best to steer the conversation onto something a little less personal. "Oh," I said modestly, "I took a psychology course in college. I assume you ran a missing-persons check, sis?"

Deborah flipped her hand dismissively at that. "First thing we did," she said. "Come on, Dex; let's get serious." She put her arms on her thighs and leaned toward me. "I really want to collar this bastard, and I want him before Anderson fucks up the trail. And before this guy does it again. Because you know he's going to do it again."

"Probably," I said, overriding the mean little voice inside me that was chortling, *Almost Certainly*.

"So come on," she said. "Give me something to go on." She stared at me intently, without blinking, and even more unsettling, Jackie leaned toward me and did exactly the same thing. I was surrounded by Deborahs, all of them impatiently waiting for me to perform a miracle. It was an awful lot of expectation for one lonely Dark Dabbler, no matter how righteously wicked. Luckily for me, Robert provided a perfect counterbalance by recrossing his arms and leaning back again with a skeptical expression on his face.

"Hey, come on," he said. "Profiling is serious shit. I mean, these FBI guys who do it, it takes *years*, and they're still only right, like, fifty percent of the time." Everybody looked at him, which was a great relief to me. He shrugged. "Well, so, I'm just saying," he said.

"Dexter does a little better than that," Deborah said.

"Very cool," Jackie said. She gave me an encouraging smile, and I couldn't decide whether to crouch at her feet and let her scratch behind my ear, or slap my sister for bringing it up in the first place.

"All right, well, so," Robert said. He sounded a little defiant, as if he'd decided that we were all against him, so he might as well push back. He jutted his chin at me. "Let's see something."

It was really very thoughtful of him to provide me with a motivation to do something besides wishing I was somewhere else. His Show Me attitude was so annoying it made me forget that I was hesitant to talk about something this intimate, because I wanted so much to say something wonderful that would push his face in the dirt.

"Well," I said. I thought about the body as I'd seen it: the degree of damage, the strange variety of slash, bite, smash—and, of course, that final optical assault. Everyone was still looking at me, and I realized I had to say something.

"It, um . . ." I said. "It starts with the eyes. . . ."

"All right," Deborah said expectantly. "What about 'em?"

"That's the most important thing," I said. "What he's trying to say about her *seeing*. And, um, *not* seeing."

Deborah snorted. "I didn't know that?" she said. "I mean, he rips out her eye and shoots his wad into her eye socket, and I'm supposed to think that's an accident? I know he blinded her, so he had a thing about the eyes. So what?"

"But that's exactly it, Debs," I said.

"What is?" Jackie demanded, sounding very much like Deborah.

"He didn't blind her," I said. "He left her one good eye. He wanted her to see what he was doing."

"Jesus Christ," Robert muttered.

"And I still don't know why, or what it means," Deborah snarled, her normal cranky self once more.

"The whole thing for him is centered around it," I said, and I felt a soft rustle of encouragement from the Passenger, almost as if it was whispering, *Good, go on.* . . . "Vision, watching, *seeing* . . . It's all about that. It's not just part of it; it's the whole point."

"What the fuck does that mean?" Deborah snapped.

"I'm not sure yet," I said, and Robert cleared his throat to show he wasn't going to say what he was thinking.

"I don't understand," Jackie said. "I mean, okay, the thing with the eye socket. But how does that say anything except he's a sick bastard?"

"You have to try to go inside his mind," I said, and I took a deep breath. "Try to picture what he was thinking."

"I'd rather not," Jackie said softly, but I was already hearing the far-off whisper of wings and the slow rising of shadows and I closed my eyes and tried to *see* it, reaching down into the Dark Basement and stroking the thing that uncurled there, petting it until it purred, stretched, and sprang up into the black interior sky and showed me all the pictures of Eternal Nighttime pleasure. . . .

*And I see her, see the way she thrashes, moans, twists wildly against the ropes, fighting to get a scream past the gag, seeing nothing but her approaching death and not even seeing the all-important Why of it, the reason it must be, the Me who is doing this to her because she has refused to notice—and even now her eyes are on the knife and not the hand holding it and I need to make her see ME, need to make her pay attention to ME, and I drop the knife and I move closer, more direct, more intimate, and I begin to use hands, feet, fingernails, teeth—and still she will not see ME and so I grab her by the hair, that perfect golden hair, and I haul her face around to look and she has to see ME at last.*

*And she does.*

*She sees me. For the first time, she looks at ME and she sees ME and she knows me for who I really am and at last at last I can show her how I can care for her like no one else ever could, show her that this was meant to be, this was how it was always supposed to be, and at last at last I can show her my Truth, my Self, my Reason for Being.*

*I can show her my love.*

*And so I will know that she will always see my love I take her eye and I will keep it with me forever so I will remember, too.*

*And so she will really and truly see how I love her I put my love there where her eye used to be.*

*And then I am done. And I feel the sadness again. Because nothing is forever. But love is supposed to be forever, and I want this love to last. And so she will know that, and so this love will be forever and can never change and never end, and so it can never be anything else, there is one more thing. Nothing else can ever happen that will tarnish this matchless love or make this perfect moment less than forever. It's important.*

*And so I kill her.*

Somebody cleared their throat; I opened my eyes, and the first thing I saw was Jackie. She was looking at me with a very strange expression on her face, a mix of fascination and fright, almost as if she had heard the soft and leathery whispers that were still fluttering through my brain.

"What?" I said to her.

She shook her head. Her ponytail flopped to one side, then back. "Nothing," she said. "I just . . ." She bit her lip and frowned. "Where did you go just now?"

"Oh," I said, and I could feel a hot flush mounting into my cheeks. "I, uh, it's hard to explain."

Deborah snickered, which I thought was extremely unkind. "Try," she said. "I want to hear it, too."

"Well, uh," I said, which was not up to my usual stellar standards of wit. "I, um . . . I try to imagine it, you know. What the killer was thinking, and feeling."

Jackie was still staring, still frowning. She hadn't even blinked. "Uh-huh," she said.

"Um," I said, still wallowing in uninspired monosyllables. "So, you know. I work backward from what we can see. Using what I know. I mean," I added quickly, "what I know from *research*, and, uh, studying these things. In books, and . . ."

"Work backward," Jackie said. "What does that mean?"

"It's, um, you know," I said, feeling exceptionally awkward. "There's something unique about every murder, so you try to see what would make somebody do that."

Jackie blinked at last. "Okay," she said. "So this time, he rips off her nipple. And that tells you what?"

"It depends on how it was taken off," I said. "If it's slashed off, that means, 'I am punishing you for having a nipple, and now you don't.'"

"This was *bitten* off," Deborah said. "What does that say?"

"'I love you,'" I said without thinking, but a happy hiss from the Passenger said I was right.

Deborah made a throat-clearing sound and Robert muttered, "For fuck's sake." But Jackie looked completely floored. "'I *love* you'?" she said. "He bites her nipple off to say, 'I *love* you'?"

"It's, um," I said. "It's not absolutely normal love as we might know it."

"No shit," Deborah said.

"But the whole thing with this guy, it's sexual," I said. I felt a bit defensive, and was not quite sure why. "It's a mix of compulsion and sex and love, and it's all so powerful and so frustrating that he can't even express it except, um"—I shrugged—"like he did."

I looked around at my little audience. Deborah had resumed her normal stone-faced cop expression, and Robert looked like he was trying very hard not to laugh out loud. But Jackie looked past me, somewhere in the great distance over my shoulder, and slowly began to nod her head. "I think I see it," she said.

Deborah twitched her head in disbelief. "You do?" she said. "Jesus Christ, how do you see that?"

Jackie looked at her. "It's kind of like acting," she said. "I mean, like, when you're doing Shakespeare? He doesn't tell you anything in the script, like how you should react, or how you should say things. So you look at what he has you *do*, what he has you *say*, and you work backward from that." She turned and gave me a quick smile. "Like Dexter said."

The warmth I'd been feeling in my face suddenly slid down into my chest. Somebody understood me. Jackie understood what I had done. It was so wildly unlikely that this goddess of the silver screen should understand anything, let alone something like me, that I just stood and looked at her and felt a small and grateful smile creep up onto my lips.

But of course, Robert could not allow me to feel any real happiness. "Oh, for Christ's sake," he said. "This isn't fucking Shakespeare, sweetheart. This isn't your goddamn *thee*-ate-ter. This is the *real* world. This is a fucking wacko, psycho, out-of-his-skull asshole who likes to bite your tits off, and playing Neighborhood Playhouse acting games in your head isn't going to catch him."

"Neither is throwing up every time you see a little blood, Bob," Jackie said sweetly.

Robert opened his mouth, closed it, and then opened it again. But Deborah spoke before he could get out his no-doubt-stinging reply.

"All right, fine," Debs said. "I'm glad you see it, Jackie. I don't see it, but what the fuck; that's why I put up with Dexter."

"What about my stunning competence?" I said. "And my understated wit? And—"

"What I still don't see," Deborah said, riding over the rest of my modest list of good qualities, "is how it connects to where you started. About the eyes. I mean," she said, holding up a hand to stop me from saying something I wasn't going to say, "all right, he rips out an eye, he fucks the eye socket, and he kills her."

"And he keeps the eyeball," I said.

"You don't know that," Robert blurted out.

"I think I do," I said.

"Most of these guys keep souvenirs," Deborah said, and I enjoyed a rare moment of having a sister who backed me up now and then. "That's cold fact, right out of the book."

"So we're supposed to look for a guy carrying around a bunch of eyeballs?" Robert said, making a face of great disbelief and distaste. "Jesus fuck."

Jackie snorted. "Good idea, Bob," she said. "Let's just start frisking people, and when we find somebody with a baggie full of eyeballs, he's our guy."

"I'm not the one who brought it up," Robert said, and he was going to say more, but Deborah stopped him.

"Shut the fuck up, both of you," she said, and they both did. She looked at me. "What are the odds he's done something like this before?" she asked me.

I thought about it. "Pretty good," I said. "Maybe not a lot, but almost certainly once or twice before."

Jackie frowned and cocked her head. "How do you get that?" she said.

"The first time couldn't be this, uh . . . this *complete*," I said. "Just killing for the first time would be too distracting, too powerful. He would rush through it, and then panic and run, quickly. But then he doesn't get caught; he starts thinking about what he should have done. . . ." I nodded at her, nearly overwhelmed with the idea that she understood. "You know."

"Yeah," she said. "And so he thinks, 'That was too fast; I didn't get caught—next time I'll try *this*. . . .'" Her eyes got far away again as she saw it. It was a real pleasure to watch her—a pleasure that was quickly shattered, of course, by Deborah.

"All right," my sister said. "Let's put this out on the wire, see if there's anything like it out there."

"What good does that do?" Robert said. "I mean, even if he did it before, nobody caught him."

"A truly keen grasp of the obvious," Jackie said.

"It beats the hell out of psychic detective work," Robert sneered back.

Deborah looked at me and shook her head wearily. "Get him out of here," she said.

# SEVEN

I SPENT THE REST OF THE MORNING SHOWING ROBERT HOW TO find latent blood with Bluestar. It isn't very hard; you spray it on something and whatever traces of blood there might be glow at you, no matter how much it has been scrubbed. Good stuff, and it didn't degrade the DNA, which was becoming more important every day. Robert didn't seem to mind blood in the minute amounts we were working with, and the hours passed quickly enough with no more than minor irritation when Robert's questions got too persistent. But at least he wasn't being aggressively obnoxious. When Jackie wasn't around, he wasn't nearly as annoying, and as the clock approached noon it occurred to me that if I could put up with him a little longer, he would probably pay for lunch again.

So I endured him patiently, working with him as he happily used up almost an entire bottle of Bluestar, and I was just about to drop a casual hint to him that lunch might be a good idea when my phone began to chirp at me.

"Morgan," I said into the phone.

"Get up here," Deborah said. "We got a hit."

"What?" I said, very surprised. "You mean you got a reply from the wire?"

"Yeah," she said. "Two of 'em."

"That isn't possible," I said. And it wasn't. It was much too soon for anyone to respond to the query she had sent out. It should have taken days, even weeks for some cop somewhere in the country to get around to reading it, checking his files, finding a match, and then responding. Most cops have a life, and a caseload that is already overwhelming, and so although professional cooperation with a brother officer is a great idea, it's never quite as important as finishing a report before the captain chews your ass, with a little time left over to make it to your kid's soccer game.

But Deborah was claiming she'd had not one but *two* replies, and before I could question her any more she said, "Now," and she hung up.

Deborah was alone when Robert and I got back to her desk. She was frowning at her computer screen, and she looked up and tapped it to show me her e-mail when we walked in. "Look at this," she said. "*Two* of 'em, in two different cities, and it's absolutely our guy, no question." She flipped her finger at the screen. "Body found in a Dumpster, right nipple missing, same kind of marks on it—"

"What about the eyes?" I said.

She nodded. "The first one, over a year ago in New York, both eyes ripped out; one found near the body, the other never found. The second one, um . . ." She looked down at the paper, nodded. "Yeah. Vegas. Like, four months ago." She looked up and smiled triumphantly. "One eye missing, semen traces on the face. It's him, Dex. It's gotta be."

I nodded. It probably was him. But knowing that didn't catch him, and it left a crucial question, maybe the most important of all. "New York, Vegas, and now Miami," I said. "Why?"

"He's harder to catch if he moves around?" Robert offered.

"Most serial killers don't even think about getting caught," Deborah said. "They stay in one place, even in one neighborhood."

Robert looked at me. "Really?" he said.

I nodded. "Yup, pretty much," I said. "So if this one doesn't, it's for an important reason."

"Okay. So why?" Robert said.

"He could be chasing something—or someone—specific," I said.

"Or . . ." A very small idea popped into my head. "Those are all cities that have a lot of conventions," I said.

"Right," Deborah said. "We can cross-check the lists, see if anything matches."

"What are you saying?" Robert said. "He could be going to all these conventions, like, he's a Shriner or something?"

Deborah shook her head wearily, and I took pity on her and came to the rescue. "Shriner sounds plausible," I told Robert patiently. "He could make his getaway on one of those little tricycles they ride in parades."

"The case files are coming by e-mail," Deborah said. "But I got detectives in two different cities wanting to fly down here and shoot somebody."

"Tell them to stay home," I said. "We have enough of our own shooters in Miami." I looked around the room, and it felt a little bit empty. "Where's Jackie?"

Debs waved a hand. "She had an interview," she said. "Matthews told her she could use the conference room."

Before I could arrange my face to show that I was impressed by Matthews letting anyone use his conference room, Robert blurted out, "Interview? With who?"

It might have been my imagination, but it seemed to me that his face lost a little bit of color, and he definitely looked unhappy.

"She didn't say who," Deborah said. "One of the magazines, I think."

"Magazine," Robert said. "Like a local one?" he added hopefully.

"The captain would never let her use the conference room for a local magazine," Debs told him, and she said it with such a complete lack of expression that I realized she had picked up on Robert's apprehension and was playing him a little.

"Shit," he said. "They should have— She really didn't say which one? I'll be right back," he said, heading for the door. "Gotta call my agent."

Debs and I watched him go, and I said, "You have a very nice wicked streak, sis."

She nodded, stone-faced. "It passes the time," she said. She turned to her computer, and after scrabbling at the keyboard for a moment, she said, "Case files are here." She frowned and hit a few more keys, mumbling, "Goddamn it" under her breath; my sister had many sterling qualities, but computer competence was not one of them. Even so, after a moment her printer began to whir, and she pushed back from the computer with a look of satisfaction.

"New York got here first," she said.

"Naturally," I said, and I leaned forward to look at the pages as the printer spit them out. The first few pages came out quickly; they were standard typed cop report, and Deborah snatched them up and began to read eagerly. Page three took a long time to print—a photograph, probably of the victim as she had been found—and I waited impatiently as it came out one line at a time. It finally sputtered all the way out and I grabbed it eagerly.

Nowadays, digital technology has made police photography much more colorful and detailed than in days of yore. My adoptive father, Harry, had been forced to look at grainy black-and-white pictures of dead bodies. It can't have been nearly as much fun. Because of the high-resolution color cameras we use now, I could see the wonderful rainbow of pigments left by the various punches, bites, and slashes on the body, ranging from bright pink down through the spectrum to deep purple. In fact, the image was clear enough that I could make out the mark of individual teeth in one of the bites, and I made a mental note to tell Deborah to check dental records for a match.

I studied the picture carefully, looking for any hints that might tell me something new. The similarities were striking. This victim, like ours, was a young woman who had almost certainly been attractive before the series of unfortunate events that had led to this picture. She had a very nice, trim figure, and shoulder-length hair of the same golden color our local victim had. I worked my way down the body, noticing that the knife wounds were in the same places, and I was so engrossed that it was several moments before I became aware of a soft floral aroma nearby, and realized that somebody was standing behind me. I glanced up quickly, startled, to see that Jackie had come silently back into the room and was standing very close to me, peering around my shoulder at the photograph. Her hair was down now, hanging around her face in a way that was disturbingly like the victim's. "Oh," I said. "I didn't hear you."

"I was a Girl Scout," she said. "Merit badge in woodcraft." She didn't move away, and for a very long moment I forgot about the photo in my hand and just inhaled the subtle perfume she was wearing. Jackie finally reached a finger around me and tapped the picture. "This is different," she said. "I mean, it's not the one we've been working on."

"That's right," I said.

"What is it?" she said, sliding her finger down the image of the body.

"We got an answer to the query Deborah sent out," I said.

"Really," Jackie said. "I thought it was supposed to take a while?"

"It always does," I said. "Unless it's a really high-profile case."

"What would make it high-profile?" she said.

"A lot of things," I said. "She might be somebody's daughter."

"Almost certainly," Jackie murmured.

"Or it could just be because she's young, pretty, not a hooker."

Jackie looked up and raised one eyebrow at me. "And white?"

I nodded. "Sure. But nobody ever admits that. How did you know?"

She looked back at the picture. "I did an after-school special about that," she said. "An African American girl goes missing, and the family can't get the cops to do anything."

"I'm sure they did something," I said. "Just not as much."

"Where did this come from?" she asked.

"New York," I told her, and I realized that this was a wonderful opportunity to further her forensic education. And to be truthful, I didn't want her to move away, either. So I added, "How many things do you see that are different?"

She glanced up at me and gave me a quizzical half smile. "What, like one of those puzzles for kids? How many things are not the same?"

"This is the homicide version," I said. "For grown-ups."

"All right," she said, and she began to study the picture in earnest. She bent her head forward so that her hair brushed against my bare arm. She pulled it back and tucked it behind her ear, revealing her neck, and I could see the pulse fluttering in her carotid artery.

"Vegas," Deborah said. She said it softly, under her breath, but I still jumped; I'd forgotten there was someone else in the room. Debs gave the keyboard a few more irritated pokes and the second file began to print. Once again the first few pages were the report, and they whirred out quickly. When the photograph finally slid out I stepped around Jackie and grabbed it, and it was just like the other two: a young woman with a good, athletic figure and shoulder-length golden hair. There could no longer be any question about the pattern; now it was a matter of trying to figure out *why* this specific type was necessary.

"I found something," Jackie said, pointing at the picture. I looked at where her finger rested on the victim's face. There was nothing there but smooth skin.

"What?" I said.

"Well," Jackie said, "the Miami victim has a slash mark here. Lemme see Vegas." She held out her hand, and I gave her the second picture, leaning in to look with her. "Yeah, see? This one has it, too. Just one quick slash, right across the face." She looked up at me, her violet eyes bright. "What does that mean?"

"Anger," I said.

"About what?" she said. "Because right there on the face is like—"

But before she could say anything more, Robert came bustling back into the room.

"I'm going to have to wrap up here early," he said happily. "I got *Screen Time* magazine in ninety minutes." He waited for somebody to congratulate him, but nobody did, so he nodded at the papers Deborah held, frowned, and said, "Is there anything in the report? You think it's our guy?"

"Yeah, I think so," Deborah said. "It's pretty much the same handwriting." And maybe because I had already complimented her on her wicked streak, she added, "Take a look at the pictures; see for yourself."

Jackie looked up at him expectantly and held out the pictures. Robert stared at her, and then his jaw muscles tightened and he leaned forward and took them. He swallowed, visibly steeled himself, and began to look them over. "Jesus," he said. "Oh, my God." He handed the pictures back to Jackie. "Sure looks like the same guy. I mean, there couldn't be two guys doing like that, right?"

"Probably not," Deborah said.

"So, what do we do with this stuff?" Robert said.

"We compare all three," I said.

"Right," Robert said, nodding. "What are we looking for?"

"We don't know until we see it," I said. "But he's done this three times, and every time the odds increase that he made a mistake, left some kind of clue."

"Okay," Robert said. He raised his eyebrows and added, "Hey, I did this feature a few years back? I played an alcoholic detective, and there's a serial killer killing young girls. And this guy, my character, he's divorced? But he has a daughter, and it turns out the killer is stalking *her*, so I have to go sober and catch the killer before my daughter is killed." He shrugged. "Low-budget thing, Israeli money. But very authentic, and it got great reviews." Deborah cleared her throat and Robert flashed her a quick smile. "Right. Sorry. Anyway," he said, "he looks at *when* the serial killer strikes, you know. He sets up a time line, and it turns out he kills somebody every six weeks? So I set up a trap for the guy at the right time, and that's how I catch him." He looked at Deborah, and when she didn't say anything, he looked at me. "So I thought, maybe it turns out to be nothing, but should we do that with this one?"

"Why?" Jackie said. "We don't even know what city he'll do it in next time. So how does it help to know when?"

"We could just look," Robert said stubbornly. He raised an eyebrow at me and said, with a kind of boyish eagerness, "Whaddaya say, Dexter?"

I couldn't think of any way that knowing the interval between kills could possibly tell Robert anything useful. On the other hand, Robert happy and busy was a lot easier to take than Robert sulking. "All right," I said. "It can't actually hurt anything."

Deborah shrugged and held out the two reports. "Knock yourself out," she told me.

I took the reports from Debs, and Robert came over and stood beside me, forcing Jackie to step away. She moved to Deborah's desk and leaned one haunch on the corner, while Robert bent over the pages I was holding. He didn't smell nearly as good as Jackie.

"All right," he mumbled, and he scrabbled at the pages, trying to see all of them at the same time.

I pushed the papers at him. "Here," I said. "Vegas is on top, New York under that." He grabbed the papers and leaned on the window-sill again, studying them.

"Right, right," he said softly, and then he frowned and shook his head. "No, that doesn't make sense. September 2012 in New York, then Las Vegas in June 2013, and now October in Miami." He looked up, disappointment visible on his face. "It doesn't work out," he said. "The interval is different."

"Oh, well," I said.

He stared at the papers some more, trying to make them behave, but it didn't seem to work. "Well, shit," he said at last. "I guess it was a long shot."

Nobody argued with that. Robert leaned over and tossed the papers on Deb's desk, shuffled his feet, crossed his arms, uncrossed them, and then stood up straight. "Well," he said. "I, uh, I should go get ready. For my interview." He smiled. "Put on a clean shirt, do the hair, you know. For the photographer. So . . ." He looked at Deborah and then at me, possibly waiting for us to object. When we didn't, he shrugged and said to me, "So all right. I'll see you tomorrow?"

"Bright and early," I said.

He pointed a finger-gun at me and dropped his thumb. *Pow.* "Bright and early," he said. He nodded at Deborah, gave Jackie a half glance, and then sauntered out the door.

Nobody said anything for a few moments. Jackie picked up the papers Robert had thrown down and studied them. She frowned. "Funny," she said.

"What?" I said.

She shook her head. "Oh, nothing," she said. "It's just . . . I mean, it sounds like I'm doing a diva: 'It's all about me!' And I'm not, so . . . forget it."

"I can't forget it if you don't tell me," I said.

Jackie crossed her arms across her chest and gave me a kind of rueful smile. "Dexter, it's nothing," she said, and while I was still pondering the realization that this was the first time she'd called me by my name, she went on. "I mean, it's just a stupid coincidence. When Robert said the dates, it's just . . . I was there, on those dates. Working on a couple of films. New York in September, Vegas in June." She shook her head and waved the papers dismissively. "Like I said, just forget I said it." She uncrossed her arms and slapped her thighs. "So," she said, looking at Deborah. "What's our next move?"

Deborah might very well have answered her, but if she did I didn't hear it. Because as I watched Jackie swing her head toward Deborah, golden hair flipping with the movement, something clicked in the Deep Shadows of Dexter's Dark Closet, and I looked down at the pictures in my hand, both of them so very similar, and then—

*All light is gone and I am answering the urgent rattle of black wings and I climb on and lean into it and let them lift me up on a dark wind and we soar up and up and up into a black night sky, up far above, up to where we can see, and we rise and circle faster and faster until we are there in the cold and starless sky and we look and then it is there, a single bright scarlet patch of the landscape below that is as clear and sharp and unavoidable as if it was illuminated by a dozen noonday suns—and I see them. And we swoop down into the red-tinged light and I am with them again, with the women in the pictures, standing above them and watching them twist and bulge out against their bonds, and every one of their muscles locks and every inch of skin, every nerve, every bone, screams in pain and it does not even slow me; it drives me instead to new and more exciting things, and I begin to do them to her and she turns away so she will not see what I am going to do and she must see it, she must see me, she must watch, because that is why I am doing this, that is what this is all about, it is about her seeing me, and so I grab her by her hair, that perfect golden hair, and I pull her head around and see her face—*

*—and it is the wrong face.*

*And that makes me furious, and I yank her hair even harder, that almost-perfect golden hair, the not-quite-right hair that is so close and looks so very much like hers but it is still not her hair and the face is not her face and it is just not right anymore even though I picture her face instead as I finish but when I look down at what I have done I can feel it all drain away because it is not right, it is not her, and a bright flash of rage runs down from the top of my skull and all the way down my arm and I pick up the knife, the cold impersonal knife, and I slash at that face, that so very wrong face, because it is not—*

"Oh," I said, and my eyes pop open to the fluorescent light of Deborah's office, and no matter how hard I try to push it away and find a way not to believe it, the things I saw do not change. Even in the harsh and ugly light of the office the picture is the same, and even worse, I now see Deb and Jackie staring at me uncertainly, as if they had been watching me urinate on a busy street. "Oh, um," I say. "It's, you know. I just thought of something."

"What?" Jackie said, sounding very unsure of what she was asking, and as if she was deliberately mocking me and mocking my vision, she flipped her hair around and over her shoulder—her hair, her perfect golden hair. . . .

"It is you," I told her. "I mean, it really is about you."

Jackie blushed and fidgeted with her hair. "That's not, I mean . . ."

But Deborah cut right across Jackie's modest dithering. "What do you mean, it's about her?" she demanded. "What are you saying?"

"That's why he did it," I said, and I realized that I was still feeling the bat-wing rush of my interior flight with the Passenger and I was not actually making real-time sense. I took a deep breath and slapped the photos onto the desk beside Jackie. "The hair is like yours," I said. "They both have a similar kind of figure. The same locations at the same time as you." I looked up and locked eyes with Jackie, and she stared unblinking back with a small flicker of fear growing in those violet eyes. "And then the knife slash across the face, the rage—because it's the wrong face. Because it isn't you."

I watched the long and elegant muscles in her throat move as she swallowed and then began to slowly shake her head. But as much as I wanted to be wrong, I knew that I was not.

"It's you," I said. "He killed them because they looked like you."

# EIGHT

For a few moments there was utter silence in Deborah's office. Debs just stared, and Jackie simply sat there clutching white-knuckled at her hair, lips slightly parted, looking very pale, and apparently not even breathing. "I, I, how can, um . . ." she said.

"Where the fuck does that come from?" Deborah said.

"It, um—it just makes sense," I said.

"Not to me," Deborah said.

"I don't think . . ." Jackie said faintly. "I . . . I don't know if . . ."

Deborah pushed her chair back against the desk, making a noise that seemed horribly loud all of a sudden.

"It's bullshit, Dexter," Deborah said. "Unless you got something *concrete* to back it up."

"You've got the dates and places," I said. "And the victims all look like her."

Deborah shook her head, lips pursed. "Lots of women look like her," she said.

"Deborah, I'm sure about this—"

"Well, I'm not," she snapped. "You got nothing to go on but one of your . . . hunches? And that's not enough. I can't go to the captain and say, 'Look what we found when Dexter closed his eyes.' Not when it isn't even my case. I need evidence. Not just more of your psychic detective crap."

It stung a little more than it should have. After all, she was the one who had forced me to perform, far too publicly for my liking, and now she was scolding me for doing something I hadn't wanted to do at all. And I had done it just for her, because family is supposed to count for something—and done it quite well, too. And now she spurned me, mocked me, accused me of sophistry. So I reached down deep for a truly hurtful comeback, something that would really smack her down. But before I could even say, "Oh, yeah?" Jackie spoke.

"Oh, shit," she said, staring at me and shaking her head jerkily from side to side. "Oh, my God, Deborah . . ." She twitched her head sideways and said, "I mean, Sergeant. I mean— Oh, shit."

"What?" Deborah said.

Jackie continued her series of quick, jerky shakes of her head. "I think he's right," she said in a very small voice.

"Why?" Deborah demanded.

Jackie finally realized that she was still shaking her head and stopped. She took a deep breath, closed her eyes, opened them and blinked at me, and then looked at Debs. "I have a stalker," she said. "He's been . . . He sent a bunch of letters."

"What kind of letters?" Deborah said.

Jackie licked her lips. "They started out, you know. A little creepy, but just regular fan stuff." She shrugged. "I get lots of those. And, you know, there's a standard reply my assistant sends out. Sometimes with a picture. And he didn't like that. He wanted something more . . . real." She raised her hands and fluttered them like two small helpless birds. "Something *personal*," she said. She dropped her hands into her lap. "Which I *don't* do, ever. I mean, if it's a kid with cancer or something, okay, but just a regular male fan letter? I usually don't even see 'em, let alone answer 'em. My assistant brushes 'em off, and if they don't take the hint we just ignore 'em. Send their letters back."

Jackie bit her lip and looked down at her hands. "Which we did. We sent his letters back, and . . . he really hated that. And he wrote again, but . . . the letters turned really . . . nasty. And he sent my picture back all . . . shredded. Hacked up, and things drawn on it, and, um . . ." She actually gulped, took a deep breath, looked right at me, and said, "And one of the eyes poked out."

"Fuck," Deborah said softly.

"And the letters said some very bad things. Bad enough so Kathy—" She looked up. "Kathy is my assistant," she said.

"Okay," Deborah said.

"The letters were so dark and twisted and threatening that Kathy got worried. She showed them to me. I, uh . . . I don't know. I didn't really believe it was serious, but . . ." She shrugged and lifted her hands and then dropped them into her lap again. "I told her to show them to the police."

"Did she?" Deborah asked.

"Yes," Jackie said. "I mean, I assume so. I didn't really . . . I mean, Kathy is very good at her job, so I'm sure she did."

"Okay," Deborah said. "And then what?"

Jackie shook her head. "Then nothing," she said. "I mean, I didn't think about it anymore; I just figured it was taken care of, and I had work to do. You know."

"Where are the letters now?" Deborah said.

Jackie blinked. "Um. I don't have any idea. I mean, I could ask Kathy?"

"Where is she?"

"She's here, with me," Jackie said. "I mean, here in Miami."

"Call her," Deborah said. "I need to see those letters. And I want the name of the cop who saw them—in L.A.?"

Jackie nodded, chewing at her lower lip. "Yes," she said. "I mean, the Valley, but—"

"All right," Deborah said. "Where's your assistant now?"

"I, uh . . . probably at the hotel?" Jackie said.

"Call her," Deborah said again.

Jackie nodded and turned away to her purse, which was over in the corner beside the desk. She took out a cell phone and tapped a number, turning away from us to talk. She spoke a few soft sentences, then disconnected, slid the phone back into her purse, and faced us again. "I talked to Kathy," she said, which would have been my first guess. "The cop in L.A. still has the letters? And she's going to find his business card and call me back." She shook her head and looked at us, and then, almost as if somebody had pulled the plug and let all the air out of her, she sank into the visitor's chair beside the desk. "Holy shit," she said softly. She closed her eyes and blew out a long breath. "Holy shit," she said again. She opened her eyes and looked from Deborah to me. "Do you think he's . . . I mean, do you think I'm in any real danger?"

"Yes," Deborah and I said in unison.

Jackie blinked several times. Her eyes got moist and the violet color seemed to go a few shades darker. "Oh, boy," she said. "What am I supposed to do?"

"I'll ask the captain to assign somebody to stay with you," Deborah said.

"Somebody—you mean like a bodyguard? Like another cop?" Jackie said anxiously.

Deborah raised her eyebrows. "Is there something wrong with that?" she asked.

Jackie hesitated, pursed her lips, then clasped her hands in front of her mouth. "Just," she said. "Oh, boy, this is gonna sound really . . ." She looked at me, then at Deborah. "Can I be totally honest with you?"

"I hope so," Deborah said, with an expression of mild disbelief on her face.

"This is . . . How to put this," Jackie said. She shook her head, stood up, and went to look out the window. There wasn't a whole lot to see out there, but she kept looking. "My career is kind of . . . what. Fading? It's not really . . . The offers aren't coming so fast anymore. And they're not as good." She bit her lip and gave her head one slow shake. "It happens. For a woman in this business it's all over at thirty, and I'm thirty-three."

Jackie looked up and forced a quick smile. "That's confidential information," she said, and Deborah and I nodded.

Jackie looked back out the window. "Anyway," she said, "the reality is, I need this show to go, and I need it to be a hit, or my career is pretty much over, and I've got nothing left except maybe marry a Greek arms dealer or something." She sighed. "And those offers are slowing down, too," she said.

It was hard enough to feel a great deal of pain and sorrow for

Jackie simply because she was not getting enough marriage propos-als from billionaires—and it was even harder to see how that affected our current situation. "I'm sorry," I said. "But, um . . . ?"

Jackie nodded. "I know," she said. "Poor pitiful me." She blew out a breath and turned briskly away from the window at last. "The point is," she said, "if the network finds out that there have been serious threats on my life, they have to tell the insurance, and the insurance premiums for the shoot go way up—I mean, *millions*—and since we haven't even started shooting yet, suddenly it's a whole lot cheaper to get rid of me and recast the part with somebody younger and prob-ably better-looking."

"Not possible," I said without thinking, and Jackie gave me a quick bright smile.

"Cheaper," Deborah said. "You mean, they'd just dump you to save money?"

"That's a joke, right?" Jackie said. "They'd dump Jesus to save fifty bucks."

"Shit," Deborah said.

"We start shooting next week," she said. "If I can get, say, a week of film in the can before they find out, I should be okay." She inhaled deeply and looked at Deborah very seriously. "I know it's a lot to ask. But . . . can we not tell them for a week?"

Deborah shrugged. "I don't have to tell the network," she said. "I don't owe them shit."

"What about Robert?" I said. After all, he was my nearly constant companion nowadays.

Jackie actually shuddered. "Oh, Jesus," she said. "If he finds out he'll tell *everybody*. He'd do anything to get me fired from this show."

"It could be kind of hard to keep him from finding out," I said. "He's with me all day long."

"Please," she said. "It's just for a couple of days."

"Well," I said, "I'll do my best."

"Thanks," Jackie said, and Deborah cleared her throat.

"I don't have to tell the network," she said, "and I don't have to tell Robert." Her face dropped into the cold-forged cop face, the one that kept her from showing anything, no matter what she felt. "I *do* have to tell Detective Anderson. It's his case."

"What? But that's— No!" Jackie said.

Deborah clenched her jaw. "I *have* to," she said. "I am a sworn officer of the law now in possession of some vital information pertaining to a homicide case, and Anderson is lead on it. If I don't tell him, I lose my job. I probably do jail time."

"Oh," Jackie said, looking very deflated. "But that's . . . I mean, do you think Anderson would, um, not tell anybody?"

Deborah looked away. "He'll tell," she said.

"He'll probably call a press conference," I said.

"Shit," Jackie said. "Shit, shit, *shit*." She sank into a chair, looking for all the world like a forlorn rag doll. "I can't—I won't ask you to risk your career," she said, and she said it with such hopeless, noble resignation that I wanted to kill something for her—like Anderson, for instance. But as that happy thought flashed through my mind, it was instantly replaced by one of those wonderful moments of insight that come only once in a lifetime, and only to the Just. "Oh," I said, and some of my gleeful surprise clearly showed in my voice, because Jackie looked up, and Deborah frowned at me.

"What?" Jackie said.

"Deborah has to tell Anderson," I said happily, and I said it again for emphasis. *"Anderson."*

"I know his fucking name," Debs said.

"And you know his fucking character, too," I said.

"For fuck's sake, Dex, what the—"

"Deborah, think a minute," I said. "It might not hurt very much."

She glared at me for a moment longer, then blew out a vicious breath. "All right, fuck, I'm thinking," she said, and her face took on the look of a mean-spirited, slightly constipated grouper.

"Wonderful," I said. "Now, picture this in your thoughts: You, Sergeant Deborah Morgan, Defender of the Faith and Champion of Justice—"

"Cut to the fucking chase, huh?" she said.

"You go to Detective Anderson," I said patiently. "You, a person he thinks very highly of."

"He hates my fucking guts," she snarled. "So what?"

"So that's just the point," I said, and I let the glee creep back into my voice. "He really does hate your fucking guts. And you take him your file on this stuff, and you tell him you have a very important lead—*you* tell him, Deborah. Not me or Jackie or Captain Matthews—*you* tell him. With witnesses." I looked at her expectantly and, I have to admit, I smirked, too. "What does he do?"

Deborah opened her mouth to say something that looked like it would be rather venomous—and then her jaw snapped shut audibly, her eyes got very wide, and she took a very deep breath. "Holy shit," she breathed, and she looked at me with something approaching awe. "He does *nothing*. He loses the fucking file. Because it's *me*."

"Bingo," I said, which was something I'd always wanted to say. "He's afraid you would get the credit, so he does nothing—but *you* have done *everything*, by the book, with witnesses. You're in the clear; Jackie's secret is safe; all's right with the world."

"Would that really *work*?" Jackie said softly.

Debs squinted, jutted her jaw, and then nodded once. "It might," she said.

"Oh, come on," I said. "It's at least a probably."

"All right, it will probably work," she said.

"And if you maybe twist the knife a little?" I said. "You know, like how important this lead is, and he should drop everything he's doing to work on what *you* found?"

Debs snorted. "Yeah," she said. "That would do it."

"Oh," Jackie said, "that's— Dexter, you're so— Thank you, thank you both so much."

"But even if it does," Debs said, turning to a suddenly hopeful Jackie, "that doesn't keep you safe."

"Oh," Jackie said, and she looked deflated again.

"We've got to find this guy before he finds you," Deborah said. "And in the meantime, we have to put you where he can't get to you."

"I, um . . . I can just stay with you, here at headquarters, during the day?" Jackie said. "And then the hotel at night, with the door chained and bolted."

It's always nice to encounter innocence, but in this case I thought I should say something. "Hotels are not safe," I said. "It's much too easy to get into the room and grab somebody." I tried to say it as if I was very sure, which I was, but without sounding too much like I knew it was true from personal experience, which I did. It must have worked, because Jackie looked like she believed me.

"Well, then, um," she said. She looked imploringly at Debs. "Where do I go?"

"You can't stay with me," Deborah said. She shrugged. "Sorry. I won't put Nicholas at risk." Nicholas was her son, born a few months after the father had disappeared in a fit of noble sacrifice. He was a very nice baby, only a few months younger than my daughter, Lily Anne, and Deborah doted on him.

"I could hire a bodyguard, but they're always so . . ." She sighed again. "Some muscle-bound retired SEAL with a pistol and an attitude. And if the Taliban are after me, I'd be safe. But this? I mean, a homicidal psychopath? I need somebody who really understands that." She looked directly at me as she said it, which I suppose was only fair, but it was still a bit unsettling. "Not just somebody who can shoot." She looked back at Debs. "Of course, it's nice if they can shoot, too, but . . ." She looked back at me and blinked, her eyes huge and moist. "I need somebody I can really *trust*," she said. "Like I trust you guys." She shook her head.

She kept looking at me, and if I was really as smart as I like to think I am, I would have known where this was going—but for some reason, I didn't. "Dexter," she said. "I know this is a huge thing, but . . . is there any way that, you know."

I must have looked like I didn't know, because she stepped toward me and put a hand on my arm. "It's just for a few days," she said. "And I'll pay you whatever you ask, but . . . could you?"

I was certainly ready to agree in theory, but I still didn't know what she was asking me. I understood that she wanted me to help, but I didn't really see how I could help her find a safe place to stay. All I got was a mental picture of Jackie sleeping on my couch, with Cody and Astor tiptoeing around her to get to school, and the image was so unlikely I couldn't even respond, except to say, "Uh—"

"Please . . . ?" she said, in a voice that was suddenly soft and a little hoarse and a lot more intimate than a kiss. And even though I still didn't know what she was asking me to do, I wanted very badly to do it.

"Well, um," I said, trying to sound very willing, which can be difficult when you don't know what you're agreeing to.

"It's not a bad idea," Deborah said helpfully. "I can help you square it with Rita." She nodded at Jackie. "He can actually shoot, too," she said. She reached into her bottom desk drawer and brought out a Glock 9mm pistol in a clip-on belt holster. "You can use my backup piece."

I looked at the Glock, and I looked at Jackie's pleading face, and the light began to dawn at last. "You mean . . ." I said. "I mean, you . . . That's, that's . . ." And although in normal times Eloquence is Dexter's middle name, nothing would come out that was even intelligible.

"Please?" Jackie said again, and the look she gave me would have melted a marble statue.

Dexter, of course, is made of sterner stuff than any mere mortal, and imploring looks from a beautiful woman have never had any power over Our Wicked Warrior. And it was an absurd idea, something far too strange even to contemplate—me, a bodyguard? It was out of the question.

And yet somehow, when the workday ended that evening and all good wage slaves trotted dutifully away to hearth and home, I found myself on the balcony of a suite at the Grove Isle Hotel, sipping a mojito and watching as a spectacular sunset blew up the sky behind us, reflecting orange and red and pink onto the water of Biscayne Bay. There was a tray of cheese and fresh fruit on the table beside me, and the Glock was an uncomfortable lump in my side, and I was filled with wonder at the unavoidable notion that Life makes no sense at all, especially when things have taken a sudden and extravagant turn into surreal and unearned luxury. Terror, pain, and nausea I can understand, but this? I could only assume I was being set up for something even worse. Still, the mojito was very good, and one of the cheeses had a very nice bite to it.

I wondered if anyone ever really got used to living like this. It didn't seem possible; weren't we all made to sweat and suffer and endure painful hardship as we toiled endlessly in the vile cesspit of life on earth? How did sharp cheese, fresh strawberries, and utter luxury fit in with that?

I looked at Jackie. She didn't look like she had ever set foot in the vile cesspit. She still looked fresh, composed, and perfectly at home in this opulent setting, like a demigoddess lounging around Olympus. It was a very sharp contrast to the scene that had greeted me at my house a little earlier.

I had left Jackie at headquarters with Deborah and gone home to get a toothbrush and a change of clothes. After all, even bodyguards should practice good hygiene. I went to my bedroom and pulled out a blue nylon gym bag. I put some socks and underwear in; funny— the last time I had used the bag, I had filled it with duct tape and a few casual blades and gone for an evening of light merriment with a brand-new friend, a charming man who lured young women out on his boat and somehow always came back alone. I had helped him learn that it wasn't nice to treat others as disposable toys—learn it by helping him become disposable himself. It had been a real pleasure to work with him, a thoroughly enjoyable evening. Had that really been three whole months ago?

My fond reverie was shattered by a great crashing sound from the front door, followed immediately by a shrill nasal howling, an inhuman sound that could only be Astor in full preteen snit. Rita's voice rose up to meet it, the door slammed even louder, and then there was a flurry of foot stomping, shouting, and another, closer door slam.

Rita came into the bedroom with Lily Anne under her arm, the baby's day-care bag over one shoulder and her own purse on the other. Her face was red, shiny with sweat, and the frown lines around her mouth looked like they had suddenly become permanent. And it hit me that she no longer looked like the picture of her I had been carrying around in my head. She had aged, and for some reason I was seeing it for the first time.

"Oh, Dexter, you're home early," she said, thrusting Lily Anne at me. "Can you change her, please? Astor is absolutely— I don't know what to do."

Lily Anne burbled at me happily and called out, "Dadoo!" and I carried her over to the changing table as Rita threw the bags on the bed.

"Oh," Rita said. I glanced over at her; she was holding up my gym bag. "But this is— I mean, you can't—"

"Wonderful news," I said, taking a very wet diaper off Lily Anne. "I have a chance to make a lot of money—enough to pay for a new pool cage at the new house."

"But that's— Do you *know* how much they cost?" She shook her head, and a drop of sweat flew off her face and hit my gym bag.

"Doesn't matter," I said. I threw the wet diaper away and reached for the baby wipes. "I will make that much and more."

"Doing what?"

I hesitated—not just because Jackie's need for a bodyguard was confidential, but also because it suddenly seemed like a good idea not to tell Rita I would be cooped up with a beautiful movie star for several nights. "It's confidential," I said. I wiped Lily Anne thoroughly and reached for a fresh diaper.

Rita was silent. I looked up at her. She was frowning, and the lines in her forehead looked very deep. A limp, damp strand of hair fell down across the lines. She pushed it back. "Well, but . . ." she said. "I mean, is it legal? Because . . ." She shook her head again.

"Perfectly legal," I said. "And very well paid." I fastened the new diaper and picked up the baby. "Deborah said she would call and talk to you about it."

"Oh, well," she said. "If Deborah is— But can't you tell me what it is?"

"Sorry," I said.

"It's just, there's so much right now," Rita said. "Moving day is coming—and Astor is being completely . . ." She dropped my gym bag and crossed her arms over her chest. "I mean, Dexter . . ." she said.

"I know," I said, which was a lie, since I didn't know, because she hadn't finished a sentence yet. "But it's just for a few days, and we can really use the extra money."

For a long moment Rita just looked at me. Her face was like a mask of uncertain misery, and she seemed to sag all over. I wondered what she was thinking that could make her look so much like a damp and tattered dish rag. She gave me no clues, but she finally said, "Well . . . We really could use some extra money. . . ."

"Exactly," I said. I handed Lily Anne back to her and picked up my gym bag. "So I will see you in just a few days?"

"You'll call me?" she said.

"Of course," I told her, and she leaned forward and gave me a sweaty kiss on the cheek.

"All right," she said.

# NINE

AND NOW HERE I WAS IN THE LAP OF LUXURY, FAR FROM THE hooting and screeching and dirty socks of my normal domestic life. It probably wasn't fair to compare, of course, which was a good thing. This hotel made even my new, swimming-pooled house seem squalid—made my whole little life seem just a bit less bright and shiny.

I watched Jackie. She was lifting a large red strawberry off the platter and she looked as fresh and perfect as a human being can look. It definitely wasn't fair to compare her to Rita.

"The seafood is very good here," Jackie said, biting the end off the strawberry. She swallowed and licked her lips. "I guess it should be." She smiled and sipped from her own mojito. "You probably get great seafood all the time," she said.

"Actually, I don't," I said. "The kids won't eat it."

"Kids," she said, and she gave me a strange and quizzical look.

"What?" I said.

Jackie shook her head. "Nothing. It's just . . . you seem so, um." She fluttered one hand while she took another sip of the drink. "I don't know," she said, putting the glass on the table. "So . . . independent? Self-contained? I mean, I don't really know you that well, and maybe I'm being, um . . ." She touched my arm, very lightly, and then took her hand away again. "Tell me if I'm being too personal," she said. "I just got this feeling like I know you? And it seems like, you know." She reached for a slice of kiwi fruit. "Like you are complete all by yourself. It's hard for me to picture you with kids."

"It's even harder for me," I said, and Jackie laughed. It was a nice sound.

"What's your wife like?" she asked.

"What, Rita?" I said. The question took me just a little bit by surprise. "Why, she's, um." Jackie watched me, unblinking, and from the hours of daytime drama I have watched in order to understand human behavior, I knew that I was supposed to say something flattering about Rita, since she was, after all, my wife. And I thought about it, thought about how worn she had looked earlier, and I tried to think of a nice phrase for her, but all that came to mind was that I was used to her, that she was blind to my harmless little foibles with knives and felons, and that didn't seem to be what the situation demanded. I thought some more. Jackie kept looking at me. The expectant silence grew, and in desperation I finally said, "She's a terrific cook."

Jackie tilted her head to one side and kept looking at me until I began to wonder whether I had said something wrong. "That's kind of funny," she said at last.

"What?"

A small smile flickered on and then off her face. "If you ask most guys about their wife, the first thing they say is, 'Oh, she's really beautiful, wonderful.' Something like that. And you think about it forever and all you come up with is, 'She's a good cook'?"

I wanted to tell her that, after all, I had my priorities, and as far as I was concerned Rita could have looked like Shrek as long as she made mango paella the way she did. But it didn't seem like quite the right note to hit, and I wasn't really sure what was, so I stammered out, "Well, but you know. I mean, she's very nice-looking."

"She should be," Jackie said, reaching for her glass again. "Married to a hunk like you."

Human conversation is something I have studied diligently, since it makes no sense at all to me unless it follows the comfortable path of cliché, which it does ninety-nine percent of the time. So in order to fit in, I have learned the formulas of small talk, and I must follow them or I am lost in a jungle of feelings and impulses and notions that I do not share. I am blind to nuance. But I would have had to be deaf and dumb as well not to realize that Jackie was paying me a compliment, and I groped for an appropriate response, only managing to say, "Oh, thank you," which sounded pretty feeble, even to me.

Jackie clutched her glass with both hands and looked out across Biscayne Bay. "Sometimes I catch myself wondering," she said. "You know. Like . . . maybe I should have found a nice guy like you and settled down. Had a real life." She went very still, just holding the glass and staring at the horizon, and I watched her. I admit I was surprised to hear what sounded like wistful regret in her voice—after all, she was beautiful, rich and famous, a star, and even the most levelheaded observer would have to say she had just about every-thing one could wish for.

And to her very great credit, she proved to be rather levelheaded herself, because she gave a small laugh and shook her glass. It rattled; it was empty, except for the ice. "I know," she said. "It's not very con-vincing, even to me. Besides, I've met plenty of nice guys and none of 'em made me want to give this up." She made a rueful face and set the glass on the table. "Plenty of not-so-nice guys, too," she said. "But the real truth is, I wouldn't trade my life for anything."

"Not even a Greek arms dealer?" I said.

"Not even two," she said, smirking at me. "And anyway, those guys are horribly possessive, so I'd be like his *property*, you know. I guess they have to be that way, but . . ." She shrugged. "That doesn't work for me."

She looked at me, and I looked back, and the moment seemed to stretch past what was comfortable, but I couldn't think of anything appropriate to say, and since she didn't appear to feel uneasy with the silence, I decided not to, either. Behind us the sun was just starting to sink into the horizon, and the water in front of us had that golden glow it gets at sunset, and that reflected up onto Jackie's face, and I suppose onto mine, too. Finally, the corners of her mouth went up into a smile, and she said, "Anyway. We should probably think about dinner. Are you hungry?"

I might have said that of course I was hungry; the mighty engine that is Dexter's body runs perpetually at a very high level, and requires regular fuel. But I settled for a polite, "Actually, I am a bit," and Jackie nodded, suddenly looking very serious.

"All right," she said. "Is there a really good place nearby? The network is paying, so don't be stingy."

Truthfully, my taste in food tends to be more robust than refined, but in any case, there were other considerations at the moment that were more important than what might be on the menu. "Um," I said. "How about room service?"

Jackie raised an eyebrow at me and started to say something, then seemed to catch herself. "Oh," she said. "You mean because . . ." She frowned and shook her head. "You think it might be dangerous to go out," she said.

"Yes," I said. "It's getting dark, and I have to assume he's figured out where you're staying by now."

"Oh," she said again, and she seemed to deflate a bit, slumping down into her chair and letting her chin sink onto her chest. "I keep forgetting," she said. "I was just enjoying . . ." She sighed heavily, which seemed like a strange reaction, unless she really wanted a fancy high-priced dinner. "Anyway, room service is fine. Since you are"—she waved one hand vaguely—"looking after my safety."

"That is why I'm here," I said.

She looked at me just a moment too long. "I'll try to remember that," she said. And before I could figure out what that meant, I heard a kind of scrabbling noise coming from the direction of the suite's door.

"That's—" she started to say, but I held up a hand and cut her off, listening hard for a second. There was no doubt; somebody was trying to open the door and get in.

We had not ordered anything yet, and since Jackie had been here almost a week I didn't think the management would be sending up a fruit basket. That left one very obvious and unpleasant possibility.

I got carefully to my feet and pulled the Glock from its holster. "Dexter," Jackie said. "I think it's—"

"Lock yourself into the bathroom," I said. "Take your phone, just in case."

"But I just—"

"Quickly!" I hissed at her, and I moved rapidly and silently toward the door, making sure the pistol's safety was off and holding it in the ready position, just the way my adoptive father, Harry, had taught me so long ago. I don't like guns—they're noisy and impersonal and really leave very little room for true artistic expression. But they are effective, and Harry had taught me how to use them as only a combat veteran and career cop could teach, and with a weapon as good as this one I could put holes in things at a very good distance.

In this case, however, I was hoping I wouldn't have to shoot. So I hurried across the floor to one side of the door, holding myself and my Glock in readiness.

As I got there the door began to ease open slowly, almost shyly; whoever it was, they were being very careful not to alert anyone that they were coming in. Unfortunately for them, I was already alerted. With my left hand I grabbed the edge of the door and yanked it open. I stepped quickly around, snatched at the arm holding the doorknob, and jerked hard, and as a head of short brown hair followed the arm into the room I slid behind and pressed the barrel of the Glock into the right ear.

A clatter of papers, keys, cell phone, and a Starbucks cup fell to the floor, and as they hit I heard a soft moan of terror, and I looked at what I was holding at gunpoint.

She was a square, plain-looking woman in her mid-thirties, wearing large Elton John–style glasses and a lightweight tropical sundress, not at all what I had pictured as our killer, and she was trembling violently. "Please," she croaked. "Please don't kill me." There was an unpleasant smell, and I looked down at the floor by my feet. Coffee was puddling out of the Starbucks cup, and a pool of urine around the woman's feet was growing to meet it—and spreading now toward my shoes, too, a very nice pair of New Balance running shoes, practically brand-new.

"Please," the woman whispered again, and she was shaking so hard now I could barely keep the gun in her ear.

"Ahem," said Jackie, and I looked up. She was standing about ten feet away, looking at us with an expression of real concern. "That was very impressive," she said. "I mean, it's nice to see you really know what you're doing, but . . ." She bit her lip. "I, uh, I tried to tell you," she said, and nodded at the woman I had captured.

"Um . . ." Jackie said with a kind of appalled flutter of her hands. She gave an embarrassed half smile and waved one hand at my prisoner. "Can I introduce my assistant, Kathy?"

I looked at the woman I was holding. She was still trembling, and she looked back at me with wide and terrified eyes. "Pleased to meet you," I said.

# TEN

I F YOU ARE JACKIE FORREST AND YOU ARE STAYING AT THE Grove Isle Hotel, you do not get the kind of room service normal people must put up with, even very rich normal people. I have stayed in some very nice hotels, but it always takes somewhere between one hour and three days to get a response to a call for service. And when help finally arrives, it is usually one surly man with a bad back who only speaks Urdu and refuses to understand the simplest request unless he sees dollar bills of a large denomination.

But for Jackie, the hotel had apparently hired a team of Olympic sprinters with a pathological need to please. Within thirty seconds of Jackie's call for a mop, a trio of young women arrived, eager and smiling. They wore hotel name tags that said NADIA, MARIA, and AMILA, and they fell on the puddle as if they were starving and it was manna rather than urine, while poor Kathy was still staggering away from the door and collapsing into a chair.

One of the maids, Amila, looked strangely familiar, and I stared longer than one really should look at a hotel maid mopping up pee. She looked up and smiled at me and then tossed her head, flinging her golden hair to one side. "I make my hair as Chackie," she said shyly, with a very thick accent from some Central European country.

"Very important star, yes?" She glanced over to the chair where Jackie was soothing Kathy's nerves.

And sure enough, it was true. Amila had styled her hair just the way Jackie did, which explained why she had looked familiar. "It's very nice," I said, and Amila blushed and returned her attention to her mop. She and her business associates had our little accident cleaned up in no time. They put the Starbucks cup, keys, and the cell phone on a side table, and they vanished, still smiling and leaving behind no more than a pleasant lemon smell, before Kathy managed to say, "Oh, God," more than two times. Amila paused at the door, briefly, and looked hungrily at Jackie. She touched her own hair, sighed, and disappeared into the hall.

Kathy said, "Oh, God," another twenty or thirty times while Jackie cooed at her in an attempt to soothe her jangled nerves. I am sure it is very unsettling to have a gun jammed into your ear, even a gun as nice as the Glock, but after five or six minutes of monotone monosyllabic misery, I began to wonder whether Kathy might be overdoing it a bit. I hadn't actually shot her; I'd done no more than grab her and point the pistol. But the way she carried on you would have thought I'd taken out her liver and offered her a bite.

Still, she finally calmed down enough to stop saying, "Oh, God"—and she immediately switched to staring at me and saying, "You bastard. You horrible bastard. Oh, you bastard."

Jackie glanced at me to see if I minded the rough language, and when I shrugged she twitched me a quick smile and went back to soothing Kathy.

"Dexter is here to protect me, Kathy," she said. "I'm really sorry; this is my fault; I should have told him you were coming."

"Oh, God, that bastard," Kathy said, cleverly combining both of her annoying chants.

"It's my fault," Jackie said. "I am so sorry."

"My phone!" Kathy choked out. She leaped out of the chair. "My God, if you ruined my phone . . . !"

"I'm sure it's all right," Jackie said.

Kathy jumped over to the side table where Amila had put her things. "All of your appointments! The contact list—everything!" She grabbed up her phone, and Jackie followed behind and took her arm, leading her back to her chair. But Kathy refused to sit until she made sure the phone had not been ruined by exposure to her own urine.

"It works," she said at last. "Oh, thank God, it still works." And she glared extra hard at me, as if I was the one who had peed on it. "Bastard," she said.

"All right, Kathy, we're all right now; everything's fine," Jackie murmured.

It was several more minutes before Kathy calmed down enough to resume normal human behavior. I filled the time by reholstering my Glock, bolting the door, and sitting down on a chair on the opposite side of the room from Kathy and her tedious meltdown. But even the most irritating things must end, and eventually Kathy remembered that she was, after all, an employee—and an employee who had wet herself in front of her boss, too. She finally fluttered to her feet and began to babble apologies to Jackie, alternating them with venomous glares at me. She straightened the heap of papers she'd brought in, reminded Jackie about a couple of telephone interviews in the morning, and finally stumbled out the door and away with one final hateful glower at me.

I secured the door behind her and turned to see that Jackie was watching me with a kind of amused caution. "What?"

She shook her head. "Nothing," she said. "Just . . . sorry about that. Poor Kathy really is very devoted to me. Very good at her job."

"She must be," I said. "If you let her pee on your floor."

Jackie giggled, a sound that was as contagious as it was surprising, and I found that I was smiling in response. "She did pee, didn't she," Jackie said.

"If she didn't," I said, "Starbucks coffee has gone way downhill."

Jackie giggled again, and started to sink down into the chair where Kathy had been sitting. She caught herself halfway down and jerked upright. "Oh!" she said. "That's, um—I think I'd prefer a chair with a dry seat."

"Good thinking," I said, and I watched Jackie move to one end of the couch, where she sat down and relaxed into a kind of contented sprawl. She sighed, and then she glanced at the heap of papers Kathy had piled on the end table. She immediately tensed up; her shoulders went up an inch and the half smile fell off her face.

"The letters," she said.

It may have been the strain of being called a bastard so many times, but I didn't know what she meant. "What letters?" I said.

Jackie nodded at the papers. "From him," she said. "The psycho. Kathy brought them for you."

"Oh," I said. It was very thoughtful, even though I really didn't want them.

Jackie kept looking at the pile with an expression that was halfway between loathing and anxiety.

When nothing else happened for a full minute, I cleared my throat politely. "Well," I said. "Should we order some dinner?"

Jackie looked at me with an expression I couldn't read, for just a moment too long, before she finally said, "All right."

Dinner was a somewhat somber affair. The chummy, lighthearted mood of cocktail hour had vanished, and Jackie spent most of the meal staring at her plate, picking at the food without actually eating very much of it. That was a shame, because it was really very good food. I had ordered tournedos of beef; I'd always wondered what a tournedo was, and when I saw it listed on the menu I decided there was no time like the present to find out. I knew it was some kind of beef, so it seemed like a rather low-risk gamble, and it turned out to be two very tasty chunks of beef, cooked in a wine-and-mango sauce. I was fairly sure that mango was not part of the original recipe—after all, what's the French word for mango?—but it was a nice addition, and I had no trouble eating everything, including a large mound of garlic mashed potatoes and a helping of broccoli, steamed just right.

Jackie had stone crab, or at any rate, she had it served to her. She cracked a claw open and poked at it for a while before she nibbled at one small chunk, without even dipping it in the melted butter. She also ate one spear of grilled asparagus, and half a forkful of wild rice. Altogether, though, it was quite clear that she was having trouble with the whole idea of eating. I wondered briefly whether she would think I was rude if I offered to finish her meal for her—after all, stone crab does not grow on trees. But upon sober reflection, I decided it was not quite the thing.

That was the last chance for sober reflection of any kind that evening, since Jackie had ordered a bottle of wine for each of us—red for my tournedos and white for her crab. The shyness she exhibited toward solid food did not extend to the wine, and she had finished about three-quarters of the bottle by the time she pushed her plate away. On top of the mojito she'd had earlier, it should have made her very unsteady, but her movements seemed perfectly crisp and her speech did not slur, what little there was of it. For the first part of the meal I didn't really notice how quiet she was, since my attention was all on my plate. But as the happy sounds of eating began to slow down, I became aware that no conversation arose to take its place, and I watched as Jackie slouched over her plate in moody silence and played with her food without eating.

Even the excellent dessert didn't improve her mood. I had something called Decadent Lava Cake, which was very good, although the decadence escaped me. Jackie had ordered a kind of crème brûlée, but once again she didn't really eat it. She picked a small piece of caramelized crust off the top and crunched on it, but that was all. I began to wonder whether perhaps she took vitamin shots in secret; she certainly didn't eat enough to sustain human life.

The waiters came and cleared away the wretched refuse of our meal, and I bolted the door behind them. Jackie still sat at the table in a kind of introspective slouch. I wondered how long it would last. I wondered if I should do something to help her snap out of it. If so, my study of daytime TV drama gave me two clear choices: either therapeutic release by getting her to talk about it, or cheerful chatter to change the subject. But it was impossible to say which one was right, and in any case, I couldn't be sure it was actually in my job description.

And seriously: What was my real role here? Earlier this evening we had been chatting away like true pals, but I was not really a friend—she had probably just been putting me at ease. After all, she was a rich and famous person—a star, in fact—and I was no more than a modest and unassuming forensics geek with an interesting hobby. As far as I knew, this was a situation Emily Post had never covered, and I did not know how to proceed. Should I keep things formal and businesslike, because I was a technical consultant turned bodyguard? Or was I now an employee—and if so, should I follow Kathy's lead and pee on the floor? After a mojito and most of a bottle of wine, that option was starting to look appealing, but it would almost certainly nudge the tone of the evening in an unclear direction, so I decided against it.

So I stood there uncertainly, watching Jackie stare into blank, bleak space for what seemed like a very long time. But finally her head snapped up and her eyes met mine. "What," she said.

"Nothing," I said. "I just wasn't sure, um . . ." And I realized I wasn't even sure what I wasn't sure of, so I stumbled back into awkward silence.

Jackie smiled with just the right side of her mouth, a kind of rueful acknowledgment. "Yeah, I know," she said. "Sorry." She shook her head. "I guess I wasn't very good company for dinner."

"Oh, well," I said. "That's all right. I mean, it was a very good dinner."

She smiled again, using both sides of her mouth this time, although she still didn't look entirely happy. "Right," she said. "Glad you liked it." She got up and wandered over to the sliding glass door that led out onto the balcony, and for a moment she just stood there looking out. I was afraid we were going right back into moody silence again, and I began to wish I'd brought a good book. But apparently she saw something out on the Bay that snapped her out of it; she suddenly turned around and, with a cheerful energy that was clearly forced, she said, "Well, then! It's too early for bed. So what should we do?"

It took me by surprise, and I blinked stupidly. "Um," I said. "I don't know." I looked around the room for a clue that wasn't there. "I don't see any board games," I said.

"Damn," Jackie said. "I could really go for a good round of Monopoly." She crossed her arms over her chest and tilted her head to one side. "So, what would you do if you were at home? With your wife and kids?"

"Oh, probably watch TV," I said.

Jackie made a face. "Yuck," she said, and I must have looked surprised, because she laughed. "I know," she said. "But just because I make TV shows doesn't mean I have to like them."

"It doesn't?" I said, and it was really sort of hard to imagine. I mean, I enjoy my job—both of them, in fact. Why else would I do them?

"No," Jackie said. "I mean, there's some good stuff now and then. But mostly, I'd rather stare at the wall. In fact, I usually can't tell the difference." She shrugged. "It's the business. You do an awful lot of crap, just to get into a position where you get a chance at something worth doing. But then you get a reputation as somebody who's really good at doing crap, and the good stuff never comes along, and the money is too good to turn down. . . . Eh," she said, spreading her hands in a what-the-hell gesture. "It's a good life. No complaints." She frowned and was silent for a moment, and then she shook herself and said, "Hey, look at me. Sliding back into the dumps again." She clapped her hands together. "Fuck it. How about a nightcap?" And without waiting for an answer she disappeared into her bedroom.

I stood uncertainly for a moment, wondering whether I was supposed to follow her. Before I could decide, she came back out, holding a bottle in her hands. "Get a couple of glasses," she said, nodding at the sideboard. "You know, tumblers."

I followed her nod to the large silver tray that stood on the table beneath a mirror. It held a silver ice bucket with silver tongs, four wineglasses, and four tumblers. I took two tumblers and joined Jackie on the couch. She set the bottle reverently on the coffee table and I looked at it as I sat. It was a very nice bottle, with a large wooden stopper on top and a palm tree etched onto the front, and it was filled with a brown liquid.

"What is it?" I asked politely.

Jackie smiled. "Panamonte," she said. "The best dark rum I ever tasted."

"Oh," I said. "Should I get some ice?"

Jackie gave me a look of mock horror. "Oh, my God, no," she said. "Putting ice in this stuff is a capital crime."

"Sorry," I said. "I don't know much about rum. Except the kind you mix with Coke."

Jackie shook her head vigorously. "This ain't it," she said. "Mixing this with anything is like drawing a mustache on the *Mona Lisa*." She pulled the cork out of the bottle and poured a little rum into each tumbler. "Try it," she said. She picked up both glasses, passing me one and raising the other in front of her face. "*Sláinte*," she said.

"*Salud*," I told her.

I sipped. It was not at all what I'd expected. I have never been a real Drinker, but there are times when Social Custom demands that you drink, and so I have from time to time, and I usually don't like it. And I have found that most brown liquors that are served after dinner are smoky, with a sharp taste that I don't like, no matter how much someone insists that it is very rare and the best ever, and I have never been a real fan of such things. But this was like nothing I'd ever tried before. It was sweet but not cloying, dark and rich and crisp, and probably the smoothest thing I'd ever tasted. "Wow," I said. It seemed like the only appropriate thing to say.

Jackie sipped from her glass and nodded. "Yup," she said, and for several minutes we just sat and sipped.

The rum seemed to take the dark edge off things for Jackie. She visibly relaxed as the level in her glass went down. To my surprise, I did, too. I suppose it was only natural; as I said, I am not a drinker, and I'd already had a mojito and several glasses of wine this evening. I probably should have been worried that all the alcohol would make me too dopey to be really effective as a bodyguard. But I didn't feel drunk, and it would have been a shame to spoil the experience of sitting on a couch and drinking rare dark rum with a celebrity. So I didn't: I sat; I enjoyed; I drank the rum slowly, savoring each sip.

Jackie finished hers first and reached for the bottle. "More?" she said, holding it toward me.

"I probably shouldn't," I said. She shrugged and poured a splash into her glass. "But it's very good," I said. "I'll have to get a bottle."

She laughed. "Good luck," she said. "You won't find it at the corner store."

"Oh," I said. "Where do you get it?"

"I don't know," she said. "This was a gift." She lifted her glass in a half toast and sipped. She rolled it around in her mouth for a moment and then put the glass back down. "Those letters," she blurted. "They scare the shit out of me."

"I'm sorry," I said.

"I mean, why?" she said, hunched over and staring down into the glass. "What did I do to make him hate me?"

"He doesn't hate you," I said.

Jackie looked up. "He's trying to kill me," she said.

"That's not hate," I said. "In his own way, he actually loves you."

"Jesus fuck," she said. She looked back down at the glass. "I think I'd rather have hate next time." She picked up the glass and sipped, and then swung her eyes to me. "How come you understand this rotten psycho bastard so good?" she said.

I suppose it was a fair question, but it was an awkward one, too. If I told her the truth—I understood him because I was a rotten psycho bastard, too—it would seriously undermine our relationship, which would have been a shame. So I shrugged and said, "Oh, you know." I took a small sip from my glass. "It's like you were saying before. It's kind of like acting."

"Uh-huh," she said. She didn't sound convinced, and she didn't look away from me. "Thing is, in acting, you find a piece of the character inside your own self. You expand it, you shape it a little, but it has to be *in* there or you don't get the job done." She took a small sip, still looking at me over the rim of the tumbler. "So what you're really saying is, there's something inside *you*"—she tipped the glass at me—"that is like this crazy asshole." She raised an eyebrow at me. "So? Is there?" She sipped. "You got a killer in there, Dexter?"

I looked at her with astonishment, and deep in Dexter's Dungeon I could feel the Passenger squirming with discomfort. I have lived my life among cops, people who spend every waking hour hunting down predators like me. I have worked among them for years, for my entire professional life, and not a single one of them had ever had the faintest misgiving about Dexter's snow-white character. Only one of them, in fact—Dear Sergeant Doakes—had ever suspected that I am what I am. And yet, here was Jackie—a *TV actress*, of all things!— asking me point-blank if there was a Wicked Other inside me, behind Dexter's carefully crafted smile.

I was too amazed to speak, and no amount of sipping could cover the growing, horribly awkward silence as I groped for something to say. Short of admitting she was right, or denying everything and calling for a lawyer, nothing occurred to me.

"Cat got your tongue?" she said.

"Oh," I said. "Just . . . just . . . more like rum got my tongue." I lifted the glass. "I'm not used to this stuff," I said, sounding rather lame even to myself.

"Uh-huh," Jackie said. "But you're not answering my question, either."

She was very insistent for someone who should have been a mental lightweight, and I began to wonder whether I had been too quick to decide I liked her. She was clearly not going to accept any cautiously phrased evasions, and that left Dexter somewhat on the ropes. But I am renowned for my conversational quick feet, and seldom at a loss. In this case, I decided that the best defense really was an all-out cavalry charge, so I put down my glass and turned fully toward her.

"Close your eyes," I ordered.

Jackie blinked. "Excuse me?"

"Acting exercise. Close your eyes."

"Uh—okay . . ." She put her glass down, settled back into the couch, and closed her eyes. "All right."

"Now," I said. "It's night. You're all alone, in a dark alley."

She took a deep, controlled breath. "Okay . . ."

"There's someone behind you," I said. "He's getting closer, closer. . . ."

"Oh," she said softly, and several emotions flicked rapidly across her face.

"You turn around," I said. "And it's *him*."

Jackie breathed out sharply.

"He's holding a knife and smiling at you. It's a terrible smile. And he speaks." I leaned close and whispered, " 'Hello, bitch.' "

Jackie flinched.

"But you have a gun," I said.

Her hand went up and she pulled an imaginary trigger. "Pow," she said, and her eyes fluttered open.

"Just like that?" I said.

"Damn straight."

"Did you kill him?" I said.

"Shit, yeah. I hope so."

"How do you feel?"

She took another deep breath and then let it out. "Relieved," she said.

I nodded. "QED," I said. She blinked at me. "I think it's Latin," I explained. "It means, 'I have proved it.' "

"Proved what?"

"There's a killer in everybody," I said.

She looked at me for a long moment. Then she picked up her glass and took a sip. "Maybe," she said. "But you seem pretty comfy with the one in you."

And I was, of course. But I was not at all comfy with having her guess it, so I was relieved that the subject seemed to be closed for now when Jackie put her empty glass on the table and stood up.

"Bedtime," she said. She stretched and yawned, looking like some kind of golden cat. She looked at me and raised an eyebrow. "Where do guard dogs sleep?" she said. "At the foot of the bed?"

"I'll sleep on the couch," I said. "That way I can watch the door and the balcony."

She blinked. "The balcony?"

"Anyone can get in from the roof," I said. "All you need is twenty feet of nylon rope and a screwdriver."

Jackie looked a little bit stunned. "You mean he might— What's the screwdriver for?"

"I don't know if he might," I said. "I know he could. Anybody could: just drop down from the roof, with the rope. The screwdriver is to jimmy open the sliding glass door. A ten-year-old could do it."

"Jesus," she said. She stared at me, but she wasn't actually seeing me. "I really fucking hate this," she said. And then she shook herself slightly, focused on me for a moment, and said again, "*Hate* it . . ." She stood very still, looking at me, breathing in, then out, watching me for some sign that I didn't know how to give her, and then she shook her head, turned away, and went slowly off to bed.

# ELEVEN

FELL ASLEEP QUICKLY AND COMPLETELY, AND WHEN I OPENED my eyes it seemed like no time had passed, but the first orange gleam of light was hammering its way in through the balcony door, so either it was morning or a UFO was landing on the chaise longue.

I blinked and decided it was probably morning. UFOs wouldn't dare land in Miami—somebody would chop them up and haul them off to sell for scrap metal. I started to stretch and sit up, but froze midway as I realized there was a strange whirring sound coming from Jackie's bedroom. It did not seem particularly sinister, but I had no idea what it was. As the bodyguard, it seemed incumbent upon me to investigate, so I stood up quietly, took the Glock from the coffee table beside me, and tiptoed to Jackie's door. I turned the handle silently, pushed the door open, and peeked in.

Jackie sat on a stationary bicycle, pedaling vigorously, and already a light sheen of sweat covered her face. That is, on a lesser human being it would have been sweat; on her it was *glow*. She wore a skintight leotard that did nothing to make her ugly, and there were earbuds plugged into the sides of her head, and as she looked up and saw me she pried one of them out. "Good morning," she called out, a little too loudly. "I'll just be about half an hour—you want to order some breakfast?"

Of course I did; the finely tuned machine that is Dexter requires frequent fuel. But I managed to conceal my unseemly eagerness, and simply gave her a nod and a cheery, "Okay!"

"Great!" she called back. "Wheat toast, grapefruit juice, and some Greek yogurt, please." And she put her head back down, plugged the earbud back into her ear, and pedaled faster.

I left her on her bicycle trip to nowhere and went to call room service. I tried very hard to admire Jackie for her spartan breakfast order, but it didn't work. To me, the whole point of eating is lost if you don't actually *eat* something, and it seemed to me that toast and grapefruit juice didn't quite qualify. It was really no more than an upscale version of bread and water, and was not nearly enough to sustain life as I had come to know it.

But at least I felt no compulsion to follow her lead, and I did not. I ordered a ham-and-cheese omelet, rye toast with jam, orange juice, and a fruit bowl. And, of course, the largest pot of dark Miami coffee they could muster in their high-priced kitchen.

Breakfast arrived a mere ten minutes later, and I had the garçon set it up on the balcony. I let him out, put the chain back on the door, and went back outside. The sun had clawed its way aggressively up the horizon, but its heat was not yet as brutal as it would soon be, and there was a light breeze coming off the Bay, so the balcony seemed like an ideal setting. I sat and sipped coffee while I waited for Jackie, looking out over the water and thinking that there was a great deal to be said for my new career as a bodyguard. True, it was potentially dangerous, and the hours were rather long. But on the plus side, I was living like a millionaire without paying higher taxes, and I got to hang out with a Real Live Hollywood Star and eat haute cuisine. Of course, Rita's food was far from being swill, but it had to be said that she was not truly a five-star gourmet chef, and not a famous and beautiful celebrity, either, and comparing her to Jackie was really no contest. It was an unkind thought, but since no one else could hear it, I didn't bother to pretend I hadn't thought it.

Instead, I thought about it some more. It was really nothing but a pleasant mental game, a goofy and nearly human fantasy, but it passed the time. I tried to imagine swapping my drab little existence for the life of a Celebrity Bodyguard. I pictured Me as part of an Entourage, the hawk-eyed presence at Jackie's shoulder, ever vigilant on the Red Carpets of the world. Dexter the Human Shield, Living It Large in Hollywood, Cannes, and all the great cities of the world. Breakfast on the balcony in Maui and Singapore and Bali. It would not be hard to get used to living like that, and if I had to give up scrabbling for a mortgage on a new house, and do without all the shrieks and squeals and door-slamming that went with family life, what had I really lost except shattered eardrums and frequent headaches? Of course, there was Lily Anne, the living extension of all that is Me, my DNA shipment into the future. And I had, after all, promised to lead Cody and Astor into a safe, well-planned Dark Future. My path was already laid out, and I was completely satisfied with it. Really I was. I did not need to enhance it with private jets and crème brûlée every night and a golden-haired goddess leading me through an existence of pure, diamond-studded pleasure. No matter how much I liked it.

The glass door slid open, interrupting my pleasant daydream, and Jackie stepped out into the sunlight. "Good morning," she said, and sat beside me. Her hair was damp, and she smelled of shampoo and the same very faint perfume I had noticed yesterday.

"Good morning," I said. "Coffee?"

"Oh, God, yes," she said, and she pushed a cup toward me. I poured it full, and watched as she stirred in artificial sweetener. She slurped it and said, "Aahhh," just like a normal person, and set the cup down, glancing up at me and smiling. "I hope I didn't wake you up?" she said.

"Oh, well," I said uncertainly, since she had, after all, but it didn't really seem politic to say so. "I mean, I have to be awake. . . ."

"Sorry," she said, reaching for the coffee cup and slurping again. "I have to work out every morning, no matter where I am, or I get fat."

"That's hard to believe," I said.

She reached over and patted my hand. "Bless you," she said. "But it's true. I miss one morning, and then missing two seems like no big deal, and then why not three, and before you know it I weigh a hundred fifty pounds and I'm out of work." She shrugged. "Part of the job. I don't mind." She took another noisy sip of coffee and raised an eyebrow at me. "What about you?"

"Me?" I said, a little surprised. "What do you mean?"

Jackie gestured with the cup. "You obviously work out. I mean," she said with a wicked smile, "I can see you have a pretty good appetite, but you look pretty fit." She actually winked at me. "Just like a real bodyguard should."

"Oh, well," I said, still a bit uncomfortable. "I like to run. And, um, some tai chi . . . ?"

She nodded. "Thought so," she said. "The way you moved, when you made Kathy pee on the floor." She smiled again and finished her coffee. "Which reminds me," she said, setting down the empty cup and reaching for a piece of toast. "Kathy will be here in a few minutes, so you might want to take the chain off the door, and remember not to shoot her this time."

"I'll try to remember," I said.

I had just barely finished my omelet when I heard a knock on the door. "That's probably her," Jackie said, and started to stand up.

"Let me get it," I said, and Jackie paused halfway to her feet. She held the awkward position for a moment, blinking, and then said, "Oh, right," and settled back down into her chair and slouched over her grapefruit juice.

I opened the door with the chain still on and looked out. Kathy stood in the hall with an armful of papers, her smartphone, and another Starbucks cup. She gave me a poisonous glare. "Let. Me. In," she said through her teeth, and I could tell that my legendary charm had not yet melted through the awkwardness of our first encounter. But that would almost certainly come with time. So I closed the door and undid the chain anyway, and Kathy huffed past me and into Jackie's bedroom before I could direct her to the balcony. A moment later she huffed back out, gave me an even more venomous look, and went out onto the balcony.

By the time I got back outside to where the remains of my breakfast were waiting, Kathy had taken my chair, pushed my plate onto the floor, and spread several sheaves of paper across the tabletop, and she was busily pointing to the different documents with a pen and babbling on at a rapid rate.

" . . . except the ancillary rights, which Myron says is the best we can do right now, so go ahead and sign it, here, here, and here— Oh. And then the Morocco thing? Which Valerie says is actually a *very* good deal, and publicity we couldn't buy, so here's the packet for that. And *Reel Magic* magazine wants a photo shoot; they're on your call list for this morning. . . ."

It went on like that for several minutes, with Kathy shoving papers around, Jackie occasionally signing something as she chewed toast and sipped her juice and tried to look like she was paying attention. Once or twice she looked up at me and made a wry face, which Kathy didn't see. I contented myself with lurking in the background and trying to seem vigilant, and eventually Kathy ran out of breath, gathered up the papers, and huffed out, favoring me with one last angry snarl as she went by.

I came back from letting her out and rechaining the door to find Jackie sipping another cup of coffee. She had eaten one of the toast halves and one bite of another, and about two-thirds of the small serving of yogurt. It didn't seem like quite enough to sustain human life, and certainly not nearly enough for nonhuman life like me, but she seemed content. I sat in my chair and poured myself another cup of the coffee.

"I don't think she likes you," Jackie said, in a throaty voice filled with coffee and dark amusement.

"Inconceivable," I said.

"I don't think that word means what you think it means," she said.

I sipped my coffee. "It may take a little time," I said. "But someday she will come to appreciate my many virtues."

"It may take a little longer than usual," Jackie said. "She really doesn't like you."

I was sure she was right, but it didn't seem terribly important— especially since there were three chunks of perfectly ripe cantaloupe left in my fruit bowl, and a full cup of coffee to go with it, so I shrugged it off and finished my breakfast.

The room's phone rang a few minutes later to tell us that a Town Car was waiting for us downstairs. We went down in the elevator together, and I went out front first to look around, which was standard bodyguard protocol. I left Jackie in the lobby with a doorman who was all too eager to watch her for as long as possible. I walked out and across the cobblestoned driveway, and looked into the Town Car; it was the same driver we'd had the night before, and he nodded at me. I nodded back and turned to look at the rest of the area around the entrance.

It took only a few moments to search around the hotel's front door. There were a few people standing around near the door, presumably waiting for their cars. I looked them over carefully, but they seemed to be no more than my fellow hotel guests: wealthy, well-fed people, looking rather pleased with themselves, and I passed them by and stepped out into the courtyard.

The sun was already shining brightly, and I had to blink for a moment, and then squint around me. Down at the far end of the drive, where the island's only real road led away to the bridge, there were two cars pulled over and parked rather informally. But they were too far away to do any real harm; I was not expecting a sniper attack. So I took a quick circuit around the circular driveway. There were a couple of cars parked ostentatiously along the edge of the pavement: a Ferrari, a Bentley, and a Corniche. I didn't think our killer would be driving anything that cost more than a new house on the water, but I looked inside anyway. They were empty.

The valet parking attendant watched me skeptically as I came back from looking into the Corniche. "You like it?" he asked me.

"Very nice," I said. "Is it yours?"

He snorted. "We just park it there. For looks," he said.

I nodded as if that made sense. "Right," I said. "A design moment." He shrugged. I went back inside.

The doorman was enthusiastically telling Jackie about his nephew, a really good-looking kid who could really act and sang like an angel, not like these hip-hop guys nowadays but really *sing*, and Jackie was smiling and nodding and trying to keep her eyes from crossing with the strain of enduring the doorman's blather without slapping him.

I took pity on her and interrupted without waiting for the end of the story. "We're running late, Miss Forrest," I said, sounding as Official as I could.

Jackie gave me a grateful smile and then nodded at the doorman.

"Tell him not to give up," she told the man. "Always follow the dream."

He beamed at her like she had knighted him. "Yes, ma'am, I'll tell him; thank you, Miss Forrest." And he leaped ahead of us and held the door as I led Jackie out to the waiting car.

As we came out into the sunlight I heard a sort of murmur of excitement from the handful of people waiting there, and I turned to see that they were all looking at me with bright and mindless smiles on their faces. Not actually Me, of course, which became crystal clear when someone called out, "Yo, Jackie!" She smiled and waved and I led her on past the minicrowd to the waiting Town Car. I felt the eyes following us, and I wondered why that didn't make me nervous. I checked the Dark Passenger; far from being anxious, he actually seemed to be *purring*. Someone in the throng yelled, "Whoo!" and I felt myself smiling with pleasure. I knew it was for Jackie—but I was *with* her, part of her entourage, and in a moment of truly bizarre insight, I realized I liked it. I enjoyed having idiot smiles following in my wake. It was totally unthinkable, of course; Dexter must maintain a low profile or cease to be Dexter. Still, I found that I felt larger, more handsome, certain that great wit fell from my lips every time I parted them to speak. It was invigorating, intoxicating, and I enjoyed it so much that I did not hear the rising rattle of warning from the watchtower of Castle Dexter until I opened the car's door.

But then I did hear it, loud and insistent, and I put two protective arms around Jackie and turned to survey the area.

"What?" she said, and she pushed up close against me, suddenly as edgy as I felt.

"I don't know," I said. I scanned; the people at the hotel's entrance were doing no more than beaming at us. No danger there. But I felt a sharp tickle of *something*, a kind of intense focus on Us, over to the right somewhere. I turned to look.

Down at the end of the drive, a man stood beside one of the two cars pulled over and parked at the mouth of the hotel's driveway. The man raised something up, pointed it at us—and just before I could fling Jackie to the hard uneven bricks of the driveway, I recognized it: a camera, with a large telephoto lens.

*Click. Click. Click.*

"Paparazzi," Jackie said. "They're everywhere." She looked at me with a strange expression of puzzled concern. "How did you know he was there?"

"Um, I didn't really," I said. The thought of describing my Passenger's Distant Early Warning System was unthinkable. "I just, um, I saw him move out of the corner of my eye."

She kept looking. "Uh-huh," she said, sounding very much unconvinced.

I held the back door of the car open for her. "Shall we go?" I said.

She finally nodded, turned away, and climbed into the car, and I turned to look at our audience one last time. The photographer clicked a few more shots, and as I turned away, I heard the sound of a motorcycle starting up.

Around the hotel's front door, the people were still smiling. Even the doorman was still watching and waving as I put Jackie into the backseat, but to be fair, everybody else in the area was watching her, too, watching with a kind of lustful adoration, as if Jackie was a cross between a pinup and the pope. They did not actually applaud as she slid onto the seat and I closed the door, but I got the idea that they would have if this wasn't such a classy hotel.

I got in on the other side, feeling another surge of that strange satisfaction at being the center of attention. I pushed it away half-heartedly, but it didn't want to go, and I was still feeling beautiful and important as the car started down the drive, across the bridge, and into the happy mayhem of morning traffic in Miami.

I tried to lean back and enjoy the ride, but I found it a very odd experience to creep through the havoc in the backseat of the Town Car. For the first time I was a spectator instead of a participant, and although the horns blared and the middle fingers went up just as much as ever, it was almost like it was happening in another time and place as I watched it all go by in a movie.

Jackie looked out the window and, when she felt me looking at her, turned and smiled.

"The traffic is pretty bad this morning," I said.

She raised an eyebrow in mock surprise. "This?" she said. "You call this traffic?" She shook her head. "Don't ever drive in Los Angeles. It makes this look like a sunny day in the park."

"Really," I said.

"Really," she told me. And she gave me a condescending smile and said, "You get used to it."

I've noticed before that people from New York and L.A. tend to have an attitude about their cities, a kind of survivor's confidence that says, *I'm from Real Life, and if you live in this hick town, you're not even in the game.* Always before I'd found this kind of amusing; Miami natives, after all, are just as rude and aggressive as New Yorkers, and just as sun-drenched and vacuous as Angelenos, and the combination is a unique and lethal challenge every time you drive. But something about the way Jackie said it made me feel a little bit provincial, and I wanted to say something to defend the ferocity of Miami traffic.

Happily for my city's reputation, I didn't need to say a thing. As we finally made it up onto the Dolphin Expressway and came to a stop in the bumper-to-bumper snarl, a large and shiny Cadillac Escalade went rocketing by us on the shoulder. It was going at least fifty miles per hour, and there was no more than two inches of room between it and the line of cars it hurtled past. Jackie flinched away from it and watched it go by with her mouth slightly open in surprise, and I felt a small warm glow of pride.

This was my city; these were my people.

"Oh," she said. "Does that sort of thing happen a lot?"

"Almost constantly," I said. And because I can be just as condescending as any Angeleno, I added, "You get used to it."

Jackie stared at me, and then smiled, shaking her head. "Point for the home team," she said. But before I could do a victory dance, her cell phone began to chirp. "Shit," she said. "My first interview, and I can't remember who it is." She fumbled out her phone and tossed it to me. "Please?" she said. "Just find out who it is so I don't look like a dope?"

It seemed like a reasonable request. I took the phone and answered. "Hello?"

"Hi, Sarah Tessorro, *Reel Magic* magazine; can I speak to Jacqueline Forrest, please?"

I covered the mouthpiece. "Sarah Tessorro, *Reel Magic*," I said to Jackie, and she nodded. I handed her the phone.

"Sarah!" Jackie said enthusiastically. "How are you?" And then the two of them were off into a five-minute chat in which Jackie talked about the new show, her character, how wonderful the script was, and how great it was to work with a wonderful pro like Robert. I listened to that part with real surprise, and not merely because she overused the word "wonderful," which was not her style at all. But I had watched Jackie with Robert for a week now, and I didn't need to read the script to know they detested each other. Still, Jackie said it very convincingly, and my estimation of her acting talent went up several notches.

By the time the Town Car pulled up in front of the headquarters building, she'd said it with equal conviction in two more interviews. It must have been hard work, and I decided that being a star was a little more difficult than I'd thought. Clearly, it wasn't all mojitos and sunsets; sometimes you had to repeat terrible lies in a very convincing way. Of course, that seemed like something I could be very good at—I'd had so much practice, after all—and I began to wonder again whether I was too old to switch careers.

We got out right at the front door and I took Jackie upstairs and delivered her to Deborah, who was already hard at work at her desk. She looked up at us as we came in with an expression I could not read; it was partly her Standard Cop Face, but with one eyebrow raised in cynical disbelief.

"How'd it go?" she asked us.

"No problem," I said.

"Except when he tried to shoot my assistant," Jackie said sweetly. But before I could add even a syllable in defense of my honor, she pulled the stack of psychotic fan letters from her bag and dumped them on Deborah's desk. "She brought these," she said. "The letters."

Deborah snatched them up eagerly. "Great," she said, and began to read them with ferocious concentration. Jackie watched her, then looked up at me. "Um," she said.

"You'll be fine with Debs," I said. "I'll see you later."

"All right," she said, and I turned away and headed out the door. I would much rather have stayed with Jackie and my sister, especially since I was joining Robert instead. But my duty was clear, so I left them and trudged away down the hall to my cubicle.

# TWELVE

WASN'T REALLY STALLING TO AVOID ROBERT, BUT I TOOK MY time, sauntering down the hall and savoring the memories of last night's golden extravaganza. The food, the dark rum, the company—sheer perfection. And I had another evening just like it to look forward to at the end of today's painful grind. It didn't seem quite right that someone like me should have it so good, but happily, that didn't stop me from enjoying it.

I stopped briefly for a cup of coffee and tried to savor that, too, but it proved to be beyond my abilities. The brew smelled like old pencil shavings mixed with burned toast, nothing at all like the ambrosial nectar I'd been sipping only an hour ago. Still, it would probably meet the narrowest legal definition of coffee, and life isn't perfect—at least, not during the workday. I filled a cup and trudged off to fulfill my Duty.

Robert was waiting for me behind my desk again, but to his very great credit he had brought doughnuts—including a couple of Boston creams this time, and if you give one of these to Dexter, you will find that he is suddenly in a mood to forgive a great deal. We ate doughnuts and sipped the truly awful coffee, and I listened to Robert tell a long and no doubt fascinating story about a crazy British stuntman on a movie he had made many years ago. The point of the story seemed to escape us both, but might have had something to do with Robert facing him down over some obscure point of honor. Whatever it was, Robert enjoyed telling it, and luckily, he was so distracted by his own eloquence that I managed to sneak the second Boston cream out of the box and into my mouth before he noticed.

After the doughnuts were gone, we spent several hours playing with the microscope and learning how to prepare the slides properly. Oddly enough, in spite of the revulsion to blood he'd shown so far, he seemed fascinated with it in its microscopic state. "Wow," he said. "This is actually very cool." He looked up at me with a smile. "It's not that bad when it's dry and on a slide," he said. "I mean, I could actually get to like this."

I could have told him that I felt just the same, that I liked blood in its dried state so much that I had a rosewood box at home with fifty-seven drops of dried blood, each on its own slide, every one a small memento of a very special friend, now departed. But I have never quite believed in this newfangled notion of sharing your thoughts and feelings, especially on such a personal subject, so I just smiled and nodded and handed him a few more sample slides to play with. He went at them eagerly, and we whiled away the happy hours.

Just when I was thinking I should look in the doughnut box to see whether I had missed anything, the phone rang, and I grabbed it.

"Morgan," I said.

"We got an ID on Jackie's pervert," my sister said. "Come on up."

I looked at Robert, who was happily twiddling the fine-focus knob on my microscope. I could not very well take him along to hear about a stalker he wasn't supposed to know about. "What about my associate?" I asked.

"Think of something," she said, and hung up.

I put the phone down and looked at Robert. In spite of being very annoying, he was not really all that stupid, and I had to tell him something plausible. Happily for me, my stomach gurgled, providing a perfect excuse. "That coffee has gone right through me," I said.

"Yeah, it was pretty bad," he said without looking up.

"I may be a while," I said, and he waved a hand at me to indicate that my intestinal issues were none of his concern and he would be fine. I slipped out and hurried away to answer my sister's summons.

"Patrick Bergmann," Deborah said when I stepped into her office a few minutes later. It seemed like an odd greeting, but I had to assume she meant that was our stalker's name.

"That was fast," I said. "How'd you do it?"

Deborah made a face and shook her head. "The letters," she said. "He signed them. Even put his address."

"That's practically cheating," I said. "So the real question is, why did it take you so long?"

"He lives in some shit-hole place in Tennessee," Deborah said. "I couldn't get anybody local to go check, see if he was still there."

Jackie beamed at me. "So I checked Facebook," she said. She gave Deborah a fondly amused glance. "Your sister didn't know anything about it."

"I heard of it," Deborah said defensively. She shook her head with disbelief. "But shit. It's fucking nutso. People put *any* fucking thing on there."

Jackie nodded at Debs. "I showed her how it works, and we found him. Patrick Bergmann, Laramie, Tennessee. With pictures, and postings about where he is." The smile dropped off her face. "Um," she said slowly, "he's here. In Miami."

"Well," I said, "but we already knew that."

Jackie shrugged and seemed to pull herself into a smaller shape, abruptly making herself look like a lost little girl. "I know," she said. "But it kind of . . . I mean, I know this is stupid, but—to see it on Facebook? That kind of makes it more real."

I'm sure that Jackie was actually making sense—just not to me. Facebook made it more real? More real than the tattered body of the young woman in the Dumpster? Of course, I am not, and never will be, a fan of Facebook. It can be a very helpful way to track people I am interested in interviewing in connection with my hobby, but the idea of a Dexter page seems a little bit counterintuitive. Attended University of Miami. Friends: None, really. Interests: Human vivisection. I'm sure I would get plenty of friend requests, especially locally, but . . .

Still, I suppose the important point was that it was, in fact, more real for Jackie. It was hard work to guard somebody from a determined psychotic killer, and if the guardee didn't believe in the reality of the threat, it was even harder.

So for once, Facebook proved to be practical. Better, it also gave us a photo of our new friend Patrick. Like I said, it was practically cheating.

"Could I see his picture?" I said.

Deborah's mouth twitched into a slight smile, and she handed me a sheet of paper from her desk. It was a printout of a picture from Facebook and it showed a guy in his twenties, squatting down beside a deer. The deer looked very, very dead, and the guy looked just a little too happy about it. I have seen enough Hunting Trophy pictures to know what they are supposed to look like: Noble Beast settling into Eternal Rest while the Mighty Hunter stands beside it, clutching his rifle and looking solemnly proud.

This picture was nothing like that. To begin with, the deer was not merely dead; it was eviscerated. The body cavity had been opened up and emptied out, and the Mighty Hunter's arms were covered with its blood almost up to his shoulders. He held up what looked like a bowie knife and smirked at the camera, a coil of intestines at his feet.

I tried to focus on his face, and as I studied his features the Passenger muttered sibilant encouragement. Patrick Bergmann was not an awful-looking person—wiry, athletic build, dirty-blond hair in a shaggy cut, regular features—but something about him was not quite right. Beyond his obvious enjoyment of the horrible blood-soaked mess he wallowed in, his eyes were open just a little too wide, and his smirk had an unsettling feeling to it, as if he was posing naked for the first time and liking it. His face was saying, just as clearly as possible, that this was a portrait of the real Him, his Secret Self. This was who he was, somebody who lived to feel the blood run down his blade and crouch in the viscera piled at his feet. I did not need to hear the Passenger chanting, *One of Us, One of Us,* to know what he was.

I tuned back in to the conversation as Deborah said, "Which means we gotta tell Anderson about this, too. I mean, we got an ID, an actual fucking photo. . . ." She held up both hands, palms up: portrait of a helpless detective. "I can't sit on that," she said.

Jackie looked dismayed, and then she actually wrung her hands. I had always thought "wringing your hands" was only an expression, or at most something actors did in old movies—but Jackie did it. She lifted both hands chest-high and shook them from the wrist, and I very clearly thought, *Wow. She's wringing her hands.*

"Isn't that kind of, oh, you know," Jackie said, "pushing our luck?"

"You gave Anderson your file already?" I said.

Deborah nodded. "First thing this morning," she said.

"And what happened?"

She made a face and then added, rather grudgingly, "Just like you said. He stuck it in a drawer—didn't even wait for me to leave the room."

"Well, then," I said. "This shouldn't be a problem."

"Yes, but, I mean," Jackie said, and she looked very worried, "it's his name, and picture, and everything. Even Anderson can't ignore that."

Deborah snorted. "Man could lose his own ass in a chair," she said.

"It's just, the rest of the cast gets here today and tomorrow, and then we start shooting and—I mean, it's my *career*," Jackie said.

Debs looked dubious. "It's your *life*, too," she said. "That counts for something."

"My career *is* my life," Jackie said. "I've given up everything for this, and if I lose this show, too . . ." She took a ragged breath and grabbed her left hand with her right, squeezing them together. "I'm just worried, I guess."

"I got no choice," Deborah said. "I got to pass it on to him."

"But he'll ignore it," I said. "And in the meantime, we will find Patrick and keep you safe."

Jackie gave me a smile of gratitude that made me feel four inches taller.

"Thank you," she said. "And, Dexter—"

She raised a hand and took a step toward me, and I believe she was going to say something exceptionally nice, but I never got to hear it. Somebody cleared their throat, and as I realized it was not Jackie, Debs, nor even me, I turned as a man stepped forward into Deborah's cubicle. He was maybe forty-five, about five-ten, and in decent physical shape, except for some extra bulk around the waist. He had dark hair and eyes, and wore something that was almost certainly supposed to be a suit, except that it looked like it had been made out of a slipcover taken from the couch in an old disco lounge. And even though I did not recognize him, he also wore that indefinable look that said he was a cop.

He raised one eyebrow at Deborah. "Detective Morgan?" he said.

Deborah gave him the same look. "Yes?"

The man held up a badge, and then stepped forward and stuck out his hand. "Detective Echeverria, NYPD," he said, and his speech very much matched what we have all come to think of as a New York Accent.

Deborah looked him over for a moment, then stuck out her hand. "Right," she said. "I got your e-mails."

They shook hands briefly, and then Echeverria stepped back and looked at Jackie. "Hey," he said. "Jackie Forrest. How 'bout that."

She gave him a small, low-wattage smile. "Detective," she said. He looked at her without blinking for a few seconds too long, until finally Deborah cleared her throat, and Echeverria snapped his head back around to face my sister.

"What can I do for you?" Deborah said, putting a slight ironic twist on the words so he would know his ogling had been observed.

"Yeah, right," he said. "What you can do, you can let me see what you got on this psycho you're working on."

Deborah gave him a very thin, Professional Courtesy smile. "Can't do that," she said.

Echeverria frowned and blinked twice. "Why not," he said.

"It's not my case," she said.

He shook his head. "What the fuck," he said.

"I know," Deborah said. "But I told you not to fly down here."

Echeverria shook his head again. His mouth twitched. "You know how many Brooks Brothers suits I got crawling up my ass on this thing?" he said.

"Yeah," Debs said. "We got 'em here, too."

"Except here the suits are a nice, tropical-weight fabric," I added, always eager to be helpful.

Echeverria looked at me. Oddly enough, it was not a glance filled with warmth, camaraderie, and appreciation of my vast knowledge of sartorial standards. It was closer to the kind of look you give somebody you caught jaywalking to spit on nuns. Then he looked back at Deborah. "Okay," he said. "So what the fuck." He frowned and nodded at Jackie. "'Scuse me, Miss Forrest." She showed him five or six teeth, and he looked back at Deborah. Apparently it was all right to say "fuck" without apologizing to my sister, because he said it to her again. "What's the fucking deal here, Morgan?"

Deborah, of course, is no slouch in the dirty-words department, and she rose to the occasion with her customary flair. "The fucking deal is the same old shit," she said.

"Which is what," he said.

Deborah's face twitched into a very small and angry smile. "Does it ever happen in New York that the captain gives a big case to some limp-dick asshole who couldn't find a shit heap if he was wearing it for a hat, and everybody else has to stand around and watch him fuck up another one?" she said.

"Never happens," he said with a matching smile that said even he didn't believe what he was saying.

"Course not," Deborah said. "Doesn't happen here, either. Our whole department is made up of highly skilled professionals."

Echeverria nodded. "Right," he said. "So who's the limp-dick asshole?"

"If you mean, who is the officer in charge of the investigation," Debs said, "that would be Detective Anderson."

Echeverria looked surprised. "Billy Anderson?" he said, and Debs nodded. "I'm s'posed to look him up for drinks. I was told he's a good guy."

Deborah managed not to give a wild hoot of laughter, but her mouth twitched several times, which is the same thing for her. "Who told you that?" she said. "Somebody you'd want watching your back?"

"Uh," Echeverria said, frowning, "maybe not."

"He might be able to find drinks," I offered. "But that's about it."

Echeverria looked at me again, and then decided he'd rather look at Jackie. He did, and then he frowned and turned back to face Debs. "Okay, I get it," he said. "But, uh—what's the deal with you? What are you doing working on it if it's not your case?"

Deborah's face froze into her official Talking to the Captain Face. "I am on detached duty as a technical adviser to the Big Ticket Network, which is shooting a pilot here. Starring," she said with a nod at Jackie, "Miss Forrest."

Echeverria looked at Jackie again.

"And so," Debs said, and Echeverria tore his eyes off Jackie and looked back at my sister, "Miss Forrest and I are conducting a parallel *mock* investigation of our own in order to teach her proper police investigative technique and procedure."

Echeverria looked at Deborah with new respect. "Fucking brilliant," he said.

Deborah just nodded.

"So, what," Echeverria said. "I gotta go talk to Anderson, ask him if I can see the case file?"

"I'm afraid so," Deborah said.

"And he really is a total fucking dope?"

"Or worse," she said. "But I never said that."

"Well, shit," he said.

"Pretty much," Deborah said.

# THIRTEEN

E CHEVERRIA LEFT TO FIND ANDERSON, WITH ONE MORE LONG
look at Jackie, and I was not particularly unhappy to see him go.
Of course, he had a right to ogle whoever he wanted, and Jackie
was certainly ogle-worthy. But for some reason, I didn't like it. Perhaps I was merely getting overzealous in my role as her bodyguard.
Maybe it was something else.

In any case, I was glad to see the last of Echeverria, and it gave me
a chance to think a little bit more about Patrick Bergmann. Knowing
what he looked like was very nice, of course, but for my purposes it
was more important to know what he *thought* like. Would he stalk
Jackie as if she were a deer, staying in heavy cover and then leaping
out when she wasn't expecting it? Or would he be the kind of freak
who showed himself to his victim a few times, just to build suspense?
Would he approach in some bizarre, brilliant, unimaginable manner?
Or just charge her with a lasso?

I knew what he liked to do after he caught his victims—I had seen
it three times already. But I didn't know how he liked to stalk, and
it would certainly help if I could figure that out. And all that aside, I
naturally enough felt a certain amount of curiosity about somebody
who shared my interests.

"Could I read the letters?" I asked Deborah. She looked at me blankly. "The letters Patrick wrote to Jackie," I said as patiently as possible.

Deborah cocked her head to one side. "Patrick," she said. "He's already 'Patrick' to you."

"It *is* his name," I said, trying very hard not to sound cranky.

"His name is sicko," she said. "Or fucking psycho. Or the suspect or the perp." She shook her head. "But to you he's *Patrick*."

"Oh, my God, he's doing that *thing* again," Jackie said, staring at me as if I was a piece of alien technology that had just turned itself on. "You know, where he goes inside the guy's head."

"If you'd rather," I said with all the dignity I could muster under the circumstances, "I can go back to drinking awful coffee with Robert."

Deborah made a snorting sound. "I wouldn't wish that on anybody," she said. She picked up the sheaf of papers from her desk. "Read the fucking letters," she said, holding them out to me. "Go away into your fucking trance. Bring back something I can use."

"Thank you," I said, and although I thought I had managed a tone of quiet but injured self-possession, Jackie and Deborah snickered in unison. But I fought down my quite natural impulse to lay about me with a chair and took the letters, settling into the folding chair beside Deborah's desk as I began to read. The letters were all printed out from a standard computer printer.

"Dear Miss Forrest," the first one began.

> I guess I should just say Jackie but I wanted to be polite the first time, so here goes. I got to say I seen a lot of beautiful girls in my time and not all of them on the internet hahaha but you are something special. First I seen you I new you are something rilly special and now I watched everything you done and I new that you and me was spose to be together like it was something just spose to happen. I no I don't have to try and discripe it to you because you are goin to feel it to soon as you see me and so I will just say for rite now I rilly need you to send me something maybe you were wearing

and you don't have to wash it first if you no what I mean. I
no you will see me real soon.

> youre soul mate Patrick Bergmann

I flipped through the next few letters; they were pretty much the
same, telling her with increasing frustration that she was meant to be
with him; anybody could see it, and she had to see it, too, and would
definitely see it as soon as she saw him. They didn't get really interesting until the fifth letter.

"I am sick of heering from that dum bitch you got working for
you," it started, and it just got better.

> You dint anser me your own self and I told you you should.
> You dint sent me the thing you were wearing and I told you
> I need that. You have to start listing to me or this goin to
> turn rilly bad. Why cant you see what is so cristal clear and
> plain as day that you and me are goin to be together? You
> no I rilly love you and you will rilly love me if you just see
> me for two seconds. And you got to no that one way or other
> you are going to see me!!!

The next letter was even angrier, starting out with a string of mis-
spelled curse words that really made me lament the state of public
education in our once-great nation, and then settling down into a
steady stream of thinly veiled and completely naked threats.

> You better jus get it thru youre head that this is goin to
> happen and that is all there is to it and if you cant see it I
> am goin to MAKE you see it and make you see ME. I am not
> afraid to do some pretty bad things if its goin to make you
> open up youre eyes and look at me and no what I am sayin
> about you and me is the total hunred percent true.

Given what had led up to it, the final letter was fairly standard
stuff, disappointingly predictable in its turn to cold rage, threats of
violence, and general psychotic unhappiness. I read it twice, pausing

in between to think grateful thoughts about the education I had been lucky enough to receive from Harry—and, as unlikely as it seemed, from the Miami-Dade public school system, which was really starting to look good compared to what Patrick got in Laramie, Tennessee. But of course, as I reminded myself, the schools in Tennessee were not totally to blame; several intelligent people had come from that state, and I was almost certain that another one could come along any day now.

I read through the last letter one more time.

If that is the way how you want to play it than that is the way how I am goin to do it. You want to go all cold and mean on me that's fine because I can play that game even better and you will be so sorry you ever did that. I will fine you and I will make you see me and I will make you see what you could have had and than I will take it all away from you one little piece at a time. And I do mean ALL of it. I will show you that you are no diffrent but just a hore like all the other girls think they are so special and I will make you SEE what you could have had and that will be the last thing you ever see and I am coming for you bitch and you better believe it.

This last letter was not signed, "youre soulmate"; love is so fragile, isn't it? And again, it really was just a little bit disappointing in the blunt and ignorant mind it revealed. I do not absolutely demand that every sick and twisted killer must show a bright gleam of intelligence and originality, but really. Something this pedestrian did seem to be letting down the side just a bit, don't you think?

In any case, it was clear to me that this was not a subtle brain, searching for visceral poetry. This was a very direct, rather dull and ordinary sick and twisted killer. He was psychotic, yes, and capable of almost any kind of perverted violence, but he lacked all refinement, and altogether seemed to be without a single subtle or interesting thought on what was, after all, a very important subject.

Disappointing, but at least it meant he should be quite easy to find, once I put my own sharp and wonderful mind to it and began to track him to his lair and then . . .

... and then nothing at all, because my mind would not be track-ing anything right now; my mind was firmly locked in place inside my skull, riding high atop my body as it performed its chores as Jackie's protector. I could not step out into the bright and welcom-ing moonlight and slide through the shadows to find Patrick in what would certainly be a terribly obvious little hidey-hole, could not take him and tape him and end things the right way, my way . . . because I would be spending those precious dark hours hovering over Jackie with vigilance and cunning, and perhaps a little more dark rum.

I became aware that conversation had stopped in Deborah's little office, and I looked up from the letters to see Jackie and my sister both staring at me. "What," I said.

Jackie smiled encouragingly. "We were waiting for you to close your eyes and, you know," she said, waving one hand vaguely. "Do that thing where you go inside his head."

"I'm afraid I won't fit," I said, trying not to sound too smug. "This is a small and very ordinary mind."

Deborah snorted and Jackie said, "Ordinary?! My God, after what he's done—and you call him *ordinary*?!"

"That's right," I said. "Ordinary, garden-variety, demented, psy-chotic killer." I shrugged. "Very predictable."

"Then predict him," Deborah said.

"Easy," I told her. "He's going to come after Jackie." And I nodded at Jackie with a reassuring smile.

For some reason, that didn't seem to reassure Jackie very much. She threw up her hands with an expression of sarcastic relief. "Well, shit, that's good to know," she said, shaking her head. "I mean, come after me, that's great—but didn't we already know that?"

Deborah, at least, wasn't quite so far gone that she had to resort to sarcasm. Of course, Patrick wasn't after *her*. "How will he do it?" Deborah said.

"Very directly," I told them. "Nothing subtle, nothing too clever. He's a hammer, not a scalpel."

"Well, goddamn it," Jackie said, "a hammer can sure as hell cave in my skull just the same."

"Not with me there," I said, and although I admit it sounded rather boastful, not at all my usual style of modest self-effacement, I really did believe it. "Really, Jackie, this guy is not capable of any real surprises."

"He surprised the shit out of those three other girls," she said darkly.

"They didn't know what he was. And," I said, trying very hard to sound quietly, modestly confident, "they didn't have me."

She looked at me long and hard, her eyes scanning my face for some sign that I had secret superpowers. I don't think she saw any such sign, but she did seem to relax a little bit. "Well," she said, and she looked over to Deborah. "I mean, so, um . . . what?"

"Nothing has changed," Debs told her. "I got you in daylight; Dexter has you covered all night."

"Oh, covered," Jackie said. And she opened her mouth to say more, then closed it again, looked at me, and, for some reason, she blushed.

"I mean . . ." She trickled off and looked away from me quickly, and for a moment she seemed so flustered that even her masterful use of sarcasm fled her. "Then, okay, so, right." She nodded a few times and cleared her throat. "All right," she said at last. "If you're both so . . . confident?"

I simply stood there and, since I had no idea what had just gone through Jackie's mind, I tried to look relaxed and overwhelmingly confident, leaving it to my sister to say, "Yeah, I think so. Dexter is usually right about this stuff." And then she cocked her head and looked at Jackie thoughtfully. "You want to hire somebody else?" she said.

"Oh, no," Jackie blurted quickly. "I mean, no. Dexter is very . . ." She cleared her throat and looked at me, and then looked away. "I trust you. Both of you," she said.

Deborah continued to regard her with one eyebrow raised, and then at last she started to shake her head. "Well, shit, who'da thunk it," she said softly, but before she could complete what must have been a very interesting thought, her desk phone buzzed loudly, and she turned away to grab it up. "Morgan," she said into the receiver. She looked over at me, and then said, "Yeah, I just saw him. I'll send him right down." She hung up the phone and gave me a mean little smile. "Robert," she said. "He's lonely." She jerked her head toward the hall door. "Git," she said.

It didn't seem quite right that babysitting a somewhat spoiled actor should take my time when there was a killer to catch—especially when it was a killer whose vulgar, pedestrian efforts were giving the craft a bad name—but life in the workforce seldom actually makes sense for the foot soldiers, and my nonsense job was to be with Robert. I gitted.

Robert was right where I'd left him, in the lab. But he was no longer alone. Standing beside him was a pudgy African American man in his mid-thirties, with a shaved head and large horn-rimmed glasses. He had five or six gold and diamond piercings in his left ear, and he wore a worn black T-shirt that said METALLICA in ornate letters, and a pair of baggy, faded madras shorts that hung down much too low. I looked at him, and he looked back blankly. Robert saved us all from what might have been a very awkward social situation by shouting out, "Hey! Jesus, that must have been the dump from hell, huh?"

I am known far and wide for my sophisticated poise and ready banter, but I had no idea what that was supposed to mean, and on top of the difficulty of having a stranger in my space, I'm afraid it had me momentarily at a loss. I just stared at Robert and muttered something like, "Oh, well, you know," before I remembered that my excuse for leaving him had been gastric difficulty. "Actually," I amended, "I got kind of sidetracked."

"Yeah, I figured," Robert said. "Just kidding. Hey! Look who's here!" And he nudged the other man forward a step.

"Oh," I said. "Um, who?"

The African American man rolled his eyes, but Robert said, "He's just kidding, Renny. Dexter Morgan, this is Renny Boudreaux!"

He pronounced it "boo-*drow*," and since I am a man of the world and recognize a French name when I hear one, I nodded to him and said, "*Enchanté, m'sieu.*"

Boudreaux stared at me and then, with a look of wonder on his face, he said, "Is that *French*?! Goddamn, you are *smooth*. I like that. French, that's— Tell me, Dexter, you ever fuck a black man?"

I really wanted to believe I had misheard him, but he'd said it so loud and clear that there could be no mistake. So I just shook my head and said, "Not yet, no. But the day is young."

Robert shouted with laughter, but Renny just nodded as if we were having a real conversation, and said, "Uh-huh. Well, you ain't gonna start with *me*, motherfucker. So you put your goddamn French back up your ass where it belongs." He shook his head, eyeing me warily, and said, "French. Shit."

I have always felt that the Art of Conversation is best served when all the parties involved have some vague idea of what they are talking about, and in this case, I had been left out of the loop. I was beginning to feel like I had wandered into some kind of Surrealist Performance piece—maybe one of those that tries to provoke the audience to some extreme reaction. But at least Robert seemed to be having a good time. He laughed again, a loud and brassy laugh that didn't sound quite sane, and he pushed Renny toward me one more time.

"Renny is playing Aaron Crait, my forensics sidekick," Robert said. "You know, in the show." He winked and added, "Kinda like you and Vince, right?"

I had never thought of myself as having a sidekick at all, and if I did it would certainly not be someone like Vince, and suddenly to think of him in that role took me even further aback. But Robert gave me no time to ponder that uncomfortable relationship; he plowed right on cheerfully.

"Renny hit town this morning and I told him to swing by, 'cause I thought you wouldn't mind giving him a crash course in forensics, right?" Possibly my mouth was still hanging open, because Robert suddenly looked a little uncomfortable, even a little anxious. "Um, you don't mind, do you, Dexter?" he said. "Because it's, you know, I thought it was important. That, you know, we're all on the same page . . . So we get it right." He lowered his voice and spoke confidentially, almost pleadingly. "Just a couple of hours, this afternoon . . . ?"

"Well, I suppose," I said. I was, after all, required to be at the beck and call of Big Ticket Network in general and Robert in person, and a few hours spent instructing Renny probably wouldn't hurt.

"Thanks, that's great, right, Renny?" He winked again, and added, "You've probably seen Renny on Leno or something."

"I don't watch Leno," I said.

"Yeah, well, I don't blame you," Robert said. "Anyway, Renny does stand-up comedy when he's not acting."

"Motherfucker, I told you *twice!*" Renny said, glaring at Robert, and I couldn't tell whether he was actually angry. "I don't do comedy—I do Social Commentary!" He shook his head and looked back at me. "God made this man so pretty 'cause he's so fucking *dumb,*" he told me.

"Oh, I thought I was the only one who noticed," I said, and Robert gave another of his awful shouts of laughter.

"Which part you notice, the dumb?" Renny said. "Or just the pretty—he hit on you yet, Dexter?"

"Not yet," I said. "Is he likely to?"

"I ain't sayin'," Renny said. "But if he ask you to take a shower—"

"Take a rain check?" I said.

"No, dummy. Don't drop the soap," Renny said.

"Ha!" Robert cawed. "This is great; I knew you two would hit it off," he said. And since I now knew that Renny and I were hitting it off, I knew exactly the right thing to do in the situation. I stepped forward and took his hand.

"Anyway—very pleased to meet you, Renny," I said.

Renny stared for a moment, and then took my hand, and as he did he met my eyes, and time faltered into a slow and shadowed crawl—

—and for just a second I thought I saw *something* behind the veil of his eyes, something dark and wicked, and it was looking back at me and baring its fangs. I couldn't be absolutely sure; it was just a brief flash, just enough to make the Dark Passenger hiss and unwind one small coil. But it startled me; I dropped Renny's hand and took a step back, looking for some confirmation in his face. There was none; he just looked at me, and then turned away to Robert. "So what the fuck, isn't it lunchtime yet? Your lover Dexter know someplace to eat where they got *real* food? Or is it all Cuban honky shit?" He looked back at me and added, "You ain't gonna take me for no *French* food, are you, faggot?"

"Well," I said, and I admit I was pleased by my quick and smooth recovery from what had so far been a very disconcerting encounter. But I gave him my best fake smile. "If you can't eat Cuban honky, and you don't like French faggot, there's always Chinese."

Renny stared at me, and then slowly nodded his head. "First smart thing you said," he told me.

# FOURTEEN

T HE AFTERNOON PASSED PLEASANTLY ENOUGH, CONSIDERING I spent it with a shallow, self-involved twit and a very loud comic who might possibly be carrying a Dark Passenger. Renny was apparently well known, in spite of the fact that I'd never heard of him, and at lunch both he and Robert were besieged by simpering well-wishers seeking autographs, pictures, and some small glimmer of reflected glow from my two famous pupils. They both took it all in stride, although Renny harangued his fans with loud and profane insults. They seemed to like it, and it certainly kept Robert amused.

And once again, as I had with Jackie, I found that I got a strange sense of enjoyment out of being an Insider, one of the Few, at the center of attention for all mere mortals who saw us. I began to wonder whether I had slipped a gear somewhere; surely there was some mistake. This was not appropriate for Our Dark Scout: gloating at the attention, smirking at the mob from inside the coveted Inner Circle, and soaking up reflected glow as if it were some kind of tonic. To be constantly gazed upon, to have every eye follow my every move, and worse, to like it—this was an impossible fantasy for the Thing that was Me. It was a lifestyle that would utterly shatter everything I was, everything I stood for. It was unthinkable. But apparently I liked it. I really liked it.

I thought about this as I watched Renny; he certainly enjoyed the attention—and yet I had seen what I had seen. Hadn't I? If so, he had clearly found a way to live in the spotlight and still feed the beast. Could I do that, too? I thought about following Jackie around the world, every now and then slipping away for some quiet relaxation. And I had to wonder: Did they have duct tape in Cannes?

A trio of beaming, giggling fans interrupted; Renny insulted them while Robert signed autographs, and then Renny signed, too, and the three fans went away with their feet hardly touching the floor. I had just managed to contain my hurt feelings that they had barely looked at me, when I became aware that Robert was arguing that Renny's Character on the Show, Crait, should have an ambivalent sexuality.

"Why you want me gay, mofo?" Renny said. "You looking for a date?"

"Not gay," Robert insisted. *"Ambivalent."*

"Ambi, shit," Renny said. "So you want me to swing both ways? What the fuck for?"

"No, no, ambi, just—it's like, we never really *know*—is he straight? Is he gay?" Robert said. "I mean, maybe we see him with some really hot chick."

"More like it," Renny said, nodding.

"And then there's a party, and he shows up dressed as Carmen Miranda." He glanced at me, frowned, then looked back at Renny. "Or, you know," he added. "Diana Ross."

"The *fuck* you say."

"It's so *authentic*, it's— Don't you see how *powerful* that could be?"

With the word "authentic," coming on top of the Carmen Miranda reference, I suddenly realized what Robert was doing. When he'd said that he and Renny were just like me and Vince Masuoka, he hadn't simply been making conversation. He had been stating a basic aesthetic principle. Just like he had learned to copy all my unconscious mannerisms, he wanted Renny to *become* Vince for the TV show. So that Art, if that's what it was, literally did imitate Life.

I shook my head and tuned them out; so much for the Act of Creation.

After lunch we went back to the lab and I gave Renny his quickie forensics course, while Robert hopped around behind me and interrupted constantly to show how much he already knew. In all fairness, Renny seemed much brighter than Robert; he concentrated, asked very intelligent questions, and quickly picked up enough of the basics to fool the finest TV camera. Even so, I couldn't quite shake the feeling of unease I got from wondering if I really had seen That Something behind Renny's eyes, and if so, what he might do with it.

By quitting time, I was more than ready to escape into luxurious vigilance once more, and it was with a ludicrous sense of anticipation that I skipped away to Deborah's lair to collect Jackie. I heard their voices before I saw them, but when I popped in with a cheery hello, they both fell abruptly silent and looked at me very seriously.

"I didn't mean to be quite such a buzz-kill," I said.

"No buzz here," Deborah said, and Jackie shook her head.

"Well, then, what," I said. "Did you give Anderson Patrick Bergmann's name and photo?"

"Nope!" Jackie said happily.

"What? Why not?"

"Captain Matthews's orders," Debs said solemnly.

I blinked, and I admit that was the only thing I could think of, except to say "but," so I did that, too. "But," I said.

"I know, right?" Jackie said, still with what seemed to be far too much lighthearted levity.

"Um, okay," I said. "Any particular reason?"

"Anderson totally blew off Detective Echeverria," Debs said. "So his captain called Matthews and demanded an explanation, and now I am in the shit house."

"You?" I said. "For what?"

"For interfering with Anderson's investigation," Debs said. "Which he doesn't actually have."

"And for luring Echeverria down here from New York," Jackie said. "Apparently, it breaks the unwritten code."

"Somebody should write that down," I said.

"And so now," Deborah said, with an ironic wave of her hands, "we have a free hand and we will catch this sick cocksucker and fuck 'em all." She shrugged. "While I am being punished."

"Bread and water in the stockade?" I said.

"Worse," she said. "I have been officially notified to stay away from Anderson's investigation—"

"Which includes," Jackie butted in, very bubbly, "*not* giving him any more leads, tips, or conjectures that might interfere with his case-work."

"Well, then," I said. "That's a perfect punishment."

"And," Deborah said, making a face, "I have to stay on as techni-cal adviser to Jackie's show during the whole shoot." She gave me an ironic smile. "So do you."

"Oh," I said, wondering how I could possibly survive being around Robert for so long. I guess my face showed what I was think-ing, because Jackie made a snorting noise.

"Guys," Jackie said. "It's not *that* bad. I mean, there's really great food on the set, and it's all free."

"Great," Deborah said. "I can eat doughnuts while the bodies pile up around Anderson."

"Well, if there's doughnuts," I said.

Deborah shook her head. "And that's all it takes to make you happy?"

"That—and the party going on down in the lab. It's really very festive."

"A festive forensics lab?" Jackie said, a smile twitching at the cor-ners of her mouth. "That's quite a trick."

"One of the other actors arrived," I said. "Renny Boudreaux?"

"Oh, God, he's a scream," Jackie said, shaking her head. She looked at Debs, who raised one eyebrow. "A terrific comedian. I mean, he's a total dick, but a really funny one."

Deborah snorted. "A funny dick," she said. "Great concept," and the two of them snickered like sorority sisters.

The Town Car was waiting for us at the front door. It was the same driver again, and I waved Jackie into the backseat, sliding in next to her on the other side. We rode in silence most of the way. Jackie looked out the window at the traffic, every now and then glancing at me. I glanced back, wondering what she was thinking, but she gave me no clue, except for an occasional small and weary smile. She was clearly far too busy thinking deep thoughts to make light conversation, so I let her think, and I drifted away into a mellow reverie of my own.

Just before we went up the on-ramp onto the expressway, a loud *bang!* sounded behind our car, and we both jumped several inches off the seat. I looked out the back window; a motorcycle had backfired as it wove its way along the white line between the far more ponderous cars. I gave Jackie a reassuring smile, and she sank back into her thoughtful silence.

At the intersection with the Dolphin Expressway traffic slowed to a crawl as everyone paused to look at an ivory-colored Jaguar pulled halfway onto the shoulder. A thick stream of smoke came out one window, and a very large man stood beside it, yelling at a thin, elegantly dressed woman. She puffed on a huge cigar and looked bored as the man shouted at her, the veins in his neck visibly bulging.

"I think I'm starting to like Miami," Jackie said as we crept past the Jaguar and its little piece of theater.

"More than L.A.?" I said.

She made a face. "Nobody really likes L.A.," she said. "We just have to live there. Part of our deal with the devil." And then she went quiet again, just looking out the window of the Town Car and thinking her thoughts, until we pulled up in front of the hotel at last.

The doorman with the talented nephew held the front door for us, and Jackie rewarded him with a smile. "Thank you, Benny," she said. "Are you working late tonight?"

Benny beamed at her. "I took a double shift, Miss Forrest," he said. "I can use the dough, and anyway, I gotta be honest, while you're here? I don't wanna go home."

Jackie widened her smile and patted him on the arm. "Well, I wouldn't want anybody else on the door, either," she said, and Benny smiled so widely that I thought his face might split. But there were no screams of pain from bursting cheeks behind us as I escorted Jackie to the elevator, and when the doors slid shut Jackie closed her eyes and shook her head.

"Jesus," she said. "Did that sound really stupid?"

"Him or you?" I asked, genuinely puzzled.

She leaned back against the wall of the elevator car, eyes still

closed. "It's a kind of—what do they call it? Noblesse oblige." She
opened one eye and pointed it at me. "Which sounds pretty pompous, I know."

"Only a little," I said encouragingly.

"Yeah, thanks," she said. She closed the eye again. "What the hell.
You have to say something, and it doesn't have to be Shakespeare to
make somebody's day." She sighed heavily. "It goes with the job. And
Benny seems like a nice guy. So . . . *normal* . . ."

I said nothing. After all, you really should understand a remark
before you respond to it, and I didn't. Clearly Jackie was in a philo-
sophical mood—but whether the evening would turn toward Aris-
totle or existentialism, I couldn't tell from her comment on Benny's
Normalness. And as the best philosophers will tell you, the rest is
silence anyway, so I kept quiet.

I got Jackie into the suite without any outbursts of Kantian Dia-
lectic, and as we settled into our chairs on the balcony and waited for
mojitos, Kathy knocked on the door, bustling past me with a haughty
glare when I let her in, and heading straight out to Jackie, her hands
full of papers and her eternal phone and Starbucks cup.

The mojitos came. Kathy waved papers and yammered for another ten minutes, while Jackie nodded, interrupting a few times
with blunt questions, signing a couple of papers and nodding wearily
at the nearly endless flow of details. When Kathy finally gathered
up the papers, and her coffee cup, Jackie looked tired and a little bit
bleak. I wondered why. She had endured Kathy's fusillade, which
had been an exhausting tirade from a rather unpleasant person, but
even so, I was surprised at how *mortal* Jackie looked all of a sudden.
She picked up her mojito and sipped as I led Kathy out and chained
the door behind her, pondering the heavy price of fame. It had all
seemed so attractive, but now I found myself wondering.

Jackie had said she gave up *everything* for this; was it worth it? I
mean, not just having to endure an annoying lump like Kathy a few
times a day, although that certainly looked like a very great burden.
But to trade away all the other stuff that *normal* people lived for, the
things they claimed made them happy: home, marriage, kids—all
the stuff I had gathered as props for my disguise. They didn't make
*me* happy, of course, but I am probably not actually capable of hap-

piness. Moments of very rewarding satisfaction, yes—but were they the result of my Happy Normal Life? I could not offhand think of any such moments. I had never glanced at a pile of dirty laundry and felt ecstasy, never smiled blissfully as Astor bellowed at her mother and threw shoes across the room. To be honest, I had never even held my own child, Lily Anne, and thought, *This is Paradise.* . . .

I had my moments, of course. But most of them seemed to come while I stood above a securely taped, carefully chosen playmate as he squirmed away from the silver music of the knife—not quite the same thing as enjoying a quiet night at home with the wife and kids. Maybe not even happiness at all, but it worked for me.

On the more legal side of things, I had certainly been enjoying my time as Jackie's entourage. Living in the lap of luxury, admired everywhere I went—it was living high on the hog, life without a care. Except, of course, for the very small care of knowing that a wild psychotic killer might be knocking on the door momentarily. Other than that, I couldn't think of anything else I could reasonably want in a lifestyle.

But was this real Happiness? Probably not, or I wouldn't be feeling it.

Did Jackie feel it? Was she happy with her life of limitless luxury, admired and even feted everywhere she went? Was it really as wonderful as it looked? Did it fulfill her? None of my business, of course—but it suddenly seemed like a question I wanted to hear her answer.

I came back out onto the balcony to find Jackie staring out over the water, still looking moody.

"Everything okay?" I said.

She nodded. "Never better," she said, and I had to hope that she would be more convincing when the cameras began to roll.

I sat down in my chair and took a sip of my mojito. Perhaps the rum loosened my tongue, but as my drink shrank, the silence grew, and I finally just blurted it out.

"Are you happy?" I said.

"Me?" Jackie said, looking at me as if I had suggested something improper. She shook her head and looked out over the water of Biscayne Bay, and then picked up her mojito and gulped down the rest of it, and, still looking out at the Bay, she said, "Of course I'm happy. I have everything that anybody could ever want." She looked down at her empty glass. "Except more mojitos. Call down for a pitcher, okay?" She put her glass on the table and stood up. "I have to use the bathroom," she said, and in a faint swirl of perfume she was gone.

I sniffed at her vapor trail and settled back into my chair, feeling like a total ninny. Why was I thinking such things, asking such stupid questions? I tried to remember the warning signs of the apocalypse; I was pretty sure they didn't include talking philosophy with a TV star, but maybe the Council of Nicea had cut that one from the list.

I called room service for more mojitos. They arrived just as Jackie returned, and the waiter nearly fell over the railing as he tried to hold the tray and pull out the chair for Jackie at the same time. Jackie settled into her chair and gave him a tired smile, and he bounced back out the door, beaming as if he had just been elected fifth-grade class president.

I put the chain on the door behind him and came back out onto the balcony. Jackie was slumped down in her chair, looking out over the water with the rim of her glass resting on her lower lip. I sat down, wondering what had turned her mood so sour. I supposed it was just the strain of being stalked. But what if it was me? What if something I had said or done—or *not* said or done—was making her upset? That would be disastrous; it would totally demolish my new fantasy life as Captain Entourage. I tried to think of how I might have offended, and came up empty. My behavior had been exemplary.

Yet something was clearly bothering her. Perhaps it was her blood sugar—she didn't eat enough to keep a hamster alive, and the unerring bioclock inside Dexter was saying it was definitely time for dinner.

But before I could frame a polite suggestion that food might be just the thing to restore her physical and mental health, my cell phone began to chirp. I took it out and looked at the screen; it was Rita. "Oh," I said to Jackie. "Excuse me." She just nodded without looking up, and I answered the phone.

"Hi," I said, with as much good cheer as I could manufacture.

"You said you would call," Rita said. "And that was Monday—and Deborah says it's something risky? But I can't really tell what she means, and— Do you have clean socks?"

"Yes, I have socks," I said, glancing at Jackie and hoping she was too busy musing to hear me.

"You always lose your socks," Rita said. "And you hate when they're dirty—remember that time in Key West? And they cost twice as much down there."

"Well, I'm not in Key West," I said. "And I have some clean socks."

The corner of Jackie's mouth began to twitch, and although I hoped she was only remembering a really good knock-knock joke, I had the distinct and unpleasant feeling that she was trying very hard not to laugh at me.

"Do you have any idea how long?" Rita said. "And there are some heavy boxes here, stuff from the garage; I can't carry them. But they have to go to— Oh. The power is on now? And the insurance company said the new house has a market value much higher than— Astor, I'm talking on the phone. Astor, please! Are you still there, Dexter?"

"I'm here," I said. "How are the kids?"

"Lily Anne has a tooth coming in," she said. "She's very cranky, and I can't even— What? No, you have to do your homework first. No. Because you *have* to," she said. To Astor again? Or was it Cody this time? There was really no way to know, and I discovered that I didn't care. I was beginning to find the whole conversation annoying, and the way Jackie was so clearly fighting off an attack of derisive laughter didn't help at all. I turned away from her and lowered my voice.

"I'm sorry I didn't call," I said, trying to inject a note of finality into my voice. "But I'll try to call again tomorrow, okay?"

"Tomorrow is the conference with Cody's teacher," she said. "At three o'clock, and you said— *Damn* it, Astor, just let me talk for a minute!"

I was fairly sure I'd said nothing of the kind, but I did remember saying I would be at Cody's parent-teacher conference. "I'll try to be there," I said. "But I am pretty busy."

"Well, you did promise," Rita said. "And it's important to him, so— Oh lord, the baby. I have to go."

"All right," I said. "Good-bye."

I put my phone down and turned back toward Jackie. She was watching me with a very strange expression on her face, part amusement and part—what? Something else I couldn't quite define. "What?" I asked her, but she just shook her head and took another sip of her drink.

"Nothing," she said. "Just . . . nothing." She looked at me over the rim of her glass, her eyes filled with liquid amusement, among other things. "Your wife seems like a very nice person."

"Yes, she is," I said.

"*And* a good cook, too . . ."

I just nodded.

She cocked her head to one side and stared at me very seriously. "So it's worth it. The whole"—she waved a hand to indicate almost everything—"this *marriage* thing? It works for you?" she said.

It seemed like a strange question, which made it just right for the way this evening was going. "I guess so," I said.

"You guess so," she said, still staring, and I shrugged and nodded. "That's not really an overwhelming endorsement."

"Well, I mean," I said, trying to think of an appropriate response, "it has its ups and downs."

"Uh-huh," she said. "What are the ups?"

"Oh, the, um . . . We're moving into a new house," I said. "It, ah . . . There's a pool?" It sounded pretty lame, even to me, and Jackie let it hang there for a few seconds, the silence making it sound even lamer.

"Uh-huh," she said at last. "The pool that needs a new cage."

"That's right—and it has a much bigger kitchen," I just blurted out; I don't know why, except I felt I had to say something.

"Right," Jackie said. "So Rita can cook even more."

"Yes, that's right," I said. I grabbed for my mojito, mostly because I was floundering through very boggy ground and really needed the security of having something to do with my hands.

"Uh-huh," she said. She sipped her drink and studied me with one eyebrow raised. "So does marriage make you happy?"

"It's . . . it's, um," I said with my usual eloquence. "I mean, you know."

"No, I don't," she said. "Never had it." She tilted her head and shrugged. "But it doesn't sound like it's exactly thrilling you." And although I have to admit that I was starting to think so, too, it didn't seem like something I should say out loud.

"You still haven't said what Rita looks like," Jackie said with a frown.

"Oh," I said. "Well, um—I mean, she was very good-looking, when—"

"*Was* good-looking?" Jackie interrupted. She took a big slug from her glass. I watched her throat muscles glide as she swallowed. "Jesus, I'd cut your heart out if you said that about me."

"Oh, but that's . . ." I said, wondering how this had all gotten so far out of hand. "I mean, I would never say that about you. . . ."

She eyed me for a moment. "You'd better not," she said.

She drained the last two inches of mojito from her glass and set it on the table with a loud *takk*. "What about dinner?"

After wrestling with philosophy, the phone call from Rita, and Jackie's merciless grilling, it was nice that there was finally something real and rewarding to latch onto. "Absolutely," I said, with the very best hearty good cheer I could simulate under the circumstances. Jackie gave me a somewhat cynical smile, and nodded toward the house phone.

I called in our order.

# FIFTEEN

I WAS SITTING ON THE BALCONY EARLY THE NEXT MORNING, nursing my second cup of coffee, when Jackie came out and sat across from me. "Good morning," she said brightly, brushing back a strand of still-wet hair that flopped over her forehead. She reached for the coffeepot and poured herself a cup. "Um," she said. "I'm sorry if last night was a little . . ." She fluttered one hand. "I don't know. I just got thinking that, you know." She shrugged. "I really don't know what to do with you."

I must have given her a look that showed how strange her statement sounded, because she blushed, looked away, and waved a hand in the air.

"I mean," she said, "I've never had a bodyguard before."

"To be honest, I've never been one before, either," I said.

"Right," she said. She sipped the coffee. "But seeing you there all the time I forget why you're here and I kind of . . . you know. There aren't that many people I can just sort of *hang* with." She made a wry face. "Especially men." She gave me a half smile. "But I feel very . . . *comfortable* with you."

I might have told her that this was not really a strong endorsement of her good sense, but she sipped her coffee and went on.

"You treat me like a human being," she said. "Not like I'm a rare piece of china, or the Second Coming or something, and that's . . . Do you know how unusual that is, for me? To be treated like . . . normal?"

"Not really," I said. "But I think I'm starting to get an idea."

"It's very unusual," she said. "I mean, I know it goes with the territory, and there are even some people who like it."

"Yes," I said, thinking of Robert. "I *have* noticed that."

Jackie looked at me, and then smirked. "Yeah, he really does, doesn't he?" she said, to show she knew what I was thinking.

"He certainly seems to."

She shrugged and sipped a little more coffee. "Well, I don't. I mean, it's nice to have everyone think you're wonderful, but sometimes I just want to feel like . . . you know." She threw both hands up, almost as if she was indicating half a touchdown, and then quickly dropped them again. "Stupid, huh?"

"Not at all," I said politely, only a little bit baffled.

"So to have you around, talking to me like we're just a couple of ordinary people, it makes me . . . I start to relax, and really *feel* normal, and it's really nice."

She sipped again, looking down at the table. "And then I remember why you're here, and . . . Oh, I don't know." She sipped again and then put the cup down. "I guess, you know. How things might have been different. If . . ." She stuck out her lower lip and blew out a breath. "Forget it," she said, and she picked up the coffee cup again. "It's stupid."

"Not at all," I said, and it really wasn't stupid. Incomprehensible, yes, but not stupid.

"Anyway," she said, with a strange forced smile. "Just a couple more days, and you can get back to your normal life."

"Oh, but . . ." I said. "I mean, I really don't mind."

Jackie raised one eyebrow at me over the rim of her cup. "Really," she said.

"Yes, really," I said. I waved a hand at the suite, the balcony, the view. "All this is new to me. I don't get to live like this very often." I smiled my best Bumpkin in the Big City smile and said, "I mean really, this is fun."

She looked at me for a long moment, then snorted. "Well, good," she said. "Glad I can provide some entertainment."

Jackie stared into her cup, and I wondered what I had said wrong. I had clearly hit a sour note somewhere, and I didn't want to. I have always found it dangerous to flounder into unknown conversational waters, especially involving human feelings, but I didn't want Jackie to slump back into her moodiness—especially if she would blame me for it. So I gave it my best shot, and said, "Jackie, really. I am having fun. I like being around you." She looked up at me without changing her expression, so I added, "I like *you*."

She looked at me over the rim of her cup with no expression. Her eyes flicked left and then right across my face. Finally, she sipped her coffee and then smiled. "Well, good," she said. "I was beginning to think it was just the room service."

"To be perfectly honest," I said, "that's pretty good, too."

Jackie laughed, a short and musical sound, and her face lost its worry lines and changed back to perfection. "All right," she said.

We finished our breakfast with scattered bursts of lighthearted chat and a brief infestation of Kathy—more paperwork and reminders of impending phoners—and in no time at all we were down in the lobby and hoping to get past Benny, the doorman, without hearing another hundred pages of his life story.

"Hey, Miss Forrest!" he called out cheerfully as we stepped out of the elevator. He completely ignored me, and although I couldn't really blame him for preferring to look at Jackie, I still felt the snub.

Jackie, of course, took it right in stride. She gave him a big smile and said, "Benny! Don't you ever sleep?"

"I can sleep when I'm dead," he said. "But right now I got the world's most beautiful star at my hotel."

Jackie put a hand on Benny's arm. "Very sweet," she said, and the man actually blushed.

"No, listen, I mean it," Benny said.

"Well, thank you," Jackie said, patting his arm, and attempting to move past.

"Lemme get the door," Benny said, rushing past us to hold the front door open and then waving Jackie through with a huge smile.

Jackie looked at me inquiringly. "Wait here while I check," I said, and she nodded.

I stepped through the front door and nodded at Benny. "Thank you, my good man," I told him, but I think his smile had stretched too wide and sealed his ears shut, because he kept looking toward Jackie and didn't seem to hear me.

I went outside and went through my little security ritual. The Corniche was still parked ostentatiously in front, and our shiny new Town Car was pulled in behind it. Next to the Corniche, it looked like a wino crouching there and begging for spare change.

But the driver was the same, and all else seemed good, and so I went back in and pried Jackie away from Benny's eager paws and handed her into the backseat of the Town Car. Just like yesterday, a small gaggle of onlookers clustered at the hotel's front door and loudly wished us well. The car was already moving down the driveway as I buckled my seat belt, and as the driver turned onto the causeway leading to the mainland I heard the same popping backfire sound I'd heard last night. I remembered hearing a cycle starting yesterday morning, too, and I wondered whether they were everywhere now. Maybe there was a Harley convention in town. Or maybe the price of gas was forcing more people out of their SUVs and onto two wheels.

Or maybe it was more than that.

I felt a dry rustle of interior bat wings as the Dark Passenger stirred in its sleep and muttered, *It's only coincidence when you're not paying attention*, and I thought about that.

What if it wasn't coincidence? What if it was not many motorcycles, but only one very persistent motorcycle, and it was following us?

Of course, even if that were true, it might be no more than a paparazzo hoping to snap a picture of Jackie without a bra, or picking her nose, or dancing drunkenly in a South Beach club. People like that were drawn to celebrities like moths to a flame. There were bound to be a few hanging around, and that was probably all it was: just somebody looking for a photo op.

On the other hand . . .

I have an extremely healthy natural sense of paranoia, and Jackie was, after all, paying me to exercise it. Our stalker might very well choose to follow on a motorcycle—it was an ideal vehicle for slipping in and out of traffic easily, and for escaping pursuit if you were spotted. And three encounters with a motorcycle seemed a little bit suspicious.

I turned in my seat to look out the back window, hoping for a glimpse of the cyclist, but my seat belt jammed, nearly strangling me, and I could get only halfway around. I reached for the release—but before I could snap the belt open, Jackie's cell phone began to chime.

"Shit," Jackie said urgently. "I think it's the *Times*. Could you please get that, Dexter?"

I answered the phone; it was, in fact, the *Times*—the Los Angeles one. Jackie took the call, and by the time I could get unhooked from my homicidal seat belt and turned around to look, there was nothing to see except the usual mad, gleaming pack of angry, overpowered vehicles. I scanned in all directions a couple of times, but I saw no cycles, and I heard no more popping backfire sounds. So I shrugged it off before we were even halfway to work, and thought no more about motorcycles.

There was no real pause for contemplation when we got in to work, either. I delivered Jackie into Deborah's care, and trudged down to my lab and the weary drudgery of another day as Robert's shepherd.

I had expected Renny to be there, too, but I found Robert all by himself, feet up on my desk, staring intensely and raptly at a folded-back newspaper. As I came in, he looked up with a startled and oddly guilty look on his face, and immediately dropped the newspaper on the desk. I stopped in the doorway, and he looked up and remembered to smile. "Oh! Hey!" he said. Then he looked very guilty and whipped his feet off the desk and onto the floor. "I mean, good morning!"

"Isn't Renny coming in today?" I asked him.

Robert shrugged. "He'll be here later," he said. "He's never on time."

It seemed to me like a strange habit for someone in show business, and I grew up in Miami, where Cuban time is a universal standard, and showing up early means you're only twenty minutes late. "Why not?" I said.

Robert made a sort of what'd-you-expect face. "He's a *comedian*," he said, like that explained everything.

"Well," I said. "As long as he's here for lunch."

"Oh, he won't miss lunch," Robert said. He snorted, adding, "He won't pay for it, either."

That was fine with me, as long as Robert paid for it. And I was just as happy not to have Renny there, since I still couldn't decide what he was. So Robert and I spent the next ninety minutes going over gas chromatography, and then, just as advertised, Renny wandered in, wearing the same Metallica T-shirt, but a different pair of faded, low-slung madras shorts.

"Greetings," he said, slouching to a stop with one side of his butt perched on the lab's counter.

"Hey," Robert said. "Aren't you supposed to say 'what up' or something?"

Renny stared at Robert with his head tilted, one eyebrow raised and one lowered. "You gonna teach me how to talk *black*, Robert?" he said. "Damn, that's great; I been wanting to learn that."

"Ha!" said Robert, a very artificial sound, even for him. "Okay. My bad. Hey! Take a look at this, Ren." He held up the graph we had been looking at. "Gas chromography," he said, pronouncing it carefully even though he was mangling it.

"Uh-huh," Renny said. "You want to graph *my* gas, you're going to be pretty busy." He crossed his arms and looked very pleased with himself, which in my opinion was not justified by the feeble joke. But he stared at both of us with that smug expression anyway, until I was ready to fling a microscope at his head, and Robert finally said, "What's up, Renny?"

Renny smiled broadly. "Just come from a production meeting," he said. "For my *special*."

"Your what?" Robert said. "When did you get a special?"

Renny looked at him and shook his head pityingly. "Bobby, Bobby, Bobby, don't you read anything but the *Advocate*?"

"Aw, come on, Ren. . . ."

"'Cause it was all over the trades, Bobby."

"Um, not, you know," Robert said. "I guess I didn't see it."

"Yeah, I know," Renny said. "You don't read it unless your name is in there."

"Heh, heh, yeah, okay," Robert said. "But when does it tape?"

"Saturday night," Renny said, looking very pleased.

"Saturday—*this* Saturday night?"

"Uh-huh."

"What?" Robert said. He looked so very alarmed that I had to assume Special Taping was some kind of threat to him personally. "I mean, hey, that's great, but I mean, you can't leave, or—you have to be here for the show, right?"

Renny stared at him with a superior expression—not hard, since Robert was practically hyperventilating. "Bobby," Renny said.

"It's Robert," Robert said automatically.

"Bobby, you been sniffing that fart analyzer too long. Don't you know shit about showbiz?"

I had to give Renny very small props for extending his gas joke by turning gas chromatography into fart analysis, but Robert did not seem to notice. "I mean, sure, it's great for you," Robert said, rubbing his hands together unconsciously, "but we have to start shooting, and . . . does the network know about this?"

Renny showed him a large selection of gleaming teeth. "Yup," he said. "Their idea."

"What?!" Robert said.

Renny let him suffer for a second longer before saying, "My special is *on* Big Ticket Network." He pointed at Robert, still smiling. "That's the same network the show is on. Did you know that, Robby?"

Robert turned pale. "Shit," he said. "They pulled the plug on us."

Renny laughed. In spite of his near-constant joking, this was the first time I'd heard him do that, and I was very glad he had kept it to himself until now. It was a high-pitched laugh, but not terribly merry; the sound of it made me a little uneasy, and I felt a small sympathetic stirring from the Passenger.

But Renny laughed on for several seconds, clapping his hands to keep time, before he finally took pity on Robert. "Oh, Bobby. Oh, Bert. Man. It's always about you, isn't it?" He laughed louder, which truly set my nerves on edge. It didn't seem to reassure Robert, either. "Oh, man. The actor's life just plain sucks, doesn't it? Got you all fucked up in the head."

"I don't think it's funny," Robert said. "Because, you know. This show is very . . . I've put a lot of my eggs into this . . ." He frowned and shook his head, and then looked at Renny with very faint hope on his face. "I mean—what do you mean?"

"I mean," Renny said, "way back when, I was supposed to do the special in Vegas." He showed his teeth again. "But then I land *this* part? And so *Mr.* Eissen says, 'Let's shoot it in Miami and use it to promo the show.' " He raised one eyebrow at Robert. "Could mean my part gets a little bigger. I know you like big parts, Bo."

"Robert," Robert said.

Renny ignored him. "*So*—we tape it *here, this* Saturday night, with the whole cast in the house. I say I'm here in Miami to tape the show. Make a joke about all the bodies we got to work with here. Camera cuts to Jackie Forrest laughing her sweet white ass off at . . . *moi.*" He raised both hands, palms up. "Everybody gets a plug. Everybody happy."

"Why Jackie?" Robert said. I was glad to see he had already moved on to his next neurotic worry. "Why does *she* get on camera? I mean, I can laugh harder than she can any day."

Renny looked at Robert, shook his head, and then turned to me. "Glad you're here, Dexter," he said. "Robert's just too easy."

"I don't want to disappoint you," I said, "but what does all this mean in English?" And because he was staring at me exactly the way he had looked at Robert, I added, "Or in Spanish, if you'd rather."

Renny folded his hands and looked down at them in mock prayer. At least, I assumed it was mock. "Lord," he called out, "deliver me from the dummies. Please, Lord—help me out here." He looked at me and said, as if to a child, "A special, Dexter. A one-hour *comedy* special. Starring me, because that's what I do. Comedy. Because I am a *comedian*, and that is somebody who *does* comedy. And the network is shooting my special *here*, this Saturday night, and using it to promote Bobby's show, okay?"

"So wait, so what," Robert said, sounding jittery but a little hopeful. "So they use *your* special to promo the show—"

"Thank you, Jesus," Renny said devoutly.

"So the show isn't canceled?"

"We are *on*, brothers and sisters, and Renny Boudreaux is even *more* on 'cuz he is on *first* and he is gonna make you laugh until you *hurt*—'cuz my shit has been cooking awhile and I am going to *kill.*"

And as he said "kill" he looked at me—and there it was again, that sudden flutter of dark flame—and then Robert interrupted, and it was gone, and once more I was left wondering whether I had seen anything at all.

"Yeah, but . . ." Robert said. He frowned, and then said, "Oh, well, hey, I guess—I mean, that's great, you know. I mean, as long as they're not— Hey, one hand washes the other anyhow, right?"

"Riiiiight," Renny said. He looked at me.

Since I was new to showbiz, I wasn't sure what was expected of me here, so I just said, "Congratulations," and that seemed to go down all right. Renny nodded at me, frowned, and then looked back at Robert.

"Oh," Renny said. "Almost forgot. Wardrobe wants to see you. They're at the hotel, suite twenty-four seventeen."

"Wardrobe," Robert said, sounding slightly alarmed again for some reason of his own.

Renny looked at him with pity on his face. "Yeah, you know, wardrobe. There's that mean woman and her two gay friends, and they dress you up for this shit," he said. "You remember wardrobe, don't you, Robert?"

Robert looked at him for half a second and then gave his peculiar artificial laugh again. "Ha! Ha! Yeah, okay, well, then, I'm outta here." He turned and aired out a few bright teeth in my direction. "See ya later, Dexter," he said. He made a clicking sound, accompanied by that annoying my-finger-is-a-pistol-and-you-are-dead gesture again, and he sauntered away.

Renny watched him go and then shook his head and said, "Can't decide if that man is dumb as shit or just really weird." And then he turned and frowned at me. "You're easy. You just weird."

"Thank you," I said.

"But that's okay; I can *use* weird," he said. And then he smiled again, and the kind of smile it seemed to be sent a tiny shiver of alarm through the coiled tentacles of the dozing Passenger. "You like to come see my show, Dexter?"

I admit he had taken me by surprise; I had no ready response other than a blink and a very feeble-sounding, "Oh. Well, I mean, it's *this* Saturday?"

"Good, you been listening. I knew you weren't a dummy," he said.

In truth, I did not want to see his show, not this Saturday nor any other. But, of course, if Jackie was going to be there, I would have to go along, too. So I nodded and said, "Well, um, sure, that would be very nice."

"Oh, it won't be *nice*," he said. "But I just might get you to laugh some. And your wife. You got a wife, right, Dexter? 'Cuz I know you want everybody to think you're *normal* and shit."

Once again I felt an uncomfortable shifting of coils deep inside; Renny's dig at me was much too close to home to be entirely innocent, but it was still nothing definite enough for me to be sure. My only real choice was to keep playing Weird Normal—for now.

"Ah, yes, I do," I said. "I do have a wife."

"Uh-huh, good," Renny said. "Mr. Eissen wants the technical advisers there, on camera." He winked at me. "That's you. And that really tough lady."

"Deborah," I said. "Sergeant Morgan."

"Uh-huh. Mr. Eissen says it's like support our troops, show the cops out there laughing. And it gives the show Cop Cred, and it even shows everybody I can get along with cops when I want to. Which, to be honest . . ." He raised an eyebrow at me, as if I was supposed to say something about that, but I had no idea what, so I just nodded.

Renny shrugged. "Your boss gonna be there, too," he said. "He wants to make sure you show up, *with* your wife."

"Well, then," I said. "I guess we'll be there."

"I'll put you on the list for two."

"Thank you," I said. And because that seemed like a slightly inadequate response for being railroaded into accepting two free tickets to a show, I added, "Would you like some coffee?"

"Yes, I would," Renny said. He straightened up and pushed off the bench. "And that is why I am going to go find a Starbucks and not drink that poison shit you all make here." He turned and headed for the door. "See you later, man."

And suddenly, there I was, all alone again.

# SIXTEEN

STOOD FOR A MOMENT IN MY ABRUPTLY UNCLUTTERED WORK space and looked around fondly. It seemed like a long time since I'd been here without Robert leaning over my shoulder and solemnly mocking all my unconscious gestures, and to see the place without him and Renny in it was almost like coming home from a long and exhausting trip. I spent a few minutes tidying up, putting things where they belonged instead of where Robert had moved them because they *looked* better there. And then I just stood for a moment, looking around with quiet satisfaction, and wondering what to do with the rest of my morning. I had been assigned two important jobs: instructing Robert and guarding Jackie. But at the moment I couldn't do either one; Robert and Renny were gone, and Jackie was off somewhere with Deborah.

For a moment I was at a loss; what should I do when there was nothing to do? I cast my brain back and forth, and came up with nothing more than a reminder that I was supposed to go to a meeting with Cody's teacher at three o'clock. It was ten twenty-two right now, which left a rather large gap in the day's activities, and in the meantime, I felt like I should do something positive, powerful, dynamic, and smart, and there was nothing of the kind immediately obvious.

But Dexter is renowned for his resourcefulness, and it took no more than a few moments of deep thought for me to hit on exactly the right course of action. I strode manfully into my own little office space, and with a vibrant and masculine vitality, I sat in my chair, leaned back, and took a deep breath: in through the nose—

And very quickly out through the mouth, and with some irritation. Because in front of me on my desk, where there should have been nothing but a neat blotter, Robert had left his newspaper. I don't like clutter, especially someone else's, dumped into my space. I leaned forward to pick it up—and saw that, under it, lying on the blotter when it should have been standing neatly at the back of my desk, was a picture of Dexter and Family.

Last Christmas, Rita had insisted that we all visit a real photographer and pose for a real Family Portrait. It had been quite an ordeal getting everybody to dress up, comb their hair, scrub their faces, and—hardest of all—make a convincingly pleasant face for the camera. But we had done it, and here was the result: Rita and Astor on the left with Cody sitting in front of them, Dexter holding Lily Anne—and if Cody was not actually smiling, at least you couldn't tell that he was thinking about sticking a knife into the photographer.

I had framed the picture and put it on my desk, because that's what Humans did. And Robert had been staring at it furtively—and felt guilty enough that he'd hidden it under a newspaper. Of all the truly annoying things he'd done, this one rankled even more, and I could not say why. But I refused to let it ruin my opportunity for unspecified pondering; I polished the picture's silver frame, rubbed imaginary thumbprints off the glass, and set it back where it belonged, at the back of my desk. And then I leaned back, took a deep breath, pushed Robert out of my mind, and pondered.

Naturally enough, my first thought was about Robert, and it was a somewhat grumpy thought. I had always assumed that actors, writers, artists, and other borderline psychotics were an odd lot—but Robert was in a league of his own, and he annoyed me far more than he should have. People don't usually bother me very much, since they are, after all, only flesh and blood, and I know very well just how fragile and transitory that is. But there was something about Robert that cut through my customary indifference to the human species, and it went beyond his apish imitation of my unconscious behavior. Did I really pinch my nose like that when I was reading departmental memos?

And in any case, why should it bother me if I did, and Robert copied me? If all my tics and twitches made it to the little silver screen, wasn't that a form of immortality—even better for me, anonymous immortality? But even that thought did not make me warm to him, and I wondered whether my dislike for the man was rooted in aesthetics. I had been taught to value originality in art, and when you came right down to it, Robert was trying to make an art out of mere imitation. Art History 102, spring semester at University of Miami, had taught me that this could not be done. Art was creating something *new*, not mimicking something already in existence. What Robert was trying to do so intently was, in fact, no more than craft. He did no more than copy my tics and twitches—even to the point of staring at my family portrait, a very personal part of my disguise, for his character research—

—which didn't actually make any sense, because his character was single. So had it been pure nosiness? But then, why the intensity? No—it had to be something else.

Could it be that he truly felt a sad and absurd longing for a family of his own? Of course, that's what he'd said—but it had not been terribly convincing. And yet, there was no other explanation, unless I was willing to believe that, with his pick of all the glamorous beauties in the world, he was staring with longing at Rita. With all due respect for Rita, I found that even harder to believe.

Not his character, not Rita, not the kids; so there was no possible reason for his fascination with the picture. There was nothing else to see in the picture, except for . . .

Somewhere, deep in the Intelligence Analysis Section of the Department of Human Studies, University of Dexter, a tiny little bell chimed softly, announcing that a new report had just drifted into the in-box, and I paused in midponder to look it over. Actually, the report stated, there was one more thing in the family portrait: Me. Dexter himself.

But, of course, there was no conceivable reason that Robert might stare at a picture of *me*. Certainly not; he was an ultramasculine leading man—except that he never got married, seemed to avoid beautiful women, had a perfect haircut and fabulous shoes, insisted on Robert-not-Bob, and always groomed himself very well—with Product! He has been seen, on more than one occasion, staring at Dexter with an expression of abstract longing, which caused the Passenger to issue a hesitant, uncertain, unspecified whisper of unease. The only man I knew who routinely dressed up as Carmen Miranda worshiped him. And on top of everything else Robert was, for God's sake, an *actor*.

Dexter takes great pride in having a brain that usually works well, more or less. And so on those rare occasions when it works a little slower than I would ideally like it to, I have to pause and wonder if I should eat more fish. Because quite clearly, I had been staring at a long list of very plain hints and failing to see the obvious conclusion.

Robert was gay.

And somehow, probably because of his intense study of Dexter in all his charm and glory, Robert had developed an infatuation with his subject—*moi*.

Of course, it was completely reasonable. To know me is to love me, and I was very fond of me, too. A list of my finer qualities would easily occupy almost half the front side of a three-by-five card. Although the list does taper off rather dramatically after "good with a knife." But such sterling traits would mean nothing to a shallow clot like Robert; he was all about surface appearances. And speaking of, I had been told on more than one occasion that I am not completely horrible to look upon, for those who like that sort of thing. It meant nothing to me, since the only purpose of good looks is to acquire sex, and I am largely uninterested. But it clearly meant something to Robert. Even with half of Hollywood to pick from, he had settled on Dexter.

He liked me. He really *liked* me.

Really, this was too much—and it confirmed my low opinion of Robert's intelligence. Me? Really? Of course, it was flattering, but it was impossible. How was I supposed to work with him when I knew he was gazing longingly at me, mooning, and fighting back declarations of the Love That Dare Not Speak Its Name?

Somehow I would have to. I had my orders, and Robert had his, and he would just have to moon on his own time—and at his own desk. I flipped the newspaper into the trash can, brushed some

mostly imaginary filth off my blotter, and set the photograph back in
its place. I leaned back again to think, trying to push Robert out of
my thoughts, but it was difficult. Even without this absurd devotion
to me, Robert was a strange and unsettling presence, and after a week
in his company I was definitely feeling that I had been pushed off
center. And to be fair, it wasn't just Robert. The whole week had been
strange, and I had not really had time to reflect on it until now, and
as I relaxed and let my powerful brain roam where it would, I found
myself thinking about Jackie.

She was a very odd person, too, judged by my limited experience, and from my even odder perspective—in a much nicer way
than Robert, of course, but still: She seemed unhappy with being a
celebrity, although from what I could see she was quite good at it. She
mooned over the idea of Ordinary Life—and yet, she was risking her
own Extraordinary one to keep herself from falling out of the lime-
light, exposing herself to an attack from a slavering beast merely to
preserve her role on this still hypothetical TV show. It seemed need-
lessly complicated to me; why not relax and enjoy the ride? I certainly
was.

But for me, it would all end, and soon. Did that make it different?
Perhaps it all got cloying if it was permanent—"Death is the mother
of beauty," as someone once said. I had always taken that to mean
something a little different, but I could see how it might apply here.
It was quite likely that I enjoyed Jackie's lifestyle because I knew very
well that even the most thrilling roller coaster runs out of track sooner
or later, and no one had offered me any kind of permanent exemp-
tion from this basic law of nature. My vacation in Valhalla would end
soon, and I would be flung from Paradise back into the Pit where I
belonged. Unfair and unwanted, but unavoidable. Of course, I could
probably run off with Robert, but the idea was not quite as appealing.
I would just have to accept that my beautiful interlude would come
to an end.

Ah, well. Some very great poet whose name escapes me had put
it best when he said, "Gather ye rosebuds while ye may." For the next
few days I could still gather me rosebuds, and I might as well enjoy
it. And because Computer Dexter is nothing if not thorough, a tiny
wheel turned over with a muffled click and called up the end of the

rosebud poem: a quaint reminder that today's rosebud *something something* "tomorrow will be dying." Ah, Death: a lovely sentiment, and it reminded me that I was collecting rosebuds in the first place because I was being paid to keep Jackie from dying at the hands of a dull and brutal psycho.

A shame; I could enjoy the flower gathering a great deal more if I didn't have to worry about that. If only I had a few lazy hours to stroll out of my workaday rags and into the slithery skin of Dexter the Devil, I could set this whole thing right and concentrate on admiring the view from Jackie's balcony. It wouldn't take long—I had more than enough proof of Patrick's guilt to satisfy the Harry Code. I would simply have to find him and let Dark Nature take its course. And I did not think it would be terribly hard to find a blunt object like Patrick Bergmann. If only I had the time . . .

Somewhere far away, deep inside the high-walled Fortress of Dexter Keep, a tiny little figure stepped up into the tower and rang a delicate silver bell, and as its dulcet note rang out through the thin and bitter air, I sat up straight in my chair and thought, *Aha*. I know it sounds pretentious, even melodramatic, but there it is: I really did think, *Aha*. Because I had just recalled that I did, in fact, have the time. I actually had a small window of perhaps three hours to work my magic—until my afternoon appointment with Cody's teacher.

But would three hours be enough? I do hate to rush these things, and there was a very minor obstacle in my way—I didn't know where Patrick was. Even if I did find him quickly, I would have very little time to dispatch him and dispose of the leftovers. It would be best, in fact, if I simply stuck the knife in and dumped the body in the handiest hidey-hole with no lingering over the good parts.

And oddly enough, the thought of that made me shudder. I had never done anything quite so cold before, and I wasn't sure I could do it now. It just didn't seem *right*. What I normally do—if "normal" is the right word—is far more deliberate, even contemplative. It proceeds from a standard start and winds through its unhurried course according to a long-standing set of rules dictated by a great deal of practice and, of course, the Harry Code. And when I finished, I had satisfied all of them, and therefore myself, Harry, and the Muse. It had to be done Just That Way, or it would not feel *right*.

And there was that awful un-Dexter word: "feel." I am not ruled by what I feel, because for the most part I do not. I am a well-adjusted, nonfeeling Monster, and quite happy to be one, and feelings were something I gave to my Playtime Friends—sharp and immediate feelings. If I could not give them to Patrick it would be incomplete, unfulfilling, Dexter Interruptus.

But, of course, that did not matter. I was not really doing this for me, aside from the fact that I would gain a few days of worry-free lounging in the lap of luxury. No, I was doing this for Jackie—and in a way, for the human race as a whole. I was removing a terrible blemish on the pockmarked face of humanity, a threat to one and all—why, this was really a good deed! Perhaps I could convince Cody's Cub Scout troop to give me a merit badge in Altruistic Homicide. And if I had to hurry things along more than I would like—well, too bad. This was not playtime. It was a job to be done, and I was just the fiend to do it.

All righty then: There would be no time for any kind of sport with Patrick Bergmann. I would simply find him, finish him, and fling him away, decisively and rapidly—and once more I faltered at the thought. To rush through it like that, and in broad daylight? Distasteful, even dirty; it seemed a little bit too much like . . . well, like murder.

Of all the odd thoughts I could have, that might seem the oddest, but there it was. Dexter was in a dither over doing what he does best, merely because it would be a rush job. Was my new life of luxury rotting away the hard and happy core of the monster that is me? Turning me into an old maid incapable of the simplest and most well-justified endings? Was I really so straitlaced?

I gave myself a stern lecture, told myself to buck up, play the man, be a mensch, do what must be done, and after several similar clichés I began to believe I could do it, but the thought of it still tickled at me.

Squeamish? *Moi?*

No matter; it must be done, and so it would. And today was my one real shot at doing it, and I would not dither it away. I looked up at the clock: ten twenty-eight. I would need to leave at around two fifteen to make it down to Cody's school for a three-o'clock meeting—and I would have to show up at the meeting for the sake of duty, propriety, and an ironclad alibi. But if I went to lunch a little early, say twelve thirty, that would give me two hours before the meeting, assuming I could bring myself to rush the actual *lunch* part of lunch. It seemed like a terrible sacrifice—but I told myself I was doing it for a noble purpose, and I could always order something extra-nice from room service tonight when it was all over.

So be it. I would swallow my silly objections, and do the thing as it must be done. I turned to my computer to begin my search.

Out of nothing more than habit, I checked my in-box and found the usual odd assortment of absurdity, improbability, and immorality. But there was also an official Memo from the Office of Captain Matthews, informing me that my presence would be required on Saturday night at the Gusman, and I was further ordered to bring my wife, dress nicely, and laugh when the camera pointed at me. I found that I was pinching my nose, and stopped with some irritation.

So Renny had told the truth when he said the captain wanted me there—to further the positive image of the department, no doubt. Well, it was just one more minor burden in this endless life of pain, and somehow I would bear it and survive. In the meantime, I would try to make sure that Patrick did not.

I do have some modest competence in the area of finding things with a computer, and I also have resources available to me that most people do not, courtesy of my job with Miami's Finest. In just a few minutes I had confirmed that Bergmann, Patrick M., of Laramie, Tennessee, was the proud owner of a red Kawasaki Ninja 650. So I had been right about the motorcycle following us. It was not another aha moment. The only real news was the model and color, and neither told me where he might be right now. But again, this was not a complicated person. If I could not find him in an hour or so, I would simply have to resign from the International Order of Modest Genius. I didn't know where he was staying: fine. Work backward from where I knew he *was*.

He had been following us for several days, biding his time while he learned our routine. He had patience, the patience of a deer hunter, and for him this was a lot like hunting deer: Learn their habits, learn how they think, and the rest is easy.

He would know our routine by now, know that from nine to five

Jackie was either here in headquarters, inaccessible, or out at a crime scene with armed officers all around her. Even a dolt like Patrick would know he had little chance of getting to Jackie when she was surrounded by cops. So he would watch, learn the rituals, and look for the times of maximum vulnerability.

And of course, it was obvious when those vulnerable intervals were. The only two times I had seen him had been at the hotel, in the morning. I had not seen him arrive at night—but he was there waiting in the morning. Sometime between sixish, when Jackie and I returned to the hotel, and seven thirty a.m., when we left, he took up his post at the end of the hotel's driveway and waited.

And how patient would he really be? Probably not terribly—this was important to him, more important than anything else in his life. So important, in fact, that he had abandoned everything else in his life in order to do it. He had been following Jackie for quite some time now, which can often have a negative effect on one's earning power.

Savings? Enough for a year or more on the road? I did not think that Laramie, Tennessee, was a hotbed of billionaires, and I was certain that Patrick Bergmann's resources were limited. He would not be staying at the Setai in South Beach, nor even the Sonesta in the Grove. In fact, it was probably safe to assume that he could not even afford an ordinary downscale Miami fleabag hotel—not if he had been on the road pursuing Jackie for so long. Even so, he had to sleep, eat, and so forth. When Jackie was untouchably surrounded by armed cops, did he trundle off to his hidey-hole for a peanut butter sandwich and a nap? He would have to do these things, but where would he go that he could do them on the cheap?

Patrick's Facebook page had shown that he was an outdoorsy type. Would he try to camp out? He could not know ahead of time that the opportunities for sleeping under the stars are somewhat limited within the city of Miami. There are no campgrounds in Miami, other than a few RV parks. So would he sleep on a park bench? Not likely—in a city that depends so heavily on tourism, such things were vigorously discouraged. But the idea of camping seemed right—it was cheap and anonymous, and it fit what I knew of him. So how would he do it?

Hoping for no more than some small visual confirmation, I

clicked onto the Web and went once more to his Facebook page. And there, lo and behold . . .

As I have mentioned, I am not a fan of Facebook. It seems to me like a kind of quiet and subtle virus that worms its way into every aspect of the living tissue of daily existence, until it is impossible to think about cereal without finding an ad for Raisin Bran in your inbox. I am sure the endless intrusive connections can be a great deal of fun for some people, but it really doesn't make sense for Dexter.

It would make no more sense for Patrick, but he had made himself a second home there anyway, so I flipped to his page for a look—and spent a full half minute staring in disbelief.

As we have observed earlier, people really do put some surprising things on their Facebook pages, almost as if they are trying to make it easier for the thing to take control of their lives. Still, there really ought to be limits, don't you think? Especially if one is on a killing spree—shouldn't one maintain a certain discreet silence, assuming one has all one's mental facilities? I mean, seriously, could anyone really be this stupid?

Apparently, someone could, especially Patrick Bergmann. And so I stared, thinking that I was surely hallucinating, because in consensus reality, nothing is ever this easy. But for all my staring, the page didn't change. It still showed a picture of Patrick standing next to some kind of cement pillar with Biscayne Bay in the background. Behind him and across the water the skyline of downtown Miami stuck up aggressively, and underneath the picture it said, CAMPING IN MIAMI!

I had hoped for some tiny hint, but this—I had to fight down an irrational moment of affection for good old Facebook and remember that, after all, I was the one who had thought to look there, based on my uncannily accurate assessment of Patrick's personality. And there it was, right where I had hoped it would be.

If I had been feeling a little squeamish about taking out Patrick without Dexter's Due Process, all such tender feelings vanished now. Anyone this completely clueless did not deserve another day of using up oxygen that I might want someday. It was a clear civic duty to yank this idiot out of existence ASAP, before he had a chance to contaminate the gene pool.

I studied the picture; for some reason I thought I had seen this spot before, and it was more than the familiarity of the Miami skyline and water. I suppose I could have figured out the location by triangulating the angle on the high-rise buildings in the background with the azimuth of the sun's arc times pi or something, but I was sure I had seen this exact spot before, and almost as sure I would remember why if I stared at it long enough. And sure enough, after only a few minutes of Zen concentration, I had it.

As noted earlier, there are not really very many places in Miami where camping is encouraged. But there is one place where it is absolutely *required*. And this picture had been taken there, beyond all reasonable doubt.

Miami Law has its own peculiar logic—or lack of it—and Patrick had landed in one of the most shining examples. An ordinance had passed forbidding sexual predators from living within twenty-five hundred feet of anything that might contain children. But these same poor benighted pedophiles were required by the parole board to live within those same city limits. Because twenty-five hundred feet is, when you think about it, a relatively long distance, it turned out that there was only one place where these people could live that satisfied both requirements—underneath the Julia Tuttle Causeway, on a spoil island halfway between Miami and Miami Beach.

Patrick was there. It could be nowhere else. Still, Due Diligence is Dexter's middle name, so I Googled the location and looked at a few pictures: They matched up perfectly. Patrick was indeed camping out in the sexual predators' colony, under a bridge on the Julia Tuttle Causeway. A small leathery something stirred within me, and a jittery twinge of excitement rose up to meet it.

I had him.

# SEVENTEEN

MIDDAY MIAMI. THE SUN WAS HIGH AND HOT, ALTHOUGH not as hot in this mild autumn as it had been just a few months ago. Still, the number of license plates on cars from the North said very clearly that it was more pleasantly hot here than it was in New Jersey or Michigan at this time of year. It felt very odd to drive among the mildly vacuous tourists in the bright afternoon, cuddling my intended shadows to my breast and whispering soft promises to them that yes, indeed, we really were on our way to do what only we can do so well, no matter that it was day and not night, no matter that there was no sound track from a silver-red moon floating down to us, no soft chorus of sweet anticipation from a deep blue nighttime sky. Here there is only the alien noise of the docile and happy early afternoon traffic on the throughway, not even the homicidal comfort of rush hour, and this is the wrong music, tempo far too easy, harmonies off or missing; it is all different, unsettling, wrong, not at all what we are used to.

Midday and moonless, idling along among the families from Ohio and retired couples from Iowa and the businessmen from Brazil, instead of lurking in the shade of a night meant for mischief, and it all seems so improper, as if we have wandered into a church and found everyone naked.

But it is what we have, it is where and when we are, what we must deal with, no matter that it all feels so unsuitable, so unreal, so very much not right now. How can it be? Here in the sunlight—how can it happen? How can we swim through the glare of a beach-perfect day to do our night-dark best? There has never before been a Dexter by Daylight, and the shadow babies inside that slither out so happily into the dark of a Joyful Night are not happy to come out and play in this high-noon shimmer of light and breeze and bright red sunburns on pale white bodies. They are not happy at all, and the Dark Passenger is not happy, and so Dexter, too, is far from pleased with things as they are.

But things are, inarguably, what they are. We must take them as we find them, and in the very short time given us we must prepare. And so we meander through the traffic and down onto Eighth Street. Calle Ocho, home of *cafecitas* and *pastelitas*, and, as tempting as these things usually are, we bypass them this time and pull into the parking lot of a pool supply store. We blink once more at the unwanted sun, and then go into the store, where we buy a small plastic water-testing kit, paying cash, and then head back out to the parking lot, where we open the trunk.

From inside the trunk we lift out a short-sleeved white shirt, and standing there in the very scant shelter beside our little car we change into it. There is a skinny black clip-on tie in its pocket and this, too, we put on. Finally and very importantly, we take out a clipboard, and now our disguise is complete and we are ready. We are no longer Dexter Daystalker; we have magically morphed into Anonymous Official Man.

It is an old disguise, but it is always effective. People see a clipboard and a tie and they see nothing else. In this case they will see Nameless Official Water Tester, and as we mosey through the predators' camp, scanning for a red Ninja or any other sign of our prey, we will pause now and then to take water samples and scribble notes, secure in the knowledge that a clipboard provides better invisibility than Harry Potter's cloak.

In the car we unwrap our water-testing kit and place it on top of the clipboard in the passenger seat, and then we are away, out onto Ocho and north to NE 36th Street, and then out onto the Julia Tuttle Causeway.

Traffic is thin by Miami standards and we move easily out the causeway. We drive past the predators' colony, looking casually-carefully for any sign of Patrick and, seeing none, we pull over onto the shoulder some fifty yards past. We gather the props for our little costume drama, and then we open the door and step out into the dreadful wrongness of that bright noontime sun. We stand for a moment and blink, hoping that somehow it will grow slightly darker for our purpose, or at least that we may become slightly easier with the ceaseless blinding light that assaults us so unpleasantly.

But neither of these things happens. The sun hammers down, and we are still uneasy, and we have so very little time. So we take a deep breath, hold our clipboard firmly in our hand, and march back toward the bridge that shelters the colony.

The sun seems hotter on the walk back to the bridge and we are sweating freely by the time we step off the road and down into the shade under the bridge—sweating when we should be all icy cool control, sweating with the strangeness as well as the heat, watching with mild alarm as great hot drops roll down off our forehead, skitter down our nose, and splat onto the concrete. We are sweating, and it is daylight, and there are people all around and these things should not be, and it makes our footsteps seem a size too large as they slap the cement in their too-loud awkward off-rhythm. But we move ahead because we must, past the first tent, where a hairless middle-aged black man is weight-lifting with two one-gallon plastic milk containers filled, apparently, with water. His arms are thin, but the veins stand out as he curls his arms open and shut, open and shut. He stares at us and we nod; he looks away quickly, and we step past him to the water's edge, where we kneel and fill our little plastic analyzer with water. We hold it up to the sun and squint at it for a moment, and then we dump it, stand, scribble on the clipboard, and move on.

On to the second tent, which is quiet and unoccupied, and then deeper into the shadow under the bridge, and seeing the day turn even three small shades darker makes us breathe a little easier; it is far from night, but it is moving in the right direction, and we move with it, staying in the shadows and easing slowly along the water's edge, stopping twice more for our dumb show with the water and the clipboard.

We are in the heart of it now and we pause, looking around at the otherworldly sprawl of the camp. There are lean-tos made of cardboard, and some made of wood with tin roofs, and others no more than sheets of plastic stretched tight to make a tent, and a few actual tents, all mixed together as if they had been scooped up at random and then tumbled out carelessly onto the concrete under the bridge.

At my right, the concrete slopes upward to meet the surface of the road, and nestled into the junction where road and concrete meet, a woman stares down at me from a sleeping bag, lifeless eyes following me without any interest at all. We stroll on through the camp, looking for anything at all that might speak the name of our speed date, Patrick, and finally, on the far edge of the camp, right at the water's edge, we find it.

It is a very nice-looking dome tent, somewhat battered and stained, but still quite clearly a serious, good-quality piece of outdoorsman's equipment. There is no red motorcycle parked beside it, and no sign of Patrick himself, but we are just as sure as we can be that this is his tent, because he has decorated it as only Patrick could.

On each side of the zippered flap that serves as the tent's only door, there is a one-gallon milk jug, the same kind used by the hairless weight lifter. These, too, are filled with water, to hold them steadily in place as they support their top-heavy burden.

A stick has been jammed into the mouth of each jug, and on top of each stick is a cat's head.

The heads have been very neatly cut from the bodies, and they look to be freshly dead, and they stare out at us with identical expressions of openmouthed kitty horror.

Between them, propped against the tent's door flap, is a crude hand-lettered sign. It says, THIS CUD HAPPIN 2 U, and underneath in smaller letters, STAY OUT!

The combination of poor spelling and neat cat butchery is as telling as a photograph; this is Patrick's tent. And we feel at last the chill all-ready steady-handed glee of impending wickedness and almost see the light around us creep slowly down the spectrum past the wretched bright yellow of noon and deep into the orange, and red, and—

But red. But wait; where is the red motorcycle? We see it nowhere and we know he would keep it close—even a hillbilly like Patrick would know he could not leave it unguarded near the road.

We look around; there is no place visible where a bike could be stored, and the happy shadows bleach away from us and back into daytime dinginess. There is no motorcycle—unless it was in the tent? But it is a small tent, and the warning sign was leaning against the tent's flap in a way that indicated he had placed it there from the outside, probably as he left, and there are no small flaps or wrinkles across the canvas to tell of movement, not even a small and sleepy breath, and we watch another fat bead of sweat roll off our nose as we come crashing back to daylight and disappointment.

Patrick is not here.

In the middle of the day, in our only small window of opportunity, Patrick has wandered away where he should not be. He has spoiled everything.

We fight down the ornery urge to give the tent a spiteful kick, and just to be completely safely thorough we move past the tent to the water, listening very carefully for any soft snoring or rumbling from inside the tent. There is nothing, no sound, and we are thinking very unhappy thoughts as we kneel down and perform our watery pantomime one more time.

Just to be very sure, we stand up and turn too fast, pretending to stumble, and giving the tent a hearty "accidental" thump. There is no response from inside.

"Sorry!" we say in a loud official voice, and we wait for an answer. "Hello? Anybody home?" Again there is no response.

It is definite. Patrick is not here.

And although we loiter for another twenty minutes, performing meaningless tricks with the clipboard, he does not return, and we finally have to admit that staying any longer would be highly suspicious, and we must pack up our toys and admit the painful obvious truth:

We have crapped out.

We thread our way back through the camp, pausing twice to scribble bad words on the clipboard, and then climb back up onto the causeway and trudge to the car in a weary, bitter, very unhappy sheen of sweat. We try very hard to think positive thoughts, to come up with some small scrap of something that will make this whole hopeless trip seem like anything other than a complete waste of time. And finally, as we thread our way through the traffic at the end of the causeway, one tiny glimmer of optimism leaks through all the cranky sludge, and we sigh and accept it as the very best we can hope for:

At least there is now time for lunch.

I had a quick lunch alone in a restaurant on Calle Ocho, a new place that had opened so recently that the waitress was still polite. The food was good. I topped it off with a *cafecita* and then drove slowly and thoughtfully back to the office. I wondered where Patrick had gone. He knew he could not get to Jackie in daylight. If he was keeping the schedule I thought he was, this was his sleeping time, and he should have been lounging there in his tent in peaceful repose. Of course, it was possible that he had run out of buffalo jerky and gone to a convenience store to get more. But after all my preparation, and my endless dithering about doing it quickly and in daylight, it was oddly deflating to come away from the afternoon with nothing to show for it except a small spot on my shirt from some spilled black beans.

Now I would have to sit around for another hour with Robert and Renny and pretend to be mild and patient—and then I would still have to go down to the meeting with Cody's teacher. That conference had seemed like a good idea when it was my excuse for slipping away, and my alibi. Now it began to seem like a great deal of dull niggling scut work, pointless and annoying posturing with an elementary school teacher, someone who could never understand Cody nor his difficulty in adjusting. The teacher would want to discuss ways to help Cody make a happy accommodation to his new grade, and strategies for success in fitting in, and the teacher could not hear the truth, would not believe it even if I spoke in plain one-syllable rhyming words accompanied by bright crayon-colored illustrations. No teacher in any school in the Dade County public school system could ever understand the simple unvarnished truth.

Cody would never adjust, never be happy, and never fit in.

Cody was not, and never would be, a normal healthy boy who wanted to play ball and tease the girls. Cody wanted other things that the school system could never give him, and his only chance of being well adjusted was to learn how to get them, and how to pretend to be human, how to live by the Harry Code—and all those things he had to learn from another monster: me.

The things Cody wanted, *needed*, are frowned upon by the intolerant society in which we live, and we could never explain it, not any part of it, not at all. And so we would sit with the teacher and dither and dance and exchange fake smiles and grandiose clichés and pretend to feel hope for a bright and shiny future for a boy who would unstoppably grow into a Dark Legacy already written in blood instead of chalk. And thinking about how I must unavoidably avoid this truth with the teacher and instead spend forty-five minutes mouthing cheerful brainless New Age buzzwords with someone who Really Cared made me want to ram my car into the Buick filled with blue-haired ladies from Minnesota that chugged along on the road beside me.

But it was all part of maintaining my disguise as Proud Papa Dexter, and there was no way around it. At least I had the evening to look forward to after that: lollygagging on a chaise longue with Jackie and eating strawberries as the sun set. It would almost make the frustration and annoyance of the rest of the day worthwhile.

And I thought again of what it might be like if only I could live Jackie's lifestyle full-time: no teacher conferences, no housepainting while standing in a mound of fire ants, no squalling and screeching and dirty diapers. Nothing but eternal vigilance in a bejeweled setting. It was a fantasy, of course, nothing more than a way to soothe the grumpy beast within after its day of disappointments. But it was a very good fantasy, and lingering inside it was good enough to put a very small smile on my face by the time I got back to my office.

The smile, as tiny as it was, lasted until I got almost to my chair, when I ran into Vince Masuoka, headed out at full speed as I was trying to head in. We collided forcefully, and because I am larger than Vince, he bounced off me and into the doorframe.

"Ouch, my elbow!" he said, quickly straightening and rubbing his arm where it had banged against the frame. "Got another one!"

"Another elbow?" I said. "Big deal. Everyone has two."

"Another body!" Vince said, straightening up and continuing his headlong rush out of the lab, pausing only to call over his shoulder, "The eye-fucker! He's killed another girl!" Then he was gone down the hall, leaving me to stand at the door and stare after him and realize that I now knew what Patrick had been doing this afternoon instead of sleeping in his tent. And very oddly indeed, I really and truly wanted to go along and see what he had done.

I went on into the lab. Robert and Renny were both there, standing uncertainly together and looking as if they didn't quite know what their characters would do when the eye-fucker struck again, and didn't really want to hear anybody tell them.

I told them anyway. "Let's go," I said.

They both blinked at me like uncertain owls. "Go?" Robert said. Renny licked his lips.

"Crime scene," I said. "Nothing like it for learning about crime scenes."

They looked at each other like they were both hoping the other would come up with a really good way to suggest we go for coffee instead, but neither of them did, and so we followed Vince downstairs and out of the building.

# EIGHTEEN

THIS TIME THE BODY HAD BEEN LEFT IN A DUMPSTER ON THE docks in Coconut Grove, near City Hall, just half a mile or so across the water from the Grove Isle Hotel, where I was staying with Jackie. I could see the high-rise profile of the hotel quite clearly as I got out of the car, standing tall above the painfully bright glare from the water.

The yellow perimeter tape was already up, with two uniformed cops in front of it, standing with that solid, meaty stance that cops everywhere seem to fall into instinctively when they put on the uniform. Even Deborah had stood like that back in the days when she wore the blue to work. Their eyes swiveled toward me, and I stepped forward, reaching for my ID.

"Yeah, hey, Dexter," Renny said from behind me, and I turned to look at him. Robert hurried past us, headed for the two cops by the yellow tape. Like he had last time, he would stand there by the perimeter, joking with the cops, so he wouldn't have to see the wonderful horror in the Dumpster. But this was Renny's first dead body, as far as I knew, and he stood uncertainly, licking his lips and glancing longingly at Robert's retreating back. "Robert says the last one was fucking sick," he said.

"Well," I said, "Robert didn't really get a good look at it."

"Ran his ass away screaming and hurling chunks, huh?" Renny said, just a ghost of a smile on his face.

"He didn't actually scream," I said.

"Yeah, right," Renny said, looking once more at Robert, and then beyond him to the Dumpster. "Hey, seriously," he said. "How bad is this gonna be?"

It may not be the very best character reference for me, but I was very eager to see whether this body was indeed the work of Bonehead Patrick, and if there was anything different about it, and I was growing annoyed listening to Renny's dithering instead of peeking in at the surprise in the Dumpster. So reassurance was not uppermost on my mind. "Oh, it's going to be very bad," I said. "Come on; I'll show you."

He didn't move. "Do I really got to look at this shit?" he said.

"Well," I said, torn between my duty to shepherd Renny and my growing desire to see the waiting wonder, "you really should see what Vince does at a crime scene. I mean, that's what your character does, right?"

Renny looked at the Dumpster out on the dock, and swallowed. "Yeah, okay," he said. Then he gave me a hard look and I saw once more the small gleam of some interior Something flaring up. "But I throw up, you cleaning it up." He took a deep breath, and then moved past me with determination in his pace and steel in his spine, and hopefully not too much in his stomach.

I followed behind Renny until he was ten feet from the Dumpster, and then he stopped dead. "I can see Vince fine from here," he said.

There didn't seem to be any point in arguing about it, so I slid past him and right up beside Vince Masuoka, who crouched in the shade of the Dumpster. "You're just in time," Vince said.

"For what?"

"Now the real fun starts," he said. He jerked his head over to one side. I looked, and about forty feet away I saw Detective Anderson talking to a thin, white-haired man in khaki pants, a pale blue polo shirt, and boat shoes. Even from this distance, the white-haired man looked badly shaken.

"Anderson has a witness," Vince said. "The old guy is off one of the big sailboats. He saw somebody dump a rolled-up carpet in here and take off in a kayak."

The kayak gave me pause; did Patrick have a new, Miami-flavored way to get around? Or was it possible that somebody else had done it this time? Feeling a small flutter of uncertainty and rising interest, I stepped past Vince and peeked inside, into the heart of the garbage.

The girl's body lay on top of a chunk of dirty brown carpet, the kind of ratty, stained carpet you can see in the garbage in any residential area where someone is remodeling. It was partially unrolled, just enough to see the top half of a very bad time, and not enough to hide the other contents of the Dumpster.

It was almost all garbage—no paper or cardboard or plastic wrappings like the last time. This Dumpster was used by the people from the rows of large yachts at the nearby dock, and by anyone who used the fish-cleaning station nearby, and the smell rising up from inside was enough to kill small animals at ten paces. But it didn't discourage the nearly solid cloud of flies that whirled around the heaps of moist, sloppy rotting leftovers. And, of course, it didn't have any effect at all on the dead girl who perched naked on top of the putrid mound of decomposing gunk.

It looked like she'd had a very hard time of it. Like the previous victim, this one had been hacked, stabbed, bitten, and clawed with an undisciplined but frenzied abandon, a wild impatience that had left very few patches of visible skin unmarked by trauma.

The state of the blood around the wounds indicated that she had been alive for most of the cuts, gashes, and punches, an entire arsenal of attacks that left the corpse looking like she had spent a week at the Academy of Psychotic Assault.

Once again a large hank of golden hair had been ripped out by the roots, leaving a raw, dark red section of scalp exposed. Under that hair, so very like Jackie's in color and cut, there was not much recognizable left of the face that wasn't slashed by fingernails, teeth, and knife blade, but something about the profile tugged at my memory for a second, before I shrugged it off. Of course she looked familiar— she looked like Jackie, just as all the other victims did. That was the whole point of it for Patrick.

I looked a moment longer, but saw nothing helpful, so I stepped back and looked down at Vince.

"Did you find anything?" I asked him, without too much hope—and truthfully, without too much interest, either. I knew who had done it, and I couldn't be more certain even if Patrick Bergmann had signed his work.

"Just this," Vince said. He held up a small plastic evidence bag. Inside I could see the outline of what looked like a small bar of soap, the kind of small soap bar hotels leave in the bathrooms for their guests. "You don't want to know where I found it," he added happily. I leaned in for a closer look, and through the plastic I could make out the crest and the words "Grove Isle Hotel and Spa" in ornate script.

Vince shook it playfully. "Maybe it'll help Anderson figure out who the victim is this time," he said.

I opened my mouth to say that it didn't seem likely, that Anderson wouldn't figure it out if he had notarized statements from the killer and the victim, and then I closed my mouth and took a step back and didn't say anything at all.

Because I knew who she was. I remembered why she looked familiar, and it was not because she looked like Jackie. It was because I had seen her, standing in a hallway and blushing, smiling, pleased with being so very near to her real-life hero, Jackie Forrest.

I rattled the handles of my memory bank and came up with it: Her name was Amila, and she was the maid at the Grove Isle Hotel who had come to clean up the mess on the floor of our suite, and told me she styled her hair to look like Jackie Forrest's hair, and it got her killed. . . .

Some small shady something tickled my spine, just a tiny breeze of unease, telling me that someone was watching, and I turned away from the Dumpster and looked, out beyond the pier with its two rows of boats, and into the painfully bright glare of the bay.

Less than fifty yards away, straight out from the end of the dock, a small yellow dot bobbed on the light chop. A paddle rose as I watched, and dipped down to make two small strokes to keep the nose pointed in at us: a double-headed kayak paddle.

Behind the kayak, as if to underline this heavy-handed hint, the

Grove Isle Hotel towered up into the bright afternoon sky: the hotel where Jackie and I stayed. The hotel where Amila had worked until Patrick ended her career.

The paddle dipped lazily again, turning the boat slightly sideways so there could be no doubt at all what it was: a kayak. It was the perfect boat for Patrick's outdoorsy lifestyle. They were light and therefore very easy to steal, and it would certainly be simpler than trying to conceal a dead body on a motorcycle. A quick trip across the half mile of water, dump the body, and then paddle away just far enough to watch the fun.

And of course he would watch. Not merely to see the excitement when his project was discovered—he would also be watching to see who showed up, because Jackie had made an appearance the last time, and he would want to see her when she came to this one, too. Without even thinking about it, I knew how important that was to him: to have Jackie look, and *see*, and know it could have been her—that it *would* be her so very soon—and to know he was watching her and waiting to make it happen again, to her. . . .

But to do it like this was pure hubris. He had taken a huge chance, dumping this body in broad daylight from a small boat. And I was quite sure it was not because he was getting bolder. This kill had come too soon, right on the heels of his last, breaking the pattern and revealing the first rift in Patrick's mountain-man armor. Because as he got closer to Jackie, as he watched the hotel through all the hours of the night, waiting for a chance—waiting for even a glimpse—his frustration had been growing, eating at him, hitting so hard that his satisfaction from the previous victim had lasted only a few pitiful days. Soon these surrogates would not be enough for him; he had to have Jackie, but he could not get to her, and so he watched and waited and the frustration grew as each day slipped past, repeating the day before, without even the smallest window of opportunity. . . .

Patrick was getting impatient. He was losing his ability to wait for just the right moment, and feeling the pressure of time racing unstoppably by, with nothing to show for it except a dwindling bank account. By killing the maid now he was trying to push things toward a climax, challenging us to see him so very nearby, daring us to do something, defying us to try to stop him, keep him from doing what he was going to do.

And oddly enough, in those two or three seconds as I squinted into the glare on the water at Patrick in his kayak, following all these little insights as they raced through my brain, I found another small thought burbling up underneath and popping into daylight with the happy snap of a bright pink bubble of chewing gum, and that thought went like this:

*All right, Patrick. I accept your challenge.*

For a moment I wasn't really sure what I meant by that, and I blinked, turning away from the glare on the Bay and staring off the dock, back toward the yellow perimeter tape, where Robert stood chatting with the two uniformed cops. No sign yet of Deborah and Jackie, which was all to the good. I looked beyond the perimeter, over the growing crowd of gawkers and into the busy streets of Coconut Grove. The Grove, that happy mecca for Miami's idle rich, with its high-priced boutiques, quaint shops, and casually posh restaurants. The Grove, where Dexter had lived for so long before his marriage, and where even now, Dexter kept his fishing boat only a mile or so from this very spot—

Oh. Fishing boat. *That* must be what I meant.

I looked at my watch; it was one forty-five, only an hour and change before the conference with Cody's teacher. I looked back at Patrick, bobbing there so insolently on his pilfered kayak, and the sight of him tripped a switch in the sinister clockwork machinery of Dexter's bleak brain. A wheel chunked into gear and hit a lever that tipped a metal plate over and onto a fulcrum that thumped into a shiny cold ball so it rolled down the chute and into the "out" basket, and I picked it up, held it in my hand, and heard it whisper, *There is just enough time.*

And there would be.

# NINETEEN

I KEPT MY BOAT BEHIND A PRIVATE HOUSE ON A CANAL, JUST south of the heart of Coconut Grove's busy center. The house was on a quiet street, and the elderly couple who owned it lived in New Jersey most of the year, coming down to this house only for the coldest months of winter. They were quite happy to take the modest rental fee from me, and I was just as happy paying less than the going rate for dockage. On top of getting a bargain, I also got a relatively private place to keep my boat, which was occasionally a very good thing, considering that I sometimes put Certain Items onto my boat and carried them away to consign them to the final briny deep, and it was probably best that no one saw me doing this.

And on this bright and suddenly eventful day, it would have been worth twice what I paid for it, because this dock was only a ten-minute drive from the redolent Dumpster where Amila lay in sloppy repose.

I don't even remember what feeble excuses I made as I hurried away from the scene and into my car. I think I said I was leaving early for my son's teacher conference because I was worried about the traffic; not my best effort, but I was in a hurry, and no one seemed to notice that it didn't make a great deal of sense.

In any case, once I got through the maddening snarl of traffic in the middle of the Grove, it was only ten minutes before I was on my boat and heading out the canal, quite a bit faster than the No Wake–Idle Speed that is generally required. But having made up my mind to do this and do it now, I had whipped myself into a lather of impatience, grinding my teeth at the thought that I would not be in time, that Patrick would paddle away, and I would miss my second and probably final chance to set things right in my own inimitable way.

And so I hurried out the canal, earning a wicked glare from a shirtless old man on the bank as I went past at a good ten knots, and a shout for good measure as I reached the mouth of the canal and nosed the boat up to full speed and onto a plane.

It was a straight line by water back to the far side of Dinner Key basin, where I devoutly hoped Patrick would still be waiting and watching, and I made the distance in half the time it had taken me to drive. There were several tricky patches of shallow water, but I headed straight through them at full speed, ignoring the possibility of hitting bottom and losing a propeller blade, and I would have gone even faster if I could have. I could not shake the worry that Patrick might be gone when I got there, and I gnashed my teeth impatiently the whole way.

It was only a bit more than twenty minutes from the time I had hurried off the dock to the time I nosed my boat around the first barrier island and into the boat basin, remarkably good time. But it was not the record-setting journey that put a smile in my heart and a song on my lips; it was the sight of the small yellow kayak, still bobbing in place, as I came off plane and slid down to idle speed inside the boat basin. Now that I knew he was still there, I could take my time, and I did not want to draw attention from anyone onshore—nor, heavens forfend, from the Marine Patrol, known as the AquaNazis by those of us who have been stopped and boarded by these diligent seagoing crime fighters.

And as I saw Patrick sitting there so placidly on his kayak, staring intently at all the fuss caused by his crude handiwork, it occurred to me that I had not even thought about *how* I would do this. I had hurried through the anxious hurly-burly of getting away, and then getting here, with never an idea of what to do when I got here, and now that I actually was here I did not know what to do next, and I took a deep and centering breath and looked at the thing from several angles. It was very bright broad daylight, and the sun would shine far too clearly on the wicked as well as the just, and I could not really be sure which one I was right now, but either way I was illuminated far too well.

Anyone onshore who saw me stick a knife into Patrick would have no such doubts about my affiliation—and there was a great crowd of possible onlookers: people on their boats at the dock, more people thronging at the yellow perimeter tape, and worse, an entire flock of law enforcement personnel. Any one of them might look up at just the wrong moment and see the very visible violence of Patrick's well-deserved demise.

I looked around. Ahead of me, on the far side of Patrick, was the last barrier island that marked the end of Dinner Key's harbor area. Onshore on the far side of that, and therefore invisible from here, was a park—had Patrick found a quiet spot there to leave his motorcycle? It would be largely deserted right now, especially with some real excitement on the nearby docks.

Off to my right, Biscayne Bay stretched away, down to Turkey Point on one side and Elliot Key on the other. There were a few boats scattered across the vast expanse of water, but nothing close enough to see what I might do.

And what might that be? I was getting closer to Patrick all the time and I had still come up with nothing, no way to do what I truly needed to do. I looked all around for inspiration, and then I looked again at Patrick floating there so smug and happy, and it sent a trickle of sharp irritation rushing through me; this was *his* fault. *He* was putting me through all this bother, the ignorant savage. The hammer-brained unrefined knuckleheaded amateur, floating there without a care, while his betters were forced to rush madly about and *improvise* a way to clean up his slapdash all-thumbs mess. It was too much, too annoying, and I hissed out a sharp and cranky breath—

And, breathing back in, I felt the brilliant light of this sun-blighted afternoon slide its way down the spectrum to a cool and deadly violet, felt the worry and the flutters drop away and drown in the bloom-ing shadows, and very slowly-happily felt all things workaday worrisome slump into the trash can and all the wonderful steady readiness of the Dark Passenger's icy calm rise up from the Dexter Deep and slither snugly into place to take control of this sun-dark day. . . .

And we are ready.

And we know what to do, and how to do it, and we know that somehow it will work.

And so we begin to do it.

We move slowly toward the drooling dolt in the kayak, one hand on the throttle, feeling the purr of ready power there, and the answering rumble of the much greater power idling just below the surface of the happy boater's smile we have tacked onto our face. *Closer* . . .

Not close enough, not yet. He does not notice us yet, does not look up, does not look away. He does nothing but lounge there, leaning back in his yellow plastic boat, staring intently in toward the dock as if this is all there is to the world and there could not possibly be some deadly slithering Something sliding toward him with such icy glee.

He stares unaware, watching only the dock, where a buzz of joy floats out at us across the water—a joy that should not be there in the presence of that clumsy horror in the Dumpster, a joy that should only be our quiet reward in this sunny midnight, and one small flicker of a glance tells us that Jackie has arrived and the crowd has forgotten all about why they have gathered and can think only about her golden presence, and my unsuspecting playmate is no different, no more aware than his kayak that we are only a handful of heartbeats from uncoiling onto his slack-jawed doze and taking him far away out of the bright warm sunshine and into the deep cold dark forever—

*Closer* . . .

And he looks up at last; some small tick or whir of the engine alerts him that we are oh so very near, and he turns to gape at us, and there is the face from Facebook, with its secret smirk of look-what-I-done, and he stares without seeing for only a moment, and then he turns away to focus again on the golden-haired woman on the dock, thinking once more his hungry thoughts and having no tiny flicker of a clue that Something much hungrier is here to gobble him up.

*Closer* . . .

And he looks at us again, and this time we are a little too close to be just casual passing traffic, and a frown creases his face, a frown that turns slowly, delightfully, into alarm—does he recognize this face we wear? Does he know us and realize at last that we have come for him, come to stop his clumsy fun and end his lethal bumbling and finish him altogether?

Perhaps he does; he lurches upright, clutching at his paddle as if it can save him from what is coming, what will soon happen, what *must* happen to him, and he digs the blades of the paddle into the water very hard—left, left, left, and right, as he spins the boat away in a growing panic that is very rewarding to watch. What does he imagine is coming for him? Arrest? Imprisonment? The mighty Hand of Justice? A steely handcuff and a stern reading of his rights, and then a long slow wait in a series of small and smelly rooms with iron bars on doors and windows?

Would he paddle away any faster if he knew that there was no iron-barred room, no handcuffs, and no arrest churning happily along in his wake? That the only justice for him will be the final kind, from the High Court of Pain, and his rights are limited to only one: He has the right to shuffle off his mortal coil and spin away into the Dark Forever, and there is no appeal, no parole, and no way out at all.

Because we are on him, no matter how rapidly he paddles. We are right there with him, quite content to take our time and watch him splash his paddles in and out of the water so very earnestly. Left, right, left, right—faster and faster. For him it is a sprint, a race to safety at truly dizzying speed, very fast indeed—for a kayak.

Not for our motorboat.

To us, with our hand on the throttle, it is an amusement, a toying with the mouse before our claws come out, and we stay with him, ever so slightly easing up closer and closer—

He is really moving very well now, digging the paddle blades into the water with a good and rapid rhythm, and glancing back to see us smiling calmly, happily slipping only a tiny bit closer, and closer, and he tries, he really does try hard, to make his little yellow boat into a wonder of speed; jaw clamped tight, veins bulging in his face and arms, he tries so hard, so valiantly, as if mere sincere effort can outrun the laws of nature, and we are so very impressed at his labors that we nearly pause and applaud.

But he is around that last barrier island now, and he is angling in toward the park onshore and quite possible escape, and he can almost taste it now, almost feel the thrill of getting away, leaping up onto the seawall and off into freedom, his hard-earned getaway from the strangely sluggish pursuer who still idles along behind him, slow and smiling, and perhaps there is a small space in his panic where he begins to wonder why.

Why do we move so slowly closer? Why don't we pounce, or shout, or shoot? Why do we simply smile, and smile, and be a villain, and ease so slightly closer a little bit at a time?

Why indeed? He does not yet know, can't hope to know, but it is really very simple. Too simple for this senseless simpleton.

We are smiling because we are happy.

And we are happy because we have been waiting for him to do just exactly this, and now he has done it for us, just as if he had studied his part in our Dark Script, and he has done all the right things just right and the time is now.

Now, when he has finally fled to the far side of the little island; now, when he is away at last from the boat basin, invisible at last to the rows of yachts, shielded from sight by the island, hidden from the dock with its crowd of cops and gawkers, and still half a mile from shore. Now, when everything is as perfectly Just Right as it can ever be and all our joyful gleaming readiness is poised and polished and ready to spring into this perfect moment—

*Now.*

And our hand flexes forward on the throttle, and the growl of our happiness swells up with the growing roar of the engine, and our boat surges forward—not too fast, but fast enough, faster than any kayak, no matter how panicked its paddler.

And he has time for no more than one startled strangled yelp of complaint, an abrupt yodel of protest that this could possibly happen to wonderful *him*, and then it has already happened. Our boat thumps the side of the kayak, thumps it hard, with all the force of our weight and greater speed, and all the wicked need that holds the wheel and still smiles, smiles even wider now, with a true delight at the lovely things that are finally happening to the ignorant and well-deserving clot in the kayak.

But he is not in the kayak, not now, not anymore. Now he is in the water and flailing away, grabbing for something that floats, or something that makes sense, and there is nothing there of either kind for him to latch onto. The kayak is already scudding away, far out of reach and upside down, and the shore is even farther away, and only one small fishing boat with a cheerfully smiling captain is anywhere in his sight. And so he flounders there in the water, and coughs and splashes, and he yells out, "What the fuck!" and we circle carefully around and slowly crawl between him and the shore.

"Sorry!" we call out, with perfect insincerity. "Didn't see you!"

And he splashes some more, but then he slows down his epic struggles, because it makes no sense that we really did hit him like that on purpose, and he is in the water right here in the sunlight, and in any case we are smiling and saying sorry and there is truly nowhere to go. So he treads water as we creep up to him, glaring up at us with suspicion and resentment, and he shouts again. "Fucking douche!" he yells, and there is a very broad smear of Tennessee on his words. "You seen me fine!"

"Sorry!" we say again, and we reach down beside us, under the gunwale, to the boat hook where it nestles in its clamps, and we pry it out and hold it up. "Grab onto this!" we call cheerfully. "We'll pull you out!"

He blinks and stares at the boat hook as it drifts closer to his face. "Who's *we*?"

It is *Us*, of course, the Dark We, the not-quite-visible but oh so very strong and cunning We of the shadowed inside smile, the happy wicked smile that spreads outward from the cold core and onto the mask of bright dopiness we wear to hide the razor teeth—but we do not tell him this; we do not tell him he is outnumbered by no more than this very real, very happy smile—we say instead no more than, "Grab the hook!" and add a cheerful, "Oops!" as the boat hook purposely-accidentally thumps against his temple. One small and careful thump, beautifully crafted to look like a mishap and perfectly calculated to stun him just enough so that for one weak and gargled moment it all goes ever-so-slightly dim for him and he breathes water.

"Sorry!" we call as he sputters back to dizzy wide-eyed panic. "Grab the boat hook!" we yell, more frightful urgency in our voice as we drift slowly away from where he flails at the endless deep that will soon be his home.

And he lunges for the boat hook, a wild and gratifying surge of panic that lifts him up and out of the water just enough so he can clamp both frantic hands onto the shaft of the boat hook.

"Great!" we call with gleeful relief—because we have him now. We have hooked our fish, set the barb unshakably into the soft flesh of his drooling gape, and so we reel him in, pulling him close and up to the side of the boat. And we haul our catch upward to where he can slap both hands onto the gunwale and let go of the pole, and we drop the boat hook to kneel on the deck and apparently offer him our left hand to help him onward, upward, into the boat.

Our left hand only, but he takes it and we pull him slightly higher. And still all unaware and dizzy and dripping wet, he dangles there half in the water and half out, just as he is now, in this perfect, wonderful, hurried, unplanned moment, already dangling half out of life.

He holds our left hand, balanced there between everything and nothing, and we hold him right there, our faces close together. Our left hand only, and he looks for our right hand to lift him out completely and he does not see it, and he looks back at us with a confusion that is tinged with anger, alarm, and desperation.

"What the fuck?" he says.

And the moment is here—the moment we have waited for, and planned for far too briefly, and we hesitate because it is not right. We have not proved his guilt, not Harry-sure, and we have not truly planned, and for just a moment we pause, bobbing in an uncertain boat on a sea of doubt.

And Patrick sees this, too, and sees that whatever might be happening, it is not what he thinks should be happening, and with his face so close to ours we can see that he is gathering himself for some purposeful thing, some sudden lunge or leap, and as ever-grateful always, just in the nick, we know exactly what to do.

"Jackie Forrest," we say.

And it works, as it always does. Patrick freezes. For a moment he forgets to breathe, and that is a shame, because his breaths are numbered now and it is a very small number. And he stares back at us, so very near, and we watch his eyes—watch and truly feel a fond and warm regard for this savage bumbler. Because we always need the Harry Proof to earn these moments of wonder and bliss, and we have nothing like that proof this time—and Patrick has come to our rescue.

We watch him, and the look that climbs up into his bright and stupid eyes is everything we need. Just from the four syllables of that name, Jackie Forrest, everything he has done and planned to do is there in his eyes, a parade of pictures as full of guilt as a twenty-page confession. He did it, beyond question; this look could not lie. It is certainly and doubtlessly him, and without waiting for any kind of no-I-didn't we bring up our right hand, the hand that has waited so patiently just out of sight, and we slide in the knife that has hovered there hoping for just this moment, slip in the blade once and carefully into just the right spot, and Patrick stiffens, gasps, and stares at us as he feels the knife go in and suddenly, terribly knows what is happening. And we watch the slow and fragile beauty of that moment as it flickers across the tiny twin screens of his pale blue eyes: the moment of indignant denial that this could ever happen to special precious *me*, then the bright bloom of world-ending agony as he knows that *yes, it can* and then *yes, it has* as the careful beat of the bioclock ticks one more time and then suddenly, unthinkably, stops. . . .

And then the most beautiful moment of all, as that thought swims away forever, that thought and all others, paddling off with every single trace of all that is *Me*; they swim away in a whirl of dark water, away from the small and pointless lump of meat and purpose that was Patrick and into the surging tide of blank and thoughtless night that has no end, away from everything he ever thought or ever was or ever wanted to be, away from the tiny bright shore that was life and into the rapid endless whirlpool of Nevermore.

And we watch and marvel as even that final flicker fades into the dim distance and the ever-same film of emptiness slides over the now-empty eyes. And the thing we are holding, the thing that was Patrick, lady-killer, alive with bright and boundless energy—that thing is now no more than an empty box, an unlovely container that will rot and fall apart faster than cheap cardboard in the rain, and as we see those eyes go dull we are truly moved, as we always are: moved, transported, lifted up for such a bright and rapid moment—

and then dropped down again, drained, emptied of everything that matters, and as close to happy as we can ever be.

It is done. We have done it and it is over.

And now the colors of the day wash upward, into the brighter end of the spectrum where they belong, and the hard dark blade of doing it melts back once more into snug and tired satisfaction of a job well done, and I pull the clumsy, empty thing the rest of the way up, over the gunwale, and onto the deck. I leave it lying there and take the boat's controls, motoring slowly away from the shore in the suddenly too-bright, too-empty afternoon.

# TWENTY

I T WAS ANOTHER HALF AN HOUR BEFORE I GOT PATRICK TUCKED snugly away in the nearest deep hole, with a large anchor securely wired to his legs. I always have an extra anchor; they come in so handy, in so many common boating situations. I like to pick them up at garage sales whenever I can, because you never know when you might need to set out an extra anchor, or give aid to a distressed fellow mariner, or hide a freshly killed body. It was a good heavy Danforth storm anchor, and I was confident it would hold him down there until the crabs had eaten him away to the bare bones. And if he did somehow bob up to the surface, it would be at some time in the future when Dexter was far away and completely innocent, and they could never trace the anchor, nor connect me to the unrecognizable fish-nibbled body, to whom I had never, after all, been formally introduced.

And it may well be that I should not have felt so very good about my strange sunlit interlude. It had been done much too quickly, and it had been done with a terribly clumsy tool, and worse, it had been done without any of my So Very Important rituals—but it had been done, and Jackie was safe, and I was now free to reap the bounty of my diligent labors. I could relax in luxury without a care, enjoying mojitos, tournedos, and sunsets over the bay, with never a care. Patrick was gone for good.

And I did not worry about anyone finding his body. It was well hidden, I could never be connected to it, and all was roses and rainbows in Dexterville. I was so wrapped up in my afterglow of complete contentment that I did not worry about anything at all, in fact, until I had cruised back up the canal to the dock—very slowly this time, earning me a grumpy nod from the shirtless old man. It was not until I had tied off the boat and started to trudge across the lawn toward my car that I glanced at my watch—and then, at last, I began to worry.

The short hand was pointing to the three and the long one to eleven, and it took only a moment of brilliant detective work to realize that it meant the time was five minutes of three, and I was going to be late to my alibi.

I hurried to my car and drove away down the little street in a way that no self-respecting shirtless old man could ever approve. Happily, no one was out on the street to see me, and in only a few minutes I was out onto Main Highway, over to Douglas, and then turning left on Dixie Highway.

Traffic was not heavy, but it was still another twenty minutes before I pulled into a space in the school parking lot. I went as quickly as I could without running, up the sidewalk and into the main office, where I signed the guest register, slapped a VISITOR sticker on my shirt, and hurried away down the hall to Cody's classroom.

Cody's teacher this year was a relentlessly cheerful middle-aged woman named Mrs. Hornberger. She was sitting at her desk when I came in, with Cody and Rita sitting in front of her, like two bad children called up before the class. The three of them looked up at me when I walked in; Cody very nearly smiled, Mrs. Hornberger raised an inquiring eyebrow, and Rita, without even taking a breath, immediately opened fire.

"Oh, Dexter, for the love of— It's twenty minutes past, and you didn't even call—really, this is just—"

"Sorry I'm late," I said. No one offered me a chair, so I dragged one of the student desks over next to Cody and squeezed into it. "How bad is it?" I whispered to Cody, and he shrugged at me.

"Okay," he said softly. Of course, he would have said exactly the same thing if the teacher had set them both on fire. I had to admit, Cody did have a slight problem in the area of communication. The trauma caused by his biological father, a mean crackhead who used to beat him and Astor until he was finally tucked away in prison, had made Cody exceptionally silent. What his father's savagery had done to Astor was not quite as clear, unless severe crabbiness is trauma-induced.

But Bio Dad's beatings had also slammed Cody out of the world of sunshine forever, into the cool dusk where the predators live. It had made him into my true heir, the Crown Prince of the Dexter Dark, eagerly awaiting my training so he could take his rightful place on the Shadow Throne. I was fairly sure the meeting today would not touch on that part of Cody's education.

"Mr. Morgan," Mrs. Hornberger said sternly. All eyes automatically swiveled to her, and even Rita stopped talking. Mrs. Hornberger looked at us each individually, to make sure we were all paying attention. Then the smile came back to her face, and everyone breathed again. "We were discussing Cody's . . . *conceptual* difficulties . . . with socialization."

"Oh," I said, and because I had no idea what else to say, I added, "Yes, of course," and she nodded at me approvingly.

And then we were off in search of Arriving at Meaningful Accommodation in a Context of Achieving Appropriate and Symmetrical Social and Educational Goals, stopping along the way to fondle every New Age–Feel Good buzzword ever coined. It was every bit as torturous as I had feared it would be, and it was clearly much worse for Cody. He could understand only one word in every four, and he squirmed and squeezed his hands together and moved his legs back and forth, and after only ten minutes he had taken fidgeting to dizzying new heights.

Rita followed every word that fell from Mrs. Hornberger's lips with breathless concentration, her brow furrowed with worry. She would interrupt now and then with one of her fragmented sentences, ending with a question mark. Mrs. Hornberger would nod as if she actually understood, and slide another cliché out of the arsenal, and

Rita would nod eagerly and go back to scrunching her face into a mask of concern.

I watched her face squeeze into its wrinkled mask, and I marveled again at how old Rita looked all of a sudden. The worry lines in her forehead seemed permanent, and they were matched by others around her mouth. Beyond that, her skin had lost color and seemed to be fading into a pale, sagging, raised relief map of some desert. Was it merely worry over Cody, or had she actually gotten as old as she looked? We were the same age—did that mean that I was getting old, too? It didn't show when I looked in the mirror—at least, not to me. Perhaps I was blind to what I really looked like and I, too, was beginning to wrinkle and blanch. I hoped not; I had a great number of important things left to do yet, and I did not want to look like a pallid walking raisin while I did them.

It is strange where the mind wanders when it is being assaulted with earnest and needless platitudes. I am quite sure I should have felt more sympathy for Rita, more empathy with Cody, and more admiration for Mrs. Hornberger's wonderful command of multisyllabic educational inanity. But I didn't; all I really felt was teeth-grinding annoyance at the Ordeal by Jargon, and faint repugnance at Rita's sudden vault into visible old age—and mild alarm at the thought that I might be sliding into senescence, too.

By the time half an hour had slogged by, I had lost every glimmer of the contentment that had so recently lit up my life and I was beginning to fidget almost as much as Cody. But it was another fifteen minutes before Mrs. Hornberger finally marched to her triumphant conclusion—Social Goals must be Integrated into an Individually Tailored Plan for Cooperative Learning, with a Full Commitment to Successful Goal Attainment at Home and at School, on Individual and Institutional Levels—and I could finally stagger weakly from the classroom, clutching my fevered brow and yearning, surprisingly but powerfully, for a cold mojito with Jackie.

I walked with Rita and Cody all the way to her car, where we paused to allow her to finish a sentence. And then she looked at me with that same faceful of worry wrinkles, and said, "Dexter—are you really . . . ? Because I mean, I don't know."

"Absolutely," I said. Surprisingly enough, I understood her, or at least I thought I did. "And I really will be home in a few days, with enough money for a brand-new pool cage." And as I said it, I felt regret stirring; was it really only a few more days?

"Well," she said. "But it's just— I only . . ." She fluttered both hands helplessly. "It would be nice if you— You really can't even tell me what you're doing?"

I opened my mouth to tell her that no, I couldn't really—and then I remembered that yes, I sort of had to, in a way: captain's orders. "Um," I said, not really sure where to begin. I suddenly felt a little bit like a kid asking permission to have a cookie after eating all but one, and I didn't know why. There was no reason for me to feel guilty or uneasy; I had done exactly what I was supposed to do, and all for the noblest motive of all—a pool cage. So I shrugged it off as a hangover from Mrs. Hornberger's tirade and plunged right into it.

"There's a TV show shooting in town," I said, and Rita lit up like a birthday cake and took off into breathless response.

"Oh!" she said. "Yes, it was in the paper? And they said that Jackie Forrest— Did you know she's thirty-three? I don't think she looks it, but of course she must have had a lot of— And Robert Chase! He is *so* handsome, but he hasn't done anything in practically— Is that what you— Oh, my God, Dexter, has something horrible happened to Robert Chase?"

"Not yet," I said, fighting to keep the regret out of my voice. "But the point is, Captain Matthews assigned me to be a technical adviser to the show. And, you know, teach Robert about what I do."

"Oh. My. *God!*" Rita said. "You've actually *met*— Dexter, I can't believe it— I mean, this is just amazing!"

"It's just more work," I said, and I admit I was a little irritated at seeing Rita so excited over the mere idea of Robert Chase. "Anyway," I said, hoping I could get the whole thing out without another of Rita's verbal frenzies, "there's another guy in the cast, a comedian, Renny Boudreaux?"

"Yes, he's very good," Rita said very seriously. "He uses some words that— And you met him, too?"

"Yes," I said. "And he's taping a special Saturday night. And the captain wants me to go."

"*Wants* you to go?" she said. "That doesn't make any— And why wouldn't you want to go anyway? Because—"

"He thinks it's good for the department's image," I said. "To show cops and the stars all together. And so I have two tickets—"

"Ohmygod ohmygod ohmy*god*!" Rita said. "Really? Oh, Dexter, oh, my God! This is *amazing*— But I can't possibly get a sitter in time!"

It took another five minutes to get Rita calmed down enough to utter a coherent agreement to meet me at seven thirty in the lobby of the Gusman Saturday night, and I found myself growing increasingly anxious for my mojito. It was very odd; I have never been a drinker, and I was pretty sure I hadn't turned into one overnight— and certainly not enough of a drinker to get the shakes when five o'clock approached without my usual dose. But I could almost taste the cool drink sliding over my tongue and down my throat, almost see Jackie looking at me over the rim of her dew-beaded glass, her large violet eyes alive with amusement at something I hadn't said yet, and I felt myself growing increasingly irritated with Rita's high-speed dithering.

And dither she did: She babbled reverentially about Jackie, and actually giggled over Robert, and tossed in several disjointed compliments to Renny and how smart he seemed, even though he *did* use some very rough language. And then she slid into a totally paralyzed frenzy because she didn't have anything at all that she could possibly wear—although I knew for a fact that her closet was overflowing with clothing—and how could I possibly expect her to appear in the same room with someone like Jackie Forrest . . . !

I'd had no notion that Rita actually knew anything about TV stars, and even less idea that she actually cared, that she would be impressed to the point of girlish incoherence at the thought of meeting Robert Chase, and seeing Jackie Forrest in a fancy dress. I mean, I sat on the couch beside Rita every night, and we did watch TV together—but to see her collapse into a kind of babbling hero worship because she was going to see Renny's show, and might even breathe the same air as Robert Chase! It was a side of her I had never even seen a hint of before, and I wasn't really sure what to do with it now.

But happily, even Rita needs to breathe every now and then, and when she finally paused to do so, I jumped in quickly and firmly.

"Rita, I have to get back," I said. "You will be there on Saturday?"

"Of course I'll be— I mean, I'll have to find some kind of dress *somewhere*, and I don't have any idea—maybe Nancy's daughter, Terri? But she's in marching band, so I don't know—"

"You don't really need to wear anything fancy," I said. "I'm not even wearing a tie."

"Dexter, I'm going to be on TV! With Jackie Forrest! Of course I have to wear something— Oh, honest to God, you don't have any idea— Maybe I could still fit into that thing from Key West? You know, that you said looked like a nightgown?"

"Perfect," I said. "I'll meet you in the lobby at seven thirty."

"Yes, of course," she said. "But I really don't know—"

I leaned in and gave her a peck on the cheek. "Bye," I said. "I'll see you Saturday."

Rita pecked me back, and I turned to go at last.

"Dexter," she called after me, and I sighed and turned back to her.

She opened her mouth to say something, and then didn't say it. For a long moment she didn't say anything at all, just looked at me, and I wondered what had derailed her frenzy. I was finally about to speak myself when she said, "It's just that . . . Do you have clean clothes?"

"Socks *and* underwear," I said.

"And a decent shirt to wear to this thing?"

"Yes," I said, extremely puzzled at the paradigm shift. "A nice guayabera."

Rita nodded, still looking at me intently. "Because it's just . . ." She fluttered one hand, like a small bird with a broken wing, and looked at Cody, then back to me. "I miss you," she said. "We all do."

"Me, too," Cody said in his husky, too-quiet voice.

I blinked at the two of them with surprise bordering on shock. Not merely because the thought of my laundry led Rita directly to saying she missed me. I found it shocking that she missed me at all. And Cody, too? Why? I know exactly what I am—although happily, no one else seems to—and what I am is no great prize, unless we are now awarding medals for inspired vivisection. And so to hear her say they all *missed* me? What did that mean? Why would anyone miss me? All I did was come home for meals, sit on the couch for an hour or two, and go to bed. Why would anyone miss that?

It was a wonderful conundrum of human behavior, the kind that I had been puzzling over my entire life, and ordinarily it would have been fun to mull it over for a while. But Rita was looking at me expectantly, and years of studying how people act, mostly on daytime dramas, has taught me to recognize a cue when I hear one. So I gave Rita a warm synthetic smile and said, "I miss you, too. But it's just a few more days. And," I added when her face stayed locked into that same worried look, "we really do need the money."

It took her several moments, but Rita finally nodded and said, "Well, yes. But it's just—you know." I didn't know, and she didn't tell me. She just shrugged and said, "All right then." She walked the three steps to me, then leaned in, and I gave her a small kiss on the cheek. I looked at Cody, who was watching with his usual alert stoicism. "Relax," I told him. "I'm not going to kiss you."

"Thanks," he said.

"And I'll see you in a couple of days," I said. "Remember to Visualize your Procedural Templates."

Cody made a horrible face and shook his head. "Yuck," he said, and I have to admit we were in complete agreement.

I turned away again and Rita called after me, "Dexter—just call a few— I mean, if it's not too much?"

"All right," I said, seeing the mojito floating in front of me in the air. "I'll call."

It was just past four o'clock. Traffic was beginning to slow with the start of rush hour, and the steady lines of cars were squeezing together, coagulating into loud, angry knots and beginning to form a motionless scab on the highways. It took me most of an hour to work my way through the snarls and get back to my office, and along the way I had plenty of time to reflect on what had been, after all, a very full day. Even though the teacher conference had washed away the afterglow of my encounter with Patrick, I felt no worry and no regret. No one would miss him, and it had been far quicker than he deserved.

Jackie's Town Car was waiting outside headquarters, motor running, when I finally got back. The driver was leaning against the front fender, smoking a cigarette, and he waved to me as I approached. I stepped over to the car, and the rear window slid down.

Jackie looked out at me with a smile that was small, but somehow made me feel like everything was going to be all right. "Hey, sailor," she said. "Would you like a lift?" And the smile got just a little bit wider as she said, "I think it's mojito time."

I thought so, too. I got in the car.

# TWENTY-ONE

ATURDAY MORNING JACKIE SLEPT LATE. I AM AN EARLY RISER, and in any case it's hard to drowse in bed half asleep when you're on the couch in a luxury hotel. So I was up at seven, and sitting on the balcony with breakfast by seven fifteen. The sun came up right on time, just the way it did on weekdays, but I tried to work through my meal a little slower, in honor of the weekend.

Far out over the water a flock of boats moved by, heading south to the Keys, or east to Bimini, the Gulf Stream, and even beyond. A large sportfisher went roaring right over the deep spot where I had put Patrick, kicking up a high rooster tail in its wake. I wondered whether it would make enough turbulence to rip him free of his anchor; perhaps he would shoot up to the surface like a nightmare cork, and bob along behind the speeding boat, all the way to the Bahamas.

Probably not. And if he did, I doubted that the big cruiser would slow down, not with marlin and sailfish waiting.

I sipped my fresh-squeezed orange juice. It was very good. So were my Belgian waffles, and the bacon was cooked just right: crisp without being dry. And the fruit on the side was excellent, too, maybe the best I'd ever had—except at breakfast yesterday. And the day before. It didn't taste like the fruit normal people can get in the supermarket, which always seems diluted, like it has been shot full of water to make it bigger and brighter. This stuff actually had real flavor. It tasted just like you always think fruit ought to taste, but never does.

I sipped. It really was wonderful to be me, at least for the time being. I wondered if you ever got used to this kind of thing, jaded enough to call the waiter and send it all back if a pear slice had a blemish. I didn't think I would, but who knew? Living this way changed people, and perhaps I would eventually turn into a self-centered dolt—like Robert, for instance. He couldn't possibly have started out in life the way he was now, or his parents would have strangled him in his cradle.

So maybe I would change, too, after a couple of years of penthouse living. Of course, we would never know; this was all ending soon, far too soon, and I would be back to the world of bruised pears and watery-tasting apples. Sad, depressing, and inevitable—but why let the future ruin the present? For the moment, life was good. I was alive, and Patrick wasn't, and I still had two strips of bacon left, and most of the fruit.

By seven forty-one I had eaten the last piece of perfectly ripe cantaloupe, pushed the plate away, and refilled my coffee cup. I had tried, but I really couldn't make the meal last any longer without moving in slow motion. So I sipped my coffee and just sat there in the sunshine waiting for Jackie. In spite of the coffee, the size of the meal and the sun on my face made me feel a little drowsy, lazy, like a large and well-fed lizard on a rock.

By eight thirty I was saturated with coffee, and filling up with impatience. There was not even anything to be impatient about; it was Saturday, after all, and I knew of nothing urgent going on anywhere that required my presence. Even so, it made me nervous to sit there and do nothing. I suppose it seems a bit much to complain about having nothing to do except sit on the penthouse balcony and drink coffee. There are worse fates, after all—I have personally delivered many of them. But the truth is, I felt ignored, even slighted, and I wanted Jackie to spring out of bed and run to me so I could protect her—doubly stupid, since I knew very well that there was nothing left to protect her from.

But it was eight forty-two before she finally made her appearance, and it was not so much a spring-and-run as it was a stumble-and-trudge. She fell into the chair opposite me as heavily as if she had been dropped from the roof, and she stared at me for several seconds before she remembered how to speak.

"Guh mornuh," she said, in a voice that was somewhere between a croak and a rasp. She cleared her throat, then closed her eyes, swaying slightly. "Coffee," she said, and if a growl can sound both demanding and plaintive, hers did. I stared at her; her face looked puffy, rumpled, and her hair was scruffy and unbrushed.

She opened one bleary eye. "Please," she croaked.

I reached for the coffeepot and she closed her one eye again. I filled a cup and put it in front of her, and when she didn't move, I leaned over, took her hand, and placed it on the handle of the cup. Still without opening her eyes, she drained the cup and held it out toward me. "More," she growled.

I refilled her cup. She drank this one a lot slower, and about half-way through it her face began to shrink back to its normal shape, and then she opened her eyes. They were violet again, and most of the red was gone from them. She finished the cup, refilled it herself this time, and sipped slowly.

"Sorry," she said after a few minutes. Her voice was still a bit raspy, and she cleared her throat. "I couldn't sleep last night," she said, and she sounded nearly human again. "So I had a few shots of dark rum." She shrugged. "Okay, more than a few. Anyway, it didn't work. So I took a couple of sleeping pills." Jackie closed her eyes and shook her head slowly. "Boy, oh, boy, did *that* work," she said. "I think I almost pulled a Marilyn."

"A what?" I said.

"Monroe," she said with a very small smile. "You know, screen goddess takes fatal overdose. Oh, my head."

"Do you want some aspirin?"

"I took four or five," she said. "They'll kick in in a minute." She pursed her lips and sighed heavily. "It's this guy. The stalker. Patrick Whatsit."

"Bergmann," I said helpfully.

"Yeah," she said. "I just kept thinking, He's out there, probably watching me right now, maybe sneaking into the hotel and picking the lock on my door. . . ."

For half a moment, I toyed with the idea of telling her that Patrick was not sneaking into anything except possibly decomposition. And in a rational world, why wouldn't I? What reasonable person could object to the removal of a brutal killer who did appalling things to human beings and liked doing them? But on sober reflection, it occurred to me that if I told her, Jackie might realize that this was an apt description for me, too, so it might not be a good idea to tell her. And after all, rotting flesh was hardly a suitable topic of conversation for the breakfast table. So I settled for more pedestrian reassurance. "There's a chain on the door," I said. "And a heavily armed and deadly Dexter on the couch."

She cleared her throat again. "I know, but this is last night, in the dark. Everything is bigger and meaner in the dark."

Of course, she was right about that, but instead of telling her so I just nodded, and she went on.

"And then I started thinking about what you had said, about how he might drop down from the roof on a clothesline, and I swear I could hear him scrabbling at the window. I'd jump up and look, and . . ." She shook her head and smiled sadly at her last-night self. "Pretty dumb, right?"

"Well," I said.

"Yeah, thanks, you don't have to agree with me." She sighed, and then eyed the large platter on the table with its silver cover. "Is that breakfast?"

"Your usual," I said.

Jackie lifted the silver lid and stared at the meager scraps of food on the plate underneath. She closed her eyes, dropped the cover, and leaned away from it. "I think I need something a little bit more substantial this morning," she said, and she stood up. "I'll call down for some eggs."

"The bacon is very good, too," I said.

Jackie's breakfast arrived so quickly they might have cooked it in the hall outside our room, and she tore into it like she hadn't eaten for a week—which she hadn't, as far as I could tell. The few miserable morsels of stuff she usually nibbled at didn't really count, in my opinion, and it was a strange kind of relief to see her eating something that actually qualified as food. Even better, she left two strips of bacon on her plate. They looked terribly lonely, so I quickly gave them a good home.

And since the waiter had left us a fresh pot of coffee, we both filled our cups, and then, almost in unison, we sipped and sat back.

"Better," Jackie said. "Much, much better."

And it was; she looked almost superhuman again. Color and shape had come back into her face. Her cheekbones had emerged from the haze, and her eyes looked clear and bright and very violet once more.

For a minute or two we just slurped our coffee in comfortable silence. I didn't feel any pressure to say clever and interesting things, and apparently neither did Jackie. Our reverie was finally shattered by the sound of the house phone, clamoring for attention. She jerked up to her feet, muttered, "Shit," and stepped back in through the sliding glass door to answer it.

She came back a moment later, frowning. "Kathy," she said. "They want to see me in wardrobe. She's going to meet us over there."

"But it's Saturday," I said. "I mean, don't people take the day off?"

Jackie shook her head with a smile that said I had a lot to learn. "We start shooting Monday morning, Dexter," she said. "The wardrobe and makeup people have tons of last-minute things to do, and they need us there to do them."

"Oh," I said, and with an effort I put on my bodyguard hat. "Will the Town Car be here to take us over?"

She nodded and sat down, reaching for her cup. "It'll be in front in ten minutes," she said. She drained the cup, put it on the table, and said, "I better get ready." But before she could stand up, her cell phone chimed. She shook her head and said, "It never ends." But when she picked it up and looked at the screen, she said, "Oh," with surprise. "It's your sister." She touched the screen and held the phone up to her ear.

"Good morning, Sergeant," she said. "No, I've already had breakfast." She glanced at me with amusement. "Of course. He even finished mine. . . . I know, he must have a high metabolism, because . . ."

It's always nice to know people are talking about you, but from the smirks Jackie sent my way, it might not have been the most flattering conversation. But short of snarling and ripping the phone from Jackie's hand, there was nothing I could do but endure, so I did, and the talk apparently changed to some other topic right after.

"Really," Jackie said. "On your day off? . . . I know; that's why I've tried to avoid it. . . . No . . . No, I have to go for a fitting. . . . A *costume* fitting. For the show . . . You did know we start shooting Monday? . . . Oh, good, because . . ."

She glanced at me again, this time with something else in her eyes—challenge? Speculation? I couldn't be sure. Her tongue poked out between her lips, and her mouth twitched as if she was trying to fight off a mischievous impulse and not succeeding. "Sure, why not?" she said. "It's a great idea; they'll love it. . . . Well, I don't mind. . . . No, she's a little bit of a witch, but I think it's okay. . . . I'll make *sure* it's okay. . . . Sure, that will be great. Bye." She touched the screen again and put the phone down. "Your sister," she said, quite unnecessarily.

"I know," I said. "How am I?"

But Jackie was already on her feet and rushing away. "I have to get ready," she called over one shoulder, and then she was gone, wafting herself away into the murky mysteries of makeup, hair, and whatever else it is that women do when they Get Ready.

Ten minutes later the doorman called on the house phone to tell me the car was here, and only two or three minutes after that, we were in the elevator and heading down to the lobby. Benny, the doorman, had finally taken a day off, and his replacement waited by the door for us, staring at Jackie with visible tension, mixed with awe.

Even though there was no actual need for it, I went through my routine of stepping outside and looking around. Everything seemed fine. There was no sign of soaking-wet, barnacle-encrusted stalker anywhere. The Corniche still looked expensive.

The driver in the Town Car was the same man, which seemed a little surprising. I opened the front door and stuck my head in. "Don't you get weekends off?"

"Not if I'm driving Jackie Forrest," he said. Then he winked at me. "Besides, I get double time."

As a fellow workingman, I was very happy for him, and I closed the door and went to get Jackie. I wondered whether I was getting double time. It occurred to me that we had never discussed an actual price for my services, and I wondered how I could bring that up without sounding mercenary. Of course, I actually *was* mercenary—more than that, with Patrick tucked into his watery grave, I was technically a contract killer now, which seemed just about as mercenary as you can get. I hadn't thought of it like that before, and I did now; it seemed unimaginable that I had killed for money. I hadn't done so on purpose—I had killed Patrick so I could relax for a few days and enjoy the life of a Celebrity Companion.

Of course, that made it seem even worse: I had killed for room service. What a terrible, low creature I was. I wondered whether I should feel cheap and tawdry, or perhaps just jaded and callous. How much lower could I sink? I was already indifferent to the suffering of my victims, so I couldn't really try to make that fit a new and colder me, if there actually was one.

I didn't think I was any different, but you are always the last to know when you have changed for the worse. Perhaps the new me was already a monster of ego and indifference. What next? Would I lose my table manners, or stop tipping in restaurants? But in the short walk back to the hotel's lobby, I couldn't really work out any details about how this new thing should make me act, so I decided not to worry about it, and I went back to wondering how I could bring the topic of Disbursement for Dexter to Jackie's attention.

By the time I handed Jackie into the backseat of the Town Car, I still hadn't come up with anything that didn't seem confrontational or boorish. So I shelved the topic for the time being and settled back to enjoy the ride.

We rolled across town through light traffic, mostly keeping our thoughts to ourselves. Several times I caught Jackie looking at me with what could only be called a secret smirk, and while it's nice to be the target of other people's happiness, I didn't get any joy from her barely suppressed amusement—especially since I had no idea what was causing it.

The crew, and most of the lesser cast members, had been put up in the Hyatt Regency downtown. It was a quick drive on a Saturday morning, and we pulled into the short circular driveway in front of

the hotel only fifteen minutes later. Once again I got out and panto-
mimed eternal vigilance, looking all around for any sign of a lurking
Patrick. I didn't see any trace of him, which was bad news for zombie
lovers, and I reached into the car and gave Jackie a hand out.

Wardrobe had a suite on the twenty-fourth floor, and we stepped
into an elevator filled with three businessmen, complete with gray
suits and briefcases, which seemed like overkill on a Saturday morning. Maybe there was a board meeting at their church. The door
slid shut, and one of them glanced importantly in our direction. He
looked away haughtily, and then did a double take. "Holy shit, Jackie
Forrest?!" he blurted out, and the other two gave a start and then
gaped at us, too.

Jackie smiled graciously and did her part, the noblesse oblige she
had talked about. I almost wished she'd been rude to them, since I
had to hold the elevator door open for a long minute while she signed
one of the briefcases with a Magic Marker. There were distant chimes,
indicating that somebody else wanted the elevator, and the door kept
thumping me as it tried to close and answer the call.

But finally, Jackie tore herself away from her adoring public and
stepped out onto the twenty-fourth floor, and as the doors slid shut
I heard the autograph hound excitedly saying to the others, "Hot
damn, what an amazing piece of—" And then, happily, the doors slid
shut on the last word, leaving me to guess what Jackie was an amazing piece of, and we fled down the hall to the suite where Wardrobe
had set up shop.

Stepping into the suite was like finding yourself in a beehive
the moment after someone has whacked it with a stick. In the eye of
the storm, a tall woman of indeterminate age stood commandingly
beside a dress dummy. Robert was parked unmoving in front of her,
wearing a hideous Hawaiian shirt as the woman tugged it closed and
began to button it. Robert looked very much like he was afraid to
move, and I looked at the woman a little more closely to see what
could inspire such dread.

Her hair was black, streaked with gray that might have been dyed,
and she had large glasses in black frames that swirled out on the
sides and glittered with rhinestones. Her face was set in an expression of permanent meanness, lips pinched and eyes squinched, as

if she automatically disapproved of absolutely everything and knew *just* what to do about fixing it and making you sorry.

A tape measure hung around her neck, and she was yelling at someone named Freddy to for *shit's* sake get the fucking hot-*glue* gun before it fucking *froze*. And a wispy young man, probably Freddy, fled from her in terror, presumably to find the fucking hot-glue gun.

Over by the floor-to-ceiling window, on a low couch and several accompanying chairs, a handful of men and women sat together, chatting. On a side table next to them was a large chrome coffee urn and a few pastry boxes.

Another slender young man ran by in the opposite direction, his arms full to overflowing with blue police uniforms. I glanced at one sleeve that dangled loose; it said, MIAMI POLICE. I wondered where they'd gotten the badges, since I had been around Miami police my whole life and I had never seen anything like them.

"Close your mouth," Jackie said, and I realized I had been staring in wonder, mouth agape, at the melee. "If Sylvia sees any weakness, it's all over."

I closed my mouth and Jackie took my elbow to steer us both to safety. But before I could take more than one step, the door to the suite bumped open, and I turned around to look. And sadly for my self-image, my mouth dropped open again.

Because standing there, framed by the doorway, stood Cody and Astor. Behind them, a baby carriage with two passengers rolled into view, and my jaw dangled even lower as I recognized the two passengers as my daughter, Lily Anne, and Deb's son, Nicholas. "Dadoo!" Lily Anne called, holding her arms out for me to pick her up, and Nicholas bounced up and down with the excitement of the moment.

And, of course, right behind them, wearing a smirk and pushing the carriage, was Sergeant Sister Deborah.

"Hi, Dexter," Astor said. "This place looks crazy. Do they have any doughnuts or anything?"

"Aunt Deborah *said*," Cody said softly.

"What, the what what," I said, sounding brain-damaged even to me.

"Move it, Dex," Deborah said. "And close your mouth."

# TWENTY-TWO

HAVE YOU EVER NOTICED THAT EVERY NOW AND THEN IT begins to feel like the entire world is a conspiracy designed to make you look like a total idiot? And if you are a reasonable being with even a nodding acquaintance with logic, you tell yourself this is mere paranoia; you talk yourself out of it and soldier on. But then something happens to make you think it's not such a far-fetched idea after all.

This was clearly one of those moments. In front of me Debs was smirking. Cody and Astor, moving around me to see into the room, glanced up and smirked, too. And when I turned around to look at Jackie, there on her face was the unkindest smirk of all.

"What, um," I said, and I was quite proud that I did not actually stutter, "what is going on here?"

"Dexter, you get to work on a *movie*," Astor said, with a certain amount of venom, though not as much as she used with Rita lately. "With stars . . ." She glanced at Jackie, and then at Robert. "And instead you didn't even tell us, or bring us here, or *anything*." She looked at me now, a cold and cranky glare. "You *know* I'm going to be an actress, and you're supposed to *care* about us, and help us learn things and do cool stuff, and you didn't even *tell* us."

"You should have told us," Cody said softly, and that hurt more than Astor's contempt.

"Yes, but, school is . . . and anyhow," I said, and regrettably, I was stuttering now.

"It's *Saturday*," Cody said.

"You're acting like a *putz*," Astor told me. And before I could wonder where she had learned that word, Deborah pushed the stroller through the door and into the room next to me.

"Rita called and asked me if I could watch the kids," Debs told me. "Some kind of awful crisis at work involving the euro and real estate prices in Germany. Which you would know if you ever called her."

"Yes, but . . ." I said. "I mean, on a Saturday . . . ?"

"You really are a putz," Debs said, shaking her head.

I glanced at Jackie; she smiled and nodded. "You are," she said happily.

They all stared at me with mild contempt and amusement; it seemed like even the two babies had learned the look, and I waited for Lily Anne to call out, "Putz, Dadoo!" Happily for me, she didn't, and I made a valiant effort to collect the tattered shreds of my dignity.

"Well," I said, "I'm very happy to see you all."

I could have continued my embarrassing groveling, but Astor had locked her eyes onto Jackie. "Are you an actress?" she asked, almost shyly, which was a very odd tone coming from Astor.

Jackie looked down at her and raised one eyebrow. "Yes, I am," she said.

"Are you *famous*?" Astor said.

Jackie gave her a polite smile. "I guess it's a matter of opinion," she said.

Astor stared a moment longer, then frowned, glanced at me, and asked Jackie, "Why are you with Dexter?"

Jackie looked at me for help, but I had nothing. The tip of her tongue poked out between her lips and she took a deep breath. "Dexter is . . . *helping* me with . . . a problem," she said.

Astor shook her head. "What kind of problem could *he* help you with?" she said, and the old, snarky tone was back in her voice; she even snickered. "Do you have a blood-spatter problem?"

"No, of course not," Jackie said.

"That's all Dexter can do," Astor said. "Except—" She caught herself just in time, looked at me, and then her jaw dropped open and she whirled back around to Jackie. "Oh, shit," she said. "You're having an *affair*." She looked back at me. "Dexter is having sex with a famous actress! That is so cool!"

Jackie actually blushed, and my sister, Deborah, helpful as ever, let out an amused snort.

"What? No!" I said. "Astor, that's ridiculous."

"Well, then, *what*?" she demanded. "Why are you hanging out with her?"

I hesitated, and Jackie didn't have anything to say, either. Deborah raised one eyebrow and shrugged, which was not terribly helpful. Apparently it was all on me, so I tried tiptoeing up to it. "It's kind of secret," I said.

"Affairs are always secret," Astor said. I wondered if anyone would notice if I flung her out a window.

"Astor, it's not an affair," I said, and then, taking a deep breath, I plunged in headfirst. "Jackie got some scary letters," I said. "I'm just . . . making sure nothing bad happens to her—"

Astor's face lit up and she beamed at Jackie. "You got a psycho stalker? Wow! You really *are* famous!" she said.

Jackie turned an appalled expression on me, and I said, "Astor, please, it's a secret."

"Why is it secret?" Astor said. "If I had a stalker, I'd want everybody to know."

"Jackie could lose her job," Deborah said.

Astor frowned and shook her head. "Why?" she said. "It's not her fault."

"It's complicated," I said. "Just please don't tell anybody." Astor looked at me like she was calculating what she might wangle out of me in exchange for her silence, and I was ready to promise her a new pony, when fate smiled on me for once. From the far end of the room, near a short hallway, there was a loud outburst of angry yelling and everyone turned to look.

Renny was holding on to Kathy, Jackie's assistant, by her wrists; she was struggling to get away and shouting at him furiously to let go or she would tell *everybody*. Renny said something soft and urgent, and Kathy yanked her arms away and slapped him. "I told you last time!" she said. "I swear to God, Renny, you just—" And then one of Sylvia's thin young men was there, stepping bravely between them and speaking soothing words. And Kathy backed off, gave Renny one last glare, and said, "I mean it, asshole!" She whirled away and steamed straight over to Jackie. For the first time, her arms were not filled with papers, and she didn't even have her trademark phone in one hand and Starbucks cup in the other. She pushed past me with a glare and stood in front of Jackie. "Sylvia said she couldn't wait for you any longer and she was going to do Robert first—"

"All right, Kathy, it's all right," Jackie said soothingly. "Are you okay?"

Kathy pushed her glasses up with one stubby finger. "I am fine," she said. "But that piece of shit Renny—"

"Okay, it's over," Jackie said, taking Kathy by the arm and leading her over toward the couch, on the opposite side of the room from Renny. He stood watching her, a look on his face that was a strange combination of anger and amusement. Then he turned and saw me looking, and as our eyes met I heard a soft hiss from a coiled Something inside and the distant rattle of leathery wings as it stretched and twitched uneasily in half readiness to rise and meet the thing that stared back at us from Renny's hissing Something—

And then Renny turned away and the Passenger yawned and turned over and went back to its lazy nap and I was left wondering once again if I had really seen that threat in Renny's eyes. What, if anything, would it steer him toward? And what had he done to Kathy? She seemed as angry at him as she had been at me—had Renny made her pee on the floor, too?

But before I could do any more than frame the questions, Astor spoke up again.

"Oh, oh," Astor said, and her voice was reverent and hushed. "That's the guy from the show Mom used to like. It's on reruns all the time. What's his name . . . ?"

I turned around to see what she was talking about. Unfortunately, she was staring directly at Robert.

"You mean Robert?" I said. "Mom watches Robert's old show?"

"Robert *Chase*," Astor said with excitement. She stared at Robert with a hungry look and licked her lips. "I've seen him on TV, like, a hundred times." There was a tone of yearning in her voice I had never heard from her before, and I realized that, as ridiculous as it might seem to me, Astor was starstruck—and with *Robert*, for God's sake.

Still, I had obligations as her stepfather, as she had already reminded me, and I was willing to do almost anything to take her mind off Jackie's little secret, so I pushed away the weary sigh that was trying to come out and replaced it with cheerful parental words. "Would you like me to introduce you?" I said. And Astor shot me a glance that made me think there might be some small hope of some-day working my way back into her good graces.

"Hell, yes," she said.

"Astor," Debs said warningly.

"I mean, yes, please, Dexter," she amended, with a completely artificial look of angelic innocence on her face. "I really want to meet him."

"Me, too," Cody said, stubbornly refusing to be left out.

"Well," I said, thinking of the Robert I had come to know far too well, "I hope you aren't disappointed."

Astor snorted and shook her head. "Dexter, he's a *star*," she said, her voice laced with pity for my stupidity. "How can we be disappointed?"

I could think of a dozen ways off the top of my head, all based on my knowledge of Robert, but it would probably be better to let him crush her dreams all by himself, so I just said, "Okay. Come on."

"You know him?" Astor said. "You really *know* him?"

"Oh, yes, I know him," I said. "Come on."

I walked over to where Robert was struggling with his repugnant Hawaiian shirt; it seemed to be a few sizes too small, and he couldn't quite get all the buttons done. "I haven't gained an *ounce*," he was say-ing to the scary woman. "Not one ounce in fifteen years—the size is wrong. Or it shrank when you cleaned it."

"I don't do shrink," the woman growled at him.

"Well, somebody did—look at this!" Robert held open the shirt and showed his bare chest. It was smooth and hairless, as if he waxed it, but it must be said that it was also lean and smoothly muscled. "There's no fat there, none at all!" he told her.

The woman—Sylvia?—stepped in to Robert and pulled at the shirt; she couldn't make it close either. She hissed loudly, and then jerked the shirt off him. "Teddy!" she snarled, and the young man who'd been carrying uniforms hurried over.

"Sylvia, the arm patches are all coming off, too, and we don't have enough hot glue for—"

Sylvia flung Robert's shirt at the poor guy, and he caught it with his face. "Take this," she snarled. "Go get another *just* like it—two sizes bigger."

"I don't know if they have any more in this pattern?" Teddy said plaintively, peeling the shirt off his face. "The man said they—"

Sylvia closed her eyes. "Go," she said quietly, but in a voice that was boiling with dreadful menace, and Teddy fled with the shirt.

"Hey, Dexter!" Robert said. He swung his eyes onto Cody and Astor. "Whatcha got here, huh?"

Astor looked at me with brand-new, never-before-seen respect in her eyes. "You *do* know him," she said. "You know Robert Chase!"

"Of course he knows me," Robert said happily. "He's been teaching me about forensics all week. For my new show." He took a step closer to the kids and held out a hand to Cody. "Howdy, partner," he said.

"Hi," Cody said, staring at him solemnly, and then slowly shaking Robert's hand.

Robert turned to Astor and held out his hand. "And what's your name, beautiful?"

Astor blushed. It was an astonishing sight, something I had never seen her do in all the long years I had known her. She blushed, and held out her hand to Robert as if she was reaching for the crown jewels.

"Astor," she said, in a voice so soft it might have been Cody's.

"Astor," Robert repeated, smiling at her. "Beautiful name for a beautiful girl." He beamed at her, holding her hand for a few seconds too long, and then turned to me. "Dexter, holy smokes, you said you had kids, but you didn't tell me your daughter was a supermodel." Astor's face turned even redder, but Cody frowned. Clearly he was feeling slightly left out.

"Well, what have we got here?" came the loud and frightening voice of Sylvia the costume witch. I turned around, prepared to draw a sword and slay her before she could eat my kids, but instead I found her beaming.

"These are Dexter's kids," Robert told her. "You know, my technical adviser."

"Well, they are *beautiful*!" Sylvia gushed. Her face split into something that was probably supposed to be a fond smile; it was hard to say, since Sylvia's face was clearly not made for such things. But she smiled and looked at Cody and Astor with maternal affection, and I could not have been more amazed if I had seen a balanced federal budget.

Sylvia knelt down between Cody and Astor with that same fond and phony-looking smile on her face. "Hello, little man," she said to Cody. She put a hand on his shoulder. "Oh, my—you're very strong— are you a football player?"

Cody was trying very hard not to look pleased. "Soccer," he said in his too-soft voice.

"That's a wonderful sport," Sylvia cooed at him. "What's your name?"

"Cody," he said. He was clearly torn between resentment at being treated like an idiot and delight at having someone pay him that much attention, but it looked like delight was winning.

"My name is Sylvia," she told him. "I'm in charge of all the clothes that the actors wear for the show."

Cody nodded. "Costumes," he said.

Sylvia clapped her hands in delight. "That's right!" she said. "So you're smart, too!"

Naturally enough, Astor didn't like being left out. She rolled her eyes and said, "Oh, brother," and Sylvia glanced her way.

"And what's your name, dear?" Sylvia said.

"My name is Astor," she said. "I'm going to be an actress."

"Well," Sylvia said, "all little girls think that."

Astor made a sound that was almost a Sylvia-like hiss. "I'm almost *twelve*," she said.

"Hey, she could do it," Robert said, pushing his way in next to Astor. "I mean, she's got the looks for it; that's for sure." And Astor looked up at him even more adoringly, if possible.

"So, Dex," Robert said, "great kids, and glad you brought 'em—but what are you doing here on a Saturday? Um—and with *her* . . . ?" He nodded toward Jackie, and although I had never before seen a nod of the head express contempt, somehow he managed it. But after all, he was a working actor. "I mean, uh . . ." he said, raising an eyebrow, and clearly waiting for a reasonable explanation.

"Oh, well," I said, hoping something brilliant would occur to me.

"Has Dexter really been working with you all week, Mr. Chase?" Astor said.

"Robert," he said with a grin that showed more gleaming white teeth than any three humans should have. "Just call me Robert."

"Robert," Astor said, trying it out and liking the sound of it.

"Hey, you want to be an actress." He nodded to the far end of the suite. "I have to go get my shirt—you want to see what an actor's dressing room looks like?" he said.

"Sure, Robert," Astor said, not sounding quite as mature as she thought she did. She glanced at me with cool aloofness and added, "I'll be right back."

"We'll just be a second, Dex," he said to me, still showing too many teeth. "That okay?"

"Um," I said, with a vague notion that this was skating close to some kind of a line. But before I could frame an objection, Astor rolled her eyes.

"It's *fine*," she said. "Come on, Robert." And she gave me her best adult stare and said, "Robert and I will be right back, Dexter." She took him by the hand and the two of them went off to the short hallway at the far end of the suite, where there were three doors, presumably into bedrooms and bathrooms.

Robert glanced back at me; his face was aglow in a way I hadn't seen before, and I remembered that he did have a crush on me. He probably thought he could please me by showering attention on my sweet and innocent little girl. Well, he couldn't, and he would soon find out just how sweet and innocent Astor was. As soon as she got over her hero worship and started to act like herself, we would see how he liked it. I waved at him; he waved back and they disappeared together through the far door, and as I turned away from them I saw Jackie hurrying over to me.

"What did he say?" she said quietly but urgently. "Did he ask why you're here with me?"

"Well, actually—" I said.

"God*damn* it," she hissed. "What did you tell him?"

"We got distracted," I said. "I didn't tell him anything."

"Well, he's going to ask again—we have to think of *something*," she said. "He's the one guy who really can't know about . . . Patrick." She bit her lip and looked very worried. "Robert is . . . He would love nothing better than to spread it around that there's a psycho after me and get me fired. . . ."

She grimaced and looked around to see whether anyone had heard her; no one was close enough. Cody stood a few feet away with Sylvia, sticking pins into the dress dummy. No one else was near. "Damn it, I don't know. We could say . . ." She trailed off, frowning, and looked around. "Got it," she said, as inspiration and relief visibly flowed onto her face. "Where's Kathy?"

A door slammed, and Kathy came hurrying out of the hallway where Astor and Robert had gone. Jackie raised a hand to signal her, but Kathy didn't see her; she just chugged rapidly out the door to the suite and vanished.

"What the hell . . . ?" Jackie said.

"Maybe she ran out of coffee," I suggested, but Jackie just looked at me, and then at the outside door where Kathy had gone, frowning, and then Robert and Astor came trotting toward us. Robert was buttoning his shirt, and he looked flustered. I wondered what Astor had said to him. As I knew very well, she was capable of saying some very surprising things. Judging by Robert's expression, this one had been a doozy.

Like Cody, Astor was turned away from Normal forever. Cody enjoyed killing things, and with proper guidance he would grow up to be like me, a well-adjusted monster. But Astor—I didn't really know. Girls were different, even if the form her difference would take was not yet clear. From what I knew of the subject, she was at the age where we would soon find out.

Like me, and her brother, Astor could not feel empathy for others. She did not really have emotions, unless you count overwhelming crankiness. I'd done a little research, just to be ready, and it was most likely that Astor would find some career path that let her manipulate people somehow, and then work her way to the top by doing whatever it took, regardless of the consequences to others. She would learn to make people do exactly what she wanted them to do, sometimes merely because she could, just to see them squirm.

Beyond that, I didn't really know what she was going to be capable of someday; she hadn't shown any interest in much, other than clothes and making boys suffer, which was almost normal for a girl her age. Mostly she just seemed angry, and a lot of her anger came out verbally; she sometimes said and did things that could be quite surprising to the unprepared. From the look on Robert's face, I had to think she had done so with him.

"That's— See? We were only one minute or so, and, uh . . . where did your assistant go?" Robert said, sounding bewildered as he looked around. Astor stood beside him with a kind of superior smirk on her face.

"Don't you have an assistant of your own, Bob?" Jackie said, much too sweetly.

Robert scowled. "You know, we have to work together, so—"

"Robert wants to show me the makeup room, but he said I had to ask *you* first," Astor said. "Can I go see it? Please, Dexter?"

"It's just down the hall," Robert said quickly. And when I didn't answer, he went on. "And hey! You didn't tell me—how come you're down here? With the kids and . . ." He glanced at Jackie and then stumbled on. "And you know. On a Saturday?"

"Dexter is getting an under-five," Jackie said. "So I said I'd show him where wardrobe is." She smiled at Robert, not a happy smile. "Is that okay, Robert?" she said, as if his name was in quotation marks.

"What's an under-five?" Astor demanded.

"Well," said Robert, looking right at Jackie and showing her his teeth, "he can't be any worse at acting than some people who do it for a living."

"My thoughts exactly," Jackie said sweetly, showing her own teeth right back. "He's almost certainly better than . . . some actors."

"Mee-ow," said Sylvia, stepping over and pushing between them. "Are you two still at it? After all these years?"

"Some things are forever," Robert said, scowling. "Like herpes."

"Robert has such trouble letting go," Jackie said lightly. "And it was such a *small* thing, too."

Robert turned bright red and clenched his fists. "I guess you're the expert."

"Well," Jackie said, with that same acid-coated sweetness, "*you* certainly aren't any expert."

Robert opened his mouth to say something crushing. But he never got the chance; Sylvia took him by the arm and said, "Enough, you two. Let's get your pants fitted."

"He's going to show me the makeup room," Astor said.

"Work comes first," Sylvia said. "Come on, Bob."

"Robert," he said automatically. He smiled at Astor and added, "It'll just take two minutes." Sylvia tugged at his arm, and with a last glare at Jackie, Robert allowed Sylvia to drag him away.

Astor watched him go, pouting heavily, and then, with a sidelong glance at me to see whether I was going to stop her, she followed along.

I looked at Jackie, hoping for some hint to what was going on. This had gone beyond the normal sniping between her and Robert. It was clear from the venom, as well as the words, that they had some kind of history together, and equally clear that it was unpleasant. I waited for Jackie to say something that might fill me in. But she just watched Robert's back, and when he was finally gone into one of the suite's bedrooms, she turned to me at last and said, "Well, now we have to get you an under-five."

"Isn't that some kind of tuxedo?" I said.

Jackie smiled and patted my cheek, and even though it was a very clear statement that I was an adorable moron, her hand felt very good, so I concentrated on the "adorable" and forgave the rest.

"So much to learn," she said. "So little time." She left her hand on my cheek for just a moment, and I could smell that same faint scent of perfume coming from her wrist. Then she dropped her hand.

"With Kathy gone, I'll have to do this myself," she said. "But the director owes me a favor. So—"

She smiled and then, very much like Astor had led Robert away, she took my hand and led me out the door.

# TWENTY-THREE

**M**Y FOSTER MOTHER, DORIS, USED TO SAY THAT YOU LEARN
something new every day. I had always taken that as a subtle
threat, but in this case what I learned from Jackie was harmless
and delightfully useless. It turned out that I had been thinking of
"plus fours," and that was not a tuxedo but a kind of Three Stooges
golfing outfit. An "under-five," as it happened, was an acting part, so
called because the actor in question—and in this case he was highly
questionable—got to say *under five* lines. I wasn't completely clear on
why that number was so important; something to do with the unions,
I think. The more I learned about show business, the more it seemed
that almost everything was about one union or another.

In any case, giving a speaking part to a forensic geek with no
acting experience—at least, not in front of a camera—didn't seem to
be a big deal to the director, Victor Torrano. He just sighed and said,
"All right, what the hell, fine, stop batting your eyelashes at me." And
I was relieved to see he meant Jackie, not me.

Victor turned and looked me over, head to toe. "Huh. Okay, I got
a few parts I was gonna cast local anyway. Um, not butch enough for
a cop. Not evil-looking enough for a drug dealer . . ." He looked at my
face and squinted. "Yeah, sorry, what's your name?"

"Dexter Morgan," I said. I hoped it was all going to be this easy.

"Dexter, right. You know anything at all about forensics?"

I could not stop myself from smiling just a little as I said, "As a matter of fact . . ."

And lo! He spake the word, and Dexter was an actor.

Jackie led me back to Sylvia's lair, a note from Victor clutched in my hand, stating that I was now and henceforth for all time, or at least for one episode, Ben Webster, scene forty-nine, and was to be garbed appropriately.

"Ben Webster," I said to Jackie as we left Victor's Presence. "Wasn't he an Elizabethan playwright?"

Jackie patted my hand. "I don't think so," she said. "You're not nervous about this, are you?"

"Oh, no," I said. "Not at all.

She turned those huge violet eyes on me and gave me a crooked smile. "You'll be fine," she said. "Don't worry about it."

In fact, I was not really worried about acting. After all, I had been acting my whole life, playing the part of a human being and a very nice guy, two things I certainly was not. And since I had never yet been flung in jail or shot dead, I have to say I must have been doing a pretty good job.

We got back into the wardrobe room in time to see Cody helping Sylvia run the tape measure down Renny's arm. Renny stood there, shirtless, and I do have to say, it was not an awe-inspiring sight. He was not fat, but he certainly wasn't in the kind of shape Robert had flaunted. His muscles were all soft and rounded, clearly the body of a man more interested in eating than exercise.

"Miss Forrest?" said a musical voice at my elbow, and one of Sylvia's assistants was there.

"Yes?" Jackie said.

The assistant smiled. "Hi, I'm Freddy? By the way, I *love* your work—and Sylvia wants me to get you fitted, for the dress blues? For the funeral scene?"

Jackie nodded. "And whatever Sylvia wants—"

"Sylvia *gets*," Freddie finished. "Believe me, I know, I work with her a lot? Anyway . . ." He smiled and waved toward the small hallway. "If you could come with me?"

Jackie turned to me and said, "This might take a while—there's coffee over by the couch?" Then she smiled and walked away with Freddie.

I walked over to check on Cody. He looked up at me and nodded, which was the equivalent of a face-splitting grin from him. "Dexter," Renny said. "I knew you'd show up if I took off my shirt." He flexed, or tried to; there wasn't a whole lot to work with. "What do you think?"

"Hold still," Sylvia said, slapping his arms out of the pose and back where they belonged.

"I think you should put your shirt back on," I said.

"I know, too much temptation, right?" Renny said. "I get that all the time."

I let him have the point. "How is Cody doing?" I asked Sylvia. "Is he talking your ears off?"

She glanced at me, and then snapped at Renny, "Raise your arm. Your *left* arm." She continued to measure as she talked. "Cody is a wonderful boy and he is being a very big help," she said, and she gave Cody that awful, unnatural smile again. "But he hasn't said more than three words."

"If he said even three, it's a good sign," I said. "He must like you."

Cody glanced up without expression. "Where's your sister?" I asked him.

He jerked his head at the main door to the suite. "Robert," he said, and he put several paragraphs of disapproval in that one word.

For no logical reason, I looked toward the door. It didn't speak, and it didn't even open. I had been with Jackie and Victor for about ten minutes; I didn't see how looking at makeup could take that long—but of course, I was not an eleven-year-old girl, or an aging gay actor. Although, come to think of it, I had a piece of paper in my hand stating that actually, I *was* at least an actor now. I wondered if I would automatically become interested in makeup—or in Robert. It hadn't happened yet.

In any case, if Astor could spend this much time examining rouge and eye shadow, it was clear that she had gone completely over the edge into her fantasies of being an actress. I didn't see any harm in it; when this show was over there wouldn't be a whole lot of other chances for her to peek into the glamorous world of showbiz—unless, of course, I was so devastatingly moving in my cameo part that it launched me into an acting career of my own. It could happen, but it didn't really seem like the most probable outcome.

Still, for the moment Astor could look and dream, and I could take advantage of one of the small perks of the trade. So I went over to the coffee urn, grabbed a doughnut, and poured myself a cup.

Somehow, I survived the afternoon, and eventually we rounded up Astor and Cody and sent them on their way with their aunt Deborah. It had been a trial, made worse by the way Jackie smirked at me far too much when she caught me in the role of Daddy Dexter. Personally, I didn't find it all that funny, and I was relieved and happy when Debs finally led them away, and Jackie and I headed back to the hotel for a late lunch, and then to get ready for Renny's show that night.

Jackie was expected to do a bit more than sit in the audience and laugh for the camera. The network planned a few minutes of Behind the Scenes with the Stars, and she was a part of the plan. She'd been told to show up a little early for this, so we arrived at the Gusman at seven oh-five. The Gusman is actually the Gusman Center for the Performing Arts and, not to be too picky, the theater part of it is, in reality, a restored silent movie theater from the 1920s, the Olympia. The marquis on the front of the building says, OLYMPIA, and tonight, under the big bright letters, it said, TONIGHT ONLY! RENNY BOUDREAUX!

There was quite a crowd stacked up on the sidewalk. A churning sea of faces all turned expectantly to the Town Car as it pulled up in front of the theater. I reached for the door handle, and Jackie grabbed my arm.

"I'm scared," she said. "It was in the paper that I would be here tonight, and he could . . . He might be in the crowd, waiting for me."

"I don't think so," I said, and to be candid, I was a great deal more certain of that than I let on. "But if he is, I won't let him get to you."

She looked at me, her gaze clicking back and forth from my left eye to my right, as if she thought she might find reassurance in one of them but wasn't sure which. I had the uneasy feeling that I should say something even more reassuring, so I dredged up a line from some old movie, looked right back at her, and said, "He'll have to get me first."

Jackie looked at me for a few seconds longer, and then, quite suddenly, she leaned forward and kissed me on the lips.

"I believe you," she said.

My mouth was filled with the taste of her lipstick, and my brain was filled with numb shock. I couldn't think at all for what seemed like a very long time, and when I finally got out one coherent thought, all that came out was, "I, um, I'll get out. And check . . ." And then I saw myself jerk into motion like a clumsy teenaged robot, fumbling the door open and stepping out into the street.

The crowd had been watching the car and holding its breath, and there was a large sigh of indifference when I climbed out. Of course it hurt, but after all, they hadn't seen my cameo yet. I wondered if they had seen Jackie kiss me. I looked back at the car; the tint of the windows was too dark to see through. That explained it; if they had seen her kiss me they probably would have cheered.

I went through the dumb show of checking the area for any signs of Patrick. I found none: no seaweed, crabs, or drag marks from an anchor chain, so I went back to the car and opened the door. "All clear," I said, and Jackie held out her hand and slid across the seat.

"You have lipstick on your mouth," she said softly, and smiled. I wiped my mouth on my sleeve and took her hand, helping her out onto the sidewalk. There was a two-second pause in which we managed to get a full step toward the front door before somebody yelled, "Jackie Forrest!" and then there really was something to protect Jackie from. The crowd surged toward us, humming like a beehive on steroids. Dozens of cameras flashed right in my face, and for a moment I couldn't see anything but wildly jiggling purple dots. I blinked, and my sight came back just in time for me to duck as a barrage of hands shot out at us, clutching programs to be autographed and fluttering like rabid birds, and cries of, "Jackie! Jackie!" battered our ears in every possible accent, from Cuban and Haitian to redneck.

Jackie performed the remarkable feat of smiling broadly at the crowd and ignoring them at the same time, hunching her head down and forward and clinging to my arm as if I was the last chunk of crumbling riverbank and the only thing keeping her from being swept away to her death. I tried to shield her as much as I could while still moving forward, but it was impossible to cover all of her, and I could only hope she wasn't taking the kind of casual, accidental beating I was getting from the star-crazed fans.

Somehow we made it to the door of the theater through the wildly waving forest of arms, and as the crowd finally thinned and then fell behind us, the first thing I saw clearly was three ushers, holding the door and grinning at us. "Thanks for your help," I told them. They didn't even look at me; all their attention was on making sure Jackie got through the door without fatally injuring herself on a hinge.

Once they got us safely inside, the ushers stood and smiled proudly, as if they had just saved Jackie from certain death. I felt like conking their heads together; they had done nothing but watch smugly as the crowd tried to rip us to pieces, and now I had a tear in my brand-new guayabera. But Jackie just nodded at them and said, "Thank you," and gave me her arm. I led her into the theater.

It took a moment to recover from the savage love of the crowd, and as we walked through the ornate lobby and into the Olympia itself, I found a second hole in my shirt, three scratches on my arms, and at least two spots on my ribs so tender they would certainly turn into bruises by morning. And yet, somehow, improbably, it had been exhilarating. Once again I found that I liked the frenzied attention of a crowd of strangers. I knew they had barely seen me, that their focus was all on Jackie, but that was fine. It was even more intoxicating to know that the center of all that adoration was with me; she had actually *kissed* me, and the crowd could never have that from her. But along with that smug delight, I found that I had to push away a rising bitterness that this had to end, and so soon.

I looked at Jackie's profile; somehow, even after the pounding and pulling of the crowd, her hair was still in perfect order, and she was every bit the Goddess the crowd needed her to be—a Goddess who had kissed me, and I still didn't understand why.

She swung her head my way, and locked her violet eyes on me. "What?" she said.

"Oh," I said, suddenly embarrassed, and not sure why. "Nothing. You know."

Jackie smiled. "I *don't* know," she said. "Are you going to tell me?"

"Really, it's nothing," I said. "Just . . . the crowd. And you . . ." I meant to say, *You kissed me*, but somehow, what came out of my mouth was, "You look so . . . perfect."

"About time you noticed," she murmured, and then we were inside the theater itself and she looked up. "Oh, look at that! It's beautiful!" She stopped in her tracks and stared upward, but my eyes were drawn to the curve of her neck, and I looked at that for a long moment before I looked at the ceiling, too.

I suppose the ceiling of the Olympia really is beautiful. But I had seen it before, and I'd read in the paper too many times that it's gorgeous, wonderful, a treasure of restored glory, and so on. It's just not the kind of thing that really moves me. But Jackie needed a few moments to take in the golden swirls and the faux night sky, and I stood there politely while she goggled.

"Wow," she said at last. "Beats the hell out of the Chinese Theatre in L.A."

Down in the front of the theater, in the third row, Deborah turned around, saw us, and stood up. But before she got to us a well-dressed young man came in from the lobby and hurried over to us. I watched him carefully for any sign that he might be a sniper, or a zombie, but he just smiled and said, "Miss Forrest?"

Jackie tore her gaze away from the gaudy ceiling, and the young man beamed at her. "Hi, I'm Radym Reitman," he said. "Mr. Eissen wants you to come back to Renny's dressing room—they're shooting the preshow stuff?"

"Of course," she said, and then Deborah joined us.

"What the hell happened to you?" Debs said, eyeing the tear on the front of my shirt.

"The adoring public," I said. "I guess somebody recognized me."

Deborah snorted and turned her attention to Jackie. "Not a mark on you," she said.

"Lots of practice," Jackie said.

"I have to meet Rita in the lobby," I said to Deborah. "Can you stay with Jackie?"

"Sure," Debs said, and Reitman cleared his throat. Deborah gave him a really good Cop Look, and he fell silent and just fidgeted. "Oh," Jackie said. "I have to go backstage for a minute—okay?"

"Sure," Debs said. "But I got us a couple of beers." She nodded toward the seat she'd been in when we entered. "Lemme grab 'em first."

"Oh, good, thanks," Jackie said, and with a final smile and a pat on the arm for me, she followed Debs and Reitman away toward the front of the theater.

I watched them collect their beer, and then follow Reitman off to a side door. When they were gone, I looked at the stage. There was really nothing to it, except for a backdrop of a nighttime cityscape. Hanging from the top of that was a bright and spangly sign about eight feet tall that said, RENNY. In front of that, close to the edge of the stage, was a stool with a bottle of water on it, and a wireless microphone on a stand. No glitz, no gimmicks; it was all up to Renny.

I looked at my watch; miraculously, it had not been torn off my arm or smashed to pieces by the crowd, and it was even still working. The time was seven twenty-eight; I was supposed to meet Rita in the lobby at seven thirty, so I sauntered back up the aisle and into the lobby.

Based on Rita's past performance, I was quite sure I would have to wait for fifteen or twenty minutes; she lived on Cuban Time, even though she was a blond Anglo. She had never been less than twenty minutes late for anything in all the time I had known her.

But I had reckoned without her girlish obsession with all things Hollywood, and as I moseyed into the lobby, I stopped dead, stunned at the sight that met me. It was Rita, already there and pacing nervously as she waited for me. She reached the far end of the lobby and turned, and the filmy almost-negligee she wore swirled around her. Even at this distance I could see the worry lines on her face, and she was nervously rubbing the back of her left hand with her right. Then she saw me; her face lit up and she practically sprinted across the floor.

"Dexter, my God," she said. "I think I just saw Andy Garcia? And they said the mayor— Is that your shirt?" She put the palm of her hand on my guayabera and stroked it, as if she could turn it into something more acceptable. "Oh, Dexter, there's a *hole* in it right on the *front*—is that really what you're wearing?" She sucked her lower lip between her teeth and looked worried.

I bit down on the impulse to tell her that no, it wasn't my shirt; it belonged to Andy Garcia, and I was just about to change clothes with him, right here in the lobby. "It's perfectly all right," I said. "This isn't a formal ball—it's a comedy show."

"Yes, I know, but really, it's a *hole*," she said. "And another on the back—and what's this on your sleeve?" With a frown, she rubbed at something, and I realized it was the lipstick from Jackie's kiss that I had wiped on the sleeve.

"Oh, it's just, you know," I said with as much nonchalance as I could muster. "Somebody in the crowd or something."

Rita shook her head and, happily for me, didn't seem to hear how feeble my answer was. "The whole shirt is— You're a mess, Dexter— and it doesn't even go at all with what I— I mean, now I look like some kind of— How much time is there until— If I really . . . I could change into—"

"You look fine," I said, although in truth, when I compared her ensemble to what Jackie was wearing, she was brutally overdressed.

Rita ran both hands down the front of her dress, smoothing out wrinkles that weren't there. "Yes, well, *fine*," she said, and she shook her head dubiously. "I mean that's— You should have told me that this was— What is everybody else wearing?"

I know a great deal about many things, but I will cheerfully admit that couture is not one of them, and I did not think the lobby of the Gusman was the place to learn. So I mustered my most command- ing attitude and put a hand on her arm and pulled gently. "Let's go inside," I said. "You can see for yourself."

Rita dug both feet into the carpet and did not budge, and a look of alarm spread across her face. "Everybody? My God, I don't think I can—"

I tugged a little harder. "Come on," I said. "I'll introduce you to Robert Chase."

If I had thought Astor overreacted to Robert, it was only because I hadn't seen her mother's response yet. Rita turned bright red, and she began to tremble, and for the first time ever, she had trouble get- ting out even one word. "Ro, Ro, I real," she stammered. "Is— You— Rob . . . Robert Chase is here? And you . . . ?"

I watched her performance with annoyance. In all the time I had known Robert, he had revealed nothing to indicate he deserved to be shown even the mildest kind of respect—and here was Rita falling into a weak-kneed reverent trance at the mere thought of being in his presence. And I was pretty sure I had told her Robert would be here, so there was really no excuse at all for her collapsing into a drooling coma that threatened to ruin the Gusman's carpet. Would she be less nervous if I told her Robert was gay?

On the plus side, in her weakened state she was in no condition to resist; I tugged once more on her arm, and she stumbled forward. "Come," I said. "Miracles await within." And I led her through the lobby and inside the theater.

I had been given a pair of seats only two rows back from the stage, in the center section and on the aisle. Whether it had been the network's idea or Captain Matthews's, I was supposed to be seated right next to Robert. I suppose it had been set up that way so the cameras would find the stars sitting happily next to Real Police People. Whatever the reason, it made introducing Rita to Robert almost unavoidable, but as we came down the aisle toward the stage, Robert was nowhere in sight. But as we approached our row, he came out of the door where Jackie and Debs had disappeared, and strode toward us, smiling and waving at the crowd.

It had been my naive thought to perform a simple intro as we slid into our seats, and then get on with life. But once again, I had reckoned without the abject reverence of Rita's Robert worship. The moment she saw him she stopped dead, went pale, and started to tremble again. "Oh, no," she said, which seemed an odd thing to say if she really wanted to meet him. "Oh, my God, it's him, it's *him.* . . ." She started to bounce up and down on the balls of her feet as she said, "Oh, my God, oh, God, oh, *God!*" and similar evocations of a deity that, as far as I could tell from brief acquaintance, had absolutely nothing to do with Robert.

Around me in the theater I could see heads turning toward us, some amused and some curious. It is true that I had liked the reflected attention of the crowd as they adored Jackie, but this was very different; I smelled amusement, condescension, even scorn in the many looks that came our way, and this I did not like. I pushed

Rita forward once more and she went, with short and jerky steps. I finally got her to our seats, although she refused to sit. Instead, she just stood there jiggling and staring at Robert, until I realized that if I didn't do something we would be standing in the aisle all night.

So I stepped into the aisle and waved to him, and he came at us, smiling. "Robert," I said. "This is my wife, Rita."

Robert held out a hand. "Hey, terrific!" he said. "Really great to meet you!" Rita just stood there with her face frozen into a numb and staring mask. I hoped she wouldn't actually drool.

After an awkward pause, Robert reached over and took her hand. "Wow, I can see where Astor gets her looks," he said, shaking Rita's limp hand. "Terrific kids you've got, Rita."

Rita spoke at last. "Oh, I ahaha," she said. "Oh, my God, I can't believe— I am such a big fan of— Oh, God, it's really *you*!"

"Well, I think it is," Robert said with an easy grin. He tried to drop her hand—but now, even though she hadn't been able to reach forward to shake hands with him, Rita clamped onto Robert's hand in a desperate, sweaty death grip. "Um," he said, and he looked at me.

"Rita," I said, "I think Robert would like his hand back."

"Oh, my God," she said, and she flung his hand away and jumped back, landing firmly on my toes. "I'm so sorry, so sorry; I just—"

"Hey, don't worry about it," Robert said. "Great to meet you, Rita." And he smiled at her and then pushed past us and sank gratefully into his seat.

Rita stared for a moment longer, in spite of the way I prodded her in the back, and I finally said, "Shall we sit down now?"

"Oh!" she said, and she jumped like she had been shocked. "But I can't possibly— You sit next to him; it's only— My God, I couldn't possibly!"

"All right," I said, and I slid into the seat right next to Robert. A moment later, Rita remembered how to sit, too, and she sank bonelessly into the seat beside me.

I sat there and watched Rita fidget for several minutes; she would start to settle down and then glance at Robert and begin to blush and twitch again. I tried to ignore it, but her spasms of adoration shook my seat, too. I looked to my left, where Jackie and Deborah would be sitting. They weren't back yet; probably still sipping beer and mingling with other celebrities in Renny's dressing room. I hoped he would keep his shirt on.

My seat quivered and I glanced back at Rita. Her left leg was jumping up and down in a nervous and probably unconscious twitch. I wondered whether she would turn normal again when the show started. Renny would probably have to be very funny to take her mind off sitting so close to Robert the God. I hoped Renny was hilarious. But what had he said to Robert—that he didn't do comedy; he did social commentary? Could that possibly be funny enough to stop Rita's convulsions? Could someone with a Passenger really be funny at all? I mean, I am well known for a dry wit—but I couldn't keep a full theater in stitches.

Still, a real TV network believed in Renny enough to give him this special. Of course, that same network had cast Robert in a starring role—but they had cast Jackie, too, so I guess that made it a fifty-fifty chance. And who knows? Anything could happen. Maybe he would even make *me* laugh. I didn't think so, but stranger things have happened—many of them to me. After all, I was married, had children, and everyone thought I was wonderful.

There was a burst of gaudy music from the sound system; a cheerful-looking young man came out onstage and plucked the microphone from the stand. "Heeeeeyyyyy—*Miami*!" he called out in a happy foghorn voice, and for some reason the audience cheered enthusiastically.

He went on to tell us all that we were filming tonight, which I already knew, and he told us to turn off our cell phones, don't take flash pictures, and remember to laugh a lot. He said one or two other things that I think were supposed to be funny, and then called out, "Oooo-*kay*! Enjoy the show!" And he stuck the microphone back on the stand and strode offstage to wild applause.

A moment later, the lights went down, the noise of the crowd trickled to a whisper, and the announcer said, "Ladies and gentlemen—Mr. Renny . . . Boudreaux!"

# TWENTY-FOUR

RENNY LET THE APPLAUSE BUILD, AND BUILD, AND THEN BUILD a little more until the audience climbed to its feet and yelled and stomped and the old theater began to shake. Then he slouched out onto the stage three steps and stopped, staring at the audience with clear disapproval. The cheering got louder; Renny shook his head and walked to the microphone as the laughter grew and mixed with the cheers. He took the microphone from its holder, turned front, and just stared at the audience.

More laughter, more cheering; Renny just kept scowling. And at the exact moment when the crowd noise started to ebb, he called out, "What the fuck is *wrong* with you people?!" and we were off again into a riotous rollicking sea of glee.

Again, he timed it perfectly, and at just the right moment he said, "I'll tell you what's wrong—you're *stupid*!" Oddly enough, this got a huge laugh, which seemed to make Renny mad, and he yelled, "I'm *serious*!" and the laughter got even louder, until Renny held up a hand and, when the noise died down a little, he said, "Sit the fuck down!"

I realized with a small shock that I was standing along with everyone else, and as I sat down, everyone else did, too. Renny waited for it to get very quiet, and then he began to speak. He mentioned the pilot we were shooting and introduced Robert and then Jackie, and as she stood to acknowledge the applause, I saw Deborah looking alertly around the room, bodyguard style. I remembered that I was supposed to be protecting Jackie, too, so I turned and pretended to search for any sign of trouble. There was none, of course. Jackie sat down safely, and Renny pulled a crumpled sheet of paper from his pocket. He scowled at it and then looked up.

"I'm supposed to say thank you to the cops here in Miami." He shook his head. "That make any sense to you? *Me*—saying thank you to *cops*? But Big Ticket said please, and they're paying for this shit, so . . . Thank you, cops." He glanced at the crumpled paper. "Hey, Captain Matthews, you out there?" The captain stood up with a modest and manly smile on his face, and waved at the crowd to polite applause. "Yeah, I just asked if you're there, Captain," Renny said. "I didn't say, stand up and steal my fucking spotlight." And he smiled for the first time. "Hey, that's right—first time I can say fuck to a cop—and he's a captain, too. Hey, Captain Matthews! Fuck fuck fuck fuck fuck fuck fuck!"

Renny waited for the laughs to die down and then he began to talk about Miami: Miami traffic, Miami food, the variety of people here—and every so often when he got a big laugh for some outrageously cynical observation, he would pause, glare at the audience, and call out, "I'm *serious*!" Apparently this was his tagline, the words he was famous for, like Steve Martin's "Excuse me!" and every time he said it, half the crowd chanted, "I'm serious!" along with him.

And he really was serious; he was just very funny about it. He talked about serious issues and made the crowd look at them in a new way, a way that was provocative and funny at the same time.

He tore into politics in a fashion that would have to be called carnivorous, and that led to public education. "You all cut the funding to public schools. Take away all the money for teaching your own damn kids—and then you complain because all the doctors are from India! You rather have an American doctor who went through your public schools, and now he's so fucking stupid he thinks Moby-Dick is a social disease?

"And then you say hey! We can fix the schools—with a lottery! And all the money will go to public schools! And the lobbyists get ahold of it, and now *some* of the money goes to the schools. And then the politicians step in, and all of a sudden, a *portion* of the *profits* goes to the schools. And what you've done, now it's not just about funding—you've turned your kids' *education* into a lottery. And you know how that works, right? One outa ten million is a winner, everybody else is shit out of luck.

"I'm *serious*!

"And who gets most of the losing tickets, huh? Yeah, that's right, it's the black man. Same old shit. You all think oh, everything changed now, 'cuz we elected a black president, but it's still hard as hell to be a black man in America. Especially since I fucking *hate* basketball . . . !

"But it could be worse," he went on. "I might be gay." He peered out into the audience and said, "Show of hands—how many faggots we got here tonight?" Believe it or not, a few hands went up, but Renny shook his head. "Come on, man, I know there's more of you—I can see your shoes." He shook his head again and waited for the laugh to die. "Yeah, being gay today, that's gotta suck. . . . I mean, the rest of y'all— Give 'em a break, all right? You think it's icky, that's fine—you don't have to watch. But really—what the fuck do you care who somebody else fucks? And if they like fucking 'em so much they wanna marry 'em, what the fuck do you care?" He made a solemn face and said, in a glutinous voice, " 'Oh, but Renny, it's in the Bible.' " Renny snorted and shook his head. "Shit, yeah, it's in the Bible; I looked it up. Any of you motherfuckers done that . . . ? I didn't think so. Well, I did. Yeah, it's in the Bible. It's right there, next to where it says you can't have a round haircut and you can't eat shrimp. And I can see some round fucking haircuts out there. And how many of you faggot bashers eat shrimp? 'Cuz if you think God wants you to piss on gay people, you gotta give up that shrimp cocktail, too, sparky. . . . I'm *serious*!"

A couple of rows behind me a loud voice called out, "Faggot!" Renny looked right at the man and smiled. "Isn't that nice? See what happens when you give a beer to a man with a tiny dick?"

The crowd laughed, but the heckler wasn't done. He yelled out again, even louder, "You're a *faggot*!"

And Renny smiled and said, "You really think I'm a faggot, why don't you just suck my dick, and if I like it—damn, you were right. And if I don't like it—at least *you* got some action tonight."

The crowd gave Renny quite an ovation, and the heckler slumped back into his seat as Renny moved on. And I suppose it wasn't really a remarkable exchange, no more than the kind of routine put-down that happens every night, every place a comic stands in front of a crowd. But for me, it was very memorable—not for the high quality of the sparkling wit, but for something very different.

Because as Renny's eyes moved over me to focus just over my head at the heckler, I felt the hair go up on my neck, and deep inside Castle Dexter an alarm began to toll as my Passenger whipped up into High Alert and began to hiss warnings at me.

And as Renny focused on his heckler and crushed him, I saw the Thing behind his eyes, the Thing I thought I might have seen, and now there was no doubt, none at all. Above all the noise of the crowd I heard the sibilant roar of the huge Dark Thing that reared triumphantly from the deep shadows behind Renny's smile. And I watched it uncoil and flare up into its great shadowy length, and reach its long and sharp claw at the heckler, and it was there for all the world to see, and although no one else did see it, I saw it and I knew.

A Passenger. No doubt about it.

I don't know how or why, but I always know it when I see it. I always have. And there was no doubt now, none at all: Renny had a Dark Passenger, just like me.

Renny moved on, and I am sure the rest of his show was every bit as funny and filled with savage insight, but I did not notice. I was lost in a train of thought that took me far away down the tracks, and I would not have noticed if Renny set himself on fire.

At first I merely thought about the fact that Renny was a monster, just like me. But that led me on to thoughts that were far loftier, and much more to the point. Because Renny had a Passenger. I didn't know how he managed its care and feeding, but he had one. And if he could survive, and even flourish in Hollywood . . . why couldn't I?

I pictured it in my imagination: Dexter lounging by the pool in Bel Air, watching the shadows grow deeper as the sun drifted down into the Pacific Ocean and a slow fat moon began to creep up into the sky, and Dexter feels the old Happy Night thrill begin to take him over, and he rises from his poolside perch and with his customary care he pads into the large and airy house on his predator's feet and reaches for his ready-packed bag of toys and tools and away he slides into a night that is just as dark and welcoming, no matter that the sun sets, instead of rises, in the water.

It could work. There was no reason it shouldn't. And I could not shake the idea that I would be far happier on that western shore, in a land of new opportunity, a fresh panorama of unexplored darkness.

But of course . . . I had not actually been invited. And there was no reason to think I would be. Jackie certainly had her own life in California, with her own friends and routines and security measures, and aside from one quick kiss, she had given me no indication that I would ever be a part of that life. If I was logical about things, I had to admit that most probably, when the pilot was finished shooting here, she would thank me, hug me, and return to the West Coast, leaving Dexter behind as no more than an occasional fond memory.

And no matter how much I wanted it to be more than that, I couldn't make that happen, and I couldn't even say what that "more" would be.

So as Renny's performance wound on to its no doubt hilarious conclusion, it was a somewhat Disheartened Dexter who finally came back to his grumpy senses as he realized that everyone around him was leaping to their feet and applauding madly. And because the First Principle of the Harry Code is to fit in, Dexter stood and clapped, too.

Rita stood next to me, clapping with manic enthusiasm. Her cheeks were slightly flushed and a very big smile was plastered on her face, a smile like I had never seen before, joy and thrill mixed together with excitement. She looked ecstatic, as if she had just gotten a glimpse into a world of magical beauty. I am sure the show was enjoyable, but Rita seemed transported to another plane. I had sat beside her on the couch and watched TV with her every night for years, and never suspected that the world of entertainment and its denizens were so important and enthralling to her. I couldn't imagine how anyone with a three-digit IQ could possibly be so mesmerized— but of course, I knew Renny and Robert much better than she did.

And when the applause finally trickled to a halt, she still stood there, staring at the stage, as if she was looking at a spot where a miracle had just happened. It wasn't until Robert tapped me on the shoulder and said, "Hey, Dex—I gotta get going," that she finally stopped beaming at the empty stage and went back into shock.

"Oh," she said. "Oh my— Dexter, Mr. Chase is . . ." And she collapsed into silence, blinking and blushing.

"Just Robert," he said, predictably, and he smiled at her. "And can I call you, uh . . . ?"

"Rita," I told him.

"Rita. Right! Well, hey, Rita, you got a great guy here." He clapped me on the shoulder to show how much he approved of me. "You'd better hang on to him," he said. He winked at her, and put a hand on her upper arm. "You let him hang out with these Hollywood types, and they may try to steal him."

Rita turned even redder. "Thank you, Mr. aahh, I mean Robert, I—oh," she said. She put the knuckles of her right hand into her mouth, as if she'd said something awful and wanted to punish her teeth.

Robert didn't seem to notice. He just squeezed her arm and said, "My pleasure. Great to meet you, Rita." He gave her arm another squeeze, and looked at me. And then, with annoying inevitability, he shot me with his finger-gun again, and said, "See you Monday, partner." He pushed past us and walked away up the aisle. Rita watched him go, knuckles still in her mouth. "Oh, my God," she said.

I glanced around. Jackie was standing at her seat with Debs, but she was looking at me, and I was suddenly very tired of Rita's worshipful blathering over Robert. "Come on," I said. "I'll walk you out to your car." And to my complete surprise, she threw her arms around me and gave me a crushing hug, accompanied by a series of wet kisses on my face.

"Oh, Dexter, thank you," she said. "This has been the most amazing— To see Robert Chase, and actually *talk* to him . . . !" she said into my ear, and she planted another damp kiss on me. "And Renny Boudreaux was *wonderful*—I mean, the language was a bit rough. But seriously—thank you. Thank you so much for this."

It seemed like a bit much; the tickets hadn't cost me anything, and I had been ordered to show up with Rita. But I just said, "You're welcome," and pried myself out of her embrace. "Where did you park?"

"Oh," she said, "just a couple of blocks away—at the hotel?"

"All right," I said, and I tried to steer her out. But apparently she wasn't finished yet.

"I really— I mean it. Thank you, Dexter; this has been so, just, like a dream," she said.

There was more, and I just kept nodding and smiling, and finally she wore down and I got her moving up the aisle toward the lobby and out the door at last and into the bright downtown Miami night.

I walked her to the parking garage, listening to her recap of the show, telling me Renny's best lines—all of which I had, after all, just heard myself. But she took great delight in repeating them, and eventually I tuned her out altogether until we arrived at her car.

"Good night," I said, and I opened the car door for her. She leaned forward and kissed my cheek again.

"Thank you so much, Dexter," she said. "It really was wonderful— and when will you come home?"

"Just a few more days," I said, and I'm pretty sure I kept the regret out of my voice.

"All right," she said. "Well . . ." And I began to think she would stand there in the open door of her car until she was struck by lightning. So I planted a peck on her cheek.

"Good night," I said. "I'll see you soon." And I took a step backward to give her enough room to close the car's door, with her on the inside. She blinked at me for a moment, and then she smiled.

"Good night, Dexter," she said. And she got into the front seat, started the car, and drove away. And I went back to find Jackie, thinking I might as well enjoy myself now.

It would all be over soon enough.

# TWENTY-FIVE

I N THE NIGHT I WOKE UP TO THE SOUND OF SIRENS. THEY WERE a few miles away, winding up the scale in their flat, urgent wail, but the sound was coming closer, and without even thinking about it I knew what that meant and where they were headed: here, to this hotel, because another body had turned up, which meant—

*Patrick*, I thought. *He's done it again.* And in my half-sleeping brain I could see his eager face as he slipped out of the chains I had put so carefully around him, and in half-waking horror I watched as he slowly, happily began to swim in toward the hotel, toward *me*, his rotting face set in a dead smile—

The image was too close and far too real and I jerked my eyes open. *Impossible*, I told myself. But in the darkened room with the sirens wailing and sleep still crusting my brain it did not seem impossible. *He's dead*, I told myself, *absolutely positively dead*. And I knew this with complete certainty, but just as surely the sirens were coming closer, and just as surely I knew they were coming here.

I looked around the darkened room and tried to focus on real things: a chair, a table, a window. The ghosts began to fade back into dreams, and I took a deep breath—and then a new thought came barreling in, and in its own way it was just as troubling as the first nightmare:

*What if I killed the wrong person?*

What if that had been some Eagle Scout–innocent kayaker, who just happened to resemble a blurry picture on Facebook? And I had stabbed him and drowned him and sent him to feed the crabs, thinking it was Patrick—and now the *real* Patrick was right here, right now, in this hotel, and he had just killed someone, and he might even be on his way up here, to this room—

I was wide-awake now. I rolled off the couch and stood there for a moment, blinking stupidly, and then I picked up the Glock and padded across the floor to the door of Jackie's room. I paused there for a moment, listening for any sound, and as I put my ear against the door it jerked open and I almost fell over.

Jackie stood there, eyes wide, one hand on the doorknob and one hand at her throat. She was wearing a plain cotton nightgown that came down to midthigh, and somehow, on her it seemed more enticing than anything Frederick's of Hollywood could ever come up with. I gaped for just a moment before her voice brought me back to the real world.

"I heard the sirens," she said. "I thought . . ." She glanced down and saw the pistol in my hand and her eyes went even wider. "Oh," she said.

"I thought so, too," I said, and she nodded.

For half a minute we both just stood there, listening as the sirens wound their way closer. There was never any doubt in my mind that they were headed here, but even so, we both held our breath as we heard the high, screaming note slide down the scale and then stop right below us, in the courtyard of the hotel. I went over and slid the balcony door open. I stepped out and looked down. Two patrol cars had parked at sloppy, cop-in-a-hurry angles. Their doors hung open and the flashing lights reflected up and onto the front of the hotel, and as I watched, more cars pulled in behind them, motorpool cars filled with detectives. I went back in and stood beside Jackie and we watched the lights flashing through the open balcony door until Jackie finally remembered to breathe.

"Oh," she said. "Oh, shit."

"Yup," I said.

Jackie inhaled raggedly, and then said, "It isn't . . . I mean, we don't know . . . Shit." Even with the incomplete sentences, I followed her logic exactly. And although I wanted to reassure her, tell her it really wasn't, it really *couldn't* be, that half-dreamed image would not leave me, and I just stood there and felt the sweat come out of my hand and onto the grip of the Glock.

Jackie shook her head, and then walked quickly across the room to the couch and sat down, leaning forward, knees together, with her hands on the cushion beside them. I followed and sat beside her. There didn't seem to be a whole lot to say. I remembered that I was still holding the Glock, and I slid the safety back on.

We were still sitting like that five minutes later when the house phone rang. I picked it up and said, "Yes?"

"What the fuck is going on?" a voice said; I recognized it as my sister, Deborah, and she sounded very tense. "Are you all right?"

"We're fine, Debs," I said, as soothingly as I could manage. "Are you here at the hotel?"

Debs breathed out, sounding almost like she was expelling a lungful of cigarette smoke. "I'm downstairs, in the lobby," she said.

"What happened down there?" I asked, which was unnecessary. I was pretty sure I knew *what* had happened; I just didn't know to *whom*.

"There's a dead woman up there, one floor down from yours," Debs said, and her voice sounded very harsh. "She's pretty torn up, but she's carrying a driver's license in the name of Katherine Podrowski. That mean anything to you?"

"Podrowski?" I said, and behind me I heard Jackie gasp and then make a brief whimpering sound.

"Kathy . . . ?" she said.

"A room service waiter saw blood coming under the door. He used a passkey, took one look, and he's still crying," Debs said. "It sounds like our guy did it again."

"But . . ." I said, and happily for me, I stopped before I said anything more.

"Is it Kathy?" Jackie said in a hoarse and frightened whisper.

"She's been ripped up, gutted, and her eye is missing," Deborah went on, rather relentlessly, I thought, and very definitely harshly now.

"Which eye?" I asked her.

Deborah hissed, long and loud.

"I'm coming up," she said, and hung up the phone.

I hung up, too, and went back to sit beside Jackie. "It's Kathy," I said.

"Oh, dear God," Jackie said. She hugged herself, and then she began to shake, and then she was crying. "Oh, my God," she said. For a few moments she cried and rocked, arms locked tight around herself. Then she took a long and ragged breath, and leaned forward over her knees. "Oh, Jesus, oh, shit," she said. "This is my fault; it's all my fault." And she put her hands over her face and, after a moment, her shoulders began to shake again.

As I have mentioned, I don't really understand most of human behavior, but I do know a standard cue when I see one, and when a woman hides her face in her hands and cries, any man seated next to her is supposed to provide comfort and support. So I did that, putting one arm around Jackie and patting her shoulder gently with my hand.

"It's not your fault," I said, which was true enough to be obvious. "You didn't ask for a psychotic stalker."

She sniveled loudly, the first unattractive thing I had seen her do. "I should have told them," she said. "I should have . . . So selfish, and now Kathy is dead."

"There's no way you could have known he would do this," I said. "It's really not your fault." And it might not be completely flattering to me, but I was actually feeling very proud of the way I kept finding appropriate things to say to her. After all, most of my brainpower was devoted to trying to figure out who had killed Kathy, since I was pretty sure it wasn't Patrick.

"It is. It *is* my fault," she insisted. "If I hadn't been so concerned with my own stupid career—and now Kathy is dead for a stupid TV show I don't even like!" Her shoulders shook harder, and then she gave a wail, combined with a snuffle, and she turned to me, shoving her face against my chest, and as she did I became very aware that her nightgown was really quite thin, and I was still dressed for sleep—which is to say, bare chested and wearing only a pair of battered boxer shorts. My other arm went around her reflexively and I held her, feeling tears and other things sliding down my side and wondering why I didn't mind.

Because I didn't mind; in fact, I was rather enjoying myself. I stopped patting her and instead began to rub her shoulder, in a way I hoped was as soothing to her as it was to me. Her skin was warm and dry and very soft, and I could still smell a faint tang of perfume coming off it, and I began to imagine all kinds of unthinkable things that really didn't fit the mood of recent murder.

Luckily for all of us, an authoritative pounding sounded on the door to the suite, and I pried myself away from Jackie and went to the door. "Who is it?" I said, rather unnecessarily.

"Who the fuck do you think it is?" snarled somebody who could only be Deborah. "Open the fucking door!"

I opened the fucking door and Deborah shoved furiously past me and into the room. She stopped when she saw Jackie slumped on the couch, red eyed and runny nosed and, it must be admitted, not really looking her very best. Debs turned back to me, and for the first time seemed to notice that my attire was somewhat informal. She shook her head, still clearly smoldering about things in general and looking for something to scorch. As usual, it turned out to be me.

"Nice panties," she said, glancing pointedly at my boxers. "You plan to chase this guy like that?"

I truly wanted to tell Deborah that I wasn't going to be chasing this guy at all, not without a scuba tank—but I couldn't. Debs knows what I am, and in her limited way she almost approves—but Jackie did not, could not, and that would have made the conversation very awkward. And I was still closing my mouth when that tiny, mean-spirited uncertainty crept back in, the completely ridiculous, illogical thought that I might have killed the wrong person. So instead I simply said, "Does it really look like the same killer?"

Deborah glared at me. "How many of these freaks you think we got running around?" she said, and I had a very uncomfortable moment before she added, "I haven't seen the body yet, but it sounds the same."

"Oh," I said, with a small flutter of hope. Jackie snuffled loudly, and I remembered why. "Do they have a positive ID?"

"The driver's license picture matches up," Deborah said. "It's her, no doubt. Kathy Podrowski." And she looked at Jackie and said, rather unnecessarily, "Your assistant."

Jackie made a sound somewhere between a moan and a retch, and Deborah turned back to me. "We both know what this means," she said. "And we both know what we have to do about it."

"Yes," I said. "You have to tell the officer in charge what we've been sitting on."

"That's right," she snarled.

"Um," I said. "Who has the lead?"

Deborah's face got even angrier, which was impressive. "Anderson," she spat.

I blinked. "But that's . . ." I said, but Debs shook her head bitterly.

"Two drive-bys this week, plus a ritual beheading, and the cannibal thing in the Grove," she said. "So Anderson comes up in the rotation again, because I am busy covering up this psycho bullshit and when Captain Matthews finds out I'll be lucky if I only get busted down to Code Enforcement and— *Shit*, Dexter!"

There was a faint sound of throat clearing from the couch, and we both turned to Jackie. She was sitting up very straight, knees together, one hand held at her throat. Her eyes were red rimmed, but she had stopped sniffling and was clearly trying to control her emotions. "If it could hurt your career . . ." she said tentatively.

"Don't even say it," Deborah snapped.

Jackie looked puzzled, then shocked. She shook her head. "Oh, no," she said. "I was just . . . I was going to say, I can tell them it was my fault. Which it is, because your orders were to do what I asked, and . . ." She raised a hand, then dropped it to the couch beside her. "I just . . . I don't want anybody else to get hurt," she finished weakly. She met Deborah's glare for a moment without blinking, and then she glanced away. "It's my fault," she said, and she looked so small and vulnerable that I wanted to kill things for her.

Deborah didn't seem to feel the same way. "It doesn't matter what you tell them," she said harshly. "I'm a sworn officer and I am supposed to know better." She stared at Jackie, but Jackie didn't look up, and after a moment Deborah's look softened just a bit and she said, "It's not your fault. I'm the one who— I *do* know better than this, and

I did it anyway." Deborah straightened up like she was getting ready to face a firing squad—which she was, administratively speaking. "I fucked up. I had the responsibility, so I take the heat," she said. She took a deep breath, turned away, and headed for the door with such a precise march step that I could almost hear "Colonel Bogey" playing.

"Deborah," I said. She looked at me bleakly with one hand on the doorknob, but I couldn't think of anything to say to make it better. "Um . . . good night . . . ?"

Debs looked at me without expression for what seemed like a long time. Then she just shook her head, opened the door, and left.

I went over and put the chain and the security lock back on. I stood there for a moment, thinking about what Kathy's death meant. Whether the chat with Deborah had sent a jolt of adrenaline into my brain, or I was just coming fully awake, I began to see small and troubling inconsistencies. If somebody was able to get into Kathy's room, wouldn't it be just as easy to get in here, into our room? And even more basic: Why Kathy? She was not blond, not young, and definitely not attractive. Her body had not been dumped somewhere public, and Debs said there was blood coming under the door, which did not fit the way the other victims had been butchered. Of course, Patrick could have been rushed, might have had to hurry more than he liked, and so—

But no: absolutely not. It truly was impossible, and I pushed the thought firmly away. It was not Patrick, could not be Patrick. I had killed *him* and no other, and Patrick was dead and gone, half eaten already by hungry sea life. And no matter how popular the notion was on TV at the moment, I refused to believe that he had come back from the dead. It was very definitely not Patrick.

So who was it?

Who had killed Kathy, and why?

And what, if anything, did I do about it? After all, it really wasn't my problem. Kathy had hated me, and I had no reason to care. Her death, no matter how unpleasant, had absolutely nothing to do with me, and there was no reason at all I should give it a second thought.

Of course Jackie was upset, but she would find a new assistant. She should be more worried about losing the role that had brought her to Miami. Because Deborah really would have to report the threat of a stalker. Even if I told my sister that the stalker was no more, she could not very well tell another detective.

And so Debs was probably right—she was in trouble. How much trouble would depend on a lot of things, like what kind of spin she gave it when she told Matthews what had happened. There were possibilities; by emphasizing very carefully that she had been following orders, assisting the production, and that she had given Detective Anderson the relevant information but he had been busy making a complete mess of the investigation, it could be done. Deborah might come out of it unharmed. Of course, it would have to be done very subtly, but still—

And as that word "subtly" passed through my mind, I sighed. Deborah was as subtle as a steam shovel. She would not have even an inkling of how to go about something like this. I might be able to script it for her, but she could never perform it as written. I knew my sister well, and although she had vast ability as a cop, she had absolutely none as a politician. She had never been able to make herself play the game properly, and she wasn't going to start now. Besides, she had already worked herself up into a masochistic frenzy and was clearly almost eager to take the bullet here, because it was the Right Thing to do—as if that ever really meant anything.

No: The way things stood right now, Deb's goose was cooked. And when that happened, Dexter was bound to end up as dessert. I was supposed to know where the line was, just as clearly as she did, and I had just as certainly crossed it. I wasn't sure what my punishment would be—Code Enforcement had no forensics department— but it would almost certainly be something unpleasant. Suspension, probably loss of pay—and just when I needed the money most.

"Dexter," Jackie said softly, and I jerked around to face her. For a moment, lost in my unpleasant thoughts, I had forgotten she was there. "What will happen?" she said. "To Deborah? And to you."

I shook my head. "Too soon to say," I said.

"But it might be bad?"

"Maybe," I said, and she looked down at her knees. They were very nice knees, but I could see no overwhelming reason for her to look at them. I watched her, but she didn't do anything else interesting, and after a moment a huge yawn took me over and I realized that I was very tired. It was, after all, still the middle of the night, and pretending to be eternally vigilant really does take a lot of energy. Suddenly I wanted nothing in the world more than just to lay me down and sleep—and Jackie was sitting on my bed, which would make stretching out and going to sleep a little awkward, or at least very crowded. I had just composed a polite way to ask Jackie to move off the couch so I could lie down and sleep when she blurted out, still staring at her knees, "He'll come back, won't he."

At first I didn't know what she meant, and then I wasn't sure what to say. After a few seconds of puzzled silence she finally looked up at me and said, "The killer. Patrick. He's going to come back and try again."

"Oh, I don't know," I said.

"He will," she said. "I know he will. And next time . . ."

Jackie shuddered, but she didn't say anything more, so I went back to my prepared remarks on the subject of slumber. "Anyway," I said, "tomorrow is a long day." I went over to the couch and stood above her, looking down longingly at my place of rest. "We should try to get some sleep," I told her.

She stood up abruptly, and in trying to get out of her way I almost fell onto the coffee table. She grabbed at my arm and steadied me, but when I straightened up she didn't let go. Instead, she pulled herself closer and looked up at me, and her violet eyes were huge and seemed to go on forever.

"He will come back," she said. "I know he will." She took a deep and uneven breath. "He could even be here in the hotel right now."

She was much closer to me than she needed to be to tell me that, but I didn't complain. I just swallowed and answered her with a mouth that was suddenly very dry for some reason. "Well, maybe," I said, and somehow she found a way to move even closer.

"I don't want to be alone," she said. "Not tonight. I'm . . . scared." She raised her face up to mine with her eyes wide and wild, and I felt myself falling forward into an endless violet sea.

I didn't get very much sleep that night, but I didn't really mind. It turned out I wasn't nearly as tired as I'd thought.

# TWENTY-SIX

WOKE UP IN THE NIGHT AND FOR ALMOST A FULL MINUTE I LAY drowsing, eyes closed, with no idea where I was. That didn't seem worrisome for some reason. A soft and fragrant sheet covered me from the waist down, and a feeling of half-ecstatic numbness covered the rest of me, and I lay there between sleep and waking and wondered how I got wherever I was and why it should make me feel so good.

And then something rustled beside me and my eyes opened wide at the sound. I turned to my left and looked.

Jackie Forrest, TV star, adored by millions and pursued by Greek arms dealers, lay there next to me, naked. Her golden hair was tousled and spread unevenly across the pillow, and one hand was clenched beside her face. The sheet was pulled halfway down; I could see the faint spray of freckles that ran across her shoulders, down her chest, and over her breasts—her perfect, amazing breasts.

I had never before understood the male obsession with this female feature; breasts are, after all, no more than a functional, even utilitarian article of equipment. They were originally a necessary survival tool for raising healthy offspring, rendered slightly obsolete by bottles and modern baby formula, and to fall into a vacuous trance at the mere sight of them had always seemed to me the height of human stupidity.

But as I looked at Jackie Forrest's breasts, I understood the madness for the first time. Jackie's breasts were a thing apart from humanity; they stood alone on the plane of avatars, beautiful, perfect, iconic things, the very embodiment of all that the ideal female breast should be, so far beyond anything I had ever seen before that I could only stare at them and marvel. So *this* was what all the fuss was about. . . .

I couldn't help myself; I reached a hand out and touched the closest breast. The feel of it was soft, incredibly smooth, and invited a closer and more thorough examination. I covered it with my hand and was rewarded with a feeling of satisfaction I had never before experienced, or even believed was possible. The perfect pink nipple rubbed against the palm of my hand, and it grew harder—and that, too, was amazingly, implausibly satisfying.

Jackie moved slightly, a small shifting of hips and shoulders, and one eyelid fluttered. I took my hand away, and then, still not at all sure what I was doing or why, I moved my mouth down to her breast and rubbed my lips on it.

Jackie stirred again, and then her hand slid softly over my cheek and around to the back of my neck, and I sat up to look at her face.

Her eyes were half open and her tongue slid over her lower lip and then her mouth curved into a sleepy smile. "Again . . . ?" she said in a husky half whisper. She reached a hand up and pulled my face down onto hers, and we again'd.


Somewhere far away, in a fog of perfect bliss, an annoying buzz began to worm its way into the ethereal cloud of euphoria where Dexter floated undreaming. I tried to push it away and rise back up onto my cloud, but the sound got louder and more insistent, and the cloud began to break up, wisps of sheer happiness fading into the dull, grainy-eyed numbness of returning consciousness. I heard a rustling beside me and opened one eye as Jackie slapped at the alarm clock, and then lurched out of bed and scurried for the bathroom.

I watched her go, stupid from lack of sleep, but awake enough to marvel at what had happened to me. I was lying in a Real Star's bed, and I had spent the night doing improbable things with her—things I had never before thought about doing, but somehow I had done them quite naturally with Jackie. And I thought again about the crowds that followed her with such slack-jawed adoration, and how any one of them would have given everything they owned to be me right now—or at any rate, a few hours ago. But there was only one me, and I was it, and I had spent the night in bed with Jackie Forrest.

I heard the water start up in the bathroom, and Jackie began to splash around under the shower. I stretched and lay there for a moment, very pleased with myself. I had done a remarkable thing, and I felt quite good about it. But beyond that, I realized I was also hungry, which shouldn't have been a surprise. After all, I had burned quite a few calories in the night, and my body was never shy about asking for a refill.

I got out of bed and stared dopily around, looking for my shorts. I was pretty sure they had made it into the room, but not at all certain about just how far. I finally found them at the foot of the bed, under the crumpled bedspread. I pulled them on and padded out to the living room, site of my former bed, the elegant leather couch. Lovely to look at, delightful for lounging, but not at all the ideal spot for sleeping, and I would have been glad to move off it for a much smaller reason. But to move right off the couch and into Jackie's bed was the best of all possible worlds.

But as I caught myself sinking into a bog of fatuous self-congratulation, a nasty little thought dove in beside me. Why should I assume the move meant anything? Last night Jackie had been upset, scared, desperately in need of comfort and company. That was no guarantee that she would feel that way again tonight, or the next night, or ever. I am hugely ignorant of human sexual and emotional matters, but I knew enough to know that almost nothing in that area is ever certain. Everyone is different, everyone has different expectations, and no two humans ever have the same experience, even when they have it together. From what I can tell, the whole thing is like two people speaking different languages that have the same words; it all sounds the same, but the words have different meanings in each language. For one person *love* means sex, and for the other it means forever—two completely different meanings, and yet even the pronunciation of the syllable is the same.

So what did last night really mean?

For me? I'd had a far better time than I'd ever had without using duct tape, and I was very willing to make it the New Normal—but I had no idea what Jackie was thinking. She'd acted like she was having fun—but it could have been just that, acting. Maybe she had decided to trade a few hours of undignified exertion for the extra protection of having somebody next to her, a security blanket in case Patrick showed up. It certainly made more sense than thinking she had decided that Dexter was destined to be her one and only forever. After all, she was a world-famous beauty, and what was I? Nothing, really, no more than a simple forensics geek who moonlighted as a human vivisectionist. I had no right to assume there would be any more than one night, no logical reason to think that one evening of sweaty embrace had been the first step into a bright new future.

I stood there beside the couch in the warm sunlight that poured in through the windows, and I felt myself deflate. It would all end much too soon, and now there was a great deal more to regret than the excellent room service menu.

On the other hand, the menu truly was excellent, and deflated or not, I was still hungry. I picked up the phone and ordered breakfast.

I had finished eating and was halfway through my second cup of coffee by the time Jackie finally came out onto the balcony. She hesitated for just half a second, and then she leaned over and kissed me before she sat down. "Good morning," she said.

"It seems to be," I said cautiously. "How . . . um," I said, and I heard myself stutter off into a rather awkward silence.

"What?" Jackie said.

"Well," I said. "I was going to ask how you slept—but it suddenly sounded awfully stupid, because . . ."

"Yes," she said.

"So, um—would you like some coffee?"

"Very much."

I poured her a cup and she picked it up and held it in front of her mouth with both hands, blowing to cool it, and then sipping. When it was about half gone, she lowered the cup and took a deep breath. Then she let it out, slowly and audibly, and looked down at her lap. "I don't . . ." she said, and then bit her lip and looked up. "I feel terrible."

I did not see any way to take that remark as a compliment, and that must have shown on my face, because Jackie looked slightly startled and hurriedly added, "About Kathy. Being—dead."

"Oh," I said, with a certain amount of very selfish relief. I had been so wrapped up in my own torturous thoughts that I had actually forgotten about Kathy's murder. Very shallow, no doubt, but I have never claimed to be a compassionate person.

"It's my fault," Jackie said. "My selfishness got her killed. And then we— I just feel so *awful* about what I did. . . ."

I wanted to tell her that she really shouldn't, because she had done it quite well, but this time I knew she was talking about Kathy. Clearly, some words of comfort were called for—and surprisingly, I realized I wanted to make her feel better. "Jackie," I said. "It really wasn't your fault. If anything, it was mine."

She looked startled. "Yours?" she said, and I nodded.

"I am supposed to be the expert," I said. "And I had no idea he would attack Kathy. So you couldn't possibly know."

Jackie sipped her coffee and frowned. "Maybe," she said. "But—"

"In fact," I said, "this is so totally against Patrick's pattern that I wouldn't be at all surprised to find out it wasn't him." I did not add that I would have been even more surprised to find out it *was*.

"You mean somebody *else* killed Kathy?" she said. "But *why*?"

"I don't know," I said.

Jackie frowned and looked down, and then shook her head. "No," she said at last. "Who else could possibly— No. That's crazy."

"That's exactly my point," I said. "Sane and solid citizens usually don't do these things." And I have to say I spoke with some expertise here.

She thought about it, sipping her coffee, and finally she sighed and shook her head again. "No," she said. "I know you're trying to make me feel better, but . . . I don't believe it."

I looked at Jackie, wallowing in needless misery, and in one of the strangest moments yet, I realized I wanted her to smile, laugh, feel the sun and the wind on her face and know true joy, or at least finish her coffee without bursting into tears. "What if I can prove it was somebody else?" I said, and she looked half startled.

"How?" she said.

I smiled, and it was very nearly a real smile. "This is what I do," I said. "In all modesty, I have to admit that I am pretty good at forensics."

"And one or two other things," she said, but she heard herself being lighthearted and looked guilty. She turned away again, frowning.

"All I'm asking is to let me look at the reports and talk to Vince before you decide that you don't deserve to live anymore," I said.

A long moment later, she looked back to me, and if there was no actual hope on her face, at least she didn't look completely miserable anymore. "All right," she said. She took another sip of coffee, followed by a deep breath, and she let a determined look settle onto her face. "Fine," she said. She put the cup down and reached for the two covered dishes on the tray, then hesitated. "Which one is mine?" she asked.

"Both of them," I said, and she raised an eyebrow. "Well, I wasn't sure—I mean, I got your regular church-mouse breakfast," I said, tapping one of the silver covers, "but I thought . . . Anyway, there's also an omelet and some bacon, in case you wanted something more, because, um . . ." I finished lamely, sounding far too much like Rita.

"Because I worked up an appetite last night?" she said.

"Well—yes, I guess so."

She smiled. "I did," she said. "But we start work in front of the cameras tomorrow, so . . ." She shrugged and lifted the cover off the toast and grapefruit juice. She put the cover aside and picked up a piece of toast, crunching at it and sipping the juice.

I eyed the other cover, the one over the omelet, and whether I was truly hungry or just needed something to do, I lifted the cover. "If you're sure," I said. "I mean, it's really very good."

Jackie sipped her juice. "I'm sure," she said.

I ate the omelet.

When I was done, I poured more coffee into Jackie's cup, and then into mine. We sipped, and the silence grew, and I wondered whether I should start babbling, just to fill the silence.

"Listen," she said at last. I looked at her attentively. "Last night . . ." She sipped again, and then looked away. "It was very nice," she said.

"*Very* nice," I said. "I mean, *nice* doesn't really seem adequate."

She looked back at me and flashed a brief smile. "I'm glad you think so," she said. "But . . ." She shook her head and looked down at her feet. "There's always a *but*, isn't there?"

"I don't, um . . . Is there? I mean, always?" I asked.

Jackie looked up at me again and made a kind of rueful smile. "Yeah, always," she said. "I mean, right now it's, 'Wowee, thank you, Jesus, one more time'—but things are always different in daylight. . . ." She was probably right, and for a brief moment I wanted to try it in daylight to see how different it was, but Jackie didn't seem to share that mood; she sighed heavily and looked away again.

"I was scared last night," she said. "I was sure he was in the hotel, coming for me, and—" She paused abruptly and blinked at me. "Not that . . ." she said, looking very uncomfortable. "I mean—it was something I really wanted to do. With . . . you." She looked at her knees. "You have this . . . I don't know. Something about you that . . ." She pursed her lips and gave her head two very small shakes. "I don't know. Like you're this . . . normal *man*, secure and . . . and . . . solid? Ordinary? No, maybe comfortable?" She shook her head again. "And at the same time there's this feeling I get like you're one of the bad boys I used to like, with a switchblade in your pocket or something, and the combination is so . . ."

She looked up at me, and her tongue came out across her lower lip. She sighed, and looked down again. "I really do like you, Dexter," she said. "I mean, really. But . . . we live in different worlds, and you know. I'll go back to L.A., and you'll go back to your wife."

"I don't *have* to," I said, and it was out of my mouth before I even knew what I was saying.

She looked at me very seriously, and I looked back. Then she shook her head. "You have kids, and . . . Let's just not make this complicated, all right?"

"It's not that complicated," I said.

Jackie smiled, a little sadly, and said, "It is. It always is."

"I know I'm not a Greek arms dealer," I said. "But—"

She looked startled. "Oh!" she said. "Oh, no, it isn't that." She reached across the remnants of breakfast and took my hand. "I already have more money than I can spend," she said. "And if this show runs long enough to go into syndication, that's my F.U. money."

"Your what?"

She smiled. "F.U. money. Enough money to say, "Fuck you" to anybody or anything I don't like, and not have to worry about the consequences." She squeezed my hand, and then put it down. "Anyway, that's not the problem."

"What is the problem?" I said.

She sighed again, very deeply, and turned away to face the water. I looked at her profile. It was a very good profile, even though she was spoiling it a little with another frown, thinking her deep and unhappy thoughts about . . . what? Surely not me?

"I was selfish," she said at last. "And that got Kathy killed."

"Jackie, that's—"

"No, let me say this," she said. Her frown deepened. "So many people are just totally focused only on themselves, what *they* want, that they don't think about how it affects anybody else. Especially in my business."

"Not just *your* business," I said, thinking that it sounded like a good description of normal life.

"I've always hated that," she said. "I try to . . ." She waved a hand at the water. "There's this sense of . . . empowerment . . . that goes with being famous. And I've seen how it turns good people into . . . what . . ."

"Assholes?" I suggested, thinking of Robert.

"Uh-huh, okay," she said, still looking out over the Bay. "I don't want that." She turned back to face me, looking very serious. "I don't want to be that person."

"I don't think you are," I said.

"I will be," she said, "if I try to take you away from your family."

I looked at Jackie, and her deep violet eyes, set in that perfect, smooth, lightly freckled face, and for the first time it hit me that we were talking about exactly that: Jackie taking me away from my family. Dexter leaving Rita and the kids to gallop away into a mojito-soaked sunset and a life of top-shelf bliss. Jackie and Dexter, world without end—or at the very least, world without an end for a few more weeks.

I wanted that; I'd had a tiny taste of Jackie's world, and of Jackie, and I liked it. I liked everything about it: the swirl of the adoring crowd everywhere we went, the gratifying buzz of worship from everyone who saw us, the room service and limousines and phone interviews and the feeling of being so very important that every burp and hiccup of our life was significant—I liked it. I liked the feeling of being with Jackie, in her world—and in her bed. And I liked her. I wanted more of it, all of it.

And I thought about what that meant: to leave my familiar work-aday grind of crawling through violent traffic twice every day in an aging, battered little car, and slogging through the tired jokes and mind-less routines of my job, knee-deep in carnage and callousness. And for what? Just to bring home a far-too-meager paycheck, which vanished immediately into the continual, greedy vacuum of family life, with its mortgages and braces and new shoes and groceries. And the endless, weary grind of dealing with kids and their constant problems, always flung at you in the same self-involved, demanding whine; and the every-morning shattering clatter of finding socks and homework and the other shoe as they got ready for school, followed by more shouting and fighting and doors slamming—and then a virtually identical per-formance every night at bedtime; the diapers and arguments and new jeans and teacher conferences, and high-pitched fighting every earsplit-ting step of the way. And I thought about Rita, with her perpetually fractured sentences and eternal fussing about absolutely everything, and the lines settling into her face as she hurtled into an old age that shouldn't have come for another ten years at least, and the sense that she always wanted something from me that I couldn't give her, couldn't even identify. Could I really leave all this behind for mere perfection?

I thought I could.

I looked at Jackie. She was still watching my face, and her eyes were half filled with moisture. "Jackie," I said.

"I can't, Dexter," she said. "I just can't."

I stood up and went to sit beside her on the chaise longue. "I can," I said, and I kissed her. For just a moment she held back, and then she kissed me, too.

And it turned out that things weren't really all that different in daylight. Not even right there on the balcony . . .

# TWENTY-SEVEN

OUR UNSCHEDULED SIESTA ON THE CHAISE LONGUE BLENDED right into a surprise nap, and then a startling wake-up, which led to a second shower, and that took a great deal longer than it should have and ended up in Jackie's bed again. And the whole day passed in a lazy fog of stupid jokes and comfy dozing, and before I knew it, it was night.

And the next morning, Monday, came much too quickly and caught us both in a nearly comatose state, lost in a sleep so deep that we didn't hear the house phone until the third time it rang. I staggered out of bed and grabbed it, to learn that the limo driver was waxing wroth and demanding our immediate materialization in his car or we would be late on set and the forces of darkness would overwhelm his Town Car.

I quickly brushed my teeth and hair, and Jackie repaired her hair and makeup, and a very few minutes later we were catching our breath in the backseat of the limo, on our way to work.

We said no more about the future, but it was very much on my mind. It seemed the height of irony to me that although I had never really wanted to be saddled with a woman—except as part of my disguise—now I was hooked up to *two* of them. It was a bizarre situation for me, nearly surreal. I would never have guessed that among my other faults I was a satyr, a lecher, Don Juan Dexter, sauntering through life with a priapic smirk, eager hordes of feminine pulchritude trailing along in my wake. What a rascal I was—and how stupidly happy it made me. It was like living some absurd teen fantasy: hop out of bed with my pet goddess and then away in the limo. Off to a hard day on the set, lunch with my agent, saunter through an interview or two, always pausing along the way to allow the throngs of adoring women to bask in the glow of my radiant mojo. Dionysian Dexter, the surprise god of love.

My effervescent mood—and an accompanying silence from Jackie—lasted all the way to the soundstage the production had hired for the first day's shooting. It was a few blocks in from the river, on the north edge of the Little Havana area, and in spite of the very best efforts of our driver, we were ten minutes late.

"Shit!" Jackie said, as we drove through the gate and into the parking lot. "I hate being late. It always looks like diva bullshit."

"We have a really good excuse," I said.

She smiled and squeezed my hand. "Yes, we do," she said, "but not the kind of thing I can explain to the director."

"You want me to tell him?" I said.

"Let's just not do it again," she said. I raised an eyebrow at her and she laughed. "The late part, I mean," she added.

The car coasted to a halt in front of the big roll-up doors, and I looked up to see the driver watching us with interest in the rearview mirror. Our eyes met, and he winked. "We're here, Miss Forrest," he said.

"Thank you," Jackie said. She made a move for the door handle, but the driver was already out of the car and opening the door for her.

"I was told to say that everyone is gathering in the conference room," the driver said as I climbed out. He nodded at the smaller metal door beside the large roll-up. "At the end of the hall, on the right," he said.

"Everyone?" Jackie said. "Or just the cast?"

The driver shook his head. "I don't know, miss," he said. "They told me everyone—they didn't tell me what that meant."

Jackie bit her lip and frowned, then shook herself slightly. "Thanks," she told the driver, rewarding him with a small smile.

He bowed his head ever so slightly. "All part of the service," he said.

We went in through the door the driver had indicated, into a long-ish hallway painted a truly annoying light green color. On the right we passed two doors that opened onto the stage itself. On the left, the walls were decorated with smudges of paint, grease, and what I hoped was peanut butter. Midway we passed a large bulletin board festooned with notices, flyers, warnings from OSHA, and important safety regulations. Just beyond that we began to hear the buzz of conversation coming from the end of the hall. Jackie slowed her step and glanced at me. "You know what this means, don't you?" she said in a low and worried voice.

"The jelly doughnuts will be all gone?" I said.

Her smile was a little bit mechanical. "This is it," she said. "This is where they tell everybody about Patrick. And then they introduce my replacement." She took her lower lip between her teeth and bit down on it. "Oh, shit," she said. "I can't do this. Not with Rob—with everybody watching and secretly gloating."

I was sure she had started to say "Robert," and stopped herself after one loathsome syllable, and I felt a surge of sympathy. One of the few bits of human behavior I do understand is the natural reluctance to let your enemies see you humiliated. And since Jackie was with me now, and the enemy was an annoying pimple like Robert, I felt it, too. But I didn't see any way to avoid it, either.

So I put an arm around Jackie's shoulders and drew her close. "They can't replace you," I said.

She shook her head. "I don't see how they can avoid it. The insurance—"

"I will make them an offer they can't refuse," I said with my cheeks puffed out. It was not a very good imitation, and she did not give it a very good smile—but it was, at least, a smile.

"Thanks, Don Vito," she said. She pulled away from me, straightened her shoulders, and put on a small and confident smile. "Let's get it done," she said, and she marched toward the door at the end of the hall. I trailed behind, wondering if she was right. Would they really fire her? And if so, what happened to me? I might convince her that she still needed my special kind of protection—but what if she decided to flee? Fly back to L.A., or even someplace far away, where the hypothetical Patrick couldn't find her? Would I be invited to tag along to Sumatra, or Dubai, or Brisbane, wherever she ran to? I hoped so, but there was no way to know for sure.

Before I could decide, Jackie was there at the door to the conference room. She paused once again to compose herself, and then stepped through the doorway, with Dexter trailing behind like the tail to her comet.

Robert, Renny, and several others I didn't recognize were already seated at the large oak table that ran down the center of the room. Another cluster of people stood at the far end, where a coffee urn crouched beside several very promising-looking pastry boxes.

Somehow, Jackie fought off the siren call of the doughnuts, and marched right down the table, so I followed along. Robert called from his seat on the opposite side. "Hey, Dexter!" he said as we passed, and beside him, Renny nodded. I waved, and joined Jackie at a seat that was as far from Robert as she could get and still be in the conference room. Happily for me, there was an empty chair beside hers, and I slid into it.

Jackie immediately started chattering with the woman on her right, apparently working to establish that she was confident, light-hearted, and completely in control of a perfect universe. I looked around the room and studied the people crowded in. The group at the coffee urn seemed to be mostly technical people. They wore clothing that was worn and functional, occasionally decorated with clamps, rolls of tape, and other arcane tools.

The group at the table would have to be actors. They were not as well dressed as the crew, but their grubbiness was calculated and looked expensive. Their frequent smiles revealed universally perfect teeth, and they all glanced furtively at one another, as if to make sure no one was sneaking up behind them with a machete. I didn't see Deborah anywhere, and I couldn't decide if that was good or bad.

A moment later, Debs came in behind Mr. Eissen and Captain Matthews, and then I knew: It was bad. Her face was set in its most rigid, stony, I-Am-a-Cop mask, the one that showed that she was ruled by discipline and duty and had never had any soft feelings in her entire life. But because I knew her so well, I could see that behind

the mask she was seething, and as Detective Anderson followed her
through the doorway, smirking, I understood why. This was a public
firing squad, and the only real questions were how many bullets, and
what caliber.

Eissen went straight to the head of the table, and Captain Matthews followed right behind, with only one wistful glance at the
doughnuts to show us that he was still just a cop. Debs was one step
behind him, and Anderson brought up the rear, locking his eyes onto
Jackie with a kind of knowing, superior leer on his face.

Eissen sat down in the only empty chair; Matthews looked for
another and didn't see one, but his glance fell on Deborah, and he
frowned at her before turning back around to stand at Eissen's elbow,
in a posture that showed he really preferred to remain standing.

"Thank you for being prompt," Eissen said quietly, and the room
fell silent so quickly and completely that I wondered whether I had
gone deaf. "I know you are all eager to get to work. . . ." He gave a
very thin smile to show that this might be taken as a joke, but nobody
laughed. "So I will try to keep this brief." He glanced up at Matthews,
and then stared down the length of the table toward Jackie, and I felt
her stiffen slightly. "It has come to my attention that we have a . . . situation," he said, and he paused to tear his eyes away from Jackie and
look around the room before going on. "Miss Forrest has received a
number of very credible threats on her life."

Even Eissen's icy presence couldn't prevent the immediate mutter
of shock and wonder that blew through the room, and he waited it
out, cold blue eyes fixed on Jackie. She just smiled, outwardly unwor-
ried and carefree, and my opinion of her acting ability went up two
notches.

"In the normal course of events," Eissen went on, and the room
grew deathly still again, "we would delay the production and recast
Miss Forrest's part." He smiled, an even thinner and less humorous
twitch of the lips that made me wish I was armed. "For her own protection, of course, as well as to protect what is a considerable invest-
ment of the Big Ticket Network's time and money." He nodded at
Jackie, and she nodded back, with a much better fake smile than Eissen's.

"However," he said, and under the table I felt Jackie's hand clamp onto mine, "in this case we have come up with what we hope will be a . . . *productive* alternative." He frowned slightly, as if he was unhappy with his choice of adjective. "There are certain risks involved, but after consulting with Captain Matthews"—Eissen tilted his head to the side, and Matthews cleared his throat and then nodded—"and the detective in this case . . ." Anderson made a slight move, as if to step forward and say his name, but Eissen went right on, and Anderson settled back and continued to stare furtively, and hungrily, at Jackie.

" . . . I believe these risks can be minimized," Eissen said. He spread his hands to indicate the whole room. "The entire cast and crew are here, in a relatively expensive location, and that represents a great deal of money. If we delay the production now, that money is lost. And so I have decided"—Eissen closed his eyes and gave his tiny smile again—"in consultation with the network, of course"—he opened his eyes again—"that we will go forward as scheduled. With . . . Miss Forrest."

Jackie squeezed my hand so hard I thought she might break bones, and once again a whisper of surprise filled the room. Eissen waited for it to fade, and then went on.

"I admit I have been influenced by my publicity staff, who are . . . excited . . . by the kind of buzz this situation will create." He nodded twice, and said, "A show about a policewoman who chases killers— shot while a real killer chases her." Once more his lips moved into a thin smile. "When I say 'shot' I mean the pilot, not Miss Forrest."

Nobody laughed at this frigid flight of wit. It might have been his timing.

"In any case," Eissen went on, "this will almost certainly generate some very good publicity."

"And if I get killed," Jackie said, "it's even better publicity."

Eissen fixed his deadly stare on Jackie, but the quick bark of laughter from nearly everyone else in the room stopped him from optically flogging her, instead forcing him to put on his awful little smile again. "There is that," he said, and he got his own, slightly smaller laugh this time. "Of course, we all hope it won't come to that." Someone near the coffee urn muttered, "Of course." Eissen ignored that and went on.

"You have all signed a nondisclosure agreement," he said. "Our lawyers *assure* me"—and he paused for a moment to let us all feel the weight of that word—"that it applies to this situation. If you speak of this to *anyone* . . . Well, take my advice and don't." I looked around the room; it looked to me like nobody thought Eissen was kidding.

"Captain Matthews has assured me that his people can supply enough security to minimize the risk. For *all* of us. And I am asking you all to be extra-vigilant. This is a closed set. If you see anybody who doesn't belong, or notice anything out of the ordinary, tell a policeman. There will be plenty of them around." He glanced at Matthews, and the captain nodded.

"All right," Eissen said. "Let's go make a pilot." He gave a very slight wave of his hand. "Captain?"

Captain Matthews cleared his throat and stepped forward, frowning solemnly at all of us. "I want to reassure you all," he said. "We have this situation completely under control, and the investigation is moving forward in a very . . . ahemp. A satisfying manner." His frown deepened. "That is, we are quite confident that there is no significant danger that can't be, ah . . ." He glanced at Anderson, who just stood there, unsuccessfully trying to look serious and competent. "The investigating officer has *assured* me," Matthews said, and his tone made Anderson stand a little straighter, "that an arrest is expected very shortly." Anderson squirmed slightly, and Matthews paused for several powerful throat-clearing noises, a ploy I was quite sure he meant to let Anderson appreciate the fact that it was a threat—and probably to cover his own embarrassment at having to deliver such a dreadful Cop Cliché. "Arrest is expected" is an ancient phrase that means, freely translated, "We don't have a clue," and Matthews had used it very publicly to make certain that if an arrest did not, in fact, materialize, it would be Anderson's fault.

"And so . . . ahemp," Matthews said, "I ask you all to hmp. Be watchful, just like Mr. Eissen said." He smiled down at Eissen, who didn't appear to notice. "There is really nothing to worry about. With a few precautions. So just tell an officer if you see anything that seems, ah, dangerous." He frowned, as if he had heard the contradiction in what he had said, which didn't seem likely to me. Then he turned and stared at Deborah for a moment, before clearing his throat again. "Sergeant Morgan," he said ominously, and then turned back to face the room, "is familiar with the, ah, appearance. Of the suspect." He glared at Debs for a moment before going on. "Hmp. And she *will* be on set," he said, "for the duration of the filming process. The whole thing."

Deborah did not move, not even a twitch, but she radiated such angry unhappiness that I could feel it in my seat halfway down the table. Matthews put his stare on her for another long and awkward moment, and then turned back and gave the room a small and spasmodic smile. "So," he said. "I want to reassure you that we have given this matter our full attention. And I want to say again how happy we are to have you here, in Miami. And I hope you will all get a taste of the real Miami to, ah . . ." He paused and looked around, as if he had realized what he might be wishing on them, and wondering where he could stack the bodies. "The, uh, South Beach, you know," he said. "Nightlife. And the beaches." He nodded at the room, and gave them a manly and confident smile. "Enjoy yourselves," he said.

And while he was apparently wondering if he had any more to say, Eissen quietly slapped the palms of both hands on the table. "All right," Eissen said. "Thank you, Captain. And officers." He nodded once and glanced around the room. "We are all here to do a job. Let's do it." He scanned the crowd, possibly to see whether anybody would deny it and go on strike, and when no one did he nodded, stood up, and walked briskly out of the room.

Victor Torrano, the director, stood up from his seat near the head of the table. "All right, people," he called out, raising his voice over the babble. "We are already two hours behind schedule and we haven't started shooting yet. Let's get out there and get busy." One of the technical people yelled out, "Boo!" Victor shook his head and said, "Keep it up, Harvey. Just remember this is a right-to-work state," and people laughed and began to move off toward the door.

Victor moved toward the door, too, revealing a tense tableau behind the chair where Eissen had been sitting. Captain Matthews had turned around and was speaking quietly but firmly to Deborah, and she did not look pleased to have his full attention. Anderson stood behind them, head swiveling from one to the other as if he was watching a tennis match. I did not need to read lips to know that Debs was getting a reprimand, and Anderson was loving it.

"Thank God," Jackie murmured beside me. "Oh, thank God . . ."

I turned to face her. She was still showing the world a confident, carefree smile, but her voice trembled a bit, and her hand came back and clamped onto mine again under the table. She took a deep and slightly shaky breath, let it out, and then said, "I'm alive."

"And I'm very glad you are," I said.

She squeezed my hand, then let it go and stood up. "Let's find my dressing room," she said.

I followed her out the door and off along a branching hallway to the right. The first door we passed stood ajar. I glanced in: Both sides of the long room were covered with well-lighted mirrors, and a counter ran the whole length at waist level, a dozen chairs tucked under it. Against the back wall stood a clothing rack filled with cop uniforms, suits, shirts, and pants, with a neat row of shoes on the floor underneath. A piece of tape was stuck on the door at eye level. It said, MEN.

"That's where you'll get dressed," Jackie said. "With the other small-part guys."

"Small part?" I said.

She smiled and patted my shoulder. "Not the part that counts," she said.

The next door led to a nearly identical room, but it was labeled WOMEN this time. "You stay out of there," Jackie said, with a menacing frown. "It's filled with hussies."

"Yes, O Mighty One," I said.

The next door was closed, but labeled RENNY BOUDREAUX. Just past that was ROBERT CHASE, and as we came abreast of it, the door opened and Robert stood there in the doorway, blinking. His eyes flicked to Jackie, then to me; he froze, and he just goggled at me for a few seconds. "Oh," he said with a strange expression of some kind on his face—shock? Guilt? And then he quickly stepped back and closed the door.

Jackie shook her head. "Fucking weirdo," she muttered, and then we were at last standing in front of the door labeled JACKIE FOREST. She paused for a minute, looking at her name, and then shook her head. "At least they almost spelled it right," she said. She looked back along the hallway. "But they always put me last, farthest away." She made a face. "And right next to Bob, too."

"Robert," I said automatically, and Jackie snorted.

"Come on in," she said, and opened the door.

In most ways, Jackie's dressing room was a smaller copy of the men's and women's. But there was only one chair, in front of a smaller mirror. A table stood next to it, laden with a huge bouquet of fresh-cut flowers, a fruit basket, and a large and gaudy box of very expensive chocolates. Under the table was a small refrigerator, and along the wall opposite there was a soft-looking sofa. A door at the far end of the room stood half open to reveal a bathroom, complete with shower.

"Well," I said. "So this is how the one percent lives."

"Squalid," she said. "But you get used to it."

Before I could settle onto the sofa with the box of chocolates, a knock sounded on the door and, a moment later, it swung open and Detective Anderson sidled in. He was carrying a large cardboard box and wearing a truly annoying smirk. "Hey, Miss Forrest," he said.

Jackie raised an eyebrow and put on her smallest smile. "Yes?" she said.

Anderson put the box down on Jackie's dressing table and stuck out his hand. "Detective Anderson," he said, smiling at Jackie as if she was a jar of honey and he was a starving bear.

Jackie hesitated, and then shook his hand. "Oh, yes," she said. "I think I've heard your name."

"Yeah, listen," Anderson said, still clutching Jackie's hand. "I brought some stuff—um, your assistant? Miss Podrowski . . ."

The tiny smile left Jackie's face, and she yanked her hand away from Anderson's grip. "Yes," she said.

Anderson shifted his weight uncertainly, and then nodded at the cardboard box. "I, uh . . . I brought you her effects. From her room." He flicked the box with a finger. "Suitcase, purse, laptop. We been through it, and, uh, I was hoping you might take a look. See if you notice anything that we might miss?"

I said nothing, but I could not help thinking that what Anderson might miss would be a very long list. Jackie frowned and flicked her eyes toward me. "It might help," I said.

She looked back to Anderson. "All right," she said. "I'll take a look."

"Thank you, Miss Forrest," Anderson said. "I know how busy you are, but I'd appreciate it if you could, you know. As soon as possible."

"I'll take a look," Jackie repeated.

Anderson licked his lips and shifted his weight again. "And, uh," he said. A funny little smile flicked on and off his face. "I wanted to give you my *personal* assurance. I'm gonna get this guy, and you got nothin' to worry about."

"Thank you, Officer," Jackie said. She started to turn away from him, a clear dismissal, but Anderson touched her shoulder; she looked back at him, and he went on relentlessly.

"And, uh, you know," he said. "If you're feeling at all, you know. Like you're worried? I want you to think of me like I'm a security blanket. Totally available, twenty-four/seven." He held out a business card, nodded at her, and smiled as if he had just said something wonderful.

Jackie looked at him with a very serious and thoughtful expression on her face, and gave him a head-to-toe scan before looking him in the eye. For a few long seconds she said nothing, and Anderson got very uncomfortable, shifted his weight from foot to foot, and actually began to blush. "A blanket," Jackie said at last, deadpan. "Thank you." She smiled wickedly. "But I already have a nice warm blanket," she said, and she leaned over toward me and put a hand on the back of my neck, rubbing it lightly.

"I have to get to wardrobe," she said. "Can you walk me over, Dexter?" And she gave me a smile warm enough to singe Anderson's eyebrows.

"I'd be delighted," I said. Jackie touched my cheek, then turned away. I glanced at Anderson. His face was mottled and his mouth hung open, and he watched Jackie saunter away until I moved to follow, forcing him to step back. "Excuse me," I said. "I have to stay with Miss Forrest." He looked at me and I smiled. "I'm her blanket."

Anderson stared back at me with such pure hate that I wanted to stand there for a while and admire it, but after all, the work of a blanket is never done. "Bye now," I said, and I followed Jackie out of the room.

# TWENTY-EIGHT

I CAUGHT UP WITH JACKIE HALFWAY DOWN THE HALL, NOT AS easily as I should have, since she was practically sprinting away from Anderson. "Shit," she said when I finally stepped up beside her, "I can't deal with Kathy's stuff, not so soon." She shook her head. "And that odious dumbfuck Anderson," she said.

"Odious dumbfuck," I said, and I really was impressed with her colorful but accurate description. "You talk pretty."

But for some reason, my sincere praise did not lighten her mood. She bit her lip, and then shook her head again. "I can't— If I look at Kathy's things right now, I'll fall apart, and I can't go in front of the cameras looking like I've been crying," she said. She hesitated, then glanced at me. "Is it . . . Could there really be something important in her stuff?"

"With Anderson in charge?" I said. "The killer could be hiding in Kathy's suitcase and he wouldn't notice."

Jackie stopped walking. We were at the junction of the hallway, where the main fork led back to the set. "Could I ask . . . Would you mind looking at her things, Dexter?"

"I didn't know her at all," I said.

Jackie sighed. "I know," she said. "I just . . . it's hard enough not to burst into tears every time I think of Kathy, and I . . ." She put a hand on my arm, and blinked back a few tears. "Please? Would you?"

The way Jackie looked at me with those wonderful violet eyes starting to fill up, I would have juggled flaming chain saws if it would make her happy. "Sure," I said. "I'll take a look."

Jackie smiled. "Thank you," she said. She took a deep breath, sniffled, and straightened up. "Right now I really do have to find Sylvia." She leaned close to me and bumped her forehead against mine gently. "Thank you," she said. "See you later." And she strode away down the hall.

I watched her go for a moment. I had never before realized how much fun it can be just to watch somebody walk. Jackie was very good at it—not just because she didn't fall down or walk into a wall, although that was true, too. There was just something about the way she put one foot in front of the other that made me think of how I felt waking up next to her naked body. It didn't make any sense, but it was true. So I watched Jackie until she vanished through a doorway opposite the set.

I turned around and headed back toward Jackie's dressing room. I didn't see Anderson, which seemed odd. He certainly hadn't gone past us. He might have gone out the door at the far end of this hall, but a sign on it clearly said that an alarm would sound if the door was opened, and I hadn't heard any alarm. That seemed to mean that he was still in the dressing room, and that was very odd.

The door was ajar, and I peeked around it and into Jackie's dressing room. Anderson was still inside. He was standing at the far end, at the rack that held Jackie's costumes. He had the sleeve of one of her shirts held up to his nose, and he was apparently sniffing it. I didn't know why he was doing that, but it made me want to break a chair on his face. Still, a little good humor is almost always a better way, so I stifled the urge and stepped into the room.

"Looking for a clue?" I said cheerfully, and he jerked around, practically flinging the shirtsleeve away from his face. "Because I've heard you totally don't have one."

"Don't have— I was just . . . What do you mean?" he said.

"I said, you don't have a clue," I said. "It's common knowledge."

His forehead wrinkled, and I could probably have counted to five or six as it dawned on him that I had insulted him.

"Listen, ace," he said. "I am running a homicide investigation here—"

"By sniffing Jackie's clothing?" I said. "Is her armpit a suspect?"

Anderson turned bright red and stuttered at me, until it was very clear to both of us that nothing coherent was going to come out of his mouth. He looked around for a way to escape, and saw nothing except the toilet. So he cleared his throat, muttered something I couldn't hear, and pushed past me, giving me one last glare from the doorway before he disappeared.

I closed the door and went to look at the box of Kathy's stuff. I took the suitcase out and put it on the floor. I really doubted that there would be anything significant stuck in with her socks and underwear, and even if the urine stains had been washed out, I would rather not have to look at Kathy's underwear. The purse was a more likely place to find something, so I dumped it out on the makeup table and poked through it. There was the usual clutter of coins, gum wrappers, receipts, coupons, a large clump of keys, a packet of tissues, lipstick, a small mirror, three pens, and a handful of paper clips. A wad of one-dollar bills, wrapped around a valet parking stub. Two tampons in a bright pink plastic case. A large packet of cinnamon-flavored sugarless gum. A wallet with several credit cards, license, a few business cards, forty-three dollars in cash, three paycheck stubs.

I frowned at the heap of useless junk. Something was missing. I am not an expert on what women carry in their purses, but a tiny nagging something tugged at the edge of my brain and whispered that this picture was missing a piece.

I looked in the box, lifting out the black nylon laptop case and unzipping it. There was nothing inside but the computer, with its ubiquitous half-eaten Apple logo on top. I poked through the Velcro-sealed pockets: a power cord, a flash drive in one pocket, and nothing else—and still the whiny little voice niggled and prodded at me that there should be something else. So I opened the suitcase and, as I had feared, found only underwear, socks, clothing, a baggy bathing suit, and a pair of sandals.

I snapped the lid shut and put the suitcase back on the floor, and as I straightened up I knew what was missing: her phone. Kathy's all-important always-present phone, the one that had all her contacts and appointments. Her signature accessory, the one thing she was never without. The phone should have been here, in her purse or separate, and it was not.

Of course, it was possible that the phone was still in the lab, maybe because it was a blood-soaked mess, unfit to be released into the world. It was also possible that somebody—probably Vince, in my absence—was checking the call log, the calendar, and so on, for any hint of the killer's identity.

And it was also possible that the killer had taken it. Not for a souvenir, which was easy to understand—for me, at least—but because he was in a rush to escape the scene and wanted to make sure that no memo or note on the phone could implicate him. No time to look, so just grab the thing and dash away into the night. That's what I would have done: Get safely away, and discard the phone later, throwing it off a bridge, or into a handy canal.

It made sense, and I was sure I was right. If Kathy's phone was not still in police custody, the killer had it.

Easy enough to check, of course. All I had to do was ask—not the officer in charge of the investigation, of course. That was Anderson, and I was reasonably sure he didn't want to say anything at all to me, unless it was, "You're under arrest." But one quick call to Vince ought to clear it up.

I pulled my own phone from my pocket and sat in the chair in front of the mirror. I heard six rings, and then Vince said, in his Charlie Chan voice, "Hung Fat Noodle Company."

"I'd like some cat lo mein to go, please?"

"Depends, Grasshopper," he said. "How far you want it to go?"

"Quick question," I said. "Podrowski. The victim at the Grove Isle last night. Do you still have her phone?"

"Quick answer," he said. "Nope."

"Was it found at the scene?"

"That's two questions," Vince said. "But the same answer: nope."

"Aha," I said. "If you don't think that's too corny."

"Why aha?" he said.

"Because Kathy—the victim—was never ever without her phone. So if you don't know where it is—"

"Egads," he said. "The killer took it."

"Egads?" I said.

"Sure," he said. "Because you got to say aha. I assume you told this to Anderson?"

"I assume that's a joke?"

"Ha!" Vince said, with his terrible fake laugh—much worse than mine.

"Did it look like the same killer?"

"Well," Vince said carefully, "of course, I am no Detective Anderson. . . ."

"Thank God for that."

"But it didn't look like it. The eye was gone, and naturally Anderson jumped on that and said *quod erat demonstrandum.*"

"He said *that*?"

"Words to that effect. Fewer syllables," Vince said. "Anyway, he was sure it was the same. But the thing is, the body was a mess. Eleven stab wounds, including a couple that chopped open the carotid artery."

"Oh, my," I said, thinking of the great awful gouts of sticky wet blood.

"Yeah, really," he said. "And even worse? There was vomit all over. Like he took a look at what he'd done and then blew lunch. I really hate working with vomit."

"Cheer up," I said. "In a few hours you'll be right back with severed heads and fecal matter."

"Fascinating stuff, fecal matter," Vince said thoughtfully. "It's in all of us."

"Some more than others," I said. "Thanks, Vince."

"Hey!" he said, before I could disconnect. "Are you hanging out at the movie? With Robert?"

"He's around somewhere," I said. "I'm supposed to give technical advice—and also," I said, trying to sound very casual, "I have a small speaking part."

"Oh, my God," he said. "You're gonna be *in* this?"

I covered the phone with one hand and changed my voice. "Five minutes, Mr. Morgan!" I said, and then, back into the phone, "My call. Gotta go, Vince. Say hi for me to all the little people."

"Dexter, wait!" he said. "Is Robert—"

I broke the connection and stood up.

I wandered down the hall to Wardrobe. Jackie was still in conference with Sylvia, standing with her arms held straight out while Sylvia made marks on her shirt with a piece of chalk and her two assistants ran by; one carried an iron, the other an armful of rubber boots.

I closed the door and looked around. I had nothing to do for at least another fifteen or twenty minutes, so I indulged my curiosity and went to take a look at the soundstage. I had never seen one before, and if this was going to be part of my new life as Dexter Demosthenes, I thought I should see what it looked like.

I went through the heavy metal door and into the room. It was about the size and shape of an airplane hangar, with a high ceiling and a cement floor. Except for isolated patches of illumination from electric lights, the room was dark. There were no windows, or anything else that might let in light, and thick black curtains hung down from the walls.

The crew swarmed in and out of the pools of light like ants skittering around on a hive that someone had smacked with a stick. In twos and threes they hurried by, performing their mystical tasks, slapping tape onto the floor in precise and nonsensical patterns, moving metal light stands from place to place, rolling out thick cables, two and three bundled together, and carrying odd bits of scenery: a window, a bright red fire door, a swivel chair.

I took a few steps into the darkness and was nearly beheaded by three people carrying what looked like the back wall of Captain Matthews's office. "Hey, watch out," one of them called cheerily, a wiry young woman with short blond hair and a hammer hanging from her hip. She hustled on by with the other two, rapidly easing the wall around lights, more scenery, and other workers.

I stood and let my eyes adjust to the darkness before I began once more to edge carefully through the room, alert for any more lethal scenery. In the center of the room, rimmed by a cluster of lights, cameras, and some intense technical action, stood a scenic wall, edge facing me, and I moved toward it to see what it was. I scooted around two men fluttering large squares of colored, transparent plastic in front of a standing light, and I peered around to see what the wall might be. As the far side of the wall came into view, I stopped and stared.

I was looking at what seemed to be the inside of an apartment on Miami Beach. A sliding glass door led out onto a balcony, where the top of a palm tree waved in front of a gleaming greenish-blue expanse of Biscayne Bay. For a moment, it was very disorienting, and I actually stepped back and looked at the other side of the wall, just to be sure it was really only two-dimensional. Happily for me, it was.

I moved a few steps closer and looked again. The scene still looked very real to me, except that as I watched, a stout, red-haired man slid open the glass door and stepped off the fake balcony to stand in apparent midair in front of the palm tree, and began to fuss with the fronds. It was an eerie illusion; if the palm tree was real, then it had a red-haired giant floating in the air beside its fronds.

I admired the surreal view until someone tapped me on the shoulder. I turned around to see a bearded man, about forty-five, with three rolls of duct tape hanging from his belt.

"We gotta focus the lights," he said. "Can you stay back over there?" He waved a hand at the far wall of the room and pushed past me, pulling a long strip of tape from one of his rolls.

"Of course," I told his back, and I made a mental note to try his tape dispenser arrangement sometime soon.

I walked carefully to the area Mr. Tape had indicated, and it turned out to be a wise move. Nestled into the corner, tucked away in the sheltering half darkness, I found a long table absolutely groaning under the weight of a remarkable array of food. There were bagels, cream cheese, thin-sliced tomato and onion—and real nova lox! And there was even a large bowl filled with M&M's, and a platter with three kinds of cheese, a huge tray of yogurt, bananas, apples, oranges, and trail mix. And on the far end of the table, right next to a large coffee urn, was a pile of pastry boxes, eight high, from Muñequita Bakery, my very favorite pastry shop.

I had just grabbed a guava *pastelita* and a jelly doughnut and settled into the shadows on the edge of the set when I felt some hostile presence steaming up behind me, and I turned around, prepared to slay it with the *pastelita*. But I held my fire when I saw that it was only dear demoted Deborah, face clenched tightly enough to crack walnuts.

"Good morning, sister dearest," I said. "Isn't it wonderful to be here at the heart of Hollywood?"

"Go fuck yourself," she said.

"Perhaps a little later," I promised. "After I finish my *pastelita*." She said nothing, just stood there glaring at the set and grinding her teeth loud enough that I thought I could hear molars shattering. "Would you like a doughnut?" I asked, hoping to soothe her just a bit.

It didn't work. Before I could even blink she whipped a fist at me, landing it solidly on my upper arm hard enough that I almost dropped my jelly doughnut. "Ow," I said. "Would you prefer a bagel?"

"I would prefer to kick Anderson in the balls and get back to doing real police work," she said through her tightly clenched teeth.

"Oh," I said. "So it didn't go well when you told the captain about Patrick?"

"He ripped me a new asshole," she said, and she ground her teeth even harder. "With Anderson watching. Smirking at me the whole fucking time, while the captain told me what a fucking idiot I am."

"Ouch," I said. "But he didn't suspend you?"

"He near as fuck did," she said. "But he figured if I was suspended I'd go after the killer on my own time."

I nodded and took a bite of guava. From what I knew of Deborah, that's exactly what she would have done. It was a very shrewd guess, and my opinion of Captain Matthews's savvy went up.

"So he ordered me to stay on the set," Debs said. "So I can't do a single fucking thing except stand around and babysit. While Anderson fucks up the case and fucking laughs at me."

"Oh, he's not just fucking up the case," I said. "He told Jackie he wants to be her security blanket, twenty-four/seven."

She snorted. "He *said* that? To *Jackie*?!"

"Yup," I said.

"What did she say?"

I smiled at the memory, as close to a genuine smile as I have ever managed. "She told him she already had one," I said. And I took a very satisfied bite, getting the last third of *pastelita* into my mouth.

Deborah looked at me, a hard and searching look, and I wondered if I was unconsciously chewing with my mouth open. I put a hand up to check; I wasn't. I swallowed the pastry and looked back at her. "What?" I said.

"You son of a *bitch*," Deborah said, and somehow her anger was now focused on me and I had no idea why.

"What did I do?" I asked.

"You *fucked* her!" she hissed at me. "You fucked Jackie fucking Forrest!"

I looked at Deborah in astonishment, trying to remember whether I had said anything at all that might have tipped her off; there was nothing, but clearly she knew. Maybe there really is something to the whole Women's Intuition business we're always hearing about. Because Deborah knew, and she was obviously very upset about it.

"Deborah," I said, flailing about desperately for something to say that would explain everything, calm her down, maybe even change the subject. But nothing came to me; I stood there with my mouth hanging silently open and my sister glaring at me hard enough to dent a Buick's fender.

"You stupid piece of shit," she said. "Do you have any idea what you've done?" It was not a well-thought-out question: I had a very good idea what I had done. I had done it more than once, and had an idea that I'd like to do it again—but that did not seem to be the same idea Debs had.

"A wife and three kids," she snarled, "and you have to do this. Fucking leap into bed with Jackie Fucking Forrest."

"Yes, but, Deborah," I said, and it didn't matter that I had nothing else to say, since she went right on without waiting for my contribution.

"I swear to fucking God," she said. "I know all men think with their dicks, but I thought you were different." She poked me in the chest with a very hard finger. "And then Jackie comes along and you're just as fucking stupid as any other ball-brained asshole and you have to go and fuck her."

"She helped," I said, and it sounded horrible even to me.

"Jesus Fucking *Christ*, Dexter!" she said, and she was getting loud enough that a few technicians began to look up from their work and glance our way.

"Deborah, we're supposed to be quiet in here," I said. "Can we talk about this later?"

"There's not going to *be* a later," she said. "I don't think I ever want to talk to you again." And she slapped both hands into my chest, hard enough to make me take a step back, and then she turned and walked away to the far side of the set, pushing past the scurrying crew people and nearly knocking over two different lights.

I watched her go, wondering if she meant it. Never talk to me again? Me, her only sibling? Was it possible? I had never even thought of the possibility—had never for even a half moment considered that anything I did with Jackie could possibly affect my relationship with Debs. She was my *sister*—wasn't that supposed to be a forever kind of thing? She had stayed my sister even when she discovered my wicked true self. As I understood things, what I did on my Special Nights was considered to be far more socially unacceptable than what I had done with Jackie.

And yet Deborah had instantly flown into high, possibly permanent dudgeon, just because I had dented a few trifling marriage vows, mere ritual words, mumbled in a meaningless rite in front of a hypothetical deity—and now she would never speak to me again?

I have said many times that I do not understand human behavior—but I had always paid Deborah the compliment of excluding her from mere humanity. She was above the routine idiocy of the rat pack, with one foot on the Olympian heights I occupied. And yet here she was, acting just as foolish and fallible as any reality-show-watching couch potato. Never again speak to me, just because I had done something human for once? It couldn't be.

I looked across the set to where she stood, back turned to me. Even from this distance I could see the angry tightness in her shoulders, and she did not loosen up nor look toward me. She looked like she might really be angry enough to carry out her threat—but why? Why would such a small indiscretion spark her to such a massive reaction? How did my tryst with Jackie touch Deborah?

And why did the thought of Life Without Debs make me feel so hollow?

# TWENTY-NINE

Sadly enough, Deborah did not relent. She avoided me for the next two days, which took a certain amount of work on her part, since both of us spent twelve hours each of those days on the same soundstage. It was a relatively small space, and the areas where we were allowed to loiter were even smaller, but somehow she managed to find a way to make sure that my offensive shadow never fell across her righteous one. I had thought that a few hours of actual thought would calm her down and remind her that I was her only living family, but it didn't happen. And when I tried to speak to her, she stalked away without even a glance in my direction. If I even leaned toward her from across the room, she would stomp off, as far away from me as she could get without leaving the building.

And after a while, my ex-sister's behavior began to make me mad. Who was she to judge me, and why should I care if she did? She wanted to fling me from her life? Fine, consider me flung. It was no loss to me—we weren't really related anyway, not by blood, which is really all that matters. We had grown up in the same house, but I knew of no law stating that shared real estate was a tie that binds. What did it matter if we never spoke again? Speaking is overrated, a waste of time and energy when there were more important things to do—like sampling the *pastelitas* on the food table.

In any case, I had already left Deborah's tiny, morally constricted, hard-knocks world, and entered a new and better one. I was now flying in Jackie's lightly scented orbit, with fresh flowers and chocolates on the pillows, and I liked it a lot more than I had ever liked serving as Deborah's punching bag.

Debs wanted no more to do with me? So be it. One less messy and annoying tie to a life I was eager to leave behind.

Besides, I had work to do. I was in three scenes as Ben Webster, Forensics Whiz, and in two of them I had actual words to say. Not many of them, of course, but they were important enough to include in the script, and I felt I should give them my all. So I flung myself into the brutally hard work of remembering the twenty-two words I had to say in front of the camera—and to be fair, just remembering them was not enough. They had to come at the right time, and in the right order, and they had to be said in a way that was convincing and interesting. Acting really is much harder than most people imagine, and I spent many long hours searching for just the right way to say, "The lab results are back." I found eleven different inflections before settling on the best one.

Two long days on the set, and two more nights with Jackie, nights that seemed far too short. Our idle hours of sipping mojitos and watching the sun set were a distant memory now; after twelve hours on the set, Jackie was so tired that when we got back to the hotel, it was no more than a quick meal, a brief but intense period of studying the next day's script, and then a shower. Of course, the shower was a mutual one, and lasted a little longer than usual. But then it was straight off to bed for a few hours of precious slumber, only occasionally interrupted by nonsleep activities.

No life is without its puzzles, and my new one was no exception. For starters, Robert seemed to be avoiding me. Maybe I had broken his sweet little heart, and maybe he caught it from Deborah, but there was no doubt about it. Like my sister, he fled from my very shadow. There were no more invitations to lunch, no more vapid questions about fingerprints. He made himself unavailable and unapproachable, spending his time either in his dressing room, "studying lines," or off the set altogether, gone away to no one knew where.

Even Renny talked to me now and then, skillfully pulling a few compliments out of me about his Saturday-night performance. But Robert was elusive; if I passed him in the hall he would nod and hurry past before I could speak, and if I saw him grabbing a cup of coffee, he would give me a quick and cheery hello, and then rush away still stirring his cup. I did not actually mind not speaking to him, but it was a little bit unsettling to have it be his decision, and it made me wonder whether I should change my mouthwash. But Jackie hadn't complained, and she would certainly know better than Robert if I was suffering from Fetid Breath Syndrome.

It occurred to me that maybe Robert was avoiding me because of his animosity toward Jackie, and because I was so obviously *with* her now—and in fact, the last time he had really spoken to me was at the wardrobe room in the hotel, when he saw me arrive with Jackie. And then my kids had shown up, and we had all gone our separate ways, and of course he couldn't confront me, point an angry finger at me, and accuse me of being straight. Whatever; I did not regret the way I had gone, even if Robert probably did.

Whatever his reasons, Robert stayed away, and that made it very difficult to give him technical advice. But I managed to contain my dismay somehow and still gather my share of *pastelitas*.

And for some other reason, those two days also went by without any progress in catching Kathy's killer. It seemed impossible, at least to Anderson, but somehow he was no closer to finding his perp than he had been the day he was born. He was still convinced Kathy's murder had been the work of the same killer, and so it was naturally hard to find any leads. I would have been very glad to lead him to Patrick, especially if I could leave them together underwater, but of course that would be against the rules: Being an Odious Dumbfuck did not make Anderson eligible for my Special Attention. Besides, Patrick did not kill Kathy. And since I really had no interest in finding out who did, I let Anderson flail around in his dull and ignorant fog. I hadn't really liked Kathy, and it wasn't my job to bring her killer to justice. And in any case, I was much too busy practicing my lines, and shooting my first two scenes.

My acting seemed to be reasonably well received. At any rate, nobody actually complained, and when I finished the first scene, the one where I told Jackie, "The lab results are back," she gave me a hug.

"Can you say Emmy?" she said to me, smiling.

"Do they give one for best supporting geek?" I asked her.

"They'll have to now," she said.

Even with the strain of waiting for my award, the two days and nights went by rapidly. And then the third day of shooting was upon us.

Wednesday was our first day off the soundstage and out onto the warm and wicked streets of Miami. We were shooting downtown, a few blocks in from Biscayne Boulevard, on a side street that bordered a large parking lot. It was my big scene, too, the one where I, as Ben Webster, shuffled off my mortal coil, and Jackie, as hard-boiled detective Amber Wayne, swore dire vengeance over my cooling corpse.

The streets were cordoned off for several blocks in each direction, and the uniformed cops kept a tighter perimeter than they ever did at a homicide scene. Inside the parking lot, a handful of large, air-conditioned trailers had been set up. One was for all the male cast members, one for female—and one, to my surprise and delight, was dedicated entirely to the individual comfort and well-being of Miss Jackie Forrest—and that meant Dexter's comfort, too. It was a lovely arrangement, even though Jackie assured me that it was standard practice, one of the tangible perks of being a Leading Lady. It was understood that true artists needed privacy in direct proportion to their salary and their billing on the head credits. But as Jackie's new boy toy, I was welcome to enjoy a little semiprivacy along with her, and I did not allow any antique notions of solidarity with the working class to hold me back from taking advantage of the lush, cool trailer, nor its well-stocked refrigerator. Instead, I dressed in my Ben Webster costume in the bedroom of Jackie's trailer, and then lounged on the sofa with a cup of coffee and tried not to feel bad about all the other small-part actors who had been crammed into one trailer all together. Somehow, I managed to live through the crushing guilt, and at around ten thirty in the morning, my call came at last.

A very dark-skinned, very excited young man with a Haitian accent led me to the place on the street where I was scheduled to die. I easily could have found it on my own, since it was ringed by people, vans, and trucks—one with a large generator—as well as cameras, lights, and a blue-and-white-striped canopy where a man I recognized as Victor, the director, sat with a few others perched in high canvas-backed chairs in front of some large flat-screen monitors. Victor did not look up as we walked past. He seemed very busy giving instructions to his peeps. I looked for a megaphone, or a martini shaker—anything that spoke of Hollywood's hallowed traditions— but there were only walkie-talkies, and a huge paper cup of coffee from a nearby restaurant in each hand.

My young guide led me past the command center, explaining to me breathlessly that he was studying communications right here at Miami-Dade Community College, and his uncle Hercule was driving a scenery truck for the show and got his nephew, himself, Fabian, this fantastic job as a production assistant, which did not pay so much, but was a fantastic experience, and if I would just step over here?

I stepped. Fabian led me to a white open-sided van, where a large man with a shaved head and an ornate mustache sat on the bumper. He stood as we approached, and called out, "This him, Fabian? Brilliant!" Even without the "brilliant," his accent said he was British. He held out his hand, looming several inches taller than either me or Fabian.

"Hullo, mate," he said. "Name's Dickie Larkin. I've got to get you all blooded up."

I shook his hand and Fabian vanished at a half trot. And as Haitian Fabian handed me to British Dickie, I had to wonder: Was I seeing an example of good American jobs stolen away by foreigners?

But Dickie gave me no time to brood over socioeconomic paradigms. He took my elbow and led me to the van's side door. "Shirt off," he said, and he leaned into the double doors.

"I just put it on," I said.

"And now you'll bloody well have it off," he said. "Got to get you wired, haven't I?"

"Oh," I said. "Have you?"

He turned around holding a wire harness with four small red

tubes hanging from it. "I have," he said. "You can't die properly without your squibs."

"I thought a squib was a kind of small chicken," I said.

"That'd be a *squab*, laddie boy, and it's a pigeon." He held up his strange harness and shook it. "This is a squib. Four of the lovely little buggers." He held them toward me. "Which I can't bloody put on you if you don't take the bloody shirt off."

"Well, then," I said, and I pulled my Ben Webster shirt off, feeling a little odd to be standing in the street in a seminaked state. But I would just have to get used to such things; I was an actor now, and my body was my canvas, half bare or not. In any case, Dickie didn't give it any thought. He went to work, whistling cheerfully, and explaining squibs to me as he put them in place.

"It's nothing but a small firecracker," he said. "And a detonator." He nodded into the van. I tried to peer around him, but he was too big. "I've got a little black box," he said. "Hit the toggle and bang-o! Arms up."

I put my arms straight up as Dickie ran the harness around my back, and then reached behind him for four small plastic baggies, each one filled with something that looked disturbingly like blood. My face must have shown some slight revulsion, because Dickie shook his head. "It's fake blood, laddie," he said. "Guaranteed AIDS-free."

"Okay," I said. "Is it, um, messy?"

"No worries," he said. "You don't have to clean it up."

He was right, of course, and that was some small consolation—but I really don't like blood, and the thought of carrying it next to my skin like that was mildly repulsive. But I clamped down on my feelings with iron-handed professionalism and let Dickie do his job. He placed one of the bags on top of each of the little red tubes. "The squib fires," he said. "That pops the blood bag, and it looks like you've been shot. Cheap and lovely. There," he said, and he stepped back.

"Right," he said. "Can you move all right?"

I raised and lowered my arms, twisted from side to side, and then hopped up and down. "Yes," I said. "What, um . . . what does it feel like?"

"You'll feel a bit of a spark," he said, "and that's your cue to fall over dead, right?"

"How much is a bit?" I asked.

He winked at me. "Won't kill you, squire," he said. "I've had worse." It was not a lot of comfort, but apparently it was all I was going to get from Dickie. He made a few small adjustments, then stepped back again and looked at me with satisfaction.

"Done like a dinner," he said. "Shirt on and you're good to go."

I put my shirt back on. It was a little snugger with Dickie's fireworks strapped on underneath, but he assured me that it didn't show, and in the wink of an eye I strode over to the street to Find My Mark. Mark was not a person: It was a piece of tape on the floor that showed you where to stand so the cameras could keep you in focus. I had learned all about marks while shooting my first scene, and I felt very professional asking Martha, the assistant director, where mine was. She led me to a spot on the sidewalk, just a few feet from where an overpass loomed up and crossed over the street.

"The car goes by right over there," she said, pointing to the street. "They shoot, and you fall right here." She showed me the second taped mark, half in the gutter and half on the sidewalk. "Your head goes this way," she said, nodding in the direction of the overpass. "Try not to move too much once you're down." She patted my arm. "Continuity," she said, and then she trotted away, talking loudly into her walkie-talkie.

Making filmic art is a lot harder than most of us ever appreciate. You might think that something as simple as filming bad guys killing Dexter would be a very easy thing. After all, look at all the wonderful little movies we all make every day with our cell phones. But the real thing, like we were now making, is much harder. There are many small actions that have to be coordinated perfectly, lights and reflectors that need to be moved around, sound booms lifted in and out, and several fits of ritual yelling at people by the director. And then finally, when everything is just right, a jet goes overhead and ruins the sound so you have to start all over again.

In the grand scheme of things, my death was a mere plot point, a small and insignificant detail in the larger and more important story of beautiful but hard-boiled Detective Amber Wayne. Even so, it took seven separate attempts before everything happened to the complete satisfaction of the director, Victor. It was tedious, and it was difficult to look convincingly shocked and surprised when the same thing happens seven times in a row. But it was all part of my new craft, and if I worked my way up the ladder to larger parts someday, seven takes would multiply into many more—exponentially more if it was a theatrical feature instead of a TV show. Jackie had told me that on a feature film with a respectable budget, one hundred fifty takes was not uncommon.

So I went patiently through the simple act of looking with surprise at a passing car, over and over, until Victor was happy—and then I had to endure getting shot three times. I'm sure it would have been more if not for the fact that each time the squibs exploded and the blood packs popped, my shirt was ruined, and they had only three matching shirts. So after the third time I went through the harness routine with Dickie, and then performed Dexter the Dying Swan and gracefully collapsed in the gutter, Victor called out, "Okay, that'll have to do. Get Jackie out here. Stay put, Derrick."

"It's Dexter," I said, feeling uncomfortably like Robert objecting to being called "Bob." Victor did not respond; no doubt he had many important orders to give.

I stayed put. No one asked me if I was comfortable, which I wasn't. The sun was hot for an autumn day, and the pavement was hard. But it didn't seem very professional to ask for a pillow or a parasol, so I lay there and thought my deep dark thoughts. I wondered when Jackie would get here, and I wondered how many takes we would have to do. I wondered whether our eventual audience would be able to see a special bond between me and Jackie in this, our big scene together. I had heard that "chemistry" between actors gave an extra-special edge to their work, and we certainly had chemistry. Perhaps it would translate to the screen. Of course, I was dead, and that did limit my chemical actions. Maybe this was not the time and place to think about my Emmy.

And I wondered if there would be other scenes together in the future. Was there, in fact, a future for Jackie and Dexter? We had not really talked any more about it since I had so pleasantly changed the subject on the chaise longue on the balcony of Jackie's suite. Was this a mere on-the-job infatuation, the kind of Hollywood working hazard one always reads about in the tabloids? Or was it more than that, something longer-lasting, a new start in an entirely new setting?

As things stood right now, I would not miss my old life very much; my sister, Deborah, was apparently through with me forever, my home life had become an annoying millstone around my neck, and my job was no more than rote performance of repetitive tasks. I didn't really have any actual friends—other than my boat, there was nothing to tie me to my life in Miami. Of course, there was the Nighttime Me, the Devil Dexter who delivered the Wicked to their just deserts with a sharp blade and a hearty smile. But that other me was portable, too, and from what I had heard about the movie business, I was quite sure there were plenty of deserving Playmates in L.A.—or, for that matter, anywhere I might go. Human nature being what it is, I could be certain to find quality entertainment everywhere on this tired old globe.

There was one tiny, perhaps important detail—Jackie had not yet invited me to go with her when she left, and I had no idea whether I was actually a part of her plans for any future beyond tonight at the hotel. I have never been able to read humans—especially female humans. Just when I am sure I know exactly what they're thinking, they say or do something so surprising and outrageous that I can only marvel and realize once more that I am not the only one walking around with a total lie written on my face.

I thought Jackie liked me—and maybe more than *liked*. If not, she had certainly been giving me a wonderfully convincing imitation. But I didn't know, and didn't know how to find out, unless I simply blurted out the awkward question. And if the answer was no, what then? Could I really just shake her hand and walk away, go back to being Dull as Dishwater Dexter?

In the near distance I heard the thump of a trailer door, and then Martha stepped over to me. "Here she comes," Martha said, and then she leaned over me and said accusingly, "You moved." She adjusted my left arm, then my right. "Like this," she said, and then she turned my head an inch to the right. "And here—okay, good." She disappeared, and a moment later Jackie was standing over me.

"You look so natural," she said with a small smile.

"It's much harder than it looks," I said. "And so is the pavement."

"Well, then, let's see if we can nail it in one take," she said. And then Victor was yelling directions, the lighting people began to move around the reflectors, and the soundman moved in and hovered nearby, holding a long pole with a microphone on the end of it over Jackie's head.

Jackie looked away from me, and I watched her go through the strange transformation she always did when the cameras turned to her. Her face became colder, harder, and its lines seemed to change subtly until it was not Jackie's face anymore.

The first take began—and abruptly stopped for no reason I could see before Jackie could speak. So much for nailing it in one.

Take two went a little better. Jackie actually got to the part where she saw my shattered corpse and called out, "Ben! Oh, God, Ben!" and then a motorcycle roared past on a nearby street and Victor yelled, "Cut!"

Take three, and Jackie got all the way to where she knelt mournfully beside my body and said through gritted teeth, "I'll get the bastards who did this—I swear it!" But instead of looking vengefully off into the distance, she turned toward the director and said, "Goddamn it, Victor, there's a shadow across my face the whole goddamn time!"

And so it went. Far from nailing it in one, we were still trying to nail it after eleven takes. It was only a few words and a couple of simple actions, but each one required dozens of minute adjustments, and each adjustment took several minutes, and time does not stop, even for the director. Tempers began to fray, even Jackie's. I had learned that she was a different person during working hours: demanding, impatient, and occasionally—like right now—short-tempered. Not by any means a diva, at least not in my opinion. But she did know what she wanted in very exact terms, and she was not shy about asking for it.

The lighting people fussed about and moved things around, the soundman moved in and out and once or twice yelled some arcane phrases in Victor's direction, Jackie got crosser, and all the while poor

Dead Dexter lay unmoving on the unyielding uncomfortable pavement and wondered when his torment would end, and whether it was time for lunch yet. And finally, proving once more that the sun shines on the wicked as well as the just, I heard Victor yell, "Well, god*damn* it!" There was an urgent murmur of soothing voices, and then Victor said, "Shit. All right, people—lunch!"

# T H I R T Y

I WALKED WITH JACKIE BACK TO HER TRAILER. SHE WALKED quickly, with her head down, clearly preoccupied, and I did nothing that might break her concentration. She did not speak until we were settled comfortably onto the couch in the cool and quiet of the trailer. Someone had quite thoughtfully left lunch on the table, and I took a look.

It may seem like a paradox, but even though everything else moves so slowly on a set, gossip travels slightly faster than the speed of light. I had noticed by the second day that people who had ignored me before were now being polite and friendly. Every time I got a cup of coffee or one more small *pastelita*, someone would praise Jackie somewhere nearby, where I could hear it. Added to the sly looks and small jokes I overheard, it became apparent that everyone knew Jackie and Dexter were an Item. And so naturally enough, *two* very nice box lunches had been left in Jackie's trailer, His as well as Hers.

I opened one box: good, thick sandwich of cold cuts, cheese, lettuce, and tomato. Bag of chips, pickle, plastic bag with a large chocolate cookie.

I looked at Jackie. She sat on the couch, script beside her, arms crossed, a distracted look on her face. "Want some lunch?" I said.

She looked up as if she was seeing me for the first time. "What? Oh—sure, why not." And then she frowned and looked back into space at the same fixed point on the trailer's wall, her lips moving slightly.

I took one box, set it beside her on the couch. "Drink?" I said. "There's soda, iced tea, Perrier—"

"I don't care," she said, rather crossly, I thought.

I got her a bottle of Perrier from the trailer's small refrigerator, twisted the cap off, and held it out to her. She didn't see it, or me. "Jackie?" I said.

"For Christ's sake, what the— Oh, thanks," she said. She took the bottle from me, but didn't do anything with it.

My phone rang. I had left it in the small bedroom, on the dresser, and I went in to look. In my hurry I tripped over something I really should have seen—the large box of Kathy's possessions. It had moved into the trailer with us, and now occupied the narrow space between the bed and the dresser. Jackie still hadn't been able to make herself go through the stuff, but she kept it nearby in case she had an unfortunate fit of conscience. I stepped around it and looked at my phone.

The phone's face was lit up with the caller's ID: It was Rita. I hesitated, trying to decide whether I had anything to say to her right now. I looked back out at Jackie, still frowning, staring straight ahead, and moving her lips in some unvoiced conversation with an invisible friend. I looked back at the phone, still undecided, and it stopped ringing. A moment later it bleeped, the signal that Rita had left a voice mail.

I picked up the phone and saw that there were now twelve unanswered calls from Rita, each one with a voice-mail message.

I suppose I should have called back, or at least listened to the messages, but I didn't really want to; I did not want to get sucked back into any kind of whirlpool that might be swirling around my old life as it went down the drain. I had no patience for an argument about what color the trim should be around the pool at the new house, or why Astor's skirt was too short. These things no longer seemed to be a part of me or who I was, and I did not have any subtle yearning to go back to them, nor any feeling of obligation. I do not actually have a sense of duty; I never have—except to myself. In the old days, I would have called Rita back because I had learned that it was the kind of little detail that kept her happy, and I needed her to maintain my pretense of fitting in. She was a large part of my camouflage; people saw a married man with three kids, and therefore did not see the monster I really am.

But now? I could not raise any real interest in Cody's grade on a reading test, or Rita's opinion of my laundry. I felt a very small twinge as I thought of Lily Anne—the only direct biological connection I had to the future, my DNA's only shot at immortality. But after all, whatever happened I would certainly be allowed to see her every now and then, and in the interim, a little girl really needed her mother, much more than a father with a tendency to slice and dice whoever happened to come under his knife.

So I put the phone down and looked back out at Jackie. She was still staring, her forehead lightly creased by a frown, but at least her lips had stopped moving.

I went back out to the couch and looked down at her. She apparently didn't notice me, and she didn't move. I sat beside her. "Is something wrong?" I asked.

She looked at me, still frowning. "What? Oh, no, it's— Listen, if I said to you, 'You're a lightweight piece of crap,' what would you say?"

"I don't . . . I, um," I stammered. "I mean, *are* you going to say that to me?"

Jackie looked startled, and then gave a small laugh. "Oh, no," she said. "Not you, just—it's a line; it's something Tonio says to me in the next scene." Tonio was one of the bad guys in our gripping little drama, the one Jackie—as Amber Wayne—suspected of gunning me down.

"Oh," I said, and I admit I was relieved. "So you don't think I'm a lightweight piece of crap?" I was fishing, and rather shamelessly, but why not?

"Dexter, don't be a dope," she said, and she pulled me close to her. "I think you are the farthest thing you can be from a piece of crap."

"But still a lightweight?" I said. In spite of the long morning's work, she smelled very good.

She nuzzled in against my neck. "Heavyweight champ," she murmured. Then she bit me.

I jumped. "Ow," I said. I looked at her and, although she was still looking at me, and no longer frowning, she looked very serious.

"The question is," she said, "what are we going to do about it?"

And there it was, right out in the open.

"Well," I said, trying to feel my way ahead cautiously, "what would you like to do about it?"

Something flickered across her face—dismay? irritation? I couldn't say. And then she gave a small snort and shook her head. "One of the things I really like about you is that you are not at *all* like any other guy I've ever known," she said. "But there's a downside to that."

"What do you mean?" I said.

"Dexter—that was your cue. You were supposed to say that you want to run away with me; you can't live without me; you need me like the air you breathe—"

"All of that," I said, very uncomfortable. "But I don't . . . I mean, I wanted to know. I mean, what *you* think."

She shook her head again. "I'm the girl; you're the boy," she said, poking me with a finger so I would understand which one was me. "You're supposed to *tell* me what I think, you big dope," she said. "*Convince* me—don't you know anything about women?"

"I guess not," I said. "Is there a book . . . ?"

She punched me in the arm, not nearly as hard as Deborah did. Or used to do, I guess I should say. I rubbed it anyway. "Asshole," Jackie said. "And you're still not saying."

"Well," I said, feeling very uncomfortable, "I, um . . . I guess I . . ." She was watching me steadily, those huge violet eyes fixed unblinkingly on me. I took a deep breath. "I guess I, um . . . I need you like the air I breathe. And, um, I want to run away . . . with you?"

Jackie kept watching me for what seemed like a very long moment. And then at last she smiled and reached her hands around and clasped them behind my neck.

"Better," she purred. "Much better." And she pulled my face down to hers.

Our call to return to work came about forty minutes later. As it turned out, I had to eat my sandwich on the way back to the set.


It was another two hours before I was finally dead enough to satisfy Victor. We had moved the reflectors eight times, the cameras three, and changed one of Jackie's lines to fit more closely the excellent imitation of Deborah she was doing. By the time I was released from my corpsehood, my left leg had fallen asleep, and I had a headache, a backache, and a neck ache from lying on the pavement in such an uncomfortable contortion for so long—and it must be said that I was also thoroughly sick of lounging about in a shirt soaked with blood, fake or not. Altogether, it was enough to make me rethink my decision to become an award-winning star of the screen. Still, great art comes with a price, and today was Dexter's day to pick up the check.

It was with no reluctance at all that I yielded my spot in front of the camera. I stood and stretched and tried to get a little bit of feeling back into my leg as Jackie conferred with Victor. By the time I could walk again without looking like Long John Silver, they were already setting up for a series of close-ups of Jackie as she reacted to things that weren't really happening. As fascinating as this kind of self-induced psychosis usually is, I'd had enough after about five minutes, and so I bade a fond farewell to the hypnotic lure of the cameras and headed back to the trailer to change clothes and relax.

I could hear my phone ringing as I climbed the three steps to the trailer's door, and it did not take a rocket scientist to figure out that it was Rita calling again. I trudged through the living-dining room and in to the dresser, stepping carefully around the box of Kathy's stuff this time, and glanced down at the screen: Yes, indeed. It was Rita— and she had called seven more times while I lay dead in the street. Really, the woman was obsessed with me, and I wasn't even a star yet.

I put the phone down and started toward the kitchenette for a soda—and I paused. Nineteen phone calls seemed excessive, even for Rita, unless she was calling about something very important. The only real question was, important to whom? At first I had suspected that Deborah had told Rita everything in a fit of Dexter Hatred, and Rita was calling to screech clichés at me about my utter depravity. This was a conversation she could have quite well without me, and I preferred that she would.

And if Rita had won the lottery, wonderful; it would cushion the blow as she started her new and Dexter-less existence.

But if, on the other hand, she was calling to report a calamity of some kind . . .

It could not be something drastic enough to require an ambulance or police intervention, or I would have heard about it from one of the cops here on the set, or from Vince, or perhaps even from Deborah. And that left—

What?

It is true that I am not actually human, and I do not have the reckless illogical feelings of that wild, windblown race. But I do, unfortunately, share one or two human failings, and one of the deadliest of these is curiosity. Nineteen phone calls to report something that was incredibly significant, but neither too good nor too bad; it was a true riddle, and I do not like riddles. They are an affront to my hard-won and well-polished self-esteem, and the more impossible they seem the more I hate them—and yet, I still feel compelled to find the answer.

And so finally, after several minutes of fruitless conjecture, when I had reached the teeth-grinding stage, I surrendered, picked up my phone, and called Rita.

"Oh, Dexter, thank God," she said, instead of a more traditional "Hello," and her voice told me right away that I could safely rule out the Winning-the-Lottery option. "I have been calling and calling and— Oh, my God, where have you been? I don't know what to do, because— Why didn't you answer?"

In the present case, I didn't answer because I could not squeeze a single syllable into the spaces between Rita's words. But that wasn't really the question. "I'm sorry," I said. "But I'm working with the movie people this week."

"Television," she said irritably. "Dexter, it's just a pilot—and you don't call, and you don't *answer*—and I am going right out of my mind!"

It didn't seem like that would be a long trip, but I wanted to know what was wrong, so I just said, "Well, I am sorry, but we've been working long days—and I have a speaking part now, Rita. I mean, as an actor."

"Yes, I know, Astor said you— But that's just it!"

"What is?"

"Astor!" she wailed. "I don't know where she—she hasn't even— Oh God, I should have let her have her own phone."

I knew Rita and her conversational patterns well enough to know that, at last, we were approaching the answer. Our problem had something to do with Astor—but could it really be about Astor not having a phone? "Rita, calm down," I said. "What about Astor?"

"Calm *down*?!" she said. "When I have searched high and low and called you two dozen times and— Dexter, I don't have any idea where she went!"

"She's *missing*?" I guessed. "Astor is missing?"

"Yes, of course, that's what I've been— Dexter, what do we do?"

"Did she stay after school?" I asked hopefully.

"She didn't *go* to school!" Rita bellowed, sounding like she was tired of telling me the same thing. "She never even *got* there this morning! And then the school called to say she was absent and it was just that awful recorded message and I couldn't get through to anybody in the main office and she hasn't gone anywhere that I can find because none of her friends know oh Dexter, she's *gone*!" It was a remarkable sentence, delivered at high speed and top volume without a single breath, and I spent a moment marveling before the actual words sank in.

"Rita, are you saying she's been gone since this morning?"

"And I caught her last night; she snuck out of the house! And didn't even come home until— I heard the door, or I wouldn't even know—and now she's completely gone!"

"Last night?" I said, trying to grab onto some small chunk of floating logic. "She snuck out last night, but she came back and went to school this morning?"

"I dropped her off in front of the school like always, and Cody, and then I took Lily Anne to day care. And by the time I got to work, the school is calling and— Dexter I'm going out of my mind; I don't know what to do!" she yowled, which I took for a yes. "Please, you have to— I don't know what to do!"

"All right," I said, and because there was really nothing else I could possibly do, I added, "I'm on my way."

"Hurry!" she said, and I disconnected.

And having said that I was on my way, I realized that I was; I had to be; I could really do nothing else. Even though I had mentally cut myself away from Rita and her brood, and in spite of the fact that I do not ever really feel obligated to perform any of the painful tasks of human fatherhood, I really did not see what else I could do. I told myself that I just wanted to make sure my breakaway was unencumbered by guilt, accusations, recriminations, and anything else that might clutter up a clean escape, and to some extent that was true. But I also found myself wondering what Jackie would think of me if I ignored this kind of duty.

And finally, if I was perfectly honest, and I seldom am, I had to admit that I still felt a certain amount of . . . *ownership* for Astor. If she was missing, the odds were good that some predator had corralled her, and if that was true, he had taken her from *me*—not merely a fellow predator, and one who was much higher up on the food chain, but *me*. For someone to come onto my turf and take one of my things—it was intolerable, and I felt myself growing cold and angry and anxious for a few quiet words with this noxious creature. To prey on children—*my* children—was not just beneath contempt; it was a personal affront. They had taken something of mine; I would get it back and help them see the error of their ways.

So I didn't think about it a whole lot longer. I stuck my phone in my pocket and headed back out to where Jackie was shooting her pickups.

Luckily for me, Jackie had just finished when I got there, and she was heading back toward her trailer for a break. "Hey!" she called when she saw me. "I thought you'd be buried in a cup of coffee and a Danish."

"Something's come up," I said. "Astor is missing."

"Astor?" she said. "Your little girl?"

"Rita's girl," I said. For some reason it seemed like an important distinction. "I have to go find her."

"Oh, my God, of course you do," she said.

"I'm sure it's nothing," I said, although I wasn't sure at all.

"Go," she said. And then she frowned and plucked at my shirt. "But maybe you should change first?"

I looked down and saw that I was still wearing my bloody Ben Webster shirt. It probably would be better not to wander around on a rescue looking like I was the victim. "Oh," I said. "I think you're right."

I went back to the trailer with Jackie and began to change into my own clothes. Jackie settled onto the couch and watched me. "Do you have another scene to shoot?" I asked her.

"Not for a while," she said. "And then it's the big scene. The ultimate horror."

"What do you mean?" I said, pulling up my pants. "I already died—what could be worse?"

She made a truly appalled face, and she actually shuddered. "A love scene with Robert," she said.

"Oh," I said. I sat beside her to put on my shoes. "Can you do it?"

"Somehow," she said, and she shuddered again. "But he wants to run the lines with me, and . . . I probably should; it's a big scene." She sighed, and then shook her head. "Or I could go through Kathy's stuff, like I promised Detective Anderson," she said. "I've been putting it off and putting it off, and I really don't want to think about Kathy being . . ." She looked away from me, into the bedroom, where the box was crouching beside the bed. "Suddenly the thought of having to kiss Robert makes it bearable."

"Well, then," I said, and I stood up. "That's what you should do."

"Yeah," Jackie said, still looking at the box. And then she shook herself and stood up. "Look at me, such an actress, totally self-centered," she said. She put her arms around me. "Your little girl is missing," she said, and she hugged me with her head on my chest, and then looked up at me, those wonderful violet eyes turning suddenly moist. "Go find her, Dexter," she said. "And quickly. And . . ." She gave me a long and searching look, and quite clearly there was something else she wanted to say, but after a long moment she simply buried her head in my chest. "And then come back to me," she said.

I started to say that of course I would, but then she raised her head and her lips covered mine and it didn't seem all that important to say anything. And far too quickly, Jackie pushed herself away from me. "Go," she said. "Before I drag you into the other room." She leaned in and pecked at my cheek, and then strode in and lifted the laptop out of the big box of Kathy's stuff, and began to plug it in beside the bed. "Shit," I heard her murmur. "I hate this. . . ."

I wasn't too happy with things at the moment, either, but I headed out the door. And as I was almost out of earshot I heard the trailer door slam open, and Jackie's voice yell, "Robert!" and then, softer, "Son of a *bitch* . . ." She had clearly decided that she would rather run lines with Robert than sort through Kathy's stuff. It was a tough program either way, but I had some hard time ahead of me, too.

I headed for the perimeter.

I had left my car in the parking lot at work, since I'd been riding with Jackie in the Town Car. But I found a cop who was headed that way and hitched a ride. He had an AM radio playing a conservative talk show. The host was making some very interesting statements about the president. I don't usually pay much attention to politics, but from what the man said, I had to believe that sometime in the recent past the laws regarding sedition must have changed.

The cop who was driving, however, was nodding his head and muttering agreement, so I just rode along, grateful that I didn't have to make conversation, and in a mere twelve minutes I was getting into my car and headed for home.

# THIRTY-ONE

A T THIS TIME OF DAY, A MIDWEEK AFTERNOON, IT WAS AN EASY drive to my quiet South Miami neighborhood. The traffic was light, and I went quickly up onto I-95 and then straight down Dixie Highway with no problem, and in only about twenty minutes I pulled up in front of my house—my ex-house—and parked my car. I sat for a moment, looking at the place. It had been my home for several years, and it was still home to several things I cared about. My special private rosewood box, for instance: the carefully concealed reliquary for my ever-growing collection of memento mori. Each and every one of my Playmates was there, represented by a single drop of dried blood on a small glass slide. Not Patrick, of course, and that was too bad, but he had been rather a rush job. But all those other fond memories, fifty-seven of them, still lived here in my box. Would it come with me? It had to, of course—leaving it here was unthinkable, and so was getting rid of it. But could my beautiful and unique collection make the transition to life in the fast lane? Could I find a new and safe place for it in my new and unknown life?

That box and its slides were important to me—but under the circumstances it was a truly stupid thing to worry about. I had to find

Astor, wherever she was, and if she had been snatched by some predator, as I suspected, then there would soon be a new slide in the box.

The front door of the house banged open and Rita came chuffing
out to my car as I got out. "Oh, Dexter, thank God you're here; let's go,
quick!" she said, reaching for the handle of the passenger door.

"Go where?" I said.

Rita jerked her hand back from my car as if it had burned her.
"Oh!" she said, "I don't have— I don't know, it just seems— I mean, I
thought if we could— Oh, no . . ." she said, and she came around the
car and clamped onto me, putting her head down onto my chest and
snuffling, right where Jackie had so recently pressed her face.

I pried Rita away from me and gave her a gentle shake. "Rita," I
said. "Is there someplace to go? Have you heard from Astor?"

"No, of course not, no, but, Dexter," she said, "what do we do?"

"First," I said, "we calm down." I didn't think Rita would accept
this suggestion with any enthusiasm, and she didn't. She sniffled
again, and moaned, hopping up and down, for all the world like a
child who has to go to the bathroom. "All right," I said, taking her
elbow. "Let's go inside." And over her incoherent protests I led her
into the house and sat her down on the couch.

"Now then," I said. "When is the last time you heard from her?"

"Oh, God, Dexter, you sound just like a— I mean, it's *Astor*, for
God's sake, and you're just—"

"Yes, I am," I interrupted. "We won't find her by being hysterical."

"Oh," she said, "I suppose you're right, but . . ."

"When," I said very deliberately. "When did you hear from her?"

"I didn't," Rita said. "Just . . . like I said, this morning I dropped
her at school? In the same place as always, and then they called to
say . . ."

"All right," I said. "But you left her in front of her school."

"Yes," she said. "And then I— I mean, Cody was being so grouchy,
and Lily Anne needed a change, so I just . . . I drove away."

It took only a moment's thought for me to realize what that meant.
In a strange way, it was disappointing. I had raised my Other Self
up on point, ready to seek and destroy whatever nervy pervert had
grabbed Astor, and as always, I felt a little diminished when I had to

let all that icy glee drain away. "She wasn't snatched," I said. "She left on her own."

"What!?" Rita said, sounding horrified. "Dexter, but that's stupid! She would never—"

"She did," I said firmly. "There's a cop there at the school in the morning, and hundreds of parents, and bus drivers and teachers—all watching very carefully. Nobody could grab her there without being seen. So they didn't. She walked away."

Rita stared at me with big round eyes and a mouth stretched open in almost the same shape. "But . . . why?" she said. "Where would she go?"

"Almost anywhere," I said. "Walk up to Metrorail—it's not far— and then . . . did she have any money?"

"Her allowance," Rita said. "And . . ." She bit her lip. "I think she took some money from my purse. Forty dollars."

"Well, we can rule out Singapore," I said. Forty dollars and Astor's allowance—maybe another ten or twenty dollars, if she'd saved up— would not get her far. "Has she said anything? Like a new friend, or somebody online? Any hint at all?"

"Oh, no," Rita said. "I would never let her— You know what she's like. She doesn't make friends very easily, and— She didn't say anything."

"Okay," I said, and I stood up. "I'm going to look in her room."

"What?" Rita said. "Dexter, she's not there; I'm sure I would have— Oh! You mean look for something. . . ."

"Yes," I said, and I stepped around her and down the hall to the room Astor shared with her brother. It was a small room, too small for two growing kids of different genders, which was one of the main reasons we had bought the new and larger house, where they would each have their own room. One side of the room was taken up by the bunk bed—Cody on top—and the other side was carefully divided between His space and Hers.

The room was cluttered with all the junk you would expect a couple of ordinary kids to collect—but there were differences, because these, after all, were not ordinary kids. Their Bio Dad's violence, and probably his DNA, had set their feet on the Dark Path, and they would never ever walk in the happy-face light of Normal.

And so a few odd touches stood out to the eye of any trained observer, especially if he was also a Monster like me. For example, Cody had a number of action figures—he got very cranky if you called them dolls—as any boy his age might. But every one of them had been neatly and lovingly beheaded. The tiny plastic heads were lined up in a careful row on the top tier of his toy shelf, aligned exactly, perfectly, not a single one out of place.

The entire Cody side of the little room, in fact, was alarmingly neat. His shoes were lined up, toes together, his books stacked with the spines aligned, and even his dirty clothes lay neatly in a blue plastic laundry basket, looking like they had been folded first. Preteen boys are never that neat, but since I had been the same way myself, I didn't worry. Something in a Monster just likes things tidy. Since Cody shared my other, Darker tastes, I just assumed that his Neatness was simply part of the package.

Astor's half, on the other hand, was as chaotic as a very small space could be. She had a small desk with a hutch on it, and a chair pulled halfway out. Clothing, both clean and dirty, was piled on the chair and on top of the hutch, everything from shorts and jeans and dresses to oddly colored socks and underpants with bright patterns on them. It was a mess, even more than usual, as if she had taken every stitch of clothing she owned and sorted through it, throwing it all around as she did.

If she had, in fact, sorted through it as she prepared to leave, the things she chose to take away might be significant. I was no expert on Astor's wardrobe, but I could recognize some of the most important pieces, since I had listened to her screech about them when they were not laundered yet, or too stupid to wear, or the wrong color for Friday. I picked through the mound of shirts and skirts and sweaters and hoodies, not sure what I was really hoping to find—and finding it anyway.

There had been some kind of fall dance at school a few weeks earlier, and to my surprise, Astor had insisted on attending. Even more, she had gone into a weeklong towering tizzy about having nothing to wear, which struck me as even odder, considering that the floor of her closet was heaped with enough clothing to start a boutique.

But Rita had played along with Astor's enthusiasm, telling me only that a girl's first dance was very special, almost like first Communion, and of *course* she had to have a new dress, and of course it had to be Just Right. And so they had spent an entire weekend flitting across Miami from mall to mall until they found the perfect dress. It was a silver sheath that sparkled and gleamed and radiated blue highlights as it moved, and Astor had been more pleased with that dress than I had ever seen her. And it must have been effective, because she came home from the dance radiating a smug contempt for boys.

But the dress didn't seem to be here at the moment. I poked through the heap of clothes without finding a flicker of silver. I stepped over to the closet and peered in, moving things around until I was sure it was not there, either.

Wherever Astor had gone, she had taken her Very Special Dress.

I moved back beside her desk and thought about this. She would not have taken that dress if she planned to hitchhike through South America, climb Mount Rainier, or work her way to Australia on a tramp steamer. She would not risk getting it dirty. So where *had* she gone?

I looked around. On the far side of the rag heap, there were dozens of photos taped to the wall, jammed crazily together and even overlapping one another. I stepped over and looked at the most recent layer, hoping to see something, anything that might suggest where she was. Most of the pictures on the wall were of Astor, many of them she had clearly taken herself, by holding the camera out in front of her own face, or shooting into a mirror. There were three pictures taped on top of all the others, in the center of the wall. But they showed nothing except Astor clowning with Robert, obviously taken on the day she and her siblings had surprised me at Wardrobe. In one of them Astor had pale makeup covering her face and fake blood dripping from her mouth; she was attacking Robert as he cringed away in mock fear.

The next one showed Astor in grotesquely overdone glamour makeup, pouting at her reflection in the large, light-framed mirror of a professional makeup room; Portrait of the Actress as a Young Vamp.

In the last picture Astor, still in the awful makeup, stood in front of Robert with huge eyes and a face full of dramatic yearning straight from *Gone with the Wind*, while Robert looked away with an expression of noble longing on his face.

A fourth picture, set off to the side, was a standard publicity shot of Robert. In black marker, somebody, presumably Robert, had written, "To the Beautiful Astor with my very best," and then an illegible flourish that was probably his signature.

There was nothing else, just these silly pictures, and nothing to them but a young girl's infatuation with the idea of being an actress, and having a chance to really do it with Real Makeup and a Real Star. There was nothing else there on the wall that I hadn't seen before: no tourist brochures for Rio, no scribbled flight numbers, nothing. I poked around for another minute anyway, looking in the closet, under the bed, and even under the mattress, but I found no hint of where she might have gone, or why.

I sat on the edge of the lower bunk and pondered. I was now sure that Astor had run away—probably just *walked* away, most likely—and had not been grabbed by some drooling dolt with arrested development. Of course, that would not last. A young girl on the street alone does not stay alone for long; that is a simple law of nature. She would have company very quickly—they would find her. She would almost certainly not like her new friends, or the things they made her do, but she would not be alone. Someone with an eye out for somebody just like her would find her, and lead her away, and then Astor would disappear forever into a world of painful surprises.

In the meantime, however, there was a brief window of opportunity for me to get to her before somebody else did. And it should be easy, because I knew her very well, knew her in ways that even her mother did not, and also because I am very, very clever and I almost always figure out these little puzzles.

So where would she go? And just as important, why would she go *now*? She had grumbled about hating her family and wanting to run away, but all kids did that, and I'd never taken her seriously. Astor was too bright to throw herself out the door and into random chance, or to think she could instantly find a place where her True Greatness and Beauty were recognized and rewarded. And she had taken along her Special Dress. So if she went, it would be to someplace specific, and someplace she was sure would be better.

But what could be better than having three square meals, plus snacks, and new shoes now and then? And all this with a family who actually liked her for some reason, paid all her bills, put up with her unpleasant and furious snits—and more, a semifather who knew and understood what she was really like in the dark and damaged interior of her twisted self?

On top of everything else, she was about to move into a new house, with her very own room and a swimming pool. She had been very excited about her new house, carefully painting her room and planning where her desk and bed would go, and what she would wear to her first pool party—could she really find something better than that to run away to, something that was right here, right now, immediate and within reach?

There was a snuffling noise from the doorway, and Rita's plaintive voice called, " . . . Dexter . . . ?" and I blinked myself back to awareness. As sometimes happens when I am concentrating on some complex problem, I found that I had been staring fixedly straight ahead, without actually seeing anything. But as Rita's interruption brought me back to the here and now, I saw that I was staring straight at Astor's wall of photos.

"Dexter?" she whined again. "Have you . . . found anything?"

I opened my mouth to answer her, but the words that came out surprised me; they were not at all the words I had thought I was going to say. "Yes," I said. "I know where she went." And even stranger, I did know.

"Oh!" Rita said. "Oh, thank God!"

I barely managed to stand up and then she was on me, sobbing and yodeling into my shirtfront and leaving me coated with damp unpleasant things. I pried her back from my chest and she looked up at me with a wet, red, puffy face. "Where is she?" she said, unsuccessfully trying to sniffle some goo off her lip and back into her nose. "Where did she go? We have to— Dexter, for God's sake, we have to right *now*— Oh, why are you standing around here like this— Dexter, come *on*!"

"I'll get her," I said. "I want you to stay here."

"Stay here?! But that's— No, Dexter, I can't just— What are you talking about, stay here? That's completely— Why would I stay here?"

The real answer to *why* was that I did not want her with me, not where I was going. But because there was no way to say that without causing a full-scale nuclear war, I gave her the first thing that popped into my head: "She might come home," I said. "Somebody should be here, just in case." I put a hand on her shoulder and frowned with great seriousness. "And that somebody ought to be her mother."

I don't really know why this should be, but I have found that words like "ought" and "should" have a very special magical power, something that reaches down into a soft and gooey spot in the human heart that I do not have, thank goodness. Because aiming these words at someone who does have it—someone like Rita, for example—almost always makes them take a deep breath, straighten their shoulders, and do things they really don't want to do.

Rita did not disappoint; as if she was following a printed instruction sheet, she opened her mouth to object—and then closed it, took a deep breath, and straightened her shoulders. "All right," she said. "That's probably— I mean, of course I want to go, but—if she came back? I couldn't— I'll stay here."

"Good," I said, and I clapped her on the shoulder as if she had just agreed to parachute behind enemy lines and blow up a bridge. "I'll call you as soon as I find her," I said.

"Yes, that's— And if she comes here, I'll— But Dexter, where is she?"

I gave her a brave smile. "Someplace better," I said, and before Rita could sputter too many new objections, I was into the hall, out the front door, and driving away.

The traffic had gotten a little thicker in the last forty minutes, but most of it was going in the other direction, away from work in the city, toward home in the suburbs, and there were no serious delays all the way up Dixie Highway and back onto I-95.

I showed my credentials to a very alert-looking cop, and he waved me toward the far end of the parking lot. I parked the car there and looked around as I got out. I could see a lot more cops, all looking just as alert, wandering around the set as well as posted at the perimeter. They seemed to be taking the security thing very seriously—whether because Captain Matthews had ordered it, or because they liked the thought of keeping ordinary people away from the really cool movie action, I couldn't say. But I didn't see how Astor could have snuck onto the set without being seen, so I walked back to the cop who had scanned my credentials.

"I'm looking for a girl," I said.

"Ain't we all," he told me deadpan, looking away into the distance.

"This one is eleven years old," I said. "Blond hair, maybe a backpack?"

The cop focused on me. "Runaway?" he said.

I smiled reassuringly; I didn't want a huge and official fuss about this, not just yet. "Not yet," I said. "She wants to be a movie star, so . . ."

He nodded. "Yeah," he said. "My kid, ten years old. He wants to be a relief pitcher. So he turns up in Fort Myers, at Red Sox spring training." He snorted. "Fucking *Red Sox*?!"

"Could have been worse," I said. "Might have been the Mets."

"Got that right," he said. "Lemme call around the perimeter."

The cop turned his back and took a step away while he spoke into his radio, and a few seconds later he turned back to me and nodded. "Got her," he said. "Few hours ago. Alvarez says she came right up and asked for Robert Chase, the actor guy?"

I nodded; I was pretty sure I knew who Robert Chase was.

"So naturally, Alvarez says, 'No way, I can't do that, and why aren't you in school?' And she says she's his *niece*, and Chase is expecting her." He shrugged. "So, this is Miami. Weirder shit happens every day, right? Alvarez sends the word, and like two seconds later, here comes Chase on the run. And he leads her away by the hand."

It made sense: However angelic she might look, Astor was a predator, in her own way. She would naturally make a beeline for Robert; he had shown her weakness, and even though his first impulse would be to call me, or Deborah, Astor would not let him. I could almost hear her wheedling and bullying and lying her little tail off—and poor Robert, who thought he liked kids but had never had to deal with one, especially one like this, would have no defense at all. He would cave in to her, helpless, telling himself that he would call in just a little while, and anyway, she was safe here on the set, and where was the harm?

"Where'd they go?" I asked the cop.

He jerked his head at the row of actors' trailers. "Over to his trailer," he said. I thanked him, and I headed over there, too.

Robert's trailer was at the far end of the row. He had insisted on being put there in semi-isolation, probably because he wanted privacy so he could go into his Method trance and become his character. Since that character still had a disturbing number of habits he had stolen from me, I thought he should have been placed even farther away, maybe in the middle of the Everglades, where he might be eaten by a Burmese python.

But the end of the row was as far as he'd made it to date. I trudged along the line of sleek aluminum trailers: one for Renny, one for women and one for men, one for Victor, the director. A trailer for makeup and one for wardrobe. A thick white-noise murmur of air conditioners muffled any sounds that might have come from inside. The door of the women's trailer opened just after I passed it, and I heard laughter over the thump of hip-hop coming from inside. Then the door closed again and all was quiet.

Three steps led up to the door of Robert's trailer. I climbed them and knocked on the door. There was no response. There was no sound anywhere except the blanket of air-conditioner noise. I waited, then knocked again; still nothing.

I tried the handle, and to my surprise it turned easily and the door swung open. I paused for just a moment; a long and wicked life has taught me that, far too often, an unpleasant surprise lurks just inside the door. Of course, that surprise had usually been Me, but caution is never out of place.

I looked around the inside; nothing lurked. The trailer was dim, all the blinds pulled shut and the lights turned off, and nothing moved or made any sound. I stepped inside and looked around. It was very similar to Jackie's trailer: the same arrangement of living area with couch and kitchenette, and through a door to a bedroom with adjoining bath. I poked through the rooms, looked in all the closets and drawers, found no sign that Astor had ever been there.

For that matter, there were very few signs that Robert had ever been there, either. A couple of wardrobe items hung in the closet, and a pair of shoes sat on the floor underneath, but there were no personal touches at all: no iPod, briefcase, or book, no comfy shoes, baseball cap, or sunglasses. No vitamins, or tooth whitener, or deodorant—none of the things a Working Actor should have in his trailer on location.

It was puzzling, but not really worth any brain sweat. The important question was this: If he had gone somewhere with Astor, where? A quick jaunt off-site for ice cream? Or were they still here on the set somewhere? He might be leading Astor around to see all the really cool stuff—Dickie and his squibs, makeup, even another visit to Sylvia in Wardrobe. There was a lot to see, and if Astor wanted to see all of it—and she would—she would not give Robert a great deal of wiggle room.

So they might be anywhere in this vast forest of trailers and vans and generators, and finding them could take more time than I really wanted to spend. But it was also possible that Robert was shooting a scene, with Astor looking on raptly from the sidelines. That would be quick and easy—and it would even be quick and easy to find out. There was a fifteen-page-long shooting schedule on the table in Jackie's trailer that would tell me who, when, and where. I took a last look around, just to be sure, and then went out, closing the door behind me.

Jackie's trailer was at the other end of the row. I hurried down the line and up the steps to her door. It was not locked; I felt a silly little surge of hope that Jackie would be inside, and I stepped quickly through the doorway—

—and I froze, one foot in midair, as all the hackles went up on my neck.

There was neither sight nor sound of anything out of place, but I stood there frozen into unmoving wide-awake readiness. Deep down, but moving rapidly up the basement steps and onto the ramparts of Castle Dexter, Something had hissed and uncoiled and begun to whisper its soft and sibilant warnings that all was not what it should be, and so I did not move. I listened. I looked and I waited, and there was nothing at all but the rising rustle of that leathery whisper.

I took half a step into the trailer. A waft of frigid air from inside blew into my face, air cold enough to chill beer, and with it came a faint tang of something that sent my brain crashing back through time, far away, back to that small, awful, cold room so long ago where the Real Dexter had been born in a gelatinous lake of blood. . . .

*And I sit there unmoving in the awful sticky thickening red wetness and that smell is all there is, the smell of rotting copper, and Mommy is not moving, and I am lost and helpless and floundering in a dark world of blood and there is no way out and no help—*

And I blink and I am back here, back now, right here in Jackie's trailer, and not in that horrible wet nasty hell, not at all; I am here, and that was long ago and far away and there is no reason to remember that dreadful three-day birth, no reason at all—

Except that smell is here now, too. The chilled and cloying smell of rotting copper—the smell of blood.

I shake myself. I tell me that it is not so. It is not possible. It is no more than the smell of the roast beef from lunch and the freezing wind from the air conditioner and bad memories lurching up, because of tension and personal upheaval, and it will all go away and everything will be fine if I just remember to breathe normally and remind Dexter that he is all grown-up and will never again be trapped in the horrible cold room with its thick and sticky red floor.

I tell myself that all is just exactly what it should be and nothing could possibly be quite That Wrong and I take another step in—and the smell is still there, even stronger now, and the memories wail and moan and flail at the walls of my crumbling self and howl at me to fly, run away, sprint from the room for my life and sanity. But I push these goblins away, and I step in one more step, and another, until I can see that there is nothing to see by the couch, by the fridge, and I can see into the bedroom now, and—

She lay there at the foot of the bed with one arm flung up above her head and the other bent unnaturally under her body. Her golden hair was scattered around her as if it had been flung from a great height, and half of that hair, the half closest to me, was pasted down onto the floor by a thick dark red pool that was already congealing, and in spite of my need to fly away from that awful red copper-smelling mess I stepped toward it instead and looked down with no hope in me at all.

She did not move. She would never move again. Her face was pale and set in an expression of weary terror, and she looked up at me with clouded eyes that did not blink and did not see and would never blink or weep or see anything ever again.

Beautiful violet eyes.

# THIRTY-TWO

DON'T KNOW HOW LONG I STOOD THERE LOOKING DOWN AT Jackie's lifeless body. It seemed like forever. I had no reason for it; staring down at the mess she had turned into wouldn't bring her back, wouldn't even roll the awful sticky red blood back inside her. And it didn't help me like her being dead any better, either.

I am no stranger to death. It has been my whole life for many years, and I know what it looks like, smells like, and sounds like—but for the very first time I thought I knew what it felt like, too, because it was *her*, Jackie. And suddenly Death was something new, wrong, evil and intractable. It had no right to roll over Jackie and suck her dry and leave me here without her. It did not belong on her; Death did not fit Jackie, not someone so very much alive and beautiful and full of wonderful plans for me. It wasn't right. It wasn't fair. It shouldn't be.

But it was. She was dead and there was no going back from it. Death had breathed its ugly gray film over those violet eyes and it seemed like a very final and painful thing all of a sudden, in a way it never had before.

I am not sentimental, not at all—I believe sentiment requires some trace of humanity—but Feelings surged through me that had no place inside a Thing like me. I watched them go by in their lunatic haste: regret, anger, even guilt, a bitter sense of lost opportunity, and anger again. Feelings rippled out of the Dark Basement and up the cold stone stairs of Castle Dexter, squealing with contempt and sliding up the banister, screeching through the halls and ripping down the tapestries.

And then the feelings were gone, and they had left behind the final, most lasting feeling of all:

Emptiness.

It was done. It was over. The dream was dead, cold and bloodless as the pitiful lump of meat at my feet. Jackie was gone—but Dexter must move on somehow, move away from the magical future that had been dangling there in front of him and back into the painful squalor that had been his life before all this had swept him away into a world of bright and glittering hope—a hope that had turned out to be as solid and real as a piece of TV scenery.

I turned away from Jackie's body and went back to stand by the front door. I knew what I had to do now. It would not be much fun, but I would get used to that again. Fun was gone forever from Dexter's world.

I took out my phone and called Deborah. She didn't answer, letting the call go right to voice mail. I disconnected and called again. Still nothing. I tried a third time, and finally, she answered.

"What," she said, in a voice so flat and dead it might have been Jackie's.

"Can you find Jackie's trailer?" I said.

Silence; then finally, she said, "Yes."

"Find it now," I said. "Quickly." And I hung up.

I was certain that whatever it was that lay there between us, it would not stop Deborah from coming. She is not stupid, and she would know that I would not call her lightly at this point.

And sure enough, inside of four minutes I heard her feet on the steps outside, and then the trailer's door swung open and she was standing there, frowning into the relative darkness of the interior. "What is it," she said in that same expressionless voice.

I stepped back from the door and pointed toward the bedroom. "In there," I said. She shook her head once, still frowning, and then came inside and looked past me to where Jackie lay sprawled in her untidy heap.

Deborah froze for a second; then she hissed, "Fuck," and strode quickly in to the body. She squatted down beside it and reached her hand halfway toward Jackie's neck, and then pulled it back again as she realized there was no need to feel for a pulse. She sat there on her heels for several long seconds before she finally stood up, looked down at the body again, and then came back to me.

"What happened," she said, and there was cold rage in her voice. "Did she try to break up with you?"

For a moment I just blinked at her stupidly, with no idea what she meant, and then I understood. "I didn't do it, Debs," I said.

"I'm not going to cover this up, Dexter," she went on, as if she hadn't heard me. "I can't help you, and I wouldn't even if I could."

"Deborah, it wasn't me. I didn't do it."

I guess she heard me this time, but she still didn't believe me. She cocked her head to one side and glared at me with cold unblinking eyes, like a bird of prey deciding whether to strike. "Who did?" she said.

I shook my head. "I don't know."

"Uh-huh. Where were you?"

"I wasn't here," I said. "Rita called me—Astor ran away, and I went home to look for her."

Deborah curled her lip. "Home," she said, with heavy irony.

I ignored it. "Astor came here, to be on location, and I came to ask if Jackie had seen her, and . . ." For no good reason, I looked back to where Jackie's body lay. "And there she was," I finished, rather lamely.

Deborah was silent, and I watched her. She was still staring at me with unblinking frostiness, but at least she hadn't reached for her cuffs yet. "Where is she now?" she said at last.

I looked at her, wondering whether she had lost her mind. "Deborah, she's right *there*," I said, nodding toward the body. "She's not going anywhere."

"Astor," she said through her teeth. "Where is Astor?"

"Oh," I said, oddly relieved. "I don't know. With Robert somewhere."

Deborah looked at Jackie's body again, then shook her head. "You left her here alone," she said. "And he got her."

"What?" I said, filled with righteous indignation and certainty. "It wasn't Patrick. The stalker—it couldn't be!"

She looked back at me. "Why not?"

And she had me there, of course. If we were still enjoying our old bonhomie, I might have told her why not, explained that Patrick the stalker was no more. But as things stood between us now, I did not think I could explain away one death by confessing to another. So I did what Dexter does and temporized. "It doesn't look like the way he works," I said carefully. "And, you know. Both eyes are still there."

"Uh-huh," she said, just the way I'd heard her say it many times before when she was trying to get a suspect to keep talking. And for some reason, it worked on me.

"And anyway," I babbled, "how could he get in here? There's cops all around the perimeter, all over the place. Nobody could get past them."

"Nobody who didn't belong here," she amended.

"Yes, of course."

"Like, for instance, an extra? Maybe an extra who was also her *boyfriend*?" And she put an awful lot of venom into that word.

"All right, Deborah," I said, and if my tone of voice revealed that I was peeved past caring, fine. "If you're so mad at me that you'd rather lock me up than get whoever really did this, fine. Get the cuffs. Take me away and be a hero, the hard-ass who locked up her brother for a murder he didn't commit." I held out my hands, wrists together for the cuffs. "Go ahead," I said.

Deborah looked at me a little longer, as if she might really do it. Then she shook her head and hissed out a long breath between her teeth. "All right," she said. "One way or the other, it's not my problem."

"Deborah—"

"Don't even bother," she said. "I don't give a shit." And she turned away from me and took out her phone to call it in.

I have been on the scene of a great many homicides, profession- ally as well as personally, but I had never before been there as the person who found the body. And I had never been there as a sus- pect, either, even when I was guilty. I found it to be a vastly different experience, and I didn't like it—especially when Detective Anderson arrived to take charge.

The first thing Anderson did was to usher Deborah out the door, and then he stumped around the trailer and grumbled and hissed and bullied Angel-No-Relation, who had arrived to handle the forensic side of things. And when he finally got around to taking me aside for questioning, he did not behave like a man talking to a professional colleague caught in unfortunate circumstances. Instead, he took me by the elbow and pulled me off to stand by the refrigerator. We stood there and he gave me a long and hooded stare. I waited politely, but he just stared, obviously convinced he could soften me up before dragging an incriminating statement out of me.

My phone chirped. I reached for it, but he shot out his hand and clamped it on my wrist. I looked at him with raised eyebrows; he shook his head. It didn't seem worth fighting about, so I let go of the phone and looked at him, waiting for him to do something that might hint at an intelligence higher than the refrigerator's. I waited in vain, but he finally shook his head and favored me with a slight frown.

"Some blanket," he said.

It took me a moment to understand what he meant. It must have shown on my face, because he went on. "You said you were protecting her." He sneered. "Like a blanket."

It is usually best to stay polite and meek when being questioned by a detective, but the meekness had drained out of me with Jackie's death, and I was irritated enough by his cheap shot to give it right back. "Some detective," I said. "You said you'd find the killer."

He blushed very slightly, and then shook his head. "Maybe I have," he said, and there was no way to misunderstand him this time.

"You haven't," I said.

"Uh-huh," he said. "Except it's always the boyfriend, isn't it?"

"Sure," I said. "Even when the victim is being stalked by a homicidal psychopath who has killed before and has sworn to kill her. It makes perfect sense to suspect the boyfriend, and not the psycho stalker. At least," I said, "it makes sense to *you*."

He stared at me, and he thought he was going to say something else, some truly witty and withering put-down. But as we have all noted previously, Wit blossoms on a branch that is forever out of reach to Detective Anderson, and so he just stared, and then shook his head again as he finally realized no bon mot was on the way. "You're not out of this," he said, and he moved away to bully Angel some more.

And I wasn't out of it. Not by a long shot. I stood there for most of an hour and watched. Whenever he thought of it, Anderson would give me an intimidating stare, but other than that nothing happened.

I didn't mind. In fact, I was glad that Anderson was in charge, instead of someone like Deborah, who might actually solve this murder, because I didn't want it solved just yet. Whoever did this had done it to *me* as much as to Jackie. They had killed my whole beautiful future along with her, and thrown me back on the dung heap of cloying mundane hand-to-mouth existence in the slough of the petty, pointless life I had outgrown, and whoever did that to me, I would find them and make them pay. No, I didn't want anybody finding this killer. Nobody except Me.

So I stood there beside the refrigerator and watched Anderson stump around, the very Classical Ideal of sound and fury signifying nothing, and I looked at the two or three small factoids I had about this killer.

First, I knew it wasn't Patrick. But I was the only one who knew that, and somebody else could well have hoped to use the whole Psycho Stalker thing as a shield. They already had, in fact, if I assumed that the same person had killed Kathy. I thought only a moment, and then I went ahead and assumed it; Kathy's eye had been taken, and there was no reason to do that except as a red herring. The same killer had killed them both.

So I had two events to provide me with clues. If I had been feeling optimistic, this would have cheered me up, because two murders provide twice as many clues. But I added up what I knew without any optimism; it was gone from me forever, leaving behind only a bitter residue.

Kathy had been a nonentity, almost a nonperson. I meant no disrespect for the dead, even though they couldn't stop me if I did. But my short sweet time at the pinnacle of showbiz had taught me that a personal assistant was not even as high in the pecking order as the valet parking attendant, who might, after all, be an actor on the rise.

Kathy, though, had been a full-time professional gofer, and she could not possibly have the kind of high-octane enemies who would choose to kill her, especially not coldly, premeditatedly, and in such a vividly visceral way. But somebody had, in fact, killed her—and then taken her phone. Where she kept all Jackie's appointments, phone numbers, contacts, etc. That implied—at least to me—that Kathy's death was connected to something on the phone.

Even in Hollywood, very few people will kill to get an address or phone number—except, perhaps, the number of a really good agent. But in this case, that seemed unlikely; I was quite sure the phone had not been taken for any contact information. That left appointments, and that thought brought a small, dry rustle of interest from the Dark Detective nestled in his inner lair.

All right: The phone had been taken to hide one of the appointments. That meant that either one of Jackie's upcoming appointments was worth killing to hide—or the appointment was not Jackie's. It was Kathy's phone, after all. Why shouldn't she keep personal things on it, too? And *if* somebody made a date to meet her in her room at the hotel, and had gone there specifically to kill her, it made sense that he would take the phone away to hide the record of the date.

But wait: That made sense only if the killer knew Kathy kept all those things on her phone. And that meant it was somebody who knew her, and knew the way she did her job—and *that* meant it was either somebody from her past who flew in from L.A. just to kill her . . . Or much more likely, it was somebody here, now, involved in making this pilot. Somebody with a very strong motive for keeping Kathy from—what? Going somewhere, doing something, saying something . . .

A tiny little video clip popped onto the screen in Dexter's personal viewing room: a few days ago at wardrobe, and Kathy slapping Renny, storming away from him, yelling something like, "Next time I'll tell everybody!"

Another little clip: Renny staring at me as a dark and leathery shadow of a Something flaps its wings behind his eyes.

And another: Renny looking out at the audience at his special with that same look, a look I knew so well because it was a killer's look, and I practiced every day to hide mine with convincingly meek fake smiles.

And Renny going after the heckler with an aggressive attack that could only be called lethal, flashing his true killer colors for all to see. Renny.

It all added up: He had a motive, whatever the details were, and I knew he had that special thing inside that would make killing a simple and viable option. And so to hide this something, it didn't matter what, he had killed Kathy—and then thrown up, according to Vince, when he saw the mess he'd made? But still killed Jackie, too, in spite of this revulsion, which he should not feel if he actually had a Dark Passenger?

The roaring freight train of Dexter's Deduction slammed to a halt. It didn't make sense. Nobody capable of routine murder could possibly throw up at the sight of what he'd done. And anyway, how did that connect to the most important fact, Jackie's death?

All right, maybe it wasn't Renny. But I still had two bodies, and I was sure they were connected. So I put Renny aside for a moment and tried to get the train back on the tracks.

Somebody, possibly not Renny, killed Kathy and took her phone to keep something from getting out. And then in spite of not enjoying it, which seemed a waste, they had killed Jackie. For the same reason? But they already had the phone, so why bother?

Anderson stomped by me and out the door of the trailer, and I looked over to where Angel was calmly, methodically combing through the area around Jackie's body, directly in front of the big box of Kathy's stuff. Somewhere a small brass coin dropped into a slot with a soft chiming sound, and I blinked.

I went over to Angel. He looked up briefly, then back to a chunk of carpet he was putting into an evidence bag. "Go away," he said. "You are bad juju."

"I need to see something," I said.

"No," he said. "Anderson might shoot me."

"It will only take a second," I said. "It's very important."

Angel rocked back onto his heels and looked up at me, clearly deciding whether I was worth the risk. "What?" he said at last.

I nodded at the big cardboard box behind him. "The computer," I said. "Is it still in the case?"

He looked at me a moment longer, and then sighed heavily. He leaned over to the box, where the black nylon computer case perched on the top of the pile. With one rubber-gloved finger he flipped the case open. "No," he said. "No computer." He took away his finger and the case flopped shut. "Should it be there?"

"It was there this morning," I said.

"Shit," he said. "Well, I didn't take it."

"No," I said. "But somebody did."

Angel sighed heavily, clearly unhappy that a computer might be missing when he had forensic lead. "Is it important?" he said.

"I think so," I said.

"Why?"

"Because it's an Apple," I said.

Angel shook his head. "Dexter, *coño*, come on."

"Thanks, Angel."

He sighed again and returned to his hands and knees. "I don't think I like you anymore," he said.

I went back to my post by the refrigerator, rather pleased with myself. Now I knew why Jackie had been killed. Because if you have an Apple smartphone and an Apple computer, you synch them, so all the data on the phone goes onto the computer. And Jackie had turned on the computer, seen the appointment, and been killed for it.

But if Kathy had kept up with her updates, all that data would have been copied into the cloud, too, which meant that it should still be up there, incriminating appointment and all. But Kathy's cloud account couldn't be accessed by anybody else, not without her password. And by taking away the laptop, the killer had made sure that the information was out of reach.

I did not quite pat myself on the back, but I was very pleased. I had figured out almost everything—except, of course, the one tiny, unimportant detail of who the killer was.

I tried to make Renny fit again, and he really did, almost. But finally, I could not believe that anybody with a Passenger could throw up after the simple, relaxing, and often pleasant act of killing somebody.

On the other hand, if I eliminated Renny, who did that leave? Maybe Renny had thrown up because he'd eaten some bad oysters. It *had* to be Renny—there was nobody else who fit at all. In any case, I certainly had to poke around into his immediate past and see whether he fit. Maybe get Deborah to check into it, and . . .

Deborah. Apparently she was still not speaking to me, for the most part, and she would not be any easier to approach now, with Anderson leading his clown parade all over everything and flinging her out the door. It seemed unlikely that her ejection from the scene had softened her up so she was ready to forgive and forget.

Still, I had a lead she could use, and she was a cop down to the very marrow of her bones. She wanted to solve this thing—even more since it was Anderson's case. And it was at least possible that she would want to shove Anderson's face in the mud more than she wanted to avoid me. It was worth a try.

Of course, I could not try as long as I was standing here beside the refrigerator waiting for Anderson to come back and intimidate me. I needed to be out and about, and so I thought about my curious new position as a Person of Interest. Nobody had actually told me to stay put, don't leave town, retain an attorney. I had simply stayed around out of the reflexive urge to be useful somehow. Clearly, that was not going to happen—unless giving Anderson something to glare at is considered useful. So I looked around to see if anybody was watching me; nobody was, and I slipped nonchalantly out the door of the trailer.

Deborah was pacing back and forth outside, and she paused to watch me come down the three steps. For a moment I thought she was going to say something, and maybe she did, too. But she didn't speak. She just shook her head and turned away to resume her pacing.

"Deborah," I said to her back.

She stopped walking and her shoulders hunched up toward her ears. Then she turned and looked at me with a much more convincing version of the hostile look Anderson had attempted. "What," she said.

"I think I know who killed Jackie," I said.

She didn't say anything for a moment. Then she shook her head. "Go tell Anderson," she said.

"I'd rather tell you," I said. "So maybe some good will come of it."

She looked at me with her head tilted to one side. "You're not

going to bribe me into some goddamn forgive-and-forget Kodak
moment, Dexter. You fucked up big-time, and now because of you
Jackie is dead and Rita is—what?" she said, and her words got hotter
as she spoke. "Did you kill her yet, Dexter? Because that would make
sense to you, wouldn't it?"

"Deborah, for Christ's sake—"

"It makes more sense than walking away and leaving her alive to
fuck things up later, doesn't it?"

"I didn't kill—"

"And if you didn't, now what? You still leave Rita and your three
kids, now that you shit all over your brand-new bed? Or do you crawl
back and try to pretend it never happened? Because she may take you
back—but I don't know if I will."

"That's fine," I said. "I'll go tell Anderson." And because I can
play the game, too, I added, "And he will fuck it up, and a killer will
get away because you're too busy having a hissy fit to do anything
about it."

I was very glad to be ten feet away from her, because judging
by the look on her face, if I had been close enough, she would have
committed a felonious assault on my person, possibly resulting in
serious injury. Even from ten feet away I could hear her teeth grinding together.

"Spill it," she said at last, her teeth still locked tight.

I told her about the phone, and about the computer, and how that
meant the same person killed both Jackie and Kathy, and she listened.
She didn't suddenly burst into bright smiles and embrace me, but she
listened. When I finished, she looked at me for a moment, and then
said, "Okay. So who did it?"

"Renny Boudreaux," I said. "He had some kind of altercation with
Kathy, and she yelled that she would tell everybody next time."

Deborah looked at me, and then she sneered. I mean, really, an
actual sneer, the kind you give somebody pathetic who is beneath
your contempt but for whom you feel contempt anyway. "Renny Boudreaux is in New York," she said. "Doing the morning shows to promote his special. He left yesterday."

"What?" I said, and I admit I was at least partially stunned.

"New York," she said. "Everybody on set knows it, and you'd know it, too, if you had read the production schedule instead of spending all your time humping Jackie."

It seemed like a very low blow, but she wasn't finished with me yet. "And in the meantime," she said, moving effortlessly from the sneer back to a very good snarl, "while you dick around and waste my time with stupid bullshit, you still haven't found Astor."

I did not actually reel in shock, but her body shots definitely left me a bit wobbly and uncertain. "Well," I said feebly, "but—"

"Find your girl, asshole," she said. "Leave this alone. You've done enough damage." And she turned away and stalked toward the far end of the trailer. I stood and watched her, but she paced by me without a glance, as if I was some kind of common and rather dull plant life. I didn't want to leave this alone. I wanted to grab Deborah by the shoulders and shake her, and tell her it wasn't my fault; Patrick was dead, and somebody else had killed Jackie and ruined the only shot I'd ever had to climb out of the ooze and into the genuine gold-plated sunshine. And then I wanted to find Jackie's killer and tape him snugly under my knife and give him a very long time to reflect on what he had done. And I would; I would not leave this alone, forgotten and fumbled away by Anderson's stone-brained incompetence and Deborah's bureaucratic indifference.

But as much as it nettled to admit it, Deborah was right about one thing: I did have to find Astor, and that was a more immediate problem than my revenge.

All right: Where should I start? Robert's trailer was the obvious place, but I had already looked there. Still, that had been almost an hour ago. It was at least possible that they had returned, and if only to carry out my due diligence, I should check it again.

Deborah stalked by one more time without looking at me, and while she was still at the far end of her neurotic sentry march, I crossed over her path and headed toward Robert's trailer.

# THIRTY-THREE

ROBERT'S TRAILER WAS STILL UNLOCKED, AND AS I PUSHED the door open I saw that it was still dim inside, too. Once again I paused just outside and peered both ways, and once again I saw nothing, heard nothing, smelled nothing. I stepped through the door and looked around; still nobody home. As far as I could tell, nothing had changed. I looked in all the corners and closets anyway, because thoroughness is a virtue every bit as important as neatness, and I found exactly the same amount of Nothing as I'd found earlier.

And now what? Astor was still missing, Deborah was still not speaking to me, and Jackie was still dead. The world was not at all the happy place it had seemed to be so recently, and for just a moment there no longer seemed any point to pretending. All the purpose, all the anger and resolve and need to Do Something drained out of me, and I collapsed onto the edge of the couch in Robert's living area. It had all looked so bright and beautiful this morning, and now the world had snapped back into its true form, gray and pointless and mean-spirited, and even though that was certainly a better fit for Dismal Dexter, I didn't like it. I wanted things back the way they were. Like a little boy trapped in a dark and dreary adventure, I wanted to go home.

But I was not a little boy, and even worse, I was home. This was it, this dismal, painful, senseless trudging through sludge. This was where I lived; back in ugly old reality again. And there was nothing I could do about it, nothing at all, except to find Astor and drag her back home and start up the same old shadow show.

Home: back to dirty socks on the floor and screeching at all hours and Rita's endless, pointless, disjointed monologues. Rita: the one person still talking to me, and I didn't really want to talk to her and couldn't understand what she said. And thinking of Rita, I remembered that my phone had bleated at me while I was being grilled by Anderson. It had to be her; nobody else was left.

And so with a heavy sigh and a sense of returning to painful duty, I dragged out my phone and looked at the screen. Yup: Rita. She'd left a message, naturally—why pass up an opportunity to blather? I went to voice mail and listened.

"Dexter," she said. "I know you must be looking for her. For Astor? Because it's been a long time now and you didn't— And anyway, I thought of something, and I was going to— I know you said she might come home, and I thought, that's right, she might, but maybe not—and so anyway, I'll just be gone for twenty minutes. Oh. And I'll call you when I get back, in case." I heard her take a breath, as if she was going to go on, but instead she disconnected.

I glanced at the time. The call had come in fifty-eight minutes ago. I had been to college, so I knew that fifty-eight minutes was more than twenty minutes, but she hadn't called back.

I called her number, but it rang and rang until it went to voice mail. I disconnected. I couldn't believe Rita had left the house, and it was even harder to believe she'd gone somewhere without her phone. But apparently she had, and I would just have to wait until she got back.

In the meantime, Astor was not in any danger; she was with Robert, and she was quite probably someplace nearby, learning makeup tips. She would not want to be found, which would make things harder, but Robert would be much easier to locate. If he wasn't hovering nearby at the edge of the excitement, somebody would know where he was—Victor, the director, would be a great place to start.

I found Victor in his trailer, just two doors away. I could tell he was in there because as I started to walk past, Martha, the assistant director, came rushing out of the trailer as if she was pursued by killer bees. Before I could even frame a question to her, she sprinted past me, muttering, "Shit shit shit shit *shit*," and then vanished around the end of Trailer Row.

I went up the steps and knocked. There was no answer, but I could hear a voice inside, raised in passionate agony, so I pushed open the door and stepped inside.

Victor sat at the table, white-knuckled hand pressing his phone against his face. A large glass of water stood in front of him. He was listening to someone on the other end, shaking his head and whining, "No. No. No, impossible, fuck, no," and as I stood there watching he picked up the glass and drained the water.

And then he reached behind him for a large blue bottle, which I recognized as a popular brand of vodka, refilled the glass, and took another healthy drink. I didn't think he had filled the vodka bottle with water. He looked up at me without seeing me, and suddenly exploded in rage at whomever he was talking to on the phone.

"Well, goddamn it, what would *you* do? We got half a pilot in the can and a dead star, and the network is all over my fucking ass to fucking *do* something, and I can't do shit without her and I can't fucking raise the fucking dead!" He listened briefly—very briefly— and then snarled into the phone, "Well, then, call me back when you *do* know something." He slapped the phone to disconnect and then slammed it onto the table.

"Rewrite," he muttered angrily. "Fucking *re*write around a dead woman . . . Asshole . . ." Victor reached for his glass of "water" again, and then appeared to notice me for the first time. "What," he said, and he did not sound like he was going to invite me to join him for a drink.

"I'm looking for Robert." He just stared at me. "Robert Chase?" I said helpfully.

Victor screwed his face up and turned bright red, like he was going to give me a dose of the kind of bile he had unleashed on the phone, and I was in no mood for it. So it probably wasn't the nicest thing I could have done, but I was past caring. "He has my little girl," I said. "She's eleven years old."

All the color drained out of Victor's face. It was an amazing thing to watch; one moment he was puffed up like a big red balloon, and the next he was a greenish-white thing with cheekbones poking through sagging flesh. "Oh, Jesus fuck, I'm dead," he whispered, and he reached for his glass with two hands, lifting it numbly to his face and draining it.

When the glass was empty, Victor put it back down on the table. His hands were shaking and the glass rattled briefly before settling to a stop in front of him. He stared at the glass and then, finally, looked up at me with eyes that were nearly as dead as Jackie's. "They said it was just gossip," he said, and there was a slight slur to his words. "I never . . . I mean, you know. Richard Gere and the hamster. Tom Cruise is gay. All that shit. Just backstabbing bullshit Hollywood gossip." He lifted the glass, saw it was empty, and put it back down again. "I swear, I never thought . . . I didn't really think . . ."

Victor closed his eyes and slumped forward until his face was almost touching the tabletop. "Fuck," he said. "Why me? Why is it always me . . . ?" He began to shake his head, slowly and rhythmically. "I'm dead. It's all turned to shit on me and I am soooo . . . fucking . . . dead. . . ." And he stopped shaking his head, and stopped breathing, and just sat there slumped into a pale green heap.

I wouldn't have thought it was possible, but his face had actually turned even greener, and he sat there for a long moment, motionless. Then he jerked upright, snapped his eyes open, and took a deep breath.

"You got to understand, Chase wasn't my idea," he said. "I wanted somebody younger, but the network needs a star. They got a list; it tells everybody's TVQ—"

"Their what?" I said.

He gave me an impatient, irritated look. "TVQ. How popular they are. How many viewers they can get to watch something." He held up a hand, then let it flop back down helplessly. "Robert's is very high."

"Right," I said. "He's popular."

Victor nodded. "He's popular. A star. And people always make up awful shit about stars. It's . . . Everybody says stuff like that, you know, about anybody who makes it. It's a mean, bitchy business, but if I thought it was really true about Chase and little girls—"

He stopped and looked down at the table again. "Fuck," he said. "I woulda cast him anyway. He's got a really high TVQ." He stared at his hands for a moment, and then lurched sideways and grabbed the big blue vodka bottle and began to pour his glass full again.

I watched him, and I felt small and icy fingers tickling at the back of my neck. "What did you mean," I said, "about Chase and little girls?"

He wouldn't look at me. "It's just a rumor," he said, and he didn't sound like he even convinced himself. He put the cap back on the vodka, and as he bent to put the bottle back on the floor I sat next to him and picked up his full glass. "What the fuck," he said, and I slowly and carefully poured the entire glassful onto his lap.

Victor didn't try to stop me. He just stared at the puddle of booze as it soaked into his slacks, his mouth hanging slightly open, and then he looked up at me, and I smiled. "And what is the rumor, Victor?" I said. "About Robert Chase and little girls?"

He looked at me and his Adam's apple slid up and down, and then he finally closed his mouth and looked down again. "He *likes* them," he said in a soft and husky voice. "Really likes them." He glanced up at me briefly, then swallowed again. "He *likes* little girls."

I slid closer to him and put an arm around his shoulders, feeling him tense up as I touched him. "And when you use that word 'like,'" I said, "what does it really mean to you, Victor?"

"He has sex with them," he said in a whisper. "Robert Chase is a pedophile."

I thought about my days with Robert, and his wistful talk of kids. I thought it unconvincing and it was—but not because he didn't like kids; it was because he *really* liked them. And the family portrait he left hidden on my desk. His immediate and complete interest in Astor when they met, and the way he instantly got her alone in the makeup room—and even Robert's weekend in Mexico at a "special private resort," which probably meant a place that catered to men with his tastes; it all added up, fit together so perfectly that in retrospect, only an idiot could have missed all the obvious clues. And I was an idiot. A true and total dolt. I had thought he was gay, and because I am a fatuous conceited idiotic dolt I had even thought he had a crush on me. And all along, it had been the kids after all.

There was no longer any doubt about it. Wave after wave of contempt for my complete stupidity washed over me, and I sat there for a very long time, just letting the waves lift me up and crash me down on the rocky shore again.

Of course Robert liked little girls, girls just like Astor. And being the Child of Darkness that she was, of course Astor would have played along, loving the sense of power and control as a full-grown man, a *Star*, focused all that flattering attention on her. That Saturday at Wardrobe, moments after they met, she had rushed off with him right away, down the hall to the little dressing room. . . .

And once more a quick movie clip flashed by on the screen in Dexter's skull: Kathy going into that room where Astor and Robert had disappeared, and then flying out as if she'd seen a ghost, and vanishing out the door. She had seen them engaged in Inappropriate Behavior—and she had not said anything? Because Robert begged and pleaded for a chance to explain? Yes: Even with Kathy, his star power had counted for something. So she agreed to meet him that night, maybe even planning to blackmail him, and he killed her instead and took her phone so no one would know about their date. He'd even thrown up, which fit what I knew about him so well that the moment Vince told me about it I should have thought of him, and once again I let the tide of recrimination lift me and slam me into the seawall a few times. Even then I should have seen it, and if I had, my new and beautiful life would still be on track and Jackie would still be alive. Stupid, stupid, *stupid* Dexter.

I sat and ground my teeth and cursed myself until eventually I became aware of a very annoying sound somewhere nearby. I turned to see that I still had an arm around Victor's shoulders, and he was clearing his throat to get my attention as he tried feebly to wriggle free.

"Hey," he said. "Listen, I really didn't, you know, just . . . Are you going to . . . ?"

"I haven't decided yet," I said, and I looked at him. He flinched away, and I realized from the sound of my voice and the chilled feeling of my face that Victor was seeing the Real Dexter, seeing him the way very few have seen him and lived. "Where did they go?" I said.

He quivered at the sound of my voice, but he just shook his head.

"Don't know," he said. "Chase was here this morning and then— Shit, I really don't know; please, you're hurting me."

I looked at him just a moment longer. He was much too scared, drunk, and deflated to lie, so I let go of him and stood up.

"Fuck," Victor said, rubbing his shoulders, "scared the shit outta me."

I glanced back at him from the door of the trailer. "Fuck," he said again, and as I turned away he was picking up his glass.

I went out of Victor's trailer and left the magical world of show business behind me forever. No more lights, cameras, and squibs, and finding my mark. No more adoring crowds and sunset mojitos and chauffeured Town Cars. Farewell to the grips and gaffers and extras. And adios to hiring pedophiles because they're popular, and pretending that anything is okay if it helps the ratings and you don't actually see anything wrong.

And good-bye forever to the new me in a flimsy gaudy setting that was all bright colors and happy lies on the surface, and nothing but sickness and death underneath where it counts, just like every-thing else in this vile rotten world. There would be no escape for me, no hope of happiness, no new career.

Dexter's Debut had been derailed.

I headed for my car. I wasn't sure yet where I was going, but at least it would be away from this.

# THIRTY-FOUR

WHEN I GOT TO MY CAR I STILL DIDN'T KNOW WHERE TO GO. It seemed fairly appropriate for the total moron I had turned out to be: clueless, aimless, hopeless. The Avatar of Idiocy. No idea where to go, but an urgent need to go there fast. So naturally I just sat in my car and rested my forehead on the wheel. It wasn't much, but at least it wasn't destroying anybody close to me.

How could this be me? How could so much cool and clever confidence turn into this sorry heap of used and brainless body parts? Dexter the Doofus, who had blithely introduced Astor to a pedophile and encouraged them to play together; Dexter the Dim, who set up Jackie to be killed, and then left her alone with the killer—a killer who had been right under my nose for more than a week, and I'd never had a clue. Dexter the Destroyer, who left suffering and misery and death in his wake and moved happily on, unaware of everything behind—and apparently everything ahead, too. It was just plain luck that I hadn't strangled myself trying to tie my shoes.

And I couldn't even believe it was an aberration, a hasty left turn off a well-traveled path of cunning. I had screwed up everything in sight so effortlessly, naturally, and thoroughly that I had to believe this was the real Me emerging at last. I'd been lucky for a long stretch, never really noticing what a dolt I truly was, but my luck had finally run out, and here I was, stuck being the worst possible Me at a time when I needed most to be the smooth and clever engine of destruction I had always been before, if only in my imagination.

And so, with the world crashing around me in flames, here was me, sitting motionless in my car, massaging my temples and wondering where all the thoughts had gone. Astor could be anywhere. Robert might have taken her to his special resort in Mexico, or out to L.A., or anyplace in between. He could be doing terrible things to her right now, while she pleaded and squirmed and wondered why help didn't come. But Help, in the form of Dexter, was not going to come, because it didn't know where to go—and that might be a real stroke of luck for her, considering how I'd done so far. And of course, how I was doing now, too, because sitting here telling myself I was a dolt was no help to anyone, even if it was true.

*So think, Dexter: Try really hard to make something new and wonderful happen in that dull unmoving sandbox in your skull. Try for an actual thought, a genuine idea, before it's too late for Astor, too—if it isn't already.*

Nothing came. That was not a surprise to me, in my current state of overwhelming idiocy. I should just accept the fact that I was mentally deficient and learn to be happy. Maybe buy a banjo. Because I had no clue at all where they might be, and not even the glimmer of a hint of how to find out. I could only hope that somewhere along the way, somehow, somebody would stumble over the two of them and get Astor away from Robert. Clearly it wouldn't be me. I couldn't find them if they fell out of a tree and landed on my head. Even Rita had a better chance. At least she'd had a whatchacallit, one of them idea things. . . .

And maybe that idea had panned out. Maybe her luck was running better than mine. It couldn't be a lot worse, not unless she'd accidentally set herself on fire. So I pulled out my phone and called Rita, mostly because I was such an unvarnished blockhead that I couldn't think of anything else.

But Rita's phone rang and rang and went right to voice mail. Wherever she'd gone, she was still there. Did that mean she'd found them? Or was she just stuck in traffic? And where had she gone, anyway?

I tapped on the message she'd left earlier, and listened to it again. It hadn't changed at all. The only part of it that gave even a faint whiff of a hint was when she said, " . . . you said she might come home, and I thought, that's right, she might, but maybe not—and so anyway, I'll just be gone for twenty minutes. . . ."

"Come home but not" was typical Rita-ese, so convoluted and incomplete that it might mean almost anything. But I had been struggling to understand her for many years now, and I thought I could interpret. Of course, *thought* was proving to be a dangerous and alien activity for me, but I tried it anyway, and I took "home but not" and added it to "gone for twenty minutes," and there was only one thing it could mean. It was probably the wrong thing, but what I came up with was our new house. Home but not home, a ten-minute drive away, and definitely a place that Astor would want to go.

Of course, I had to assume that Astor had some say in where they went, but I knew how persuasive she was, or, failing that, how very stubborn. And Robert would be desperate to find a place where he could lie low. He was new at all this—except, apparently, for the pedophilia—and he would assume that the whole world was on his trail. So he'd want to find someplace quiet and unexpected, a place nobody would think to look. And ever-helpful Astor could very well suggest a place where she felt secure: the unoccupied, surrounded-by-hedges, complete-with-Her-Own-Room, very quiet New House.

And one last little shard of something that might have been thought clattered onto the floor of the dusty unused Ballroom of Dexter's Brain: If Robert and Astor had gone there to hide out, and if Rita went there and found them, Robert would not smile, autograph a picture, and send her on her way. He would, in fact, do all he could to keep her from leaving again and giving up his location. He would, very probably, tie or tape her securely. And if he had any sense at all he would gag her, too. Then he would put her in a closet, or in a bathroom, and leave her while he watched his back trail and waited to see who or what might be coming after him.

And taking everything into consideration, there was only one person left who could come after him: Me. This was not good news for the good guys, considering my recent track record, but there was no one else. And if there had been someone else, I wouldn't want them anyway.

Robert had Astor, and she was mine. She belonged to me the way a gazelle belongs to a lion, and he had snatched her away, taken something of *mine*, and I could not let him get away with that.

And Robert had killed Jackie, and left me stranded on the shore of a dark and sandy place filled with nothing but epic emptiness. He had taken away the only thing I'd ever had that felt like *feeling*, my only ever stab at happiness, and for that he could not possibly suffer enough, not if I could tape him under my knife every night for a year, each session longer and more pleasantly inventive. There was no possible payment that could make up for what he had taken from me, but what he could pay, I would take. And I would not stop taking until it was all gone, and all of him, too: every too-white tooth and too-bright smile, every studied gesture and practiced expression, all of it. I would take everything he had, everything he ever was or would be, and I would send him far away forever to the place where only pain is real, never-ending soul-destroying shattering pain. And if I left a mess big enough to lead the cops straight to me, that was fine, too. There was nothing left in this world but dumb suffering, and whether I endured it in prison or on the sofa with Rita, it was all the same to me.

This might be the very last thing I did, but I would do it. I would take Robert out of his smug, pampered, lily-gilded world, and I would drag him straight into mine: the world of Dexter's Dark Delight. He had no idea what he had unleashed when he pulled my chain. I was coming, and even if he knew it, he would be waiting for meek and mild-mannered Daytime Dexter, Doughnut Dexter, the soft-bellied blood-spatter boy from the office who was no more threat than a swivel chair. But that Dexter was gone, maybe forever, and it was something very different that was coming for Robert, and he would not like that difference, not at all.

I started my car and nosed it out of the lot, past the cop on the perimeter, and into the nighttime traffic, and the dim starless evening bled into me and filled me with the glow of very special purpose and I was ready for Robert.

It was the height of rush hour, and the traffic was snarled beyond repair. I inched along, grinding my teeth and thinking of new and special things to do to Robert. He was good-looking, and far too aware of that; that would be a help; I could use that. I could spend hours just playing with his face, slowly and carefully removing each separate bit of it and holding it up in front of his eyes so he would see Me holding permanently removed pieces of him, and see every step of the way that I was doing it, and it could not be stopped or slowed or repaired. This was happening to *him*, and this was all there was and all there would ever be, and there was no going back from it. This was the forever show in Dexterland, and tickets were nonrefundable and one-way only.

And I was so very wrapped up in my pleasant daydreams that before I knew it, I was down onto U.S. 1 and headed south to the New House. The traffic sputtered and wheezed and crawled along, but I idled along with it, thinking only of what was about to happen so very thoroughly to someone who deserved it more than anybody else ever had.

I turned left off U.S. 1, and in a few minutes I was there. I drove by once to see any sign that they were inside. A small convertible was pulled up in front of the garage door. Rita's minivan was parked slap-dash behind it. A full house, but the wild card was coming.

I went on by, scanning the area for anyone watching, and saw no one, nothing out of place, no more than the quiet middle-class neighborhood it was supposed to be. All along the street there were modest homes radiating the contented evening stillness of a day well done. Bicycles leaned against trees, Rollerblades lay in the driveways, and the muted aromas of a half-dozen dinnertimes threaded between the houses and dueled for dominance. But nothing was outside, no one was watching, and all was exactly as peaceful and unsuspecting as I wanted it to be.

I parked a block away from the house, under the canopy of a large banyan tree, took the fillet knife from under the seat, and climbed out of my car. It was full night now, and I breathed it in deeply, taking the darkness into my lungs and letting it flow out through my body and up my spine, and as it spread over my face and out to the very tips of my ears I felt the cool slithery calmness take the wheel and slowly, carefully push us forward into sharp and eager action.

We looked over the roof of the car, down the street to the house. A light gleamed beside the front door. We didn't care. Its nasty gleam would never touch Us: We would slide around to the back, hugging the hedge and following the shadows. We would stalk through pools of gloom and slip in through the tattered screen of the pool cage and up to the back door. We would use the key we had been carrying these many weeks and we would slide through the door, into the house, and onto Robert, and then we would begin, and we would not end until there was nothing else left to do.

A deep breath, a slow and steady flush of clarity and control, and all the cold dark blues of the night around us glowed warm and bright in our eyes and the night smells came alive in our nose and all the clicks and whispers of nocturnal life began to blend into the thrumming music of the hunt, and we go forward with them.

Slowly, with casual carelessness in our steps, we walk toward the house. TV glows and blathers in the neighbors' living rooms, and all is just as normal as it can be, everything peachy fine and hunky-dory—everything except for the nonchalant Monster strolling by on his way to a pleasant evening of lighthearted play that does not quite suit these sleepy suburbs.

We reach the hedge and all is still just what it should be, what it *must* be, and we pause to be sure, and when we are sure we slide without sound into the deeper darkness of the side yard and move carefully, quietly, perfectly down the shadowed hedge to the back-yard.

And moving softly soundless across one brief bright patch we pause once more behind a key lime tree only ten feet from the pool cage at a place where a large flap of ripped screen hangs loose, and we stand there and we do nothing at all except breathe, wait, listen, and watch.

Several minutes go by and we remain motionless and soundless in our predator's patience. Nothing happens. There is no sound or sight or smell and still we do not move, just waiting and watching. This side of the house is very clearly visible; one window shows a faint glimmer, as though a light is on in the hall just outside the room. Along the back of the house, facing the pool, there is my door, and then a large sliding glass door, and then another window. In this last window a bright light is on, and in the center, seen through the sliding glass door, there is a muted glow, spill from a light set back from the door.

But on our side, at our door, there is only lightless shadow, and nothing moves there, and we feel the gleaming happiness that all is right, all is ready, that once again things will go our way, as they always do when we are on the hunt, and at last, when there has been no sign of anything moving for a very long time, we move, one long smooth glide of purpose, out of the shadows and across the brownish grass and through the tattered flap of screen to the door.

We pause, one hand on the knob and one ear pressed against the door: nothing. No more than the muted rush of the central air conditioner blowing through the house. All is quiet, all is ready, and out of our pocket we take the key to Our New House, a newer and bigger and brighter and freshly painted house, ready for a wonderful new family life that will never move in now, because that dream was built on fumes from a happy hookah, a wispy picture of something that was never any more than hallucinations of hope, and that delusion has evaporated like the mirage it was and left cold dark ashes. And that does not matter. Nothing matters at all except this moment, this night, and this knife, this Right Now.

This is what *is*: Dexter with a blade and a target. This is the only Real there ever was: the sly stalk through shadows, the sudden pounce, the snicker of steel in a darkened room, and the muffled squeals and groans as the Truth slowly, gleefully pushes through the curtains and takes its bow. This is what is and what was and what shall be, and there was never really anything else in the world but this Dark Purpose, and never any time but *now*, and we push the key into the lock and with a silent twist of the wrist the door is open.

An inch, two . . . six slow and careful inches the door swings open and we pause once more. No movement, no sound, no sign of anything but the dim walls, still giving off the faint smell of fresh paint.

Still slow and careful we push the door open wider, wide enough now to slide through sideways, and we do, and as we turn to push it quietly closed we hear a melon-breaking *thump* and the dim room lights up around us like a bursting star and a bright pain blooms on the back of our head and as we pitch forward from dull surprise into painful darkness we are filled once more with the awful truth of our complete and brainless incompetence and the mean and mocking voice of our self-reproach as it calls out, *Told you so!*

And just before the blackness floods in and pushes out everything but regret, I can hear a small voice from a very great distance, a familiar voice, the snide and snarky voice of an eleven-year-old girl, as it says with great and bitter self-righteousness, "You didn't have to hit him so *hard*. . . ."

And then happily for me, or for all the stupid inept shards of self-delusion that are left of me, black nothingness takes the wheel and drives us straight into a long and lifeless tunnel.

# THIRTY-FIVE

FOR A VERY LONG TIME THERE WAS ONLY DARKNESS. NOTHING moved, or if it did, there was nothing to light its way, and nothing there to see it. There was only timeless, bottomless, thoughtless gloom, without shape or purpose, and this was very good.

And then somewhere far off on a bleak horizon, a persistent bleat of pain began to nag at the edge of the darkness. It throbbed insistently, and with each rhythmic beat of its pulse it grew bigger, brighter, sending out thorny little vines of misery that grew larger and stronger and pushed back the darkness piece by ever-shrinking piece. And at last the pain grew into a great and luminous tree with its roots driven deep into the bedrock, and it spread its branches and lit up the darkness and lo! It spake its name:

*It's me, Dexter.*

And behold, the darkness answered back:

*Hello, stupid.*

I was awake. I could not be sure that this was a good thing; it hurt an awful lot, and so far I had done much better when I was unconscious. But no matter how much I might want to roll over and go back to sleep, the throbbing pain in my head was strong enough to make sure that I had to wake up and live with my apparently boundless stupidity.

So I woke up. I was groggy and dopey and not really tracking things very well, but I was awake. I was pretty sure I hadn't gone to sleep normally, and I thought there might be some really important explanation for why I hadn't, but in my numb and painful state I couldn't quite think of it, or of anything else, and so I dove right back into the same stupidity that had landed me here and I tried to stand up.

It didn't work very well. In fact, none of my limbs seemed to be doing what they were supposed to do. I pulled on an arm; it seemed to be behind my back for some reason, and it jerked about two inches, dragging the other arm along with it, and then it stopped and flopped back to where it had been, stuck behind my back. I tried my legs; they moved a little, but not separately—they seemed to be held together by something, too.

I took a deep breath. It hurt. I tried to think, and that hurt even more. Everything hurt and I couldn't move; that didn't seem right. Had something happened to me? Maybe—but how could I know if I couldn't move and couldn't see? My head throbbed its way through one or two thoughts, and came up with an answer: *You can't know if you can't move and can't see.*

That was right; I was sure of it. I had thought up the right answer. I felt very good about that. And in a fit of overwhelming and completely unjustified self-confidence, I grabbed at another thought that floated past: I would *do* something about that.

That was good, too. I glowed with pride. Two whole ideas, all by myself. Could I possibly have another? I took a breath that turned the back of my head into a lake of molten pain, but a third idea came. *I can't move, so I will open my eyes.*

Wonderful; I was firing on all cylinders now. I would open my eyes. If I could only remember how . . .

I tried; I managed a feeble flutter. My head throbbed. Maybe both eyes was too hard; I would open *one* of them.

Slowly, very carefully, with a great deal of painful effort, I pushed one eye open.

For a moment, I could not make sense of what I was seeing. My vision was blurry, but I seemed to be looking at something cream colored, maybe a little fuzzy? I could not tell what it was, nor how far away. I squinted and that really hurt. But after a long and painful time, things began to swim into focus.

Fuzzy, underneath me, where a floor should be: *Aha*, I thought. Carpet. And it was cream colored. I knew there was something I could think of that had to do with cream-colored carpet. I thought really hard for a while, and I finally remembered: the master bedroom at the New House had cream-colored carpet. I must be in my New House. The carpet was blurry and hard to see because my eye was so very close to it.

But that meant I was lying on my face. That didn't seem to be right, not something I would usually do. Why was I doing it now? And why couldn't I move?

Something was just not right. But now I had several really good clues, and a small dim memory told me that there were things I liked to do with clues. I liked to add them up. So I closed the eye and did the math. My face was close to a carpet. My hands and legs seemed to be held together by something so I could not move. My head hurt in a way that made me want to scream—except that even the thought of any loud noise made it hurt even more.

I was pretty sure I wouldn't do all this to myself. Something unusual had happened to me. That must mean somebody else had made all this happen. Head, hands, legs, New House—all these things were connected. They added up and meant something, and if I could just push the pain aside for a moment, I would remember what they meant.

I heard a voice in another room—Astor's voice, rising up in a tone of blame and scorn. And I remembered:

I had heard that voice, that same tone, at the exact moment all these unusual things began to happen.

For a long while I just drifted with the pain, remembering small pieces. I remembered the thump on my skull that put me here, and I remembered Astor's voice as I pitched forward, and very slowly, I began to remember why I was here.

I had come here to tie up Robert. It hadn't worked. He had tied me up instead.

And slowly at first, and then with a flood of bitter memory and lizard-brain rage, it all came back to me.

Robert had killed Jackie, and by doing that he had killed my new and wonderful life. And he had taken Astor, taken her from *me*, and he had done all these things right under my very own night-sniffing nose, making me into a bungler, a booby, a complete clown: Dorky Dexter, Royal Fool at the Court of Shadows. Dress him in motley and turn him loose with his funny little knife. Watch while he stabs himself and falls down, tripping over his giant floppy shoes. Dexter the Dupe, looking right at Robert and smiling because he sees only harmless, brainless, self-centered stupidity. And still looking and smiling while the dim-witted clot outthinks him, outflanks him, and caves in his head.

For several long and bright seconds the anger took me over and I shook with it, grinding my teeth and pulling against the ropes that held me. I rolled over once, twice, and yanked my limbs furiously, and of course, nothing at all happened, except that I was now three feet away from where I had been, and my head was throbbing even worse.

All right then, brute force was not the answer. And clearly thinking was not our strong suit. That left prayer, which is really just Talking to Yourself, and Myself had not been very helpful lately. Was there anything else left?

And strangely, happily, just in time, it turned out that there was one last thing: pure, stupid, unearned Luck.

And Luck came slithering into the room where I lay.

"Dexter!" a soft voice whispered, and I turned my head to the door with great and painful effort.

Astor stood there in bright silhouette, the light from the next room behind her. She was wearing what looked like a white silk negligee, with a pale blue bow holding it closed below her throat. She tiptoed in and squatted down beside me.

"You moved," Astor whispered. "Are you okay?"

"No," I said. "My head hurts and I'm tied up."

Astor ignored that. "He hit you really hard," she said, still speaking very softly. "With a baseball bat. He hit Mom hard, too. She hasn't moved for a while." She put a hand on my forehead, then took it away and nodded. "I didn't know he would do that," she said. "I thought you might be dead."

"I will be," I said, "and you will be, too, if you don't untie me."

"He won't kill me," she said, and there was a bizarre, alien smugness in her voice. "Robert loves me."

"Astor, Robert doesn't love anybody but himself. And he's killed a couple of people."

"He did it for me," she said. "So we could be together." She smiled, a little proud, a little pleased with herself, and a bizarre and unexpected thought popped into my throbbing head: She was actually considering leaving me tied up, for Robert's sake. Unthinkable—but she was thinking about it.

"Astor," I said, and unfortunately, a little bit of Disapproving Dad crept into my voice. It was the worst possible tone to use on Astor, and she shook her head and frowned again.

"It's true," she said. "He killed them because he really loves me."

"He killed Jackie," I said.

"I know. Sorry," she said, and she patted my arm. "He kind of had to. She came busting into his trailer, yelling at him, and we were . . . together," she said, looking smug and a little shy. "She was yelling about how the computer says he killed Kathy, whoever that is. But she sees us there, you know. I let him . . . *kiss* me, and . . . and she sort of, whoa, just stopped there. And Robert jumps up and he's totally, 'No, no, wait a minute; I can explain.' And she looks at him, and says something like, 'Okay, you can explain it to Sergeant Morgan.' " She grinned briefly. "Aunt Deborah," she told me.

"Yes, I know," I said.

"So anyway, Robert jumps up and says to me, 'Stay here,' and he's gone out the door, chasing Jackie." She shrugged. "I didn't want to miss anything. I followed and I see them go into Jackie's trailer, and by the time I get there he's running out again, carrying this really nice MacBook Air." She nodded. "He says I can have it," she said. "When we get away someplace safe."

"Astor, there isn't anyplace safe," I said. "He's killed two people.

They're going to find him, and they're going to put him in prison for a long time."

Astor bit her lip. "I don't know," she said.

"I *do* know," I said. "There is nowhere he can go where they won't find him."

She didn't look convinced. "People get away with murder all the time," she said, and she looked at me with a kind of knowing, challenging smirk.

"But Robert killed somebody *famous*, Astor. The cops have to catch him or they look bad to the whole world. They'll give this everything they've got, and they'll catch him."

"Maybe," she said.

"Definitely," I told her. "They will try their very hardest—in fact, the only thing that could make the cops try any harder is if Robert also kidnapped somebody. Like an eleven-year-old girl with blond hair."

"He didn't *kidnap* me, Dexter," she said. "I went with him. He loves me."

"Do you love him?"

She snorted. "Course not," she said. "But he's going to get me into movies."

"He can't do that from prison. Or if he's dead," I said.

"But he says we can get away!" she said. "We can hide from the cops!"

"And how will he get you into movies if he's hiding from the cops?"

She put her lower lip between her teeth and frowned. "I don't know," she said. And I thought I might have convinced her at last.

"Astor," I said. "Robert's acting career is over. His *life* is over. And yours is, too, if you stay with him." I wiggled closer to her and held my wrists up as far as I could. "Now untie me."

Astor looked at me, and then turned and looked at the door. Then she looked back at me and shook her head. "I better not," she said. "Robert might get mad."

"Astor, for Christ's sake!"

She put a hand across my mouth. "Shhh," she said. "He'll hear you."

"I already did," said a voice from the door, and Robert came into the room. He flipped the light switch beside the door and the ceiling light came on. It was a lot brighter than I remembered it, and I had to squint. So I didn't see anything until Robert knelt down beside me, his head blocking the light. Then I could see, but I wished I couldn't; Robert was carrying a very large butcher knife, and he looked like he knew what he wanted to do with it.

Robert studied me for a moment, head cocked to one side. Even in the glaring light of this room, his tan looked great, his skin seemed smooth and soft, and his teeth were still perfect as he peeled his lips back to give me a brief automatic smile. He hefted the knife and there was no doubt what he was thinking, but he was still the most unlikely executioner I could ever imagine. "You shouldn't have come here, Dexter," he said, rather sorrowfully, as if it was all my fault.

"You shouldn't have killed Jackie," I said.

He grimaced briefly. "Yeah, I hate that," he said. "I just don't have the stomach for it. But I had to," he said, and he shrugged. "It gets a little easier each time." He looked at me like he thought I would be easiest of all, and I could see I was running out of time. "Anyway," he said, "I had a good reason. I did it for Astor."

He turned and looked at her, and to his credit, if that is the right word, the look he gave her was either genuine abiding affection, or he was a much better actor than I'd thought. Astor looked back at him, but she didn't look quite as smitten, and I thought I saw one small chance to save poor Dexter's bacon.

"If you like Astor so much," I said, "you never should have lied to her."

Robert jerked his head back around to face me and frowned. "I didn't lie to her," he said. "I would never do that; I really love her. She knows that." And he smiled at her again, putting the knife down on the floor beside him so he could take her hand reassuringly.

"You *lied* to her," I said, and it was the only card I had to play, so I pushed it hard. "You told her you could get her in movies, and that's a lie."

"No," he said, "I have a lot of connections and—"

"Your connections will run from you like the plague," I said. "Just as soon as they find out you're a lying, murdering pedophile."

Robert turned bright red. "You don't understand," he said. "Nobody understands."

"That's right," I said. "And the cops don't understand, either, and they will make sure you go to jail for the rest of your life—if you're lucky. We do have capital punishment in Florida, you know."

He was shaking his head, faster and faster. "No, no way," he said. "They'll never catch me. I can get away."

"How, Robert?" I said. "They're already watching the airports, the docks, even the bus depot."

"I have a car," he said, almost like he hoped that was worth something.

"And if you use your credit card to buy gas, they'll know it. They're going to get you, Robert. You snatched a little girl, and they are coming for you, and they will never, ever stop until they get you."

Robert bit his lip. A bead of sweat formed on his forehead. "I can . . . I can bargain," he said.

"You've got nothing to bargain with," I said.

"I do," he said. "I have a . . . a hostage."

"A what?" I said.

"That's right," he said. "I can get a boat and make Cuba—I just need a head start. They'll give me that if I give them Astor."

Right beside Robert I saw Astor's face change. She had been watching us like she was seeing a Ping-Pong match, head swiveling from Robert to me, while a frown slowly bloomed on her face. But when Robert said "give them Astor," her face hardened into a mask of cold dark rage, and she aimed it right at Robert.

"Give them Astor? I thought you loved her," I said.

He shook his head. "I can't go to prison," he said. "I know what they do to people like me." His jaw moved from side to side, and he blew out a breath and repeated, "I can't go to prison. I just can't. I will do anything to stay out." He leaned over me, blocking everything out of my sight except his perfectly tanned, far-too-handsome face, and he actually looked a little regretful. "So I'm really sorry," he said. "But that means I have to, um, you know." He sighed heavily. "*Kill* you. I'm really sorry, Dexter. Really. I like you. But I can't take the chance that— Urkkh," he said, and his eyes got very big. For a long moment he didn't move and didn't breathe, just knelt over me looking faintly surprised. Then he frowned and opened his mouth to say something. But instead of words, a great horrible gout of vile hot awful red blood came out and it splattered onto the floor and onto me, and even though I jerked my head to one side some of it dripped onto my face. . . .

And then Robert toppled over to one side and did not move, and behind him, snarling triumphantly down at him and holding a very bloody, very sharp knife—behind him in her little white silk negligee with its pale blue bow and a new set of bright red polka dots, was Astor.

"Stupid asshole," she told him.

# THIRTY-SIX

ASTOR USED THE KNIFE TO CUT THE ROPES OFF MY HANDS. IT was just nylon clothesline and it parted easily, and in just a few seconds I was sitting up and rubbing at the nasty wet blood on my face. I felt unclean, soiled, and very close to panic until I untied my feet, too, and stumbled in to the sink to wash the awful stuff off. I looked in the mirror above the sink to make sure I'd gotten it all, and I saw a strange, uncertain face looking back at me.

*Who are you now?* I wondered. It was a good question, and I could not answer it. I had tried to be a new and different Dexter—tried and failed. I had seen what I thought was a wonderful, shiny new life, a place where luxury was common coin and everyone was beautiful and no possibility was out of reach. I had seen it, and I had wanted it, and I had even been invited in, and I had thought that in a place that shone so brightly, even love was possible—love, for someone like me, who had never felt any emotion stronger than irritation.

And I had looked around at my little perch, a tried-and-true place of proven safety, sanctified by years of experience and the Harry Code, and suddenly it had not been enough. So I had jumped feet-first off my perch, and I had landed in the bright and gleaming New World—only to find that the bright and shining place that looked so warm and solid was no more than thin and brittle ice that could never hold my weight. And it had shattered and dumped me in the frigid salt sea.

And when I had needed most of all to be the real me, Saint Dexter of the Knife, I had taken one standard, well-practiced step into the Dark Dance, and fallen off my plié. I had been tricked and trapped by a man so dull and hollow he was practically a hologram, and he would have finished me off if I had not been saved by an eleven-year-old girl.

It was perfect; only the truly delusional can fall so far. I had tumbled out of all my illusions, new and old. And now I would fall the rest of the way, back into the stifling dullness of the plain wood-frame world behind the beautiful fake scenery.

There he is in the mirror; ladies and gentlemen, the Heavyweight Chump of the world—Dexter Delusional!

And my reflection nodded, wisely and mockingly. *This is what comes of trying to be something you are not*, it said, and I nodded back. Because no matter how far you may travel, you are what you are, and even when you are flying at thrilling new heights, circling the sun and thinking you belong in the halo of that perfect golden light, you do not. The wings always melt, and you always crash-land in your same old self.

A small and pretty face appeared in the mirror behind me. "Dexter?" Astor said. "What should we do?"

I blinked, and my narcotic self-involvement vanished. I turned to look at Astor, and beyond her, turning the cream-colored carpet into a soggy red mess, I saw a dead TV star. Directly in front of me stood an eleven-year-old girl wearing a negligee, and somewhere in the house my wife was bound and unconscious.

With a rush of paranoid insight, I realized that this was not the best possible situation to find yourself in, especially when you are so very far from top form. The whole thing suddenly seemed designed to point right at me, starting with Jackie's death, to Robert's—and even Astor in her unlikely sex suit, since I was, after all, only her *step*-father, and in cop circles "stepfather" is a code word for *Sexual Abuser*.

I could put together this scenario in my sleep, and it very definitely had a starring role for Dexter.

Ten minutes of basic cop questions with anyone involved in the pilot would reveal that I had been Jackie's new boyfriend. This automatically made me the prime suspect in her death—after all, choosing between me and World-Famous Robert Chase as a possible killer was such a simple choice that even a dolt like Anderson would pick me.

And of course, it *would* be Anderson, who had fresh and compelling reasons to hate me. And Vincent, the director, would tell him I had gone looking for Robert—and now, here I stood over Robert's body, speckled with Robert's blood. My usual trump card, Sergeant Sister, was no longer in the deck. From my last attempt to speak with her, I was quite sure she would be absolutely thrilled to watch me twist in the wind. She might not tie the noose, but she certainly wouldn't lift a finger to untie it, either. She would step back and watch as Anderson tucked Dexter neatly into this perfectly tailored scenario. And tuck he would: He had made a career out of accidentally trampling evidence and arresting the wrong person. How much better at it would he be now, when he would do it purposely, gleefully with real evidence?

There was Astor, of course—but anything she said would be largely discounted. She was a minor, and besides, everyone knows that stepfathers use intimidation and fear to keep the secret of their wicked pleasures, and a poor young thing would say whatever he told her to say.

It was a perfect blend of clichéd situations—and cops love clichés because they are true most of the time. That's how they get to be clichés.

The more I thought about it, the more I thought I might be in a great deal of trouble.

It was not mere paranoia; Jackie had been very famous. The pressure to arrest *somebody* for her death would be enormous. Adding Robert into the mix increased the pressure tenfold. And just to seal the deal, Jackie had been killed while under the publicly proclaimed protection of Miami's Finest. If a killer had slipped through that protection, the cops looked even worse. But if the killer was somebody on the *inside*, somebody who could easily pass through the Blue Wall, but not a rogue cop, it would take off a little heat. They would lunge at it with both hands.

Do cops arrest and frame someone they know is innocent? Not very often. But would the department at large refuse to look too closely when a brother officer arrested somebody plausible and said he was guilty? Would Captain Matthews keep his blinders on, merely to protect the department's image?

Is water really wet?

And Deborah—whatever she'd said earlier, she would still be half unconvinced of my innocence. But which half would win? In the past, she would have gone after the truth relentlessly, no matter what, bucking flak from above and ignoring whatever the slings and arrows might be. Old Debs would have braved anything to free an innocent man—and if that innocent was her brother, nothing would hold her back. She would willingly take on the whole department.

But now?

Now, on a case that Debs had been booted off with both of the captain's feet? Now that she was already in the Official Doghouse, her precious career hanging by a thread? She had been spanked very publicly and told to stay away. Any small rocking of the boat could tip her into the water and end something that meant more to her than anything else—would she risk that for me *now*? Now that she had said quite clearly that she thought I was such an utter scum-lump that I would even kill Rita, and that she was pretty much done with me forever?

I didn't know. But it didn't seem like a very good idea to bet my life on it.

But of course, I did have a very good way out, a simple but effective Get-Out-of-Jail-Free card: Rita. I had not, in fact, killed her. She would confirm that Robert had taken Astor, and dressed the girl in the incriminating negligee, and then attacked Rita. And that would lead back to why he killed Jackie, and even Kathy—it would all fit together, and Robert's death was suddenly well earned, a clear case of self-defense. Anderson would probably still try to stick it on me, and he might make things very unpleasant for a while, but eventually even a dolt of his very high caliber would be forced to see the truth.

Rita was the key. She would keep me safe from Justice, and that seemed like the final irony. As hard and willingly as I'd tried to escape her and the dreadful gray subsistence-level life she stood for, she was the only one who could save me now—perfect. Welcome home, Dexter.

"Dexter?" Astor said. "Hey, Dexter?"

She startled me, even though I knew she was there, and I looked at her and blinked. I saw uncertainty on her face, and something that might even be guilt. "What should we do?" she said again. For the first time in several weeks, she looked like an eleven-year-old girl: scared, unsure of herself, lost in a sudden attack of reality.

"First," I said, "we get your mom."

We found Rita on the far side of the house, near the washer and dryer. She was tied up as I had been, and she was not moving, and when I knelt down beside her I felt only a very faint, very fluttery pulse. I turned her over carefully and began to work at the knots that held her wrists, and at some point while I tugged at the ropes, her pulse stopped.

I tried my basic CPR. I gave her mouth-to-mouth. I did everything that training and desperate imagination could come up with, but after five minutes of trying she was still not breathing and her flesh had already begun to turn chill and clammy.

Rita was dead.

And so, quite possibly, was Dexter.

I looked at her body. I thought of the many years we had been together, and all the excellent meals she had cooked, and all the many things she had done for me even beyond her cooking, and I shook my head. I know I should have *felt* something—anger, sorrow, regret, almost anything at all. But my only thought was that death had smoothed out most of the wrinkles that had lately been growing on her face.

And I thought about Jackie; death had looked much worse on her. Not that it mattered, not really. They were both equally dead. I shook my head slowly, and finally I did feel something—I felt a keen appreciation of the irony Life had inflicted on Deeply Deserving Dexter. I, who never cared for women, had felt peacock-proud because I had two.

And now I had none.

I turned away from Rita's body. Astor stood behind me, chewing her lower lip. "Is she . . . is Mom . . . dead?" she asked me.

I nodded.

"But isn't there . . . Can't you . . . *do* something?"

"I did," I said. "It didn't work." And I might have added, *like every-thing else I've tried lately.*

Astor looked down at her mother's body and shook her head. For a moment I thought she might actually cry—but of course, that was not in her, any more than it was in me. Instead, she knelt beside Rita and touched her cheek. For a long moment she stared down at Rita, her face showing no more than her mother's did. Then she turned and looked up at me. "What do we do now?" she said.

I sighed. There were many things I might do—but all of them led, eventually, to the same cell in the detention center downtown. And even I had to admit that I deserved it. My entire career had never been any more than a prelude to prison. I'd kept ahead of Just Deserts for a very long time by using my wits—but recent events proved those were gone, dried up and blown away like last autumn's leaves. It was all over: inarguably, inescapably over, and as I admitted that to myself, I even felt a little bit of relief.

There was no point in prolonging this any more than I had to.

I pulled Astor to her feet. "We call the police," I said. "And then we face the music." She looked puzzled, but that didn't matter.

I took out my phone and called it in. Then I sat with Astor and waited for the music to start.

# GET READY FOR THE FINAL CUT

**DEXTER** THE FINAL SEASON

**DEXTER** THE FINAL SEASON

# DVD AND BLU-RAY
## AVAILABLE TO PRE-ORDER NOW